≈ ≈ ≈ ≈ ≈ ≈ ≈

She stepped to him slowly, and Ruben spread his legs to accommodate her. When she reached him, she put her hands on his shoulders, and the towel fell to the floor. Ruben looked her up and down slowly, his eyes devouring her nipples, belly button, every pore.

He placed his hands on her hips. He leaned forward and kissed her stomach.

"I love your skin," he whispered.

Cynthia ran both of her hands through his brunette hair, which was very different than the hair she was used to seeing on her boyfriends.

"Why?" she asked.

Ruben continued to plant soft kisses on her belly. His lips were thin, but they were warm. Each kiss sent a pulse of energy through her stomach and made her spine tingle. His white skin stood in sharp contrast to Cynthia's dark complexion, almost like zebra stripes.

"It's so deep," Ruben said between kisses. "So pure. It's beautiful."

He put a hand on her chest and traced two fingers down to her belly button. "I wish I could make your color," he said, "in a bowl, like cake mix." He kissed her areola and sucked the nipple on the opposite breast. "I would eat it raw," he whispered. "I'd lick the bowl clean. I love everything about your skin, the smell, the taste..."

≈ ≈ ≈ ≈ ≈ ≈ ≈

JACKSON MEMORIAL

KEITH THOMAS WALKER

KEITHWALKERBOOKS, INC
This is a UMS production

JACKSON MEMORIAL

KEITHWALKERBOOKS

Publishing Company
KeithWalkerBooks, Inc.
P.O. Box 331585
Fort Worth, TX 76163

For information write
KeithWalkerBooks, Inc.
P.O. Box 331585
Fort Worth, TX 76163

ISBN-13 DIGIT: 978-0-9850500-4-7
ISBN-10 DIGIT: 0985050047
Library of Congress Control Number: 2013904682
Manufactured in the United States of America

First Edition

Visit us at www.keithwalkerbooks.com

This book is for all of the health care workers who give their all for an often thankless profession. No matter how bad it gets, take pride in the fact that your hospital is not nearly as bad as Jackson Memorial! Lol.

MORE BOOKS BY
KEITH THOMAS WALKER

Fixin' Tyrone
How to Kill Your Husband
A Good Dude
Riding the Corporate Ladder
The Finley Sisters' Oath of Romance
Blow by Blow
Jewell and the Dapper Dan
Harlot
Plan C (And More KWB Shorts)
Dripping Chocolate
The Realest Ever

Visit keithwalkerbooks.com for information about
these and upcoming titles from
KeithWalkerBooks

ACKNOWLEGMENTS

Of course I would like to thank God, first and foremost, for giving me the creativity and drive to pursue my dreams and the understanding that I am nothing without Him. I would like to thank my wife for being my first and most important critic, and I would like to thank my mother for always pushing me to be the best I can be. I would like to thank Janae Hafford Hampton for being the best advisor, supporter and little sister a brother could ever have. I would also like to thank (in no particular order) Brandy Rees, Denise Bolds, Sabrina Scott, Dianne Guinn, Kierra Pease, Sharon Blount, BRAB Book Club, Trey Williams and Uncle Steven Thomas, one love. I'd like to thank everyone who purchased and enjoyed one of my books. Everything I do has always been to please you. I know there are folks who mean the world to me that I'm failing to mention. I apologize ahead of time. Rest assured I'm grateful for everything you've done for me!

JACKSON MEMORIAL

CHAPTER ONE
DAMIEN

Fridays were always special at Jackson Memorial. Friday, March 15th was especially so because this payday all of the full-timers got an incentive bonus in their check. By 8 pm the nine-to-fivers were all gone, getting a head start on their blessed weekend. But the 2:00-to-10:30 crews were stilling milling about anxiously, praying they wouldn't have to do anything too taxing during their last couple of hours on the clock.

Another thing about Fridays was they seemed to be the chosen day for mischief for the people of Overbrook Meadows, Texas. Jackson Memorial housed the city's premier trauma center, which meant they would always get the worst of the worst. When the bull riders got banged up at Will Roger's Coliseum or the bullets found fleshy targets on the south side of town, the victims all came here.

There were no major traumas in the emergency room at that moment, but the ER was humming. On the "Quick Trip" side there were nearly a dozen patients with shortness of breath, chest pain or flu-like symptoms. In the "Med/Surg" area, there were just as many people complaining of belly aches, headaches and one out-of-control nosebleed. The "Trauma" side was the temporary location for anyone with broken bones and all of the assault victims. It was relatively early, but a handful of people had already been stabbed, stomped or mugged on this beautiful spring evening.

The ER was brightly lit. It smelled of disinfectants and sanitizers with an underlying, coppery scent of blood. Multicultural employees wearing different color scrub suits rushed to and fro. From a bystander's perspective, the place looked chaotic. But everything that happened at Jackson Memorial was highly organized. Every employee had a specific function.

From the folks in admissions to the doctors, nurses and lab techs, the hospital ran with the efficiency of a huge bee hive. Even the unexpected was planned for – which was a good thing because no one in the ER knew that two of their assault patients were engaged in battle less than two hours ago, and they still had plenty of bad blood between them.

Mr. Murphy lie on a stretcher on the Trauma side, receiving aid from Dr. Dego, a nurse and an uncommonly attractive medical student named Lola. Mr. Murphy was intoxicated, disheveled and slightly belligerent, but incidentals like that would never interfere with the quality of care he received at the hospital. Murphy's wounds included head and facial contusions, a possible concussion and a superficial stab wound to the right forearm. Initially Mr. Murphy said a relative caused his injuries, but when the police were summoned to take a formal statement, Mr. Murphy recanted, saying he couldn't remember exactly what happened.

Mr. Thomas stumbled into the ER a full hour later. His injuries were also indicative of an assault, and he too was inebriated. When questioned, Mr. Thomas declined to say who attacked him. He certainly didn't say his assailant was a cousin named *Murphy*, so the pending disaster was a complete surprise to everyone involved.

As a nurse rolled Mr. Thomas' wheelchair through the Trauma side, the patient was shocked to see his dear old cousin receiving treatment in the same ER. His surprise quickly gave way to anger. Even though he won the initial fight at the trailer park, Thomas' whiskey-soaked brain determined there was but one way to handle this sticky situation: He must have revenge!

"Why you goddamned fucker!"

Dr. Dego was busy suturing his patient's stab wound. He frowned and turned quickly to see who would disrespect his work space with such a vulgar outburst. Mr. Thomas was already rising from his wheelchair by then. Dr. Dego didn't know who the patient was mad at, but he knew something ignorant was about to take place. He dropped his instruments and stepped quickly to protect his daughter, the pretty medical student named Lola.

The other patient, Mr. Murphy, recognized his cousin's voice immediately. As he pushed up on his elbows, his whiskey-drenched mind came to the same conclusion: *Revenge!* "You followed me to the hospital? You sonofabitch! You done cut me up, you dumb asshole!"

Mr. Murphy raised his wounded arm as proof. The suture needle, needle holder and thread dangled dangerously.

Lola's eyes widened.

Her father admonished Mr. Thomas with a heavy Ethiopian accent: "You, you get away from here!"

Murphy struggled to climb out of his stretcher. "I'll kick your ass again!"

"I'll kick *your* ass," Thomas countered, and the two came together with a clunky *SMACK* that was audible all the way to the waiting room.

Dr. Dego managed to usher his daughter out of the curtained room a moment before Murphy's stretcher crashed to the floor, and the two patients (who just happened to be cousins) began to thrash about like the idiots they were.

"*Help!*" Dr. Dego screamed. "Get help! We need help!" He was wide-eyed, but not particularly shocked by what he was witnessing.

His nurse wasn't all that surprised either. Rather than attempt to break up the fight, she stepped out of harm's way, threw her head back and shouted, "*SECURITY!*" so loudly Lola was sure the unruly patients would untangle themselves and back away to neutral corners.

No such luck. The tanked relatives continued to wrestle with reckless abandon. Neither was aware of a group of uniformed personnel racing to the scene like storm troopers. A couple of the security guards hollered, "*HEY!*" and "*GET OFF HIM!*" as they approached, but the leader of the pack didn't say a word. He briefly surveyed the scene and reached for the man he believed to be the aggressor.

Damien Glover's uniform wasn't the same as his cohorts because Damien wasn't really a security guard. By day he was a full-fledged police officer for the Overbrook Meadows PD. He raked in extra bread by providing security at the hospital on a part-time basis.

Damien was built like a running back. The bullet-proof vest under his uniform made his chest look even more massive. He wore his hair short and cropped. Damien was already handsome, but most thought his moustache/goatee combo added to his good looks. The muscular arms exploding from his short-sleeved shirt pushed his attractiveness up another notch.

"What are you, stupid?" Damien asked calmly. He grabbed Mr. Thomas by the arm and collar and lifted him into the air with minimal effort. Before the patient could turn or wrap his mind around what was happening, Damien slammed him hard on the floor, a few feet away from his cousin. The sound of bone hitting firm tiles was loud and sickening. No one was surprised when a fresh gash opened on Mr. Thomas' chin and began to squirt blood onto the emergency room floor.

"What the—"

Mr. Thomas' exclamation was cut off when Damien followed up his body slam with a well-placed knee to the offender's spine. Mr. Thomas twisted his neck to see who was attacking him as Damien secured one of his arms and reached to pull the handcuffs off of his belt.

"What the fuck, man!"

Mr. Thomas' eyes widened even more when he realized he was being restrained by a *black man*, but his struggles came to a sudden halt when he saw the badge on the black man's chest.

"You're going to jail," Damien told him. He still hadn't raised his voice, which was almost as shocking as the dramatic manner in which he diffused the situation.

"Get off him!" the other cousin yelled, and he actually began to crawl in Damien's direction. "Leave him alone! We just playing!"

Damien grinned slightly as his hand moved from his handcuffs to the butt of his stun gun. "You wanna get tased?" he asked Mr. Murphy. "Make another move, if you wanna. I'll whoop both your asses."

The two security guards who came with Damien were so stunned, they hesitated before approaching the unrestrained troublemaker.

"I didn't do nothing!" Mr. Murphy yelled when they finally put hands on him.

"I didn't do nothing neither!" the other cousin yelled at Damien, but with a quick CLIK-CHIK he was cuffed and fully under control.

"We're gonna move you to the other side," Damien said, still conversational, yet authoritative.

"I didn't do nothing!" Mr. Thomas squealed.

"I'm gonna help you up," Damien said, "get you back in this wheelchair."

"Let me go! I wanna go home!"

"If you refuse medical attention," Damien said as he lifted the man, "you can go to jail right now. Could you roll that chair over here?" the policeman asked one of the nurses who had come to gawk. She blinked quickly before doing as she was told.

Damien guided his prisoner to a seated position when the chair was in place. Everyone stared at the blood leaking from the handcuffed man's face. Mr. Thomas was quite a spectacle, but the ER staff saw gaping, squirting wounds on a daily basis.

"So, you wanna go to jail, or you want the doctor to check you out?" Damien asked. He moved to the back of the wheelchair and got it rolling before the injured man responded.

"I'll sue you!" Thomas promised. "You beat me up! I didn't do nothing!"

"Alright, so you wanna go to jail first?" Damien paused at the next intersection. More stunned faces looked from the policeman to the bloody patient. Everyone stared unabashedly. There was no political correctness here. If you made a damned fool of yourself in this ER, you would receive all of the attention you desired.

"Fuck you!" The patient literally spat blood. He struggled at his restraints to no avail.

Damien chuckled and turned the chair to the right. "Alright buddy. No one's gonna treat you, if you don't want 'em to."

"I wanna see a doctor!" the prisoner suddenly decided. "I wanna see a doctor right now!"

Damien didn't appreciate being ordered around, but the truth was his prisoner still had plenty of rights. No hospital in America would deny medical attention, even to the biggest of assholes.

Damien turned the wheelchair to the left and pushed his hillbilly deeper into the belly of the ER rather than head for the exit. A couple of nurses were already following so they could assess and stop the bleeding on the patient's chin whenever Damien came to a stop.

It was usually impossible to navigate the ER without saying, "Excuse me," a hundred times, but all of the employees made room for the cop and his wounded patient. Damien wasn't an attention freak, but his chest swelled a little as he rolled the wheelchair, especially when he spotted a housekeeper named Amina in the crowd.

Damien gave Amina a quick, little smile, and she looked down at her sneakers. Damien continued on his way, and no one noticed the brief interaction – except *one* person. Amina was standing with her supervisor Brenda. Brenda's eyes narrowed as she stared after the handsome policeman.

Her expression was still suspicious when she returned her gaze to Amina a moment later. Rather than meet her supervisor's eyes, Amina turned and headed in the opposite direction, the way the policeman had come. Brenda looked back at Damien once more before she shook her head and followed her coworker.

≈ ≈ ≈ ≈ ≈ ≈

Amina Perez was 23 years old, short in stature and quietly curvaceous. Her loose fitting scrubs concealed her slim waist and perky breasts, but most of the guys who worked at Jackson knew how to spot a banging body behind a *blah* uniform. The tell-tale sign was usually the booty. Amina's assets created an eye-catching bulge in the back of her pants, which was enough to give most of the horn-dogs pause.

They would then check out her face, boobs and stomach, usually in that order. Amina was pleasingly slim. She had a simple beauty that she didn't try to enhance with lipstick or blush. Her eyebrows were trimmed, but she didn't draw more attention to her hazel orbs with mascara or shadow.

Overall, she was going for the vague, unassuming, fall-through-the-cracks existence that was typical of most immigrants in corporate America. But it was impossible not to notice this housekeeper. Amina's large eyes were innocent and exotic. Her brown skin was smooth, her lips full.

She was new to the hospital, and she typically wore a confused expression that made men want to approach her, take her hand and guide her to her destination. The only thing that kept them at bay was Amina gave you the impression that she only knew a few English words, which probably were, "I'm sorry, no speak English."

But Amina did speak English, and so far she was a model employee at Jackson Memorial. Today she was stationed in the ER with two other housekeepers. Amina got stuck with the Trauma side, but that was fine with her. The steady work kept her so busy, her eight hour shift seemed to fly by.

All of the housekeepers wore pagers that assigned them "jobs" throughout the day, but Amina didn't need help staying on task. She heard the commotion a few moments ago, and she saw Damien wheeling a bleeding patient from her station. She followed the blood trail back to the scene of the fight. The curtained room was empty now, and it was a complete mess. There was blood and bloody gauze everywhere. Amina sighed slightly as she went to retrieve her cleaning cart.

When she returned to the room, she was surprised to see her supervisor waiting on her. Amina's large eyes flashed with uncertainty. Her first assumption was that she had done something wrong.

"I clean this now," she said. She pulled on a pair of gloves and bent to retrieve the larger items from the floor.

Brenda waved a hand in dismissal. She looked around and then leaned on the only real wall in the room. "Did you hear what happened in here?"

Amina shook her head without looking up. Even though she and Brenda were standing together just a minute ago, Amina wasn't surprised that her supervisor got the scoop already.

"It was a fight," Brenda said. "Two white guys going at it in here. Damien bust that dude's chin."

Amina didn't respond. Brenda nodded and brought a hand up so she could examine her fingernails.

"Yeah, Damien slammed him, like it wasn't nothing..."

At 45, Brenda was nearly twice her coworker's age. She and Amina wore identical gray scrubs, but Brenda's outfit was quite a few sizes larger. And she didn't fill hers out nearly as well. Not only did Brenda have no booty pushing the back of her pants, but she didn't have much of a neck either. And she was developing a hunch on her back. Brenda's skin was dark like Pepsi Cola. She wore thick glasses and a good deal of makeup.

Brenda knew she wasn't much to look at, but she got her hair done every week, and she was proud of her double D breasts. They would probably look more enticing if her belly wasn't so big, but what are you gonna do? Brenda liked to eat, and everyone knows fried chicken tastes better than cantaloupe.

Her physical issues aside, Brenda did have at least one thing going for her: Her job at Jackson Memorial paid $18 an hour, and she was able to make it to a supervisor position with no more than a high school education. Brenda wasn't the smartest or even the best housekeeper on her shift, but Jackson was known for promoting from within – especially if you could maintain excellent attendance for a few years.

"You like Damien, don't you?" Brenda asked her employee.

Amina didn't look up from the floor. "No, I don't understand..."

"I seen the way Damien looked at you," Brenda said. "He like you, don't he?..."

Amina looked up at her with a confused expression, but her ears turned candy apple red. She shook her head. "I don't–"

"It's alright," Brenda said. "You can tell me. I know all about Damien already. You think you the only one? You ain't. Some other housekeepers told me what he be doing..."

Amina rose to her feet and took a handful of mucky gauze to a contaminated bin. She replaced her dirty gloves with a fresh pair and knelt again to retrieve the hospital equipment strewn about the small room.

"I know he prolly came up to you when you was in a room by yourself," Brenda guessed. "He make you feel like you special, but you not. He do that to everybody. He a ho."

Amina tried to keep her mind on the task at hand, but her brain was racing. She continued to shake her head. "I don't... I don't know him."

Brenda sighed. She pushed her glasses up her nose and looked around to make sure no one was eavesdropping. "You don't have to lie to me," she said. "I ain't gon' get you in trouble. You can't get fired for this. I wanna help you. He doing you wrong, and you know it. He do it all the time. You can tell me about it. I swear I won't tell nobody..."

"I don't know him," Amina insisted.

"Yes you do," Brenda said, growing frustrated. "Damien's that black security guard. He a police. You just saw him come out of here with that man in the wheelchair. Don't tell me you don't know him."

Amina looked up at her. Brenda saw fresh droplets of sweat on her forehead. She thought the girl would break, but Amina shook her head again.

"We never talk. Did, did I do something wrong? I'm in trouble?"

Brenda hesitated. It would be easy to lie to her: *Yes, you are in trouble. I got no choice but to fire you, if you don't tell me the truth.* But a lie like that might come back and bite Brenda in the ass. Amina wasn't very talkative, but she was a sneaky kind of quiet. She might go to Human Resources tomorrow to plead her case. The folks upstairs wouldn't know what Amina was talking about. Brenda might be the one to lose her job if someone found out about this conversation.

She knew Amina was lying, but neither she nor Damien was worth getting fired for. Brenda sighed and shook her head.

"Naw, you not in trouble. I was just trying to help you. Damien be messing with a lot of girls up here. I was hoping me and you could do something about it, but if you don't wanna tell the truth—"

"I did tell the truth," Amina said. "He never talk to me."

Brenda waved a hand in dismissal. "Whatever, girl. That's on you."

Amina stood up again. She avoided eye contact as she stepped to the mop bucket she brought with her.

"Damn! Is this where they had the fight at?"

Both ladies looked up and rolled their eyes at the same time when they saw who it was.

"Yeah, they had a fight over here," Brenda said. "How you know about it already?"

"Everybody talking about it," their visitor said. He was a tall, handsome gentleman with a big smile and golden brown skin. His scrub suit was completely black. The name badge affixed to his uniform identified him as Rodney Tucker from Material Operations.

"That's all you do is run around and gossip," Brenda said, but her features softened and brightened when she saw that Rodney wasn't alone. "Oh, hi, Larry."

"How you doing, Miss Brenda," Larry said with a nod of his head. Larry Barnes wore the same colors as Rodney, and Brenda knew that he had been working in Material Operations for more than five years. Larry was taller than Rodney, and at 28 he was six years older. Larry's skin was rich and dark. His voice was deep and manly. Brenda knew she'd never have a chance with a young buck like him, but she couldn't help from flirting whenever Larry came around.

"Why you say hi to him like that?" Rodney wondered. "You wasn't smiling when you said hi to me."

"Don't nobody smile when they see *you* coming," Brenda snapped. "Not unless they up to no good, just like you."

"What you talking about?" Rodney asked.

"Boy, you know you ain't right," Brenda told him.

"I ain't do nothing," Rodney whined.

"That's the problem right there," Brenda replied. "You don't *never* do nothing."

Larry laughed and tried to diffuse the situation. "Did y'all see the fight?" he asked the housekeepers. "I heard Damien whooped somebody pretty good."

"We didn't see it," Brenda said with a quick smile. "But we saw when they wheeled him out of here. He was bleeding bad."

"What would possess somebody to fight in the ER?" Larry wondered.

"Trailer trash," Brenda replied. "They was both drunk, and they'd been fighting before they came in here. That's what they was up here for; one of them stabbed the other one."

"I heard they was cousins," Rodney said. "They still here? You know where they took 'em? I wanna see the one Damien body-slammed."

"That's your problem," Brenda said, her frown back in place. "You run around playing all the time, don't never do no work."

"I do be working," Rodney replied. Then he asked, "Why you be getting an attitude with me? Larry asked you the same questions, and you ain't rolling your eyes at him."

"We was just stopping by," Larry said, as he backed out of their workspace. "We'll let y'all get back to work. Come on, man." He gestured for Rodney to go with him. Thankfully the hothead complied without saying anything else.

Brenda watched until they were gone, and then she told Amina, "That little boy make me *sick*. Run around playing all day, and then he wonder why people don't like him. He don't understand that some of us work hard for our money. We don't wanna watch him goofing around all the goddamned time."

Amina continued to mop quietly. The hospital was filled with slackers, especially the folks in Material Operations. She didn't understand why Brenda singled Rodney out. But more importantly, Amina wished her supervisor would leave her alone. She didn't need help cleaning the room, and it wasn't like Brenda was helping anyway. She was just hanging around, gossiping; the very same thing she was supposedly upset with Rodney about.

As if reading her mind, Brenda said, "I'll talk to you later," and then she turned and left the room.

Amina wiped the sweat from her brow and finished mopping. After a few minutes she managed to get her heartbeats under control.

CHAPTER TWO
LARRY AND RODNEY

"Man, fuck Brenda."

Larry laughed at his young coworker. "Don't take that shit personal."

The two men continued their walk through the ER with no particular destination in mind. Larry was assigned to the ER for the rest of their shift, but Rodney didn't have any business there that Larry knew of.

"Why I shouldn't take it personal?" Rodney wondered.

"'Cause everybody talks bad about Material Operations," Larry said. "They think we don't do nothing."

"Brenda don't talk bad about all of us," Rodney countered. "Just me. You see she wasn't hating on you like that."

"That's 'cause I'm nice to her," Larry said. "Like how I call her '*Miss* Brenda,' and I'm always saying 'Yes, Ma'am' or 'No, Ma'am.' That kind of respect goes a long way."

"Whatever, man. You prolly fucked her," Rodney said.

Larry frowned at him. "Fool, what would possess you to say something stupid like that?"

"She wanna fuck you," Rodney said. "You know she do."

Larry shook his head but didn't offer a response. Rodney's number one problem was his immaturity. Larry would've laid it out for him, but he wasn't the kid's father or guidance counselor.

"Look at that," Rodney said, pointing to a stretcher parked against one of the walls. There were a few IV poles and IV pumps piled on the stretcher haphazardly. "Everybody else don't be doing what they supposed to," Rodney said. "Why they stacking that over there? They know that's not where that stuff goes."

"You right," Larry said, and he stepped in that direction. He released the brakes on the stretcher and started pushing it.

"What you gon' do with it?" Rodney asked.

"I'ma take it downstairs," Larry told him.

The men continued walking. Larry kept an eye out for any other miscellaneous equipment lying around.

"I woulda left it there," Rodney informed.

"This is my zone," Larry explained. "I'm supposed to take this stuff."

"Yeah, but not if somebody already got it stacked on a stretcher," Rodney said. "Whoever did that should take it."

"Maybe they stacked it up for me," Larry ventured.

"If they wanna help, they can take it all the way downstairs," Rodney said. "Everybody at this hospital *lazy*. I don't know why that bitch single me out."

Larry grinned at his friend. "I see she really got under your skin."

"I'm alright. That's why that ho got a hunchback," Rodney said and they both laughed. "Say, who's that?"

Larry followed his buddy's gaze to the nursing station on the Med/Surg side of the ER. There were more than a dozen people over there, but Larry knew who Rodney was referring to. Only one of the folks in that area was a black female. She was young, less than 25 years old. Her skin was brown like a honey bun. She wore her shoulder length hair down and layered.

"I don't know who that is," Larry said. "I never seen her here before."

"I'ma go holler at her," Rodney said, and he started that way.

Larry reached and grabbed his shoulder. "Hold up, man. You can't keep running up on every pretty face you see."

"Why not?"

"'Cause, man. Maybe *I* wanna holler at her."

"I saw her first."

"Yeah, but you not even supposed to be here. What you doing in the ER anyway? This is my zone."

"It don't matter what I'm doing here," Rodney said with a grin. "I'm here, and she here, and I saw her first."

"Quit being greedy," Larry told him. "I thought you was talking to that CNA upstairs."

"So?"

"And you got a woman at home already."

"And?"

"And you can't have this one," Larry stated. He pushed his stretcher against a wall and kicked the brake in place. "I'ma go talk to her."

"That ain't right," Rodney said, but he was smiling.

"Alright, I owe you one," Larry said, his eyes still on the new face. "I'll do your sweep tonight for you."

Rodney wasn't interested in the trade, but that was actually a big deal. Every night all of the employees in Material Operations were assigned a floor to "sweep," meaning they had to search the unit for any stretchers, wheelchairs, IV poles, oxygen tanks, or any other equipment left in places it shouldn't be. If you ran into more apparatus than you could fit in the elevator, a simple sweep could turn into a twenty minute ordeal.

"You know I don't be doing my sweeps anyway," Rodney complained.

Larry didn't have anything else to barter with, so he decided to take the woman caveman style. He shoved Rodney aside on his way to the nursing station. "Whatever, homey. *I'm* talking to her."

Rodney laughed rather than take offense. "Damn, nigga. If you want her that bad, go ahead. I gots plenty of women." He continued down the hallway, towards the staff elevators.

Larry took a deep breath as he approached the new tenderoni. She wore blue slacks with a white blouse and black pumps. Larry was a breast man, but he liked a nice booty, too. This girl had a serious onion.

My goodness, Larry said to himself. The closer he got, the better her curves looked. Her pants weren't tight, but they weren't made for a woman of her physique. Larry thought her ass was absolutely perfect. She didn't look up at him until Larry leaned on the counter next to her and said, "Hi."

The new girl looked up from the chart she was writing in and met Larry's eyes. Her features were soft and alluring. She wore glasses, but Larry saw that her orbs were dark and inquisitive. At six-foot-four, Larry was taller than her by nearly a foot. She looked up at him and raised an eyebrow rather than ask what he wanted.

"I'm Larry," he said. "What's your name?"

The woman looked from Larry's face down to the hospital ID affixed to his shirt. She frowned. That was a strange reaction, but Larry kept his award-winning smile in place. The woman turned towards him and lowered her chart, so Larry could see her ID badge. Her name was Lola Dego. Her title: MEDICAL STUDENT.

Larry's eyes widened. Lola returned her attention to her charting. Larry started to walk away, but he'd never been rejected *without words* before. He decided he didn't care for it too much.

"Sooo, what does that mean?" he asked. "You can't talk?"

She looked up again and gave him a serious once over this time. Larry was tall and dark, and even with a skeptical eye, Lola couldn't deny that he was handsome. His hair was short, styled in a bald-fade. The waves on top were deep and plentiful. Larry had a tuft of hair on his chin, but no moustache. His features were stern, jaw line rigid. His lips were nice and pinkish.

The most notable thing about Larry was his deep, rich voice. Larry sounded like the bass singer for a barbershop quartet. He couldn't tell if Lola was responding to him with indifference or annoyance.

"Can I help you?" she asked.

She had a sweet voice, but Larry could already tell her disposition didn't match. Larry thought stuck-up women were one of the worst things on God's green earth. And it was always the pretty ones. An ugly woman will smile at practically anyone who showed interest, but not these redbones. Larry almost walked away, but his pride started to swell. Medical student or not, he didn't think this woman was too good for him. When you stripped away all of the ID's, prestige and clothing, they were both just male and female, nothing more.

"Yeah, I wanted to say hi," Larry said. "I haven't seen you in the ER before. Are you new?"

"I've been here for a week," Lola said.

"Are you having a bad day?" Larry asked. "You don't look too happy."

"I'm just trying to figure out what you want," Lola said. "I'm kinda busy."

"I didn't want anything," Larry said, "just to meet you. Is that alright?"

She shrugged. "I guess." She looked away and scribbled more notes in her patient's chart. But Larry didn't disappear like she expected him to. She frowned again. "So, was there something else?"

"Well, no, not really," Larry said. "Unless you wanna tell me why you giving me the cold shoulder. Did I do something to upset you, maybe in a past life?"

She tried to fight it, but a smile crept to her lips.

Larry smiled, too. "That's what I'm talking about. You got a pretty smile. Why you hiding it behind that mean mug?"

She shook her head, but her smile remained. "What is this?"

"What you mean?"

"I mean, what are you doing?"

"I told you; I wanted to meet you."

"Are you hitting on me?"

"I think so," Larry said.

"Everybody at this hospital is screwing somebody," Lola said. "Is that what you have in mind? I'm not down with that."

Lola didn't have an accent, and she seemed familiar with American slang. But Larry knew her last name was African.

"Where are you from?" he asked.

"I'm from here."

"Overbrook Meadows?"

"All my life," Lola said.

"What about your parents?"

"Ethiopian."

Larry smiled. "So you're an African princess..."

"You didn't answer my question," she noticed.

"Which one?"

"Are you trying to hit on me?"

"I told you: All I wanted was to meet you. What college do you go to?"

"You work in Material Operations?"

Larry couldn't deny that. It was printed clearly on his badge. "Yeah."

"Have you ever been to college?"

He shook his head. "No, but I think about going sometimes."

"Do you know who that man is?" Lola asked. She pointed to a physician fifteen yards away. The doctor had his back to them.

"That's doctor, um…" Larry racked his brain. He looked around, and his eyes came back to Lola's ID badge. When he read it again, his eyes narrowed. "That's *Dr. Dego*, ain't it? Is, is that your dad?"

Lola nodded. "How do you think he'll feel about somebody from Material Operations flirting with me?"

Larry's mouth hung open. His armpits felt damp. His heart rate increased too, but his pride was still standing strong, even more so now.

"He wouldn't want *me* talking to you, or he wouldn't want somebody from Material Operations talking to you?"

"Both," Lola said. "I mean neither."

"What about you?" Larry asked, his eyes glued to the back of her father's head.

Lola hesitated and then shrugged, like she didn't want to hurt his feelings.

"You don't even know me," Larry said. "I think you should find out what kind of person I am before you start judging people. I work hard. I'm one of the best workers in my department. Your dad doesn't want a hardworking brother to approach you?"

Lola chuckled. "Are you getting offended?"

"Naw," Larry said, but he realized he was frowning. He relaxed his features. "No, I'm not offended." He looked into her eyes and smiled. "You got some pretty teeth. You used to wear braces?"

She shook her head. "Daddy's on his way back."

Larry checked and saw that Dr. Dego was indeed headed in their direction. Lola's father was shorter and smaller than Larry, but he looked a lot meaner.

"So, can I get your number before he gets here?" Larry asked.

Lola giggled and shook her head. "No."

"Why? Because your dad's watching, or because you don't want to talk to me?"

"Are you serious?"

"Hurry up, girl. He's almost here."

Lola laughed.

Larry told her, "You got a nice laugh."

Lola blushed, and then her expression changed. "I'll see you later, Larry."

Larry followed her gaze. Dr. Dego was within ten feet now. He fixed a pair of concerned eyes on his daughter and the stranger who had no business approaching her. Larry wasn't intimidated, but he didn't want to upset Lola by being disrespectful.

"Alright, Princess Lola, I'll talk to you later. Oh yes, we will meet again."

Lola looked down at her patient's chart and didn't respond.

Larry walked away. He didn't look back until he made it to the stretcher he parked against the wall. He saw Dr. Dego ask his daughter something, and then the doctor looked in Larry's direction.

Larry couldn't hear their conversation, but he knew it wasn't anything nice. He moved to the back of the stretcher and got it rolling towards the Quick Trip side.

≈≈≈≈≈≈≈

Around the same time Dr. Dego was giving Larry Barnes the evil eye, Rodney Tucker was having much more success with his love connection on the 3rd floor of the Jackson building. Certified Nursing Assistant Amy Winters wasn't able to sneak away with her new "friend" today, but she liked the attention Rodney was giving her. It always brightened her day when he visited her floor.

They first met three weeks ago. Rodney came to the oncology unit to retrieve a dozen oxygen tanks, and Amy had to unlock the utility closet for him. Rodney was immediately attracted to her figure – not that Amy was *all that*, but she did have a nice, round ass that was atypical for white girls. In fact, Rodney told her just that with his bold pick up line:

"Damn, you got a big booty for a white girl."

Amy was surprised by the comment, to say the least, but she was more flattered than offended. No one at the hospital knew that ever since she started putting on weight in high school, Amy's self esteem was pretty much nonexistent. Most of her peers were as thin as rails back then, and they never passed on an opportunity to point out Amy's "big gut" or her "thunder thighs" and "big fat ass."

Not until she enrolled in junior college did Amy become exposed to a more diverse crowd, and it was there that she learned not everyone considered her size-fourteen figure unattractive. In fact, Amy found that there was a whole population of men who liked a gal with a little junk in her trunk and some nice, healthy thighs. This new breed of men were BLACK GUYS. As an added bonus, most black guys came with BIG BLACK DICKS.

Amy backed out of the utility closet and asked Rodney, "What did you say?"

For a brief moment, Rodney thought he might get in trouble for sexual harassment. But Amy was smiling, and she blushed when he told her, "I'm just saying... I never noticed you before. You got it going on. Sho' look good to me..."

Amy looked Rodney up and down, and he sho' looked good to her, too. Rodney was tall and light-complected. His hair was styled in a mini afro. His face was clean-shaven. His eyes were cinnamon colored. He wore a gold, Cuban link chain with a matching bracelet. A diamond stud glistened in each of his ears.

"What's your name?" he asked her.

"You can't read my badge?" she flirted.

"I can read it. I wanted to hear you talk."

"Why?"

"I wanted to see if you got a tongue ring."

"What if I do?"

"You do got one," Rodney noticed. "Can I see it?"

She flicked her tongue at him.

"Can I get your number?"

She gave it to him, and Rodney left her floor with the oxygen tanks. He texted her thirty minutes later:

Still thinking about that ass. And that tongue ring.

Amy's panties got moist when she read it. She responded: Why?

Rodney said: I wanted to grab that ass. Is it soft?

Amy responded: You shoulda grabbed it then.

Rodney was getting an erection by then. He went to the Radiology break room, which was totally vacant at that time of day.

Can you meet me somewhere?

Amy said: No. I can't leave the floor right now.

Rodney said: What time you get off?

Amy said: I don't know you like that.

Rodney said: I just wanna touch that ass.

Amy left her nursing station and went to the bathroom. Her chest was knocking. This whole encounter was moving too fast, but it was exciting. She didn't want to stop. She told him: Maybe later.

Rodney said: Can you send me a pic?

Amy said: I don't know you like that.

Rodney said: I'll send you one first.

Amy said: Okay.

Rodney had several pictures of his dick saved on his phone. He sent her one of them.

A minute later, Amy responded: Damn.

Rodney said: Where mine?

Amy already had a hand in her panties at that point. Everything was nice and juicy down there. Amy never masturbated at work before, but there's a first time for everything. She put the camera between her legs and took a pic. She spread her labia with her fingers and took another one. She sent both of them, and then she went back to the pic Rodney sent her. His dick was long and thick. The head was about the size of a tangerine.

Amy rubbed her clit while she stared at the picture. She came in sixty seconds. After she cleaned up, she saw that Rodney had sent her another message:

I know you gonna let me hit that.

Amy knew it too, but her fingers were trembling so much, she couldn't respond. She left the bathroom with her head spinning, her heart racing.

She and Rodney didn't hook up that night, but they did the night after that. Amy had an apartment all to herself. Rodney knew she was a freak when she sent the two pics at work. His theory was further confirmed when he mounted Amy and slid in with no problem at all. There was a chance she stretched her own walls with huge sex toys, but it was more likely that Amy had been giving it up to a bunch of brothers who were seriously packing.

When Rodney calculated all of this information (and threw in her tongue ring), he felt comfortable enough to pull a porno stunt during their first sexual encounter. When he had Amy yipping like an excited puppy, he pulled out abruptly and told her to taste herself. Amy sat up with no complaints and sucked all of her juices off his manhood.

Rodney didn't pull out of her mouth when he came, and Amy didn't spill one drop. She drained him completely and kept sucking. She was so skillful, Rodney never lost his erection. To reward her showmanship, he lay on his back and let her ride him to her heart's content. But before he came a second time, he made her taste herself again.

Afterwards, Rodney saw that his girlfriend had called him three times since he'd been at Amy's house. He took a shower and left without so much as a "Thanks." The next day at work, Rodney told all of his homies about the "freaky white girl" on the third floor of the Jackson building.

That was three weeks ago.

Their *relationship* had been going strong ever since, even though Amy longed for more *substance*. A part of her understood that she probably ruined things already by giving up the goods so easily, but Amy convinced herself that might not be the case. Just because a relationship was founded on sex didn't mean it couldn't become something meaningful. Sometimes you have to get him hooked on the loving *before* he'll fall in love with you. Her mom might disagree with that, but Amy was old enough to make her own decisions now.

She was a big girl.

≈ ≈ ≈ ≈ ≈ ≈ ≈

When Rodney showed up on her floor that Friday, Amy knew he hadn't come to pick up any equipment. He walked by the nursing station, down to the end of the hall. He spotted Amy in the next to the last room. She saw him too, and she hurried to finish taking her patient's vitals. Rodney was waiting on her when she stepped into the hallway. Amy smiled brightly as she logged onto one of the computers mounted on the wall. She entered the patient's readings and then walked with Rodney back to the elevators.

"You been busy?" he asked her.

"No," Amy said. All of her coworkers at the nursing station gave her knowing grins when she and Rodney strolled by. That made Amy feel special. Rodney never hugged or kissed her in public, but he visited her a lot, and that was just as good.

"Did you hear about that fight in the ER?"

Amy shook her head. "Who was fighting?"

"A couple of patients," Rodney said. "Damien body-slammed one of them, bust his chin wide open."

"For real?" Amy didn't consider this "gossip" because Rodney didn't tell her the patient's name. When he left, Amy would spread the story on her floor. Half of the employees at Jackson would know about the fight before the second-shifters left at 10:30.

"Can you go with me?" Rodney asked as they neared the elevators.

"Go where?"

"For a walk." Rodney gave her a slick smile that made Amy's heart flutter.

She had gone for a *walk* with him nearly a dozen times since they first met. Rodney always led her to places where the security cameras couldn't see them. As a Material Operations employee, Rodney was required to retrieve equipment from virtually everywhere, so he knew the hospital better than any of the nurses and CNA's. He talked Amy into giving him a handjob once in the basement of the Avery building. She let him finger her in the parking garage earlier this week, but so far they hadn't gone any further than that.

"I can't leave right now," she said. "It's too close to us getting off."

Rodney nodded. He only looked mildly disappointed.

"What are you doing tonight?" Amy asked. "You wanna come by?"

"I got plans with some homies," Rodney said.

He told her that so often, Amy didn't even question it anymore.

"Well, it was nice of you to come see me," she said. "Where are you going now?"

"Nowhere," Rodney said, and then he looked over her shoulder. Amy turned, but she didn't see anything.

"What?"

"That lady in 312..." Rodney said. "Why her stuff all packed up?"

"She's leaving tonight," Amy informed. "She's going to a nursing home. They should be already on their way to get her."

Rodney rubbed his chin. Amy saw the cunning in his eyes.

"She got a laptop bag in there," Rodney said. "I saw it when I walked by. It's sitting right by the door..."

Amy shook her head, but Rodney kept talking.

"She sleep," he said. "And she real *old*. What she need a laptop for?"

Amy's smile fell. She knew Rodney stole from the hospital from time to time. Sometimes he picked up items when they were together. But Amy never helped him – not even as a look-out.

"She too old to remember if she brought it here or not," Rodney reasoned. "And even if she do remember, y'all can say somebody at the nursing home must've took it..."

Amy's frown intensified. Her face flushed with heat. Rodney looked around to make sure no one was watching them, and then he stepped closer and put an arm around her waist. He kissed her briefly, yet passionately. There was no tongue, but this was a major milestone in their relationship. Amy's dread was replaced with the warm glow of love, and suddenly she could care less about that old biddy in 312.

"I wouldn't never do nothing to get you in trouble," Rodney promised. "You ain't got to do nothing but walk away..."

Amy's heart shuddered. Rodney kissed her again, and that sealed the deal.

"Okay." She spoke in a whisper.

Rodney smiled. He was so handsome and loving. Amy didn't think she deserved a man like him. Rodney could have any woman at the hospital, but he chose her. So what if he had a stealing problem? Amy could change him, once their relationship became stronger. Even if she couldn't, there was something altogether alluring about being with a *bad boy*. The element of peril was a huge turn on.

Amy gave him another kiss, and then she backed away with a dopey smile. She turned and headed back to her nursing station. When she got there, she looked back and saw Rodney slip into room 312 with hardly any hesitance.

Amy's smile slipped, and she had to look away. She convinced herself that if she didn't see him with the laptop, then it didn't really happen. Plus it wasn't like she helped him take it. All she did was mind her own business, and there was nothing wrong with that.

Nope. Nothing at all.

CHAPTER THREE
EVA VALDEZ

At the same moment Rodney sneaked into a little, old lady's room to check out her laptop, Eva Valdez, a supervisor in Material Operations, was chilling in her office, getting the scoop on the recent violence in the ER.

Material Operations was one of the largest departments in the hospital. There were over sixty employees divided into three shifts that helped keep the hospital clutter free 24 hours a day. Each shift had a different supervisor who looked for different qualities in the workers they hired. It was no secret that 2nd shift had the worst reputation in the hospital.

Second shift started at 2:00 pm, so it was perfect for folks who didn't consider themselves *morning people*. A lot of youngsters on this shift liked to the hit the club every week and stay out until the wee hours of the morning. Second shift was also ideal for part-timers who pursued an education by day; either high school or college.

The biggest cause for second shift's awful reputation had to start with the woman in charge. Eva was thirty-seven years old, married with five children. She took the entry-level position in Material Operations more than a decade ago and gradually worked her way up the ranks with *so-so* integrity, *not bad* attendance and a wonderful motto that never seemed to fail her: *Do what you got to do – just don't get caught!*

Eva never got caught stealing food from the cafeteria to feed her family at home. She never got caught clocking out for some of her friends who didn't feel like staying all night. No one knew Eva was one of the first Material Operations employees to have sex at work. During her ten years at the hospital, Eva had never been caught taking batteries, digital thermometers, radios, calculators, ointments, gauze and other small items home for her children.

Eva knew she wasn't alone in this small-time thieving, and she knew that a hospital as big as Jackson Memorial expected *some* shrinkage. No one was going to throw a fit over a missing box of alcohol swabs. A nurse wouldn't call security if she couldn't find an electronic blood pressure cuff. And it wasn't like Eva was taking these things to sell for profit. She was putting everything to good use at home. So that wasn't as bad as *stealing* stealing.

Eva spent a nice chunk of her income at the beauty salon. Today her hair was styled in a short bob. She was of medium height and a little too chubby for her own taste, but she loved junk food too much to try dieting. Eva didn't consider herself *ugly*, but she did pile on a good deal of makeup before she left the house each day. Her lipstick was always dark red. She spent ten minutes on her eye makeup alone.

Eva's office wasn't very large, but it was big enough to fit four people comfortably, and there was usually at least that many people lounging in there. Eva sat in a padded office chair under the window because a girl named Jamie was using the computer to work on her résumé. Another girl named Roshida sat in a folding chair she brought from the break room. Another employee, a skinny teenager named Alex, sat on the corner of Eva's desk with his arms folded over his bird chest.

"I didn't see it," Alex was saying, "but I talked to a CNA who was standing right there when it happened. She said Damien came in, and he didn't say *nothing*. He just scooped that first one up, and then he slammed him down so hard his whole chin bust open!"

"Nuh-uhn!" Eva said.

"For real," Alex said.

"He was messed up," Roshida confirmed. She was 22 and attractive, a high school graduate with dreams of becoming a nurse on day. "I saw him. They hiding him on the Quick Trip side. They got his cousin on the Trauma side."

"What's they name?" Eva asked.

"The one who got arrested is, uh, *Gerald Thomas*," Roshida said. "The other one's last name is *Murphy*, but I don't know his first name."

"They white?" Eva asked. Her smile was wide and glistening.

"Yeah," Roshida said. "They both white."

"You know ain't no black people gon' be fighting in the ER," Alex said, and they all laughed.

"Boy, please," Eva said. "Black people will throw down *anywhere*. It was two crackheads fighting in the ER last year. And right before you got hired, two girls in the cafeteria went at it in front of *everybody*. It was at lunchtime, too. All kinds of doctors and managers was in there. Them bitches didn't care."

"I remember that," Roshida said with a chuckle. "That was Keisha and Tiffany. Weaves was flying all over the place!"

They all laughed again.

"What happened to Damien?" Roshida asked. "He got in trouble?"

"He can't get in trouble for that," Eva said. "He not just a security guard; he a full-time police. A cop can slam you, if you fighting somebody."

"Naw, he not in trouble," Alex confirmed. "He was still over there with the one he beat up when I went down there. You could tell he was feeling real good about hisself, too. Had his arms folded over his stomach; posted up like he a prison guard."

"I wish I woulda saw that fight," Roshida said, her eyes twinkling. "I love me some Damien..."

"You ain't never lying," Alex said. "Every time I see him, I think about going up to him with my arms behind my back: '*You can arrest me, mister officer!*'"

That brought another round of laughter.

"I heard he slept with some girls up here before," Roshida said. "I wonder if he still do..."

"I wonder if he ever hook up with some mens, on the down-low," Alex said.

"Naw, he not like that," Roshida said.

"You don't know," Alex said. "It be some of the toughest, rough neck niggas you know that be wanting to get with a dude on the side."

"Uh uhn," Roshida said. She frowned. "Naw, not Damien. He only like womens. I tried to flirt with him one time. He acted like he was interested, but it didn't go nowhere. He prolly thought I was gon' tell somebody."

Eva chuckled. It was frustrating that she couldn't tell her friends what she knew about Damien's sexuality. It happened three years ago, and it was only a couple of times, but Eva would never forget how yummy Damien's chocolate skin looked when he took off his shirt. She licked him everywhere from his thighs to his earlobes. Damien was a slow, passionate lover back then. But Eva heard he had a few strange fetishes now; things she probably wouldn't be into.

But then again, maybe she would. She'd be willing to try, if Damien ever looked her way again.

"Nigga, I'ma bust yo head!"

"What the?" Eva's erotic daydream came to a screeching halt. She shot to her feet and hurried out of her office. Alex and Roshida were right behind her.

The Material Operations department was filled with stretchers, IV poles and other equipment the crew picked up and delivered to various departments throughout the hospital. The break room had two long tables, a cluster of chairs, a fridge and a microwave. Eva was surprised (but not too shocked) to see six of her employees squatting in the middle of the room with money and die at their feet.

"I know y'all ain't playing craps in here!" she shouted.

A young man named Harold jumped up and stomped towards her. "That nigga owe me ten dollars, Eva!" He pointed to a Hispanic fellow named Edgar who had a few bills squeezed tightly in his fist.

"Nuh-uhn!" Edgar shook his head furiously. "I caught those dice, Eva. That roll didn't count."

The guy next to Edgar nodded. "He did. He caught 'em."

"You can't be catching no goddamned dice!" Harold whined.

"Yeah you can," Edgar said.

"He don't know how to play no dice," another boy added.

Sadly, this wasn't the worst thing Eva had seen in her department. She stuck a rigid finger in Harold's face. "I know you not stupid enough to gamble at work!" she growled. "If one of them managers walk up in here, don't you know *all y'all getting fired*?" She fixed evil eyes on the lot of them. "Why y'all in here anyway? Ain't no jobs? I know your pagers been going off!"

The boys looked around sheepishly.

"Jamie!" Eva yelled over her shoulder. "Check the computer to see if it's some jobs in there!"

Eva kept mean eyes on her rowdy crew while Jamie accessed the database.

When she got their system pulled up, Jamie said, "Yeah, it's a lot of them! About fifteen!"

Eva shook her head. "What y'all trying to do, get *me* fired or something?"

The boys shook their heads and looked down in embarrassment.

"Get out of here!" Eva ordered. "Go do a job! Gimme those damned dice!"

The gamblers put their money away and grumbled vague apologies on their way out of the department. Eva maintained her stern disposition until the last of them dropped the die in her hand and disappeared. When she went back to her office, Eva was surprised to see Alex and Roshida following her.

"What y'all doing? Y'all need to go do some jobs, too."

"Aww man," Alex said.

"Come on, Eva," Roshida pleaded.

"Get out of here!" Eva snapped. "You think this a game?"

Roshida didn't know how to respond to that because it usually *was* a game. Eva only buckled-down and acted like a real boss once, maybe twice a month.

When Alex and Roshida made their exit, Eva frowned at her last straggler.

"Umm, that means you, too."

"I'm almost done," Jamie said. She continued working on her résumé.

"I'm not playing," Eva said. "Close it now, or I'm deleting it."

"What about Rodney?" Jamie said.

"What about him?"

Jamie opened the tab for their job system and quickly found his name. "He been doing the same job for two and a half hours," she complained.

"What Rodney got to do with you?" Eva said.

"I'm just saying," Jamie said

"Why don't you worry about *you*, and let me worry about Rodney?" Eva suggested. "That's the problem around here: Everybody always in somebody else's business. You not supposed to be doing a résumé while you at work anyway."

Jamie smacked her lips loudly, her features set in a sneer. "*Man!*" She saved her résumé and reluctantly backed away from the computer. "I hate Harold and them! They always getting everybody in trouble!" Jamie mumbled something else as she left to do the work she was hired for.

When she was alone, Eva took a seat behind her desk and checked the job system for herself. Jamie was right; Rodney had been logged into the same assignment for more than two hours.

Rodney's scam was simple: Whenever someone in the hospital needed a piece of equipment, they put the request in the computer. "The system" would page someone in Material Operations and offer them the "job." Once an employee accepted the job, the system would list them as "Occupied," so they wouldn't get paged again until they called the system and indicated they completed their assignment.

The easiest way to avoid new assignments was to *not* tell the system you completed your current job. Eva was supposed to stay on top of anyone who tried to slack-off in this manner.

She paged Rodney once, waited a few minutes and then paged him again. Three minutes later Eva paged Rodney a third time. When he called back, Eva noted that he was calling from somewhere in the parking garage.

Rodney began their conversation with an annoyed, "What you want?"

"What you mean, *What I want*?" Eva couldn't believe his audacity. "You been on the same job for almost three hours,

Rodney! It don't take that long to take a wheelchair to the Jackson building."

"I forgot to call the system," Rodney explained.

"How you forget?" Eva demanded. "Didn't you think something was wrong when the system didn't page you for two hours? And what are you doing in the parking garage? You bet not be taking nothing to your car..."

Even as she spoke, Eva knew her threat didn't hold any weight. She didn't do anything the first time she caught Rodney stealing, and he knew she wouldn't do anything now.

"I ain't take nothing," Rodney said. "Is that it? I gotta go."

Eva's nostrils flared. "You need to watch how you talking to me. I don't know what's wrong with you today, but I'm still your boss. Don't forget that."

Rodney sighed rather loudly into the phone.

Eva was at her wit's end. "You better—"

"Where everybody at?"

Eva looked up and saw another one of her employees at her door. It was Mary; a good worker, but a notorious snitch. Mary and Eva maintained a professional, rather than friendly relationship.

"Meet me on the ground floor of the Avery building," Eva told Rodney. "By the ATM. We need to talk."

She hung up on him, rather than give Rodney a chance to undermine her authority again.

Eva stood and told Mary, "Everybody's on a job. You need to call the system, if you not on break."

Mary went straight to the phone as ordered, and Eva left to meet up with the biggest knucklehead in the hospital.

≈≈≈≈≈≈

Rodney could be a jerk at times, but he wasn't foolish enough to completely avoid his supervisor when she really wanted to talk to him. He was waiting on the ground floor of the Avery building, just as Eva instructed. She was so frustrated, she didn't want to talk to him inside, where others could hear. She stomped towards him with her arms folded over her chest. She didn't stop walking when she and Rodney locked eyes.

She told him, "Come on," and then exited the building through one of the rarely used side doors. Rodney followed her outside into the night air.

It was nine-thirty pm. The sun had completely disappeared from the sky, giving way to a bright, crescent moon. The atmosphere was cool and pleasant. The street lights attracted a frenzy of moths in search of warmth and a mate. The hospital had cameras mounted all around the exterior of the building, but Eva didn't think anyone was watching them. Even if someone was, there was nothing illicit about a supervisor taking a walk with one of her employees.

"What the hell is wrong with you?" Eva asked. She had her hands stuffed in her pockets now. Eva wore the same black scrubs everyone in her department had on, and she preferred baggy over tight-fitting garments. Most people thought she was a tomboy, but it was actually Eva's past life as a gang girl that influenced her attire.

"What I do?" Rodney asked.

"You know what you did," Eva said. "I told you, *you can't be on a job for that long*. I'm not the only one who sees your numbers. If the manager decides to check up on you, he's going to call *me* in his office first. He's gonna ask why I didn't do nothing about it."

"My bad," Rodney said. "I wasn't feeling good."

"Whatever. Ain't nothing wrong with you."

They made a right at the next corner and headed for the Meredith building.

"I *wasn't* feeling good," Rodney insisted. "I had a headache. I took some Excedrin's and sat down, waiting for my head to stop hurting."

"Why didn't you log off your job?"

"I thought I did."

Eva punched him unexpectedly in the shoulder. "Stop lying."

The punch hurt a little more than Rodney expected. He rubbed the sore spot.

"Ouch! Quit playing, man." He pushed her playfully.

Eva pushed him back with both hands, and Rodney stumbled off the sidewalk.

"Don't be putting your hands on me," Eva warned.

She looked like she was serious, but Rodney pushed her back anyway. This time it was Eva who had to take a step into the soft grass. She turned on him with her fists raised.

"Boy, you better stop pushing girls!"

Rodney threw up his hands in a defensive gesture. He was bigger and taller than Eva, but she was strong and scrappy. Rodney got into a play fight with her once, and she hit him in the chest so hard, she left a bruise that was visible for nearly a week.

"Alright, damn," Rodney said, chuckling. He put an arm around her shoulder. "What you so mad for?"

Eva pushed him away again. "Get off me, boy! It's cameras..."

Rodney looked around. "Where?"

Eva elbowed him in the ribs. "Don't *look* at 'em!"

Rodney lowered his gaze. "My bad."

"Come in here," Eva told him.

She used her ID badge to gain entry into the Meredith building through another side door. The ground floor was mostly empty, but there were still a dozen employees and patients milling about. Eva headed straight for the staff elevators (which were a lot less pretty but 100% less monitored than the visitor elevators).

Rodney followed her. The two didn't speak until their lift arrived. They stepped on together, and Eva pressed the button for the eighth floor. As soon as the doors closed, she backed Rodney into a corner and poked a rigid finger in his chest.

"Why you so hardheaded?"

"*I didn't do nothing,*" Rodney said.

"I told you; *Do what you got to do, but don't get caught,*" Eva reminded.

"What you talking about?" Rodney wanted to know. "I didn't get caught doing nothing."

"You been on the same job for two and a half hours," Eva said. "And yes you did get caught."

"Oh." Rodney grinned. He thought it was something serious.

"It ain't funny," Eva said.

Rodney wrapped his arms around her. "My bad."

"Get off me," Eva said, but she didn't push him this time.

"I said I was sorry. You don't forgive me?" Rodney asked.

His hands slipped down her back and came to a rest on her butt cheeks. Eva tried to keep a straight face, but she smiled, too. She couldn't help it. Rodney was too goddamned cute.

"You make me sick," she told him.

Rodney gave her ass a playful squeeze. "You caught me, or somebody else?"

"It was Jamie," Eva informed.

Rodney smacked his lips. "She can't do nothing."

"She can start rumors," Eva countered. "And then everybody's gonna want to know why I don't go hard on you."

"You do go hard on me," Rodney said. He fondled her ass with increased vigor.

The elevator bell rang. Eva turned away from Rodney and straightened her clothes. She stood next to him, but Rodney pulled her back in front of him.

She tried to shrug him off. "Stop, boy."

"Stand in front of me," Rodney said. "I'm hard."

His disclosure made Eva's labia tingle. She stood in front of him, facing forward, and Rodney leaned on the back wall of the elevator. The doors opened to no one, and then they closed again after a few seconds. Eva hit the B button, sending them down to the basement.

She turned back to Rodney as they descended.

"You hard?"

Rather than wait for him to respond, she reached and felt for herself. Rodney wasn't rock solid, but he was halfway there. Eva pulled the drawstring holding his scrubs up. Rodney pushed her hand away.

"We ain't got time for that." He watched the floor lights blink one by one.

7, 6, 5...

"Let me see it." Eva's eyes were wide and devilish.

"Not on no elevator," Rodney cautioned. "I ain't gon' have time to tie my pants back."

Eva looked him in the eyes. Her heart raced. She wrapped her hand around the bulge in his pants and gave it a tender squeeze. Rodney stared intensely into her eyes. Eva's lips quivered. Her expression was stuck between a smile and extreme thirst. Her husband might have thought this look was sexy, but Rodney could barely maintain eye contact.

In the beginning, he was attracted to Eva. She wasn't really fat, her titties were big, and she had a nice ass to squeeze on. But as time went on, Rodney came to understand that his attraction to Eva was never physical – it was all mental. It was the thrill of being with an older woman (who also happened to be his boss) that turned him on.

Now that he'd had his way with Eva in pretty much every way imaginable, Rodney no longer desired to be with her. Her titties were big, but they were also saggy. Her ass wasn't all that, and her gut was utterly disgusting. She didn't have a lot of stretch marks, but Eva had a saggy, fat-filled pouch that would make you throw up if you stared at it long enough.

And her face... *Jesus*. That had to be the worst of all. Eva was only thirty-seven, but she lived a hard life. And it showed. She tried to hide her wrinkles and the bags under her eyes with makeup, but that only made it worse. Rodney thought she looked like a fucking clown. The only reason his manhood responded to her now was because Eva became an excellent head hunter during her *many* years on earth. In all his conquests, Rodney never met a woman who could slob on his knob better.

The elevator dinged again. Eva turned quickly to face the front. When the doors opened, she stepped off. Rodney repositioned his erection and followed her. Eva wanted to sit him down somewhere and straddle his lap, but full intercourse was too risky at this time of day.

Instead she led Rodney into a huge storage room. It was about the size of a high school gym. It was so cluttered with equipment, you couldn't see from one side to the other. The best part about the storage room was this space belonged exclusively to Material Operations, so no one watching the cameras would become suspicious about them going in there. Plus there were no cameras on the inside.

There were plenty of spots to get busy in the storage room, but Eva was a supervisor, so she had to be extra careful. She led Rodney through a maze of hospital beds and stretchers until they reached a rarely used wash room. There was a water heater in there and a sink and a mop bucket. The room was dusty and smelled of Ajax, but Eva didn't mind. She stepped inside without flipping on the light. Rodney followed and closed the door behind himself.

The washroom was completely dark. Eva felt around until she found Rodney's stomach. She lifted his shirt and fingered the strings of his scrub pants again. She undid the knot blindly, and Rodney pushed his pants and boxers down his thighs.

Eva squeezed his manhood with both hands and whispered, "You can cum," before she got down to business.

Rodney chuckled under his breath. He grabbed Eva's head and gradually began to pump his hips as her slurping noises filled the room. Eva's mouth was wet and warm. Rodney was glad it was so dark in there. He closed his eyes and imagined Eva was someone else entirely.

CHAPTER FOUR
DAMIEN THE AUTHORITARIAN

At exactly ten-thirty that night, all of the time clocks at the hospital had to go into overdrive to keep up with the second biggest shift-change of the day. Most of the nurses had to stay and give report to the incoming crew, but the CNA's, housekeepers and Material Operations employees had no such responsibilities. Most of them had been hanging out by the time clock for the past five minutes, waiting on the exact second they could swipe their badge and speed walk to the parking garage.

In the ER, housekeeping supervisor Brenda Turner was eager to see the hospital in her rearview mirror as well. But Brenda was training a new girl, and she didn't want to teach her any bad habits.

"You see how everybody's running out of here?" Brenda asked her. The two ladies strolled through the Trauma side, following a blue line on the floor that helped visitors find their way around the ER.

"They acting like this place is on fire," Brenda continued. "It ain't a good look. Makes people think you hate your job. Everybody wanna get out of here, but some of them kids in M.O., you'll see them *running* out the door. Ain't gon' do nothing but spend they money and be broke again by Monday. Don't make no sense."

The new hire, a pretty Puerto Rican woman named Raquel, didn't know what to think of her boss. Brenda stayed with Raquel most of the day, showing her the dos and don'ts and ins and outs of the hospital. But most of what Raquel learned today was petty gossip.

Whenever Brenda taught her how to make a bed or sanitize an area, she also told Raquel about any nurse on the unit who was a ho or a bitch. Raquel knew who most of the snitches in their department were, and Brenda even showed her how to trick one of the vending machines into giving up a free soda.

Her first day at the hospital was so bizarre, Raquel began to wonder if she was on some kind of hidden camera show. The moment she accepted that her boss really was a conniving, small-minded, backstabbing slacker, a white man would appear out of nowhere with a microphone in his hand.

He'd approach her saying, "Surprise, Raquel! You're on *Jobs From Hell*! If you look this way, you'll see a camera there, and there, and all of those security cameras overhead are really for our show! Hardy har har!"

And Raquel would exclaim, "I knew it! *I knew Brenda couldn't be for real!*"

But as two hours turned into five, and five hours turned into eight, Raquel completed her first full day on the job, and no one ever stopped to tell her this wasn't real. Which meant Brenda really was the worst supervisor in history, and Jackson Memorial had more illicit stories than any soap opera that ever aired.

But all of that was just fine with Raquel. Initially she was embarrassed to take a job as a *janitor*, but hearing about all of the drama at the hospital made it a lot better. If she had to mop floors, at least she could also gossip about who was sleeping with whom. And maybe she could sneak some medical supplies home every now and then.

Hell, if Raquel played her cards right, she might garnish some attention from a young doctor or one of the handsome nurses she met today. She didn't have a lot of smarts, but Raquel was attractive and *sort of* single. Her baby-daddy just accepted a five-year prison sentence. So Raquel needed someone to help support her until he got out.

"You ain't outta here yet?" Brenda asked another housekeeper they passed in the ER.

"I'm going to leave now," Amina replied. "Just had this last room…"

"Hurry up," Brenda told her. "You know we ain't paying no overtime."

"Okay. Yes, ma'am," Amina said, and she got a little pep in her step.

"Stupid girl," Brenda muttered after she and Raquel passed her.

"What's wrong with her?" Raquel asked, eager to get the scoop on another one of her co-workers.

"Nothing," Brenda said.

Raquel was confused by her supervisor's sudden change of heart. Brenda told her plenty of rumors today about people who were cheating or stealing. She even told Raquel about a couple of folks who might have herpes. Raquel didn't understand why Brenda wouldn't air Amina's dirty laundry.

"She pissed you off?" Raquel pressed. "Is she lazy?"

"Naw," Brenda said, staring straight ahead. "She not lazy. Amina's a hard worker. She prolly the hardest worker on this shift."

"Oh," Raquel said, now even more intrigued. "She be trying to sneak her some overtime though, huh?"

"Amina's not like that," Brenda said. "She do everything I tell her to. She don't never try to get over."

"Oh." Raquel kept smiling, though she was seriously perplexed. She had only known Brenda for one day. That probably wasn't long enough to press for more details, but Brenda opened the door by being such a gossip. The ball was rolling too fast to stop now.

"She look quiet," Raquel offered. "I can tell she got a sneaky side to her…"

"Yeah, she do," Brenda said.

Raquel grinned. *Bingo.*

"Amina, she pissed me off today," Brenda confided. "I asked her to help me out with something, but she won't. But it ain't got nothing to do with work, so I can't be mad at her…"

Raquel nodded and listened, hoping Brenda would let it all out. No such luck.

"I really can't talk about it," Brenda said.

"I won't tell nobody," Raquel promised.

Brenda smiled at her. Raquel had only been working with her for one day, but Brenda had already taken a liking to her. She could tell Raquel would be one of the good ones. Sometimes when you come to work tired, and the first thing on your mind when you clock-in is when you'll get to clock-out, it helped to have a friend you can talk to; someone you can tell a secret without worrying about it coming back to hurt you. It makes the day go by faster.

But as she stared into Raquel's pretty brown eyes, Brenda began to wonder if the new-hire might be useful in another way. Raquel was young and attractive and not fat at all. She was of medium height with long, wavy hair. Raquel had lovely lady lumps in the back and in the front. A few CNA's and M.O. employees already took note of Raquel when Brenda showed her around today.

Brenda wondered if a certain police officer who provided part-time security at the hospital would notice Raquel as well. Brenda didn't know what Damien offered or threatened his mistresses with, but maybe she could get the upper hand on him if she got to his next victim *first*. Brenda chuckled. Yes, Raquel was just Damien's type, wasn't she? Brenda was pretty sure he preferred Hispanic women; the younger and more naive the better.

"I can't talk about it right now," Brenda said. "But I can tell you it's a big deal, what's going on with Amina. I tried to help her. I tried to help get her out of her situation, but she didn't want my help. I thought she was smart, but she's not. But maybe you could help me out, a little later on..."

"I'll help you," Raquel said right away. "What I got to do?"

Brenda's smile grew larger. Her heartbeats were hot and quick. "If everything go like I think it will, you won't have to do nothing," Brenda said. "Everything will come to you..."

Raquel was growing irritated with these charades. She decided to let it go for now. If Brenda didn't trust her enough to say what was going on, there was nothing Raquel could say to convince her otherwise. After a few weeks on the job, Raquel would show Brenda that she was down for almost any caper — especially if it put extra money in her pocket.

"So, are we done?" Raquel asked. "I can go home?"

"Yeah, we're done," Brenda said. "You can clock out on any clock you want to. Tomorrow you'll be working with Devin. Amina will be here too, but don't talk to her about nothing I said."

"I won't," Raquel promised. "I got your back," she threw in for good measure.

Brenda nodded. "I hope you do, but we'll see." She chuckled. "We will see."

≈ ≈ ≈ ≈ ≈ ≈

Amina Perez left the hospital at 10:38 with a knot of dread twisting in her stomach. She was anxious about her date tonight. She was also worried about the conversation she had with her supervisor at work. Brenda was a nice enough lady, but Amina thought she was the absolute *last* person who should be in a leadership position.

Brenda never did any real work herself, and Amina didn't think her boss embodied any of the hospital's core principles. The president of Jackson Memorial encouraged everyone to demonstrate *integrity, empathy* and *honor* – not the immature gossip Brenda always helped to spread. Amina thought employees like Brenda were a fungus growing within the hospital: They weren't bad enough to cripple the system, but they were annoying, contagious and virtually impossible to eradicate.

But her supervisor's work ethics aside, Amina didn't like the way Brenda questioned her about Damien. Brenda spoke like she had definite proof of some wrongdoing, but Amina knew that couldn't possibly be the case. Amina wondered if she had allayed Brenda's suspicions, or if Brenda would resume questioning her on Monday. Amina didn't know if she should report the incident to Human Resources or leave well-enough alone.

Amina also wondered if she should tell Damien that Brenda was on to them. Deep down she knew that she should, but Damien was likely to cut her off if she did. He was so careful. Damien always watched his back and paid attention to every little detail. He constantly questioned Amina, asking if anyone asked about him, if her family knew where she was when they were together or if anyone else was suspicious.

Damien would want to know about Brenda. But the more Amina thought about it, the more she convinced herself not to tell him. She and Damien had been involved for nearly three months, and Amina had come to depend on him. Sure his preferences were oddly kinky and sometimes downright degrading, but when you think about it, mopping floors and cleaning up other people's vomit was also kind of degrading.

Amina's husband was in the last stages of prostate cancer. He was bedridden, far from the provider he used to be. He couldn't give Amina the love and attention he once did, and he didn't have a solution for the bills that were piling up. Amina was her family's sole breadwinner now. She didn't think she could keep a roof over their head without Damien helping her. In fact, she knew she couldn't.

She wouldn't tell him that Brenda might be on to them. She wouldn't tell him his games were getting too weird, and she wouldn't tell him that sometimes she dreaded hooking up with him.

In the past few weeks Amina had come to understand that the things she did for Damien made her a *whore*, no better than a street prostitute, but she wouldn't tell him that, either. She had to grit her teeth and bear it until God delivered her from her sinful ways and offered a better solution to her family's financial woes. That was all there was to it.

Amina pushed her husband far from her mind as she exited the freeway and made a right on Lancaster Avenue.

≈ ≈ ≈ ≈ ≈ ≈ ≈

Damien waited for Amina in room 112 at the Great Western on Lancaster. He chose this location because it was in a rough neighborhood; the kind of place where junkies went to feed their monkey, whores performed tricks and nobody knew anyone's name. The run down hotel was dangerous by day. By night it was a virtual nightmare. If you stayed past midnight, you'd see zombies stalking shadows in the parking lot, their dead eyes

50

scanning the ground for a leaf that might really be a dollar or a stranger who might be worthy of robbing.

Damien didn't worry about any trouble befalling him at the hotel because he was THE LAW, and no matter how strung out a dopefiend was, they always respected THE LAW. Damien didn't arrive at the hotel in his patrol car, but he was wearing his full police uniform, complete with badge, handcuffs and his standard issue Glock 22. Damien didn't have to work tonight, but he liked to get dressed up for his trysts. And if you're going to play dress-up, you might as well choose an outfit that comes with a pistol.

Damien Glover was 33 years old, married with two kids. Most people thought his supreme physique was the product of a sports background, but Damien never got into basketball or football when he was younger. He grew up in a west side neighborhood called *Como,* where all of the recreational centers were boarded up, and only crack dealers hung out at the park.

Damien was bullied as a child. In his teenage years the same bullies attacked him again when he wouldn't join their gang. He started doing push-ups when he was twelve, and Damien found heaven in the weight room when he got to high school.

By the time he reached his junior year, no one was picking on Damien anymore. The coaches begged him to try out, for *any* sport, but Damien never wanted to be an athlete. Plus he could barely keep his grades above passing. Damien graduated near the bottom of his class and went straight to the Army. Four years later he returned to Overbrook Meadows and joined the police force.

Damien didn't consider himself a pervert or a sexual deviant, though he'd be the first to admit that he didn't agree with the "normal" rules of marriage and monogamy. He thought it was important to have a life partner who would be there for you in your golden years, but Damien didn't think he should limit himself to sex with just his wife. Why should he? All of the males in the animal kingdom mated with as many females as possible. Was Damien not as majestic as a lion or a tiger? Hell, even male mice got it on as much as possible during their short time on earth.

As a police officer, Damien found that sex was easy and plentiful. He slept with members of the police force. He slept with women he pulled over for speeding. He slept with prostitutes, runaways, boosters and boppers. Damien slept with so many women, he eventually grew bored and had to come up with new ways to spice up his sex life.

His first fetish wasn't that bad: Damien could only get aroused if his partner was handcuffed. Later he wanted to be with women who were high on crack or speed. Damien moved on to squirters and gaggers, but it seemed every time he satiated one appetite, a new thirst would emerge. That was not a problem because there were millions of women in the Dallas/Overbrook Meadows area. It wasn't hard to find the ones who would yield to his will.

Damien lay on his back in room 112 with his head propped up on two pillows, his legs dangling over the side of the bed. He flipped the channels on an antique remote until pornographic images appeared on the hotel television. Damien's fetish for Amina was simple: He was the bad cop, and she was the hotel maid. Damien even had a real cleaning cart in the room. The hotel manager didn't understand why he wanted it left there, and he wasn't too fond of the idea.

"We'll clean for you," the manger insisted. "You don't have to clean."

Damien greased the wheels with a fifty dollar bill. His badge helped moved things along as well. A real maid dropped the cart off three minutes after Damien entered the room. Ten minutes after that, there was a faint knock at the door.

"Who is it?" Damien growled.

"Housekeeping," someone said.

"Come in," Damien instructed.

Amina opened the door and looked around indecisively before she entered. She was still wearing her gray scrubs from the hospital. Her eyes were large and fretful, like a deer staring at two bright headlights.

"You want me to clean?" she asked.

"Yeah," Damien said. "Come on in..."

≈≈≈≈≈≈≈

Amina entered the room with a dry mouth, a cluster of goose bumps on her arms. Her fingers trembled when she turned to lock the door. She wasn't afraid of Damien, but she was always nervous about her role in his strange scenarios. The way he watched her made her feel like she was in a Broadway play, but no one bothered to give her a script.

Amina scanned the room quickly and saw a cleaning cart on the opposite side of the bed. She walked to it slowly, looking around for her mess for the day. She found it on the floor in the hallway leading to the bathroom. Someone spilled half a can of Coke on the floor. The can was nowhere to be found. The stain was roughly the size of a grapefruit.

Amina looked back at Damien. He was sitting up now, watching her. She looked away timidly and said, "I clean this," as she searched the cart for the needed supplies. The cleaning cart he provided wasn't the same as the one she used at work, but it was fully stocked. Amina found a few hand towels to blot the stain. There was also spray bottle filled with a soapy solution.

Amina dropped to her knees and got started on the task at hand. The room smelled of stale cigarettes. An unseen woman moaned on the television mounted above her. Amina's heartbeats were hard and heavy. Her breath caught when she heard a sound on the bed. She looked back and saw that Damien had scooted to the edge of the mattress, so he could watch her. He leaned forward with his forearms on his knees. His face was dark and indecipherable. His upper body was massive. The power of the uniform made him look even bigger.

Amina returned her attention to the stain. She didn't scrub in a sexy manner. She didn't shake her ass or arch her back. She worked with the same efficiency she used at the hospital. She didn't mind the cleaning. She was nervous because she never knew when Damien would take her. She knew he liked her to talk, so she told him, "This isn't that bad. I'm almost done."

Damien said, "Some more got spilled in the bathroom."

Amina nodded. "Yes, sir. I clean it all for you, Mister Damien."

"Clean it *good*," Damien told her. His voice was low, like a truck engine. "You didn't do so good last time."

Amina knew he didn't mean that. She always did an excellent job. But she said, "I'm sorry, Mister Damien. I did my best."

"Clean it like you do at the hospital," Damien ordered. There was a bulge growing against his thigh. He brought a hand to his lap and massaged it.

Amina's whole body was hot. Very hot. She sprayed a few squirts of the cleaning solution on the carpet and blotted the stain again. The scent of the chemicals filled her nostrils and triggered something strange. Amina's nipples became erect. A quiver started in her stomach and descended, settling between her legs. It was okay this time, but Amina became aroused earlier today, when she was cleaning a room at work. She now realized that it was the smell of the cleaning supplies that turned her on.

Was she becoming a freak? A pervert? Amina forced the thoughts from her mind. If you don't want to know the answer, it's best not to ask the question. She finished scrubbing the small stain and stood stiffly. She returned the cleaning supplies to the cart and pushed it towards the bathroom.

"I clean in there now," she said without looking back.

"Go ahead," Damien said. "I wanna watch." He pushed off the bed and stretched his stiff muscles.

≈ ≈ ≈ ≈ ≈ ≈

In the bathroom, Amina found another mess. It wasn't that bad. Someone splashed soda on the mirror and poured the remainder in the sink. The perpetrator tossed the empty can in the shower rather than put it in the dustbin next to the toilet.

Amina went to the shower first. She tossed the can in the trash and wiped up the few droplets that spilled near the drain. When she turned back, she saw that Damien was in the bathroom with her. He filled the doorway completely, like the immigration officers who used to harass her family when she lived in Laredo. Amina looked from his gun to his badge to his hard face that didn't look pleased at all with the work she was doing.

"That mirror's filthy," Damien said. "Why you didn't clean it?"

"I, I'm sorry," Amina said. "I clean it now." She approached him and gestured for the cart behind him. "I need, I need the spray."

Damien stepped aside so she could get to her cart. He blocked the doorway again when she started on the mirror. He watched her closely, his erection growing by degrees. He grinned, proud that he was able to turn his fantasy into reality. His ultimate goal was to have sex with Amina at the hospital, but this was just as good. In fact, it was better because here he had complete control over everything.

He approached her from behind and watched her face in the mirror. She avoided eye contact as much as possible. That was perfect. Damien told her, "Clean it good, like you do at the hospital."

Amina told him, "Yes sir, Mister Damien."

She sprayed the whole mirror again, and her face was obscured behind the soapy gloss. Damien raised her shirt and watched the muscles in her back flex slightly as she worked. He saw the top of her pink panties. He grabbed hold of her hips and pulled her butt into his lap. Amina pretended not to notice. She continued to scrub dutifully.

Damien reached around and undid the drawstring holding her pants up. He pulled them down her hips with the panties entangled. He stared at her bare ass and then looked into the mirror again. Amina wiped it, and she looked at him, too. She still looked fearful, but there was also desire in her big, brown eyes. Damien rubbed her ass and told her, "Wash that sink, too."

"Yes sir, Mis, Mister Damien."

Amina sprayed more soap.

Damien undid his belt. He placed it on the floor carefully because his holster was connected to it. He dug a condom from his front pocket before he undid his pants. He tore it open as his britches slid to his knees.

"You ain't scrubbing," Damien noticed.

"I'm sorry, Mister Damien," Amina said. She didn't have any scouring powder or pads, but she rubbed the sink harder with her hand towel. Damien pulled her hips until she took a couple of steps back. She could barely reach the sink now. She dropped the towel and held on to the porcelain as Damien rubbed between her legs. His fingers were warm and comforting on her labia. He inserted two of them with no trouble at all.

"Why you so wet?" he asked. "You want me to fuck you, don't you?"

"Yes. Yes, sir, Mister Damien."

Amina's accent was thick. She was so weak and helpless and *foreign*. Just listening to her made Damien rock hard. He rolled the condom down the length of his shaft and then rubbed her labia with the head.

"This what you want, ain't it?"

"Yes," she breathed.

Damien watched her in the mirror. Amina had her head down. She blew hot breaths down the sink drain. Damien slid in smoothly until he reached the halfway point. The harder he pushed, the tighter Amina's walls were. She gasped. She looked up, and they locked eyes.

"I told you to clean it right," Damien said. He backed out a little and plunged again. Hard. Amina yelped.

"*Aye*! I'm sorry, Mister Damien. *I'm sorry!*"

"You ain't sorry." Damien stroked, slow and steady now. Amina's kitty felt like a hot, wet glove. It gripped him tighter with each pump of his hips.

"You think about me while you're at the hospital, don't you?" Damien asked.

"Yuh, yes, Mister Damien."

"Yes what?"

"I think... *Aye. Uh.* I think about you."

"You think about what?" He grabbed her hips and pulled slowly until his pubic hair made contact with her butt. Amina screamed. She felt him all the way in her toes.

"You think about *what*?" Damien said again.

"*Your dick*," she breathed. "*Huh. Uh. Your big dick!*"

"You like black dicks, don't you?"

"*Yes!*" She lowered her head, her breaths ragged. She gripped the sink so hard her fingertips turned white.

"Look at me," Damien demanded.

Amina did as she was told. Her mouth hung open. Her hair hung in her face.

"What you think about, when you at work?" Damien wanted to know.

"*You*," Amina moaned. "Your big, black dick."

The sound of their thighs clapping was constant now, rhythmic.

"It's big, ain't it?"

"*Yes, Mister Damien! Yes!*"

His strokes increased in speed and pressure, and Amina's legs began to tremble. She could barely hold herself up. She never thought she'd commit adultery, let alone participate in a scene as bizarre as this, but she and Damien had been together nearly a dozen times now. Amina was genuinely attracted to him, and she had come to enjoy their time together, no matter how twisted his desires were.

She told him, "*I'm cumming, Mister Damien,*" because he demanded to know when she reached a climax.

He said, "Say my name while you cumming."

Amina's whole body shuddered. A wave of ecstasy rolled through her like a seizure.

"*Aye, aye! I'm cumming, Mister Damien. I'm cumming! I love it! Aye! I, huh, I love it...*"

≈≈≈≈≈≈≈

Damien took her to the bedroom and made love to her properly before their time together came to an end. Before she left, Damien asked Amina if her boys had enough clothes to get them through the rest of the school year. They did, but she told him, "No, Mister Damien."

He gave her four hundred dollars, about the same amount she made for a full week's work at the hospital. Amina left the hotel with moist stains on her underwear and next month's rent tucked safely in her purse. Later that night, she thought about Damien as she lay in bed with her ailing husband.

She wondered if Damien knew that she'd fallen in love with him, that she'd sleep with him for free if he wanted to. She wondered if Damien ever thought about her when he went home to his wife. Amina didn't think he would leave his spouse for a lowly housekeeper, but there had to be something Damien needed from her that his wife couldn't or wouldn't offer. If Amina continued to fulfill his desires, then maybe she could have him, forever.

It was foolish thinking, but Amina was an immigrant with a sick husband and little hope for a better tomorrow. She needed *something* to believe in.

SHOCKING! Drastic, amazing phenomena
Awesome: These spastic cravings for trauma
Wonderfully delicious morsels, like gumdrops
Like raindrops – this train slows *not* – no stopping
It now. Open the floodgates. It's rolling
This loathing for insipid pleasure; it's growing
It's glowing, consuming like fire, cascading
Downhill – freestyle rollerblading. This blazing
This craving, these wants, this prickling desire
Inspires the masses to die or get higher

CHAPTER FIVE
SANDRA'S ITCH

At six pm that same Friday night, registered nurse Sandra Alexander was trying to get ready for her 7pm - 7am shift at Jackson Memorial. But it was hard to maintain focus because Sandra had an itch.

Today was payday. Sandra made 26 dollars an hour, plus another two dollars an hour for working the graveyard shift. Everyone at the hospital was paid twice a month. Sandra's check was direct deposited into her checking account.

She already checked on her money today and was disappointed to see that most of her funds were already gone. The balance in her checking account had been negative for more than a week, so Bank of America took their money off the top. And then they took their mortgage payment for last month because that was late, too.

Sandra still owed more money for her cellphone, cable and electric bills, but she didn't really have to pay all of those. The electric bill was probably a must, but Sandra had a DVD player and a lot of old movies, so she didn't absolutely need cable. Her iPhone felt like a necessity, but was it really? Sandra racked her brain as she paced through her cluttered home. If she didn't pay her cable bill, then she wouldn't have internet services either. But if she paid her phone bill, she could use the iPhone to get online. Except her cellphone was past due as well!

Sandra hurried to her computer in the living room. She checked her account again to see if any other bills she forgot about had eaten away at her dwindling balance. Why the hell did she sign up for so many auto-pays in the first place? Who does that? Sandra guessed it had to be some rich person; someone who made so much money, it didn't matter how much their bills were from month to month. Sandra didn't think she had ever been that kind of person, but in the back of her mind she thought maybe she had been. Why else would she sign up for so many damned auto-pays?

Her paycheck today was $2,112.34. After the bank took what she owed them, her balance was $395.14. Her cellphone bill was $173. Her cable bill was $118. Her electric bill was $155. Sandra's knee bounced quickly as she punched the numbers in her calculator.

She yelled, "*Fuck*!" when the adding machine gave her the total. She brought a hand to her mouth and chewed on her thumbnail. Well, she tried to chew on it, but she couldn't find anything to bite down on. She looked at the digit in confusion. She saw that she already chewed halfway down the nail plate. She had been gnawing on the skin surrounding the nail plate as well. Her thumb was throbbing, completely raw. And it was bleeding a little.

It didn't even look like a thumb anymore; it looked like a big toe. It looked like someone dropped a dumbbell on their foot, and rather than go to the hospital, they let a couple of hungry rats chew on it. Sandra cursed under her breath again. She twisted her hand to and fro and finally found an angle that allowed her to nibble on some of the skin around her cuticle.

The rest of Sandra's nine digits didn't look this bad. When she was in high school, she used to chew all of her fingernails. But her aunt taught her to pick *one* nail she wanted to bite and leave the rest alone. Sandra chose this thumb more than a decade ago. She'd been nibbling on it from time to time since then, but she never went to town on it like this. She was teetering on the brink of full blown **Fuck it** mode. As she stared at the digits on her calculator, Sandra made up her mind which way she wanted to go.

"Fuck it."

She shook her head in frustration. She balled her hand into a fist and pressed it to her lips. She squeezed her eyes closed, but the tears got past anyway. She needed $446 to pay her remaining bills. She only had $395 in the bank. And today was payday. And she didn't have much food left in the fridge. And she hadn't counted the gas money it would take to get to and from work for the next two weeks.

It was impossible to pay all of her bills, so why try? Why not take her four hundred out of the bank, so at least she'd have some say so as to where it got spent? If she left it there, Lord only knew which auto-pay would come through next.

You gotta get that money out, Sandra told herself. *Don't be no fool. You worked too hard. Don't let them do you like that.*

The more she thought about it, the more Sandra agreed with this logic. It was her money. The cable company couldn't take something she didn't want to give them. Plus Sandra could get another payday loan tomorrow morning. She could get a loan for up to $500, and that would be enough to pay all three of her bills. So *technically* she didn't have a need for the four hundred dollars she had in the bank. That was *extra* money.

And everybody bought something nice for themselves on payday, didn't they? Some girls bought shoes, others a new dress. Sandra deserved something special too, didn't she? Sure she did. That's what the American dream was all about. She was—

"Ouch! *Fuck!*" Sandra shook her hand briskly and then studied her aching thumb. She saw that she pulled up a new piece of skin. The fresh scar ran from her cuticle to the first knuckle. It was bleeding pretty badly, but Sandra didn't have time to wrap it in gauze or even throw a Band-Aid on it.

It was a quarter after six. She had to leave for work at six-thirty. The trip to the bank would take fifteen minutes. The trip to the south side would take another fifteen. If Sandra went straight to work from the south side, she would be thirty minutes late – but that wasn't bad. An hour late was bad. But thirty minutes... She was pretty sure no one would notice.

Sandra sucked her whole thumb as she raced through her home in search of her purse and her keys. She was already dressed in the pink scrub suit all of the female nurses at Jackson Memorial wore.

Sandra made it out of her house at 6:18. She withdrew $380 from her checking account at 6:35. She could've made it to work on time at that point, but she headed to the south side when she left the bank. She thought about calling her floor to let them know she was running late, but Sandra knew she'd probably call-in altogether once they got the charge nurse on the phone.

No, it's better to not call at all; just show up a little late. It's always better that way.

≈≈≈≈≈≈≈

Samuel Hardcastle, better known as ManMan, was a twenty year old hood-entrepreneur. If he had been born with a silver, or even a bronze spoon in his mouth, he would've been a junior in college by now, a business major, definitely a member of one of the top fraternities.

But ManMan grew up in the Amanda Street projects in Stop Six. There was absolutely nothing glamorous about his ghetto upbringing. As a child, ManMan ate popcorn for dinner sometimes while his mother slept with random men in the next room. ManMan still had a lot of love and respect for his mother, even though she spent most of her prostitution earnings on heroin and only cared for him as an afterthought.

When he was twelve, ManMan went to live with his grandmother. That situation wasn't much better. ManMan's granny was a caring woman, but she had a mild case of dementia. When the doctors amputated her left leg, granny was even less helpful. She let ManMan run the streets until diabetes took her other leg and her life when he was sixteen. Since then, ManMan had only himself to depend on.

His story should've ended there, but the Social Security Administration tracked ManMan down when he was eighteen and gave him a check for $10,000. ManMan never knew his father, but apparently pops worked for the airport for fourteen years before he got laid off and then got killed trying to rob a liquor store. His social security money went to the only child he fathered.

The average 18 year old hoodlum would've spent the money on a used car with flashy rims and a couple of woofers in the trunk, but ManMan knew this *inheritance* was probably his only shot at a nice life for himself. So he chose to invest his money in pharmaceuticals. He picked heroin because of his mom. If a twenty dollar bag of dust could make a mother sleep with strangers and get high while her son's stomach was growling, then that had to be some very powerful powder indeed.

Two years after his initial investment, ManMan was one of the richest dealers in Overbrook Meadows. He ran seven dope houses, employed more than 30 goons to tend to his affairs, and he owned half a dozen used cars with flashy rims and a couple of woofers in the trunk.

ManMan wasn't a killer by nature, but three men lost their lives in the past year for thinking this 20 year old kid couldn't possibly be the head honcho. ManMan had plenty of triggermen, but he killed those men himself. One of them used to sell smack to his mother. After dumping his body in Sycamore Creek, ManMan felt like he avenged her, to some degree.

≈ ≈ ≈ ≈ ≈ ≈

ManMan was at his dope house on Davis Street when Sandra paid him a visit. He was in one of the back rooms playing Call of Duty on his Xbox. ManMan rarely sold drugs himself. His doorman, a bull dyke named Sammy, handled all transactions. But she knocked on ManMan's door when Sandra showed up because that's what ManMan asked her to do.

"Who is it?" he growled, not wanting to look away from his television screen.

"It's me," Sammy said, her voice deep and gruff. "That bitch here."

"What bitch?"

"The one you told me to tell you about," Sammy said, with barely concealed irritation in her tone.

"Come in!" ManMan shouted. He was playing online, so there was no way to pause the game. He had to quit the match completely, which explained the frown he fixed on Sammy when she opened the door. "Who the hell you talking about?" he asked.

ManMan was tall and thin with dark skin like mahogany. His long hair was braided to his scalp in corn rows. There was stubble on his face, but he had yet to grow a manly beard or even a full moustache. He wore new jeans, new sneakers and a sparkling white wife beater.

Sammy frowned back at him with just as much, if not more, attitude. "You the one told me to tell you when this bitch come back."

Sammy was light-skinned and burly. Her hair was trimmed short. She had big lips and full cheeks.

"What bitch?" ManMan asked again. "Who the hell is you talking about?"

"That nurse bitch!" Sammy said, and ManMan's disposition changed completely.

"Oh, she here?" He shot to his feet, rubbing his hands together. "Bring her in here."

"She prolly ain't got no money," Sammy said. "Why you keep hooking her up?"

"What's it to you?" ManMan wanted to know.

"I don't like her," Sammy said. "That ho stuck up."

"You musta tried to holler at her," ManMan said with a chuckle. "What happened, she turn you down?"

"I wouldn't even want no bougie bitch like that," Sammy said. "I can't wait till she all the way gone. I'ma make her lick my ass."

ManMan laughed. "Yeah, I knew you liked her. Go get her."

"She ain't gon' fuck you," Sammy predicted.

"You don't know," ManMan said. He sat on his bed and tried to look relaxed.

When Sandra peered through his door a moment later, he told her, "Come on in. Shut the door behind you."

Sandra stepped into the room hesitantly, but she did not close the door behind herself. Sandra was of medium height with short hair and skin the color of honey. Her lips were full. Her eyes were large and dark. She didn't look like a junkie. Her hospital attire made her appear even less so, yet here she was.

ManMan thought Sandra was beautiful, but she was already showing the telltale signs of addiction. She was about fifteen pounds lighter than she was last month. And her restless nights left bags under her eyes. She didn't have on any makeup, and she hadn't gotten her hair done recently. But she still looked good to ManMan. Compared to the women he saw on a daily basis, Sandra was downright gorgeous.

"You can come in here," he told her. "Why you acting scary?"

"What you need me to come in here for?" Sandra asked. "Ain't nothing going on."

"What you mean?"

"I can get my stuff from Sammy," Sandra said. "I got money today. I don't need no favors."

ManMan smiled. All of his teeth on the top row were gold-plated. "So that's how it is? You only want to come in here when you ain't got no money?"

Sandra looked around anxiously. She used her looks to get a couple of freebies from ManMan last month. She never touched him. She just begged and batted her eyes, and he melted like ice in hot tea. Sandra knew he wanted to sleep with her. But even at her worst, that was something she would *never* do. Once you sleep with someone for money or drugs, you might as well find a nice homeless shelter to live in, because that's where you're headed.

"I can pay you back, for last month," Sandra offered. "I got some money..." She dug in her pocket as she spoke. ManMan was not happy to see the wad of twenties she pulled out. In fact, he was very disappointed.

"You owe me eighty dollars from last month," he said as he stood. "What you want today, two or three?" He went to a tall dresser next to the bed and pulled the top drawer open. Sammy had the bulk of his dope, but ManMan had half a dozen twenty-dollar bags in there.

"Two," Sandra said, and then, "I mean three."

ManMan added quickly. "That's one-forty, counting last month's."

Sandra tried to hide her unease as she counted out the money. She only planned to spend sixty dollars in here. She knew ManMan hadn't forgotten about the packs he gave her last month, but she didn't think he'd want the money back. She cursed herself for offering to pay the debt. She held out the money, and ManMan frowned. He shook his head, staring at her hand.

"Fuck happened to your thumb, shorty?"

Sandra quickly transferred the bills to her other hand and held her wounded thumb down by her side. "Nothing. I'm alright."

"You got cut, or you been eating on that motherfucker?" ManMan asked.

"I said I'm fine. Here." She offered the money more forcefully.

ManMan laughed. He put her three bags of dope on the bed and gestured for her to do the same. "Leave it over there."

Sandra thought he did this to avoid a direct transaction, but that wasn't the case. When she turned to get her drugs, ManMan palmed and then squeezed her ass. Sandra spun on him, but she didn't do anything stupid like slap him across the face.

"Watch your hands!" She looked plenty mean, but ManMan kept smiling.

"Why you acting like that?" he asked her. "Don't you want me to hook you up? You can keep all your money *and* take them sacks, if you stop tripping."

Of course "stop tripping" meant "give me some ass." And although that was something Sandra was adamantly against, she couldn't help but consider it – just for a split second. She needed the money badly, but she needed the heroin even more. What difference would it make if she slept with this boy? No one would know. Well, all of the addicts in the dope house would know, but they were nobody to Sandra. Their opinion meant nothing.

"I told you *no*," she said, but she took a moment too long to answer, and ManMan was on to her.

He stared at her for a few seconds and then sucked his teeth. "Alright. Well take your shit, and leave all my money. I don't need you, bitch. You need me. Hurry up. Get the fuck outta here."

Sandra was stunned by his sudden change in demeanor. She knew ManMan was no Boy Scout, but he never disrespected her before. Suddenly Sandra felt like she might be in danger. She snatched up the packs and hurried out of the room.

ManMan rubbed his chin and watched her booty until she was out of sight. He wasn't really upset with her, but he wasn't used to rejection. Ever since he got his dad's social security money, ManMan could have any woman he wanted, especially if they were hooked on the big H.

If Sandra was as headstrong as she acted like she was, he knew he'd never see her again. He would barely miss her.

But if the pretty nurse was as strung out as ManMan thought she was, then she'd swallow her pride and come back. She might come back asking for a favor. And that would be the day ManMan made her drop to her knees and take his manhood into her bougie-ass mouth. Hell, he might even make her lick Sammy's ass crack. That would be something to see.

ManMan chuckled at the possibilities.

≈≈≈≈≈≈≈

Sandra's heart was still pounding when she got in her car. But the more distance she put between herself and ManMan, the better she felt. *Jesus. How did it get this bad?* But of course she knew. And she knew she couldn't blame it all on Ben, either.

Nine months ago Sandra was a regular person. She went to work on time, paid her bills, partied with her friends and took vacations to nice places; sunny beaches, tropical paradises. When she ran into Benjamin Miller at Club Ice, she was happy to see him. She and Ben hung out with the same crowds when Sandra was in college. They never dated, but there was always an attraction between them.

What Sandra remembered most about Ben was what a funny and crazy guy he was. No matter where they were, Ben was the life of the party. Plus he was six-foot-three, handsome and baldheaded with dark, lovely skin. When he approached Sandra at the club and asked her to dance, she was eager to hear what he'd been up to since they last met. When he told her he wasn't seeing anyone at the moment, she was even more interested.

Ben was happy to hear that Sandra got a nursing degree and that she'd been working at Jackson Memorial for two years. Ben was between jobs himself, but Sandra didn't hold that against him. They went out a few times before they explored each other's bodies on a rainy Saturday night, *The Best of Marvin Gaye* playing softly on Sandra's bedroom stereo.

Ben waited a couple of months, until he was sure Sandra was sufficiently in love with him, before he asked if she still got high, like she did in college. In those days, Sandra's favorite drug was marijuana. But she liked to drink and snort coke, too. The coke habit got a little out of hand during her senior year at Texas Lutheran, but Sandra pulled things together and passed all of her finals – barely.

Her advisor, Dr. Forney, told her she was going downhill fast. He advised Sandra to leave her reckless days in college and face the real world with a sane and *sober* mind after graduation. Sandra didn't know how much Dr. Forney knew about her lifestyle, but she told him she would turn things around. And she kept that promise.

Two years went by before she even thought about putting something up her nose. But Sandra wasn't upset when Ben offered her a small capsule that appeared to be filled with brown sugar.

"What is it?" she asked him.

"That's boy," Ben told her.

"What's boy?" she asked.

"That's that horse," Ben told her.

"Boy, tell me what this is," Sandra demanded.

"It's heroin," Ben stated.

"What does it do?" Sandra asked.

"Slow motion," Ben said. "Make you feel like you smoked some real good weed."

At that moment Sandra remembered the euphoric joy marijuana brought her back in the day. But rather than ask Ben for a joint instead, she cracked the pill open and made four chubby lines. She snorted one of them.

And that was all she wrote.

Ben was both right and wrong about heroin being like *some real good weed.* It was a downer, and it did slow things considerably, but weed never made Sandra sit on the couch for hours at a time, staring at absolutely nothing. Weed never made her bones ache when she didn't have any or made her stomach bubble at the sight of it. More importantly, Sandra never spent two hundred dollars in one day on weed. She never missed any work because of weed, and she certainly wouldn't go to a south side dope house all by herself for a bag of marijuana.

Three weeks after Ben gave her that first pill, Sandra caught him in the bathroom shooting up. The sight of a needle in his arm freaked her out completely. She swore she would never stoop that low, but she didn't break up with Ben like her brain told her to. Ben was her only connection to her new drug of choice. Sandra needed him to score her dope. She needed him to get high with her. No one else in her life understood her like Ben did. He became her kindred spirit.

Things proceeded in this manner for seven months, until Ben got pulled over for speeding in Sandra's car one day, and the policeman took him to jail for various misdemeanor warrants. Sandra was a nervous wreck when she went to pick up her vehicle – not because her man was in jail, but because she was a junkie, and she needed a fix very, *very* badly.

She found one when she searched her car, but it wasn't exactly what she was looking for. Ben stashed his shooter kit before he got arrested, and one of the needles was still full of dope. Sandra went through an hour long spiritual battle (crammed with crying, cursing, yelling and praying) before she wrapped a tourniquet around her arm and did the unthinkable. Afterwards she felt like a fool for dreading this inevitable graduation for so long.

Shooting dope was awesome! It was *the bee's knees,* as her grandmother would say. Sandra got ten times higher than she did when she was snorting. The next day she drove to the south side (all by herself) and asked a random prostitute where she could get more heroin. The prostitute agreed to show her a place, if Sandra bought her a bag, too. Six minutes later, Sandra was introduced to a stout lesbian named Sammy and a skinny punk named ManMan.

Two months after that, Sandra's home, spirits and finances were in complete shambles. Her chance encounter with Ben had cost her nearly everything she owned.

≈≈≈≈≈≈≈

As she drove, Sandra dug her cellphone from her purse so she could let her coworkers know she was running late. Her intestines twisted like serpents as she listened to the phone ring. Her brain raced when someone finally picked up.

"Critical Care, this is Shaley."

"Hi," Sandra said. "Who's the charge tonight?"

"Who's calling?"

"This is Sandra."

"Just a minute."

Sandra muttered to herself rather than listen to the hold music. Someone picked up after an agonizing minute and a half.

"This is Cynthia." She sounded out of breath.

"Hey, this is Sandra. I can't come in tonight." Sandra had no idea she was calling-in until the words left her mouth. But now that she said it, it sounded like an excellent idea. There was no way she could get through a twelve hour shift with her stomach bubbling like this.

"It's too late to call-in," Cynthia said. "It's already after seven. You have to call in two hours before your shift."

"I'm sorry," Sandra said. "I'm not feeling well. My stomach, I'm really sick." Technically, that wasn't a lie.

"We're already short-staffed," Cynthia complained. "I'm gonna have to call Ruben, if you don't come in. You can't keep calling-in on payday, Sandra."

Sandra reconsidered. If their manager had to come in to work tonight, he wouldn't be in a good mood. He would want to know what the hell was wrong with Sandra. There might even be some disciplinary actions.

Not surprisingly, Sandra still had plenty more *Fuck it* to go around.

71

"I'm sorry," she said. "I'm too sick."
"Alright, whatever," Cynthia said and disconnected.

CHAPTER SIX
CYNTHIA AND RUBEN

On the fourth floor of the Avery Building, registered nurse Cynthia Pullman was already having a bad day. Sandra's call-in threatened to push her completely over the edge. But Cynthia was the charge nurse tonight, and she was expected to handle stressful situations in a calm manner.

She hung up the phone and sighed and looked around her twenty bed unit. They currently had eighteen patients, with only eight nurses on the floor. As the charge, Cynthia wasn't supposed to take patients herself, but she had to take a couple to ease the workload on her peers. Two other nurses, Janice and Brenda, had three patients apiece.

That wouldn't have been too bad, except this wasn't a Med/Surg floor. This was a critical care unit; Neuro ICU, to be exact. The patients on this floor had suffered major strokes or some other brain injury that left them bedridden, clinging to life with the support of a respirator and the prayers of their family members who rarely left their side.

The two nurses who had three patients to look after were not happy at all. And Cynthia couldn't run the floor with maximum effectiveness because of the two patients she was responsible for. She told Sandra she was going to call their manager in, but Cynthia really didn't want to do that.

Ruben worked first shift. He just left the hospital an hour and a half ago. By now he'd be having dinner with his wife and children, settling in for a peaceful evening with his family. If he had to come back tonight, he'd do so with no sleep, which would probably ruin whatever plans he had for Saturday. Calling the manger was a last resort. Things were bad, but Cynthia didn't think her nurses couldn't handle it. But the night was young.

Cynthia left the nursing station, heading for her patient in 412. One of her coworkers stopped her.

"Hey, was that Sandra?" It was Janice, an attractive, dark-skinned woman with short hair and an awesome figure.

"Yeah, that was her," Cynthia confirmed. "She called-in."

With that news, Janice's whole face fell, like someone lowered the blinds. "What? She *gotta* come."

"She's not," Cynthia said. "I told her we were already short. She says her stomach hurts."

"Man, her stomach don't hurt," Janice complained. "She call-in every payday. Why y'all keep letting her get away with that?"

"It's not up to me," Cynthia said. She tried to walk away, but Janice was still talking.

"You can start documenting it."

Cynthia opened her mouth to respond, but she had to pause for a moment to make sure she didn't give her coworker any attitude. She, Janice and Sandra were the only black nurses on the unit. They got along fine for the past couple of years, but Cynthia thought things were different between them now, ever since their manager selected Cynthia to be one of the new charge nurses on the floor.

But it wasn't like that was a huge promotion. Cynthia had to take a few training courses, and she only made two more dollars an hour. She had a lot more responsibilities now, which made the extra money barely worth it. Janice never said she wanted to be a charge, but Cynthia could only describe her new behavior as *jealousy*.

"I have been documenting it," she told her. "Ruben's the one who's supposed to write her up."

"Well, have you told him how often it happens?" Janice wanted to know.

"I give him a report every time I'm charge," Cynthia said. "I'm definitely going to tell him about tonight."

"You need to call him now," Janice suggested. "If Sandra's not coming in, Ruben needs to come help us."

"I think we'll be okay tonight," Cynthia countered.

"That's 'cause you don't have three patients," Janice said. "You not the one suffering."

"I'm not supposed to have *any* patients," Cynthia reminded. "I have two. And I'm busting my ass–"

"I got *three*," Janice said.

"I know how many you have," Cynthia replied. "I'm busting my ass just like you. Everybody got–"

"No everybody don't got *three patients*," Janice said.

Cynthia rolled her eyes with a sigh. Janice put a hand on her hip and frowned. Janice was such a beautiful woman. And she was a great nurse. If her attitude was a little better, Ruben might have asked her to be the new charge instead.

"Look, I know this is gonna be a bad night," Cynthia said. "But everyone's doing the best we can. If you need me to help with one of your patients, just ask. I'll help you as much as possible."

Janice didn't have a response for that.

Cynthia thought the break in their conversation was a great opportunity to end the argument altogether. "Okay, I gotta go," she said and hurried to her patient's room.

≈≈≈≈≈≈≈

The next couple of hours were hectic, but it was nothing the critical care nurses and nursing assistants hadn't seen and endured before. When times got rough, there were a lot of complaints, but everyone buckled down and worked together towards a common cause.

Cynthia was the most stressed, but she was confident they could get through the shift – that was until a Haltom City teenager updated her Facebook status to "I'm sorry" and then tried to hang herself in her bedroom closet.

A Careflite helicopter brought the teen to Jackson Memorial's ER, where she was saved and diagnosed with an anoxic brain injury. Cynthia got a call from the nursing supervisor a few minutes later.

"I gotta give you another one," the sup' said.

"We don't have enough staff," Cynthia told him.

"Call your manager," the sup' suggested, and then he proceeded to give Cynthia the particulars about her new patient.

When she hung up the phone, Cynthia took a seat at the nursing station and shook her head woefully. She looked over her assignments again. Someone else would have to take a third patient. But a suicidal teen would need one-on-one care. That was more than her unit could handle with only eight nurses on the floor.

"We getting another patient, ain't we?"

Cynthia looked up and saw that Janice had sneaked up on her.

"Yeah," Cynthia said. "I gotta call Ruben in."

"I told you to do that two hours ago," Janice reminded.

Cynthia's nostrils flared, but she didn't get baited into another war of words. And she didn't call Ruben while Janice was standing there, either. Cynthia retreated to her office where she could close the door and collect her thoughts.

She had Ruben's cell number memorized. Cynthia didn't think she should call that line, though. She found Ruben's home number on a directory taped to her desk. Cynthia took a seat. Her heart knocked as she dialed her manager's number. It stopped beating altogether when his wife picked up after a few rings.

"Hello?"

"Hell, um, hello. Is, may I speak to Ruben?"

"Who's calling?"

"This is Cynthia, from work. I'm, um, I'm the charge nurse."

"Just a minute."

Damn. Cynthia cursed herself for sounding like a blubbering idiot. What was she so nervous about? She was at work, and Ruben was her manger. This was official hospital business. His wife was apt to make something out of nothing if Cynthia sounded like a nervous mistress when she called his home.

After a moment, Ruben came to the line. "Hello?"

"Hi," Cynthia breathed. "It's me."

Ruben said, "What's going on?"

"Sandra called-in again," Cynthia reported. "We only have eight nurses on the floor, two of them are already tripled, and we're about to get a suicide attempt. I called everybody who's off tonight, but none of them can come in. We need help."

"Alright," Ruben said. "I'll, I'll get dressed."

"I'm sorry," Cynthia said.

"It's okay," Ruben said. "It's not your fault."

"Okay. Bye."

Cynthia hung up and let out a pent up breath. It was usually cold on her unit, but her body felt very warm. She wiped her forehead and confirmed it was moist with sweat. Cynthia stood and checked her features in a small mirror affixed to her file cabinet before she left the office and returned to the chaos.

Back on the floor, the first person she encountered was Janice. Janice looked like she'd been standing in the hallway, waiting for Cynthia to return.

"Did you call him?"

"Yes," Cynthia said. "He's coming in."

"Why you tripping?" Janice wanted to know. "You acting like you scared to call him, or something."

"I don't like calling anybody in when they're supposed to be off," Cynthia said. "But I did it, he's on his way, and I gotta check on my patients."

This time she walked away without waiting to see if Miss Nosey Pants was done questioning her authority.

Janice looked after her thinking, *Some bitches make it way too obvious...*

≈≈≈≈≈≈≈

Critical Care Manager Ruben Watts returned to work at 9:35 pm. The mood on his strained unit improved almost immediately. Of the eight nurses on the floor, all of them were female, and they welcomed Ruben like a springtime rainbow after a rough storm.

Ruben was thirty-five years old, but he looked ten years younger. He had a boyish charm that could win over just about anyone he came in contact with. He stood six-foot-one, with 190 pounds distributed evenly on his frame. His face was usually clean-shaven, but he'd been sporting a light beard lately that blended well with his shoulder length hair. Dimples appeared on his cheeks when he smiled.

Ruben's nursing skills earned him countless promotions and accolades throughout his career. But it was his people skills that made him one of Jackson Memorial's brightest stars. When patients or hospital staff came to him with a problem, Ruben had a twinkle in his eye that said, *I'm listening, and I understand what you're going through.* When he told them, "Everything's going to be alright," people believed him. They trusted him. Sometimes Ruben patted his nurses on the back or gave their shoulder an encouraging squeeze, and they felt a boost of energy that was stronger than a shot of espresso.

Everyone on the unit wanted to do well for Ruben. They wanted to please him. Most of his employees had a crush on him, but the ladies rarely expressed their fondness. Ruben was so handsome and so popular, the nurses placed him on a pedestal with superstars like Brad Pitt and George Clooney. They knew Ruben was married. As far as they were concerned, he was totally untouchable on a sexual level.

But just to know him, to have him toss a smile their way or tell them, "Good job," was enough to make their sweet hearts flutter. The fact that Ruben went about his daily routine totally oblivious to his awesomeness was the icing on the cake. He was the perfect blend of power, charm, compassion and humility.

And he knew his nurses well.

He stepped off of the elevator with a big, white box in his hands, and eight tongues started to water.

"I know tonight sucks," he announced. "But to make up for it, I brought some *gourmet doughnuts*! They cost me an arm and a leg. I had to take a plane all the way to the Walmart down the street. But you know I'd do anything for my girls."

"Oh, thank you, Ruben!"

Two nurses rushed to lighten his load.

"That's so nice of you!"

"I was just thinking about doughnuts!" a third nurse said as she approached him.

"It's nothing," Ruben said. He wore khaki Dockers with a white button-down tucked in, the sleeves rolled up. "I'm glad we have eight of you here tonight. I know it's been rough. You guys are awesome, for working so hard."

The nurses grinned like school girls. Cynthia approached the crowd, but she waited on the outskirts. Her smile was just as big as the others. The sight of Ruben took a huge weight off her shoulders. She knew the work would remain just as taxing, but it wouldn't feel like it, not with Ruben there.

"We're just doing our jobs," one of the nurses told him. "It's what we went to school for."

"Yeah, but when you're in school, they don't tell you that you'll have to do all of this nonstop, with no breaks sometimes," Ruben said as he approached Cynthia. "It's times like this when you have to go above and beyond. I'm really grateful to have you here. All of y'all, seriously." He flashed his beautiful smile in 360 degrees. Suddenly everyone loved their jobs again.

"I'll check back with each one of you in a minute," Ruben said. "Let me get with Cynthia, to see who needs the most help."

"I'm okay with mine," an RN named Deidra said quickly.

"Me too," Brenda said. "I got three patients, but they're not that bad."

"It's nice of you to say that," Ruben said. He turned and looked Brenda in the eyes. "I'm glad I can count on you. You make my job a hell of a lot easier."

Brenda's ears turned cherry red. Thankfully they were concealed by her long, brunette hair.

"Thanks, Ruben." She walked away with a brood of bubbly butterflies in her belly.

≈ ≈ ≈ ≈ ≈ ≈ ≈

One of Ruben's best skills was how he could mix fun and work without there ever being any confusion about which one it was time for. A lot of managers and supervisors tried this, but it blew up in their faces more times than not. When Ruben stepped off the elevator and joked with his nurses, that was his time for fun. When he walked and talked with Cynthia, he wasn't smiling at all. She heard the stress in his voice, and their conversation was strictly business.

She told him about Sandra's call-in and about the assignments she made that night. She told him which patients were the sickest, which family members were becoming worrisome, and which nurses were struggling the most.

After they got that out of the way, Cynthia followed Ruben into his office to discuss more personal matters. She asked if she could close the door behind them, and Ruben told her, "Yes, please."

Cynthia wore the same pink scrubs required by all of the female nurses at the hospital, but she always took care to make sure her outfit was stylish. She was tall and thin, so a cinched waist was a must. Cynthia thought her hips, ass and thighs were her best features, so she bought scrubs that complimented these areas.

Cynthia's skin was smooth and rich, dark chocolaty. Her shoulder-length hair was pulled back in a ponytail, drawing attention to her beautiful visage, which was just as compelling as her curves. Cynthia's eyes were small. Her lips glistened with a thin coat of raspberry gloss. She was 26, but she possessed the maturity of an older woman.

"I'm sure you know everybody wasn't this happy before you got here," she said.

Ruben took a seat behind his desk and reclined in his office chair. Cynthia leaned on a filing cabinet rather than sit across from him.

"Who gave you the most trouble?" he asked.

"Janice always does," Cynthia reported. "But Brenda was bitching, too. I don't know when she started feeling so *comfortable* with her three patients, 'cause she wasn't thirty minutes ago."

Ruben grinned. Cynthia grinned, too.

"You like that, don't you?" she said.

"Whatever do you mean?" he asked.

"They way they act for you."

"That's what every manager wants," Ruben said. "I'm sure every floor responds differently to their manager, than they do to a supervisor or a charge."

"Yeah, but a lot of managers run their units with *fear*," Cynthia said with a smirk. "You don't do it like that."

"Nothing wrong with being nice," Ruben said. "It's not like I flirt with them."

"I don't know," Cynthia said. She went and sat on the corner of his desk. Ruben's eyes were immediately drawn to her thighs and hips. Cynthia chuckled when his gaze returned to her face. "You flirted with me," she said.

"No, I don't think so," Ruben replied.

"I remember like it was yesterday, the way you looked at me."

"Why was it so memorable?" Ruben wondered.

"Because of your eyes," Cynthia recalled. "It was the first time anyone with blue eyes ever looked at me like that."

"Like what?" Ruben said. His smile was devilish.

"Like you looking at me now," Cynthia said, her smile just as wicked. "You know, I was nervous about calling you at home tonight. I started to call your cell, but then I thought that would make your wife suspicious. But when I called your home phone, I almost freaked out when she answered."

"But it was business," Ruben replied.

"I know," Cynthia said. "But it's kinda hard to talk to a woman when you had her husband's dick in your mouth within the last 24 hours."

Ruben chuckled softly. "Now, why'd you bring that up? Are you trying to get a rise out of me?"

"I don't know," Cynthia said. "Is something rising?" She leaned over the desk and peered into his lap.

"It is now," Ruben said.

Cynthia lowered her eyes. Ruben sighed.

"It'll be just my luck if one of our patients codes right now," he said. "I'll have to run out of here with a raging boner."

"We can't have that," Cynthia said. "I'm gonna go help Tricia give 420 a bath. She said he's one big vomit/diarrhea sandwich."

"Yuck," Ruben said with a frown. "Now that's an ugly image."

"I bet it helped with your raging boner," Cynthia guessed.

Ruben smiled. "Yes, it did. You always know what's best for me."

"It would be best if you don't stare at my ass when I leave," Cynthia suggested. She stood and walked slowly to the door. She looked over her shoulder. Of course her manager's eyes were glued to her ass.

"I'm like a junkie," Ruben admitted. "I know what's best for me, but I still need my fix."

They both laughed.

When she stepped out of the office, Cynthia didn't notice anyone watching her. But two very cynical eyes glared at her from the nursing station. Janice snorted and shook her head in disappointment. She hoped that what she thought was happening wasn't really happening. But all of the tell-tale signs were there.

Janice didn't hate Cynthia because she was their new charge. And she wasn't jealous because Cynthia was taller and slightly more attractive than her. But the way Cynthia and Ruben carried on – that was too much to stomach. In fact, Janice thought she might throw up right now, just thinking about it.

CHAPTER SEVEN
RODNEY'S REAL WOMAN

A week later, the hospital was still moving along at a fevered pace. On Friday night, March 29th, all of the employees on second shift were counting down the hours until the weekend. But this wasn't payday, so there was no real anxiety. A weekend with no money was like a pizza with no toppings.

Larry Barnes, from Material Operations, was one of few low-level Jackson employees who wasn't living check to check. A few years ago he decided to start saving fifty dollars from each pay period. He surprised himself by sticking to it. At first it seemed like whenever he had a sizeable lump of money in the bank, his car would break down or another unexpected expense would pop up. But Larry worked a lot of overtime, and he easily recouped his losses.

Today he was happy to have nearly four thousand dollars in the bank. Larry didn't know if he was saving for a new car or his first home, but it felt good just to have it. It made him feel like a man.

Larry was a decent cook, and he brought his lunch from home most of the time. But on Fridays he splurged on a five dollar value meal at the Wendy's restaurant located inside the hospital. While he stood in line waiting to order, Larry spotted a beautiful medical student seated among the restaurant's patrons. When he got his food, Larry approached her table, hoping she'd be more receptive than she was a week ago.

"Hey, Lola!" He smiled like they were long, lost friends. "Fancy meeting you here."

She looked up from a thick book she was reading. Her dark hair was pulled back in a ponytail. Her glasses had a bulky, black frame that brought more attention rather than distract from her beautiful eyes. She had a half empty salad container on the table. Larry set his tray next to it.

"Can I sit with you?" he asked.

Lola looked around rather than respond. Larry looked around, too. He didn't see anything.

"What?"

"There's a lot of empty tables here," Lola noticed. She still hadn't smiled at him.

The icy reception shook Larry's confidence considerably. But his smile didn't falter.

"This is my favorite table," he said.

Lola gave him a look that said she knew he was full of shit.

"Can I sit down?" Larry asked. "I'm starting to feel like a waiter, standing next to this table."

Lola sighed. "Go ahead."

"Cool." Larry plopped down across from her.

Lola waited a moment and then returned her attention to her book.

"What you reading?" Larry asked as he unwrapped his burger.

"A medical book," she said without looking up.

"What's it about?" Larry munched on a couple of fries.

She frowned. "What do you want, Larry?"

He chuckled. "See, there I was thinking you gave me the cold shoulder because your pops was around. But he's nowhere in sight, and you still got that attitude. So it must be me, huh?" He took a big bite of his burger.

Lola's frown intensified.

"What's wrong?" Larry asked.

She shook her head. "That's really grossing me out."

"What?" He wiped his mouth. "I got something on my face?"

"No, that *meat*," she said.

"You a vegetarian?" Larry joked.

Lola nodded, still frowning.

"Oh, snap." Larry's eyes widened. "My bad." He wrapped his sandwich up and pushed it to the side. "I didn't mean to offend you." He reached for more fries. "Can I still eat these? Please? Me so hungry."

She couldn't help but smile at that. "You know, you could eat your whole meal *over there*." She gestured towards an empty table.

"Maybe," Larry said. "But I'd rather be hungry with a pretty lady than full all by myself."

Lola closed her book. She chuckled. "So, I guess you're not giving up..."

"I'm not a stalker," Larry said. "If you reject me, I'm gone."

Lola considered that. She liked Larry's height and his dark skin. She liked how he carried himself, too. A lot of the kids in Material Operations sagged their pants and strutted around with earphones stuck in their ears. But Larry was older, probably near thirty, and he tried to bring a degree of dignity to his godforsaken department.

"What'd your dad say when he saw me talking to you?" he asked.

"What do you think he said?"

"I don't know." Larry munched on his fried potatoes. "Prolly something like, '*Who was that awesome specimen of a man, Lola? And why did you not introduce us?*'"

Lola got a genuine laugh out of that.

Larry thought her voice was sweet. Her laughter was like music to his soul.

"So, that's not what he said?"

"No." Lola shook her head. "Not quite."

"What'd he say, then?"

"Do you really want to know?"

"I think you're beautiful," Larry said. "How many people told you that today, how beautiful you are?"

Lola's eyes frowned, but her smile remained. "You're the first one, Larry."

"And you're smart, too," he said. "I never met a black girl who was going to be a doctor. That's really cool. I'm proud of you."

"You're proud of me? You don't even know me."

"I don't have to know you to be proud of you," Larry said. "When I first met your father, I was proud of him, too. I'm proud of any brother or sister who makes something of themselves."

Lola nodded. "Then why haven't you made something of yourself, Larry?"

"Damn." His eyes widened. "See, if you wasn't so pretty, I'd be offended by that."

"I'm serious," Lola said. She wasn't smiling anymore.

Larry's smile faded as well. "I got a big family," he said. "My mom had eight kids with three different men. She finally stayed with the last one. That's my step-dad. He's in jail now for murder."

Lola looked like this was too much information, but Larry kept talking.

"All four of my brothers have been in jail at one point or another," he said. "Two of them are in prison right now. My big brother got killed when I was little. My big sister got killed, too. Her boyfriend choked her one day, when I was in middle school. My other two sisters, they keep having babies because the state will take care of them. One of them got herself a house already; three bedrooms, big back yard. She haven't worked in at least two years.

"Out of all of us, I'm the only one who never been to jail," Larry continued. "I never shot anybody either. I started to go to college, but I didn't have nobody at home pushing me. My mama didn't care. She wouldn't even take me to the junior college to help fill out the papers. So after high school, I just started working. I been working ever since.

"I've been at this hospital for more than five years. Nobody I grew up with has ever had a job that long. I got my own apartment and my own car. It ain't all that, but it's all mine; totally paid for. When we have family reunions, everybody thinks I'm special. They say I'm the *normal* one. Makes me feel good, to do right everyday; work hard for my money instead of stealing it.

"So when you say I haven't made nothing of myself—"

"I didn't mean—"

"Naw, let me finish," he said. "When you say I haven't made nothing of myself, I guess that all depends on what side you looking from. Maybe your family has a lot of money, and ever since you was little, your dad said you *had* to go to college. And it's good that you got it like that. But where I'm from, everybody thinks I *did* make something of myself. And I feel like I did, too."

"I'm sorry," Lola said again. "I didn't mean what I said."

"It's all good," Larry replied. "You probably went to private schools all your life, and you never really met any *regular* black people. All of us don't stay in the hood because we're lazy. We stay there because we're *stuck* there. Our parents don't have no sense, so the kids don't have no sense, either."

"But you didn't get stuck," Lola noticed.

"Thank God," Larry agreed.

Lola checked her watch. "I gotta go."

"Alright," Larry said.

"I want to apologize again," Lola said. "I feel bad about what I said."

"It's cool," Larry replied. "But you still haven't given me your phone number..."

Her beautiful smile was back.

"And I don't want you to give it to me because you feel sorry for me," Larry said. "I want you to give it to me because you think I'm a nice guy. And you think I'm cute."

She laughed. "I think you're cute?"

"Wow. Why, thank you!" Larry said.

Lola giggled. "You're funny." She turned to an empty page in the spiral notebook she toted and scribbled her name and number.

"Why'd your mom name you Lola?" Larry asked as he watched her write.

"My dad did," Lola said. "He named me after Lola Falana."

"I heard of her," Larry said. "But I've never seen her."

"You should look her up," Lola said. She tore the page from her folder and handed it to him. "She's awesome."

She stood to leave. Larry stood, too.

"Can I walk you back to the ER?" he asked.

She shook her head. "Daddy's waiting on me."

"Alright," Larry said. He stuffed her number in his pocket and returned to his seat. He reached for his burger but didn't dig in right away because Lola was still watching him.

"You can eat your dead flesh," she said.

"Oh, I plan to," Larry assured. "I can't afford to waste money like that."

"I was just going to tell you to, you know, don't try to talk to me in the ER, when I'm with my dad," Lola said. "Just out of respect."

"I like that," Larry said, "how you said *respect* instead of *embarrassment*. Respect sounds a whole lot better."

Lola chuckled. "See you later, Larry."

She took a few steps and turned back unexpectedly. Larry looked away from her ass as fast as he could, but she caught him. She shook her head.

"I know everybody at this hospital is a freak," Lola said. "But I'm not."

"I'm not, either," Larry assured her. "I don't even know any freaks here."

"How about everybody in your department," Lola offered.

Larry shrugged. "Not that I know of."

Lola rolled her eyes playfully as she walked away. "Goodbye, Larry."

"Bye," Larry said, and he kept his eyes on his burger this time. But it was hard.

≈≈≈≈≈≈≈

On the ninth floor of the parking garage next to the Meredith Building, Material Operations employee Rodney Tucker was once again having much more success with his love interest. He couldn't convince CNA Amy Winters to climb into the backseat of his '84 Lincoln, but he did stick his hand down the front of her scrub pants while they made out.

Rodney felt how wet she was, and he noticed that she shaved most of her pubic hair at his request. He rubbed her nookie expertly. He inserted two fingers, and Amy moaned her approval. She squirmed in the seat. She bucked her hips, encouraging him to probe deeper. She sucked his tongue and placed her hand over his. Rodney sensed she was about to explode at any moment.

But this was bullshit.

Rodney wasn't the type of guy to give pleasure to a female unless he was receiving as well. He withdrew his hand and pulled the drawstrings on his own scrub pants. He pushed them down, and his manhood popped up like a Jack in the Box. It was thick and stiff, engorged with blood. Amy immediately wrapped her hand around it. But Rodney was bored with her dry handjobs. It was time for Amy to stop being such a wuss.

He broke away from their kiss and clamped a hand behind Amy's neck. He eased her face towards his erection, but Amy resisted. She looked around fretfully. It was eight o'clock on a cool, Friday night. The sky was purplish black. The parking garage was mostly full, but the level they were on was quiet. No one was driving around at that exact second.

"Come on," Rodney urged.

"We can't do this here," Amy said. "Somebody will see us."

"Ain't nobody around," Rodney said. His dick jumped in her hand. Amy squeezed it tighter.

"What if somebody comes?" She spoke in a hushed voice.

"I'll watch out for you," Rodney promised.

"What about your supervisor?" Amy asked.

Eva had paged Rodney twice in the past five minutes. Rodney felt that whatever she wanted could wait. But Amy thought he should call his boss back ASAP.

"I'll call her when we get through," Rodney said.

His eyes were large and nearly desperate. In the scant light, Amy's sense of smell was heightened. Rodney's car stank of Black N Mild's, but his cologne was alluring. Amy's heart thundered. Her clit throbbed with each heartbeat. She longed for Rodney. She lived to please him. But having sex at work was taboo. What if he told someone she went down on him in the parking garage? Everyone at the hospital would know about it within a week, even the nurses on her floor.

"I can't," she told him.

Rodney let go of her head. He could get pussy whenever he wanted it. He wasn't going to beg for it. But he threw one last jab at Amy, just to see how stupid she was.

"I thought you said you loved me."

"I do," she said right away. She squeezed his dick even harder. Rodney never said he loved her back, but that was only because he wasn't used to expressing his feelings like that. Amy was confident she could break down that wall one day. "I just don't want to get in trouble," she pleaded.

"I told you, I'ma look out for you," Rodney assured her. "If somebody come up here, they can only come from one direction. I'll see them way before they see us."

Amy thought about it some more, and then she said the two magic words every manipulating man loves to hear: "Well, alright."

Rodney kept a straight face until she leaned down and her eyes were averted from his sight. As soon as her lips came in contact with his meat, Rodney's mouth fell open. His grin was big and toothy.

Fucking right! He looked down at her with pride. He couldn't believe he talked another one into giving him head at work. He'd only been working at the hospital for eight months. Amy was the ninth girl he brought to his car during that time. She was the fifth one to scream on the mic during work hours. Rodney–

Oh my damn.

He lost his train of thought when Amy took him in as far as she could. She deep-throated him, still sucking so hard her cheeks were concave. Her lips slid back up, about halfway, and then she got in to a nice rhythm. Rodney started to pump his hips, but his damned pager went off *again.* He was poised to ignore it, but Amy sat up and wiped the spittle from her mouth.

"Don't stop," Rodney urged.

Amy shook her head. "What if it's her again?"

"I'll call her in a minute," Rodney said.

"It's got to be important," Amy countered. "She keep calling. What if she knows where we are?"

"If she knew where we were, she'd come up here, wouldn't she?" Rodney spat. He found his pager and checked the display. Eva still wanted him to call her office. This time she added *911* for emphasis.

Rodney put his pager away. He reached for the back of Amy's neck again, but a pair of headlights swam around the corner at that moment. Amy rushed to lace up her pants before the car approached and then drove by slowly in front of them. The driver was a hospital visitor rather than an employee. He fixed suspicious eyes on Rodney and Amy before continuing on his way.

"Alright, come on," Rodney said. But this time Amy had made up her mind.

"I can't do this at work," she said. "It's too much going on. Cars driving by. You need to call your supervisor before you get in trouble."

Rodney started to argue, but Amy looked like she might start crying if he pressed any harder. Instead he sighed and shook his head as he got himself together.

"I'm sorry," Amy said.

"Whatever," Rodney said. He tied his scrubs and opened his car door.

Amy hesitated.

"Well, come on then," Rodney told her. "You said you wanted to go. Let's go. What you waiting for?"

"I'm sorry," Amy said again when they were both out of the car. "I can make it up to you when we get off. I swear I'll make it up to you, just like you like it."

Rodney was happy to hear that, but he didn't show it. His new thing for Amy was to have her suck him until he was on the verge, and then he'd pull out and jack-off in her open mouth. She'd swallow and suck some more, until she got every last drop.

The thought of that kind of action made Rodney want to forgive her and apologize for being such an asshole. But you don't keep a ho in check by apologizing all the damned time. Rodney was a young player, but he already knew that much.

"I got something to do tonight," he told her.

"I'll be up late," Amy said. She struggled to keep up with him now; Rodney was walking so quickly. "You can come by whenever you get done."

"Alright, we'll see," Rodney said without looking back.

When they reached the elevators, Rodney stopped to use one of the hospital telephones mounted on the wall. He told Amy, "You go ahead. I'll holler at you later."

"Are you mad at me?"

She was on the verge of tears. That was exactly the look Rodney wanted to see.

"Naw," he said, but he turned his back on her while he dialed his supervisor's number. "Go ahead. I'll catch up with you later."

Amy looked like a lost puppy as she stepped onto the elevator. Rodney didn't turn back in her direction until the doors closed and she was descending to the ground floor.

When his supervisor picked up the line, Rodney couldn't hide his irritation over the nut she just ruined. "What you want?"

"What you mean, *what I want*?" Eva snapped. "Why you ain't calling me back, boy? I paged you *three times*."

"I was busy," Rodney said.

"You full of shit," Eva replied. "Go ahead. Keep it up. You think this job don't mean nothing? Wait till you don't have one. Then you'll see how much it means."

Rodney blew a loud sigh into the receiver.

"You pissing me off," Eva growled. "I just called to tell you your girlfriend's up here."

Rodney's whole demeanor changed in the blink of an eye. He felt a chill roll down his spine. A lot of girls referred to him as their *boyfriend*, but there was only one woman Rodney claimed as his girlfriend.

"Wh, who?" he asked Eva.

"You don't know who you own girlfriend is?" his supervisor asked. "She said her name is Trish."

Rodney's eyes grew even larger. His jaw became unhinged. Of all the floozies that could've showed up at the hospital looking for him, fate delivered the one girl who wasn't a floozy at all. Trish was Rodney's *real* girlfriend, and he loved her dearly.

"I told you; you can't be having no visitors up here," Eva said. "You supposed to be here for work."

"I know," Rodney said absently. "I told her."

"Then why is she here?" Eva asked, but she was only speaking as half a supervisor. The other half was a jealous lover, which made her arguments completely ineffective.

"I'm on my way," Rodney said.

"Why is she here?" Eva demanded.

Rodney hung up and hurried to his department, his stomach doing flips the whole time. On the way, he thought about every girl at the hospital that he flirted with, felt a booty, hugged, kissed or got fellatio (and much more) from in the past eight months. Even if Trish came in through a side entrance, she was bound to have run into a dozen of them by now.

≈ ≈ ≈ ≈ ≈ ≈

When he got to his department, Rodney found his girlfriend in the break room, sitting with a bunch of loud-mouthed females. Rodney's forehead was dotted with sweat, but Trish was smiling, so he knew they hadn't told her anything damning. Not yet anyway. The only thing on Rodney's mind at that point was getting his woman far away from those heifers as soon as possible.

Trish looked up and smiled when she saw him.

"Hey, baby."

Rodney was so uptight, he couldn't even force a smile.

"Hey," he said. "What you doing here?"

"Nothing," Trish said. She stood and reached to hug him. "I brought you some lunch."

Their embrace was short and stiff. Rodney kept an arm around her waist as he quickly ushered her out of the break room and out of his department.

"Let's talk out here," he told her.

Trish craned her neck to say goodbye to her new friends. "See y'all later." She asked Rodney, "What's wrong?" when they stepped into the hallway.

"Nothing," Rodney said, but he was still moving. "Come on."

He led her through the Avery dismissal area. When they got outside, he let out a sigh of relief, like they escaped a burning building.

"What's going on?" Trish asked again. "Are you in trouble?"

Rodney turned to face her. He smiled. At 19, Trish was three years younger than her beau. She had fair skin and more curves than the Trinity River. Rodney considered himself a player ever since his high school days. Like many players, his one *real* wifey was a certified dime. Trish was tall and beautiful with full breasts, a flat stomach, juicy thighs and a perfect onion-shaped booty. Trish made some of Rodney's other *friends* (like Amy and Eva) look like mud ducks.

Tonight Trish had on black leggings with one of Rodney's long-sleeved button downs. She had the sleeves rolled up to her elbows. He auburn extensions flowed gracefully down to her shoulders. Trish could've been a model or a stripper, but she was a smart girl; an education major at Texas Lutheran. Unfortunately she was nowhere near as street-smart as she was book-smart.

"I'm sorry," Rodney told her. "I'm real busy right now." He put both arms around her waist, and her frown became a smile. "I appreciate you coming," Rodney told her. "I really do." He kissed her tenderly. He drew her body closer to his. "But you need to call me next time, to let me know you're on your way," Rodney suggested.

"I wanted to surprise you," Trish said. "Did you eat already?" She spoke softly, close to his ear.

Rodney backed away and grinned at her. "Why you treat me so good?" he wondered. "I get off in two hours. I coulda ate it when I got home."

"I know," Trish said. "But I never seen you at work before. I thought it would be more special, if I brought it to you. Are you gonna have time to eat it?"

"Yeah, I will," Rodney said. He reached for the bag she was carrying. It was rather hefty. "You made this?"

Trish nodded. She was beaming. "It's meatloaf," she said. "With mashed potatoes and cornbread."

"You made cornbread?"

"My mama helped me," Trish admitted.

"I don't deserve all this," Rodney stated, which, ironically, was the first honest thing he told a woman all day.

"Yes you do," Trish said. She threw her arms around him again.

Rodney's free hand slipped under her shirt. He palmed and then squeezed her soft rump. He loved the way Trish's body felt in panty hose and leggings. In a way, he was glad Amy didn't finish up in the parking garage. He wanted to make love to Trish when he got home, and she deserved his *first* nut – not the sloppy seconds.

"Where you parked?" he asked her.

"In the temporary parking over there."

Trish pointed, and Rodney saw her Corolla sitting in an unloading zone. He walked her to the car and got a few more hugs and kisses before she drove away.

When he returned to the building, Rodney encountered Larry in the hallway.

"Here," Rodney said, offering his lunch. "You hungry, dog?"

"I just ate," Larry said, but he took the bag and removed one of the larger Tupperware containers. "What's this, *meatloaf?*" He peered deeper into the bag of goodies. "And *cornbread!* Where you get this?"

"My girl brought it," Rodney said. "But I don't want it. You want it?"

"Can I take it home?" Larry asked. His mouth was already starting to water. "I don't have nobody to cook me nothing like this. I'll bring the containers back tomorrow..."

Rodney shook his head. "That's alright. You can keep 'em."

Larry's smile was big and appreciative. "Thanks, man!" He chuckled. "Damn. I'm eating good tonight!"

"Alright, holler at you," Rodney said. He continued to their department to see how Eva was doing. She already knew Rodney had a girlfriend, but seeing Trish in person was bound to piss her off.

Rodney hoped he wouldn't have to sleep with Eva again, but he would do it, if it shut her up for a little while. Rodney never seemed grateful, but deep down he knew how good he had it at Jackson Memorial. Not only did he get paid for doing virtually nothing all day, but he stole property whenever the opportunity

95

presented itself, and he had a whole bevy of potential sex partners to choose from at the hospital.

Working in M.O. was the best thing that ever happened to him.

CHAPTER EIGHT
THE SKIN YOU'RE IN

Around the same time Trish was hard at work on Rodney's unappreciated meal, critical care nurse Cynthia Pullman was doing the same thing in her modest two bedroom home on Overbrook Meadows' north side.

Cynthia had to work tonight, but she was in a good mood at five pm. So far it was a beautiful spring day. Cynthia woke up at noon, ran a few errands, did all of her chores around the house, and she had time to take Monster, her monstrously large Great Dane, for a relaxing walk at Circle Park.

When she got home, Cynthia diced onions and bell peppers and baked two salmon fillets at 400 degrees. By five o'clock her home was filled with delicious aromas. Cynthia made wild rice for a side dish. She packed her dinner up to take to work with her, and she fixed a plate for her boyfriend – who rang the doorbell just as she was adding cilantro to his rice.

Cynthia took his plate to the kitchen table and floated merrily to the front door. She opened it and smiled at Ruben who looked very happy to see her after his long day at work.

"Hey," she said.

Ruben stepped inside and reached to embrace her. He kicked the door closed with his foot. He held Cynthia tightly and sighed against her neck.

"I missed you so much."

His arms and strong hands on her body made Cynthia's heart feel as light as air. His words were like food to her soul. She kissed under his ear and inhaled deeply, loving every one of his scents, even his dandruff shampoo.

"I missed you, too," she whispered.

Ruben's hands swam across her form like a Texas wildfire, igniting little blazes of intimacy everywhere he touched. Both hands finally settled on her soft ass. He squeezed tenderly and drew her hips closer to his. His kissed her deeply, passionately. Cynthia tasted mint-flavored gum on his tongue. Ruben sucked her bottom lip and then peppered her neck with tiny nibbles.

"Baby, that feels *good*," Cynthia said. She threw her head back and closed her eyes.

Ruben sucked near her jugular, still fondling her ass. His hands moved to her hips when he backed away. Cynthia opened her eyes and looked into his. Her orbs were dark brown. His were electric blue. Both sets were flooded with desire.

"I thought about touching you all day," Ruben said.

"Me, too," Cynthia told him, then, "I made you dinner."

Ruben's smile ebbed slightly. "It smells great, but you know—"

Cynthia cut him off. She didn't want to hear about his wife, not now.

"You can eat a little," she said. "It's fish and rice. It's not that filling."

"But—"

"Tell her you had a sandwich at work," Cynthia offered. "You don't have to be hungry *every* day. She won't trip."

Ruben's smile returned. "Okay."

"It's in the kitchen," Cynthia said, and she stepped away from him. "I'm going to take a shower, while you're eating."

"I would much rather help you with that," Ruben said.

Cynthia would've liked that, too, but she worked just as hard on Ruben's dinner as his wife did – maybe even more so. It was little things like this that made a world of difference when you find yourself in a relationship with a married man. Cynthia found that she was constantly embroiled in a battle with her conscience about what was truly going on with her and Ruben.

Was it all about the sex, or was there something more? Ruben came to her house all the time, but they rarely went out to a restaurant or to the movies. This was obviously because they couldn't risk being seen together. But it also meant that whenever they did hook up, it was somewhere with a bedroom nearby.

Cynthia liked the way Ruben greeted her when she answered the door today, but did he really miss her, or did he miss her sex? Surely it was both, but the lines were blurred. When you added all of that to the fact that Cynthia was fully devoted to her boyfriend, but he had to split his devotion between her and his wife, a little thing like a salmon dinner became very important. It could be the difference between sanity and insanity, mistress or true love.

"No," Cynthia told him. "I don't need any help in there." She gave him a sly grin. "Eat your food. I worked hard on that. I want to know what you think."

"Of course," Ruben said. "I'll see you in a minute."

He headed for the kitchen and Cynthia disappeared into her bedroom. Ruben found his plate. He thought it looked very nice, but it was a lot more filling than Cynthia said it was. If he was at a restaurant, Ruben would have to take some of it home in a doggy bag.

He took one bite of his fish and one forkful of the rice. The flavors were mesmerizing, but Ruben had to exercise restraint. He waited until he heard the shower running before he took his plate to the backdoor and unlocked it. When he pulled it open, a terrifying beast (who was aptly named *Monster*) was waiting there to greet him.

Ruben knew that he'd been lied to all his life about dogs sensing fear, because he was terribly afraid of the Great Dane, but Monster continued to wag his tail happily. Ruben offered the animal his meal. Monster wolfed it down in exactly seven seconds. Ruben took the plate back to the kitchen and rinsed it off in the sink. He then went to the bedroom to wait for his special lady.

≈ ≈ ≈ ≈ ≈ ≈ ≈

When Cynthia turned off the shower, she heard the television on in her bedroom. She dried off and wrapped the towel around her body, holding it closed rather than tucking it. When she exited the bathroom, she saw Ruben sitting on the corner of

98

her bed. He was still dressed, except he kicked his shoes off. He looked up at her and shook his head slowly.

"This is amazing," he said. "Every time I see you, I feel like I'm noticing your beauty for the first time."

"Wow. You're full of charm today," Cynthia noticed.

She stepped to him slowly. Ruben spread his legs to accommodate her. When she reached him, Cynthia put her hands on his shoulders, and the towel fell to the floor. Ruben looked her up and down slowly, his eyes devouring her nipples, belly button, every pore.

He placed his hands on her hips. He leaned forward and kissed her stomach.

"I love your skin," he whispered.

Cynthia ran both of her hands through his brunette hair, which was very different than the hair she was used to seeing on her boyfriends.

"Why?" she asked.

Ruben continued to plant soft kisses on her belly. His lips were thin, but they were warm. Each kiss sent a pulse of energy through her stomach and made her spine tingle. His white skin stood in sharp contrast to Cynthia's dark complexion, almost like zebra stripes.

"It's so deep," Ruben said between kisses. "So pure. It's beautiful."

He put a hand on her chest and traced two fingers down to her belly button. "I wish I could make your color," he said, "in a bowl, like cake mix." He kissed her areola and sucked the nipple on the opposite breast. "I would eat it raw," he whispered. "I'd lick the bowl clean. I love everything about your skin, the smell, the taste..."

Cynthia didn't think these words were strange, coming from a white man. Instead, his comments made her feel self-confident, like no black man ever had. In her world, Cynthia was criticized more times than not because of her dark skin. In her school days, the kids came right out and called her blackie, darkie, spook, midnight, ugly and jigaboo. All of those insults came from fellow black people, who just happened to have fairer skin than hers.

In her adult years, the insults weren't so blatant, but Cynthia was reminded of how the world viewed her melanin on a daily basis: Light-skinned black folks got less jail time than dark-skinned ones. Light-skinned models were the only women rappers wanted in their music videos. And the fact that Beyonce and Rihanna were more successful than much better singers like Jazmine Sullivan and Heather Headley spoke volumes.

But Ruben, a white man, was in love with Cynthia's black skin. That was beautiful, on so many levels.

He stood and lowered Cynthia onto the bed.

He told her, "Scoot back," and she did so.

Ruben climbed on top of her, but only midway. He put a hand on each of her knees and spread them slowly while he twirled his hot tongue in her belly button. Cynthia looked up at the ceiling and then closed her eyes when she felt his mouth on her labia. Ruben licked and sucked the outer regions of her kitty for minute after mind-numbing minute before he spread the lips with his fingers and kissed her clitoris until it became erect.

Cynthia knew it was cliché to say that a white man gave her the best head she ever had, but she'd be lying to herself if she tried to deny it. The black men she had been with were pretty good at it. There were a couple Cynthia would label *cunnilingus pros*. But Ruben put them all to shame without even bringing his A game.

Cynthia thought that what separated Ruben from the rest was he never treated this as merely foreplay. He didn't lick Cynthia to get her wet, and he didn't do it because she pleased him first. For Ruben, licking the love box was as important as regular sex – sometimes even more so. There was no doubt he meant it when he told her, "I love the way you taste."

Ruben had a dozen techniques in his repertoire, any of which could make Cynthia tremble like a wet kitten. Today he employed four maneuvers: He started with the *flat tongue*, which he used to lick her from bottom to top, sometimes fast, but usually very slowly. Ruben used the flat tongue on the outer lips, but he also spread her labia and used his flat tongue on her more sensitive areas. With this move, his taste buds brushed her clitoris the entire time.

Ruben then employed his *kissing* technique as a tease. He pecked softly. Occasionally he took one side of her labia into his mouth and titillated it with his tongue while his lips massaged and sucked.

When Cynthia began to moan and squirm on the mattress, Ruben used a *stiff tongue* to jab as deeply and as hard as he could while his top lip offered continual stimulation to her clitoris.

By then Cynthia had two fistfuls of his hair. She lifted her head and stared at him dreamily, her eyes half-closed. Ruben made a smooth transition into his *sucking and drinking* phase, which was Cynthia's favorite. He sucked her clitoris, and he sucked her labia, and he sucked as far down her vagina as his lips could reach. He greedily drank her essence like a hummingbird lapping nectar.

Cynthia's blood raced through her veins, hot and fast. She moaned loudly. She pushed away from the mattress with her feet, trying to force her body deeper into Ruben's face. At the same time she pulled his head closer and harder. Her body created more and more lubrication, in anticipation of penetration. Ruben slurped and sucked it all down.

And when she came... *Sweet mercy.* When Cynthia came, Ruben went through all four phases again, always ending with the sucking and drinking.

He told her, "I feel it. Cum in my face. *Cum in my face!*"

That request was the icing on the cake.

Cynthia's explosion was a bright, white light that started in her head and rolled downward like a tidal wave. It was followed by a moment of calm. She felt herself ascending slowly, beautifully, as if onto an alien spacecraft or possibly to the heavens above.

"Tastes so good," Ruben told her. He didn't stop lapping her juices until Cynthia felt a second eruption brewing.

She loved his mouth, but the pleasure he gave only made her want *MORE.* There were depths that his tongue was biologically unable to reach.

"*Fuck me,*" she begged. "*Please, Ruben. Fuck me.*"

Ruben licked for a few moments longer before he backed away and stared at the beauty between her legs. He disrobed slowly. Cynthia almost passed out from a powerful, throbbing *wanting* while he put on a condom. Ruben didn't have the biggest dick ever, but when he mounted her, for that moment at least, Cynthia thought he did have the *best* dick.

He tongue kissed her while they made love. The taste of Cynthia's own juices in her mouth made her second climax twice as explosive as the first.

Deep down, as her toes clinched like fists, Cynthia knew that no man would ever make love to a mere mistress like this. She wasn't sure exactly what she and Ruben had, but she knew it was more than that.

Much more.

≈ ≈ ≈ ≈ ≈ ≈

Afterwards, the lovers had a few minutes for pillow talk before Cynthia had to take another shower and leave for work and Ruben had to go home to the woman he vowed to love and cherish and keep himself only unto her, until death did them part.

Among the topics they discussed was Sandra Alexander, another critical care nurse who was obliterating her attendance record as of late. Cynthia thought Sandra would call in tonight because it was Friday. Ruben didn't think she would because this was not a payday. Either way, their comments were more of a joke than serious concern.

≈ ≈ ≈ ≈ ≈ ≈ ≈

Twenty-four miles away, in a dope house on the south side of town, Sandra's ears weren't burning. But there was a fire in her soul that could only be satiated with one of the most powerful and addictive drugs known to man.

ManMan didn't have to summon the nurse to his room this time because Sandra didn't have any cash, and she asked to speak with him. ManMan wasn't there when she first arrived. Sammy offered to call and see if he could stop by. Sandra waited in the living room with the other junkies for nearly an hour until ManMan arrived. When he walked through the front door, Sandra's stomach flipped so suddenly, she couldn't stop a loud fart from escaping her.

No one cared.

ManMan told her, "Come on," and headed straight for his bedroom.

Sandra got up and followed him with her head hung in shame.

ManMan thought that if he ever saw the pretty nurse again, it meant she'd given up her last bit of self respect and was finally willing to drop her panties for drugs. Unfortunately, that wasn't the case. This was actually the fourth time he'd seen Sandra since he cursed her out, but she was still playing hard to get.

The first couple of times Sandra came by, she still had a nice wad of twenties in her pocket. The third time she only had nineteen dollars, two of which were in change. Today she reached into her pocket and produced a beautiful class ring from Texas Lutheran University. ManMan took it from her. He couldn't hide his disappointment as he checked it out.

"What I'ma do with this?" he asked her.

Sandra was scheduled to work today, but she didn't have her pink scrubs on. She wore a denim skirt with a little tee shirt that didn't have enough fabric to cover her belly button. She knew ManMan didn't want her ring, but he did want her. Sandra was not willing to sleep with him, but as long as he thought it might happen one day, he would be more pliable. Her smooth caramel legs were just a tease. Sandra didn't have a bra on, and her nipples were visible under the tee shirt.

"You can pawn it," she told him. Sandra stood uneasily in three inch heels, shifting her weight from one leg to the other.

"I can't pawn no fucking ring with your name all over it," ManMan informed. "You gotta pawn this shit yourself."

Sandra's eyes widened. She didn't know he couldn't pawn the ring. Pawning it herself was not an option because Sandra burned most of the pawnshops in the city already. They were willing to give her payday-advance loans because her check stubs from Jackson showed that she could easily pay them back.

But the pawnshops didn't know Sandra was a dopefiend. They didn't expect her to put a stop-payment on the post-dated checks she left them. The pawnshops retaliated by sending her balance to a collection agency and flagging Sandra's name in their computer so she couldn't pull the same scam or even sell items at their shops anymore.

ManMan saw the dread in her eyes. He already noticed the provocative way Sandra dressed today. He was young, but ManMan was supremely streetwise. There was no way this trifling junkie was going to play him. Sandra thought she could keep teasing him for more freebies, but ManMan was half a second from slapping the shit out of her and taking the pussy by force.

Afterwards he'd give her something to shoot-up while she cowered in the corner crying. And then he'd feed Sandra when her high came down. He'd repeat the same steps (Sex, Dope & Food) over a two to three day period. By the fourth day, Sandra would accept the fact that she was his bitch. At that point ManMan could put her on the strip and let her put that mini skirt to good use. ManMan wasn't a pimp, but he did pimp a few ho's from time to time. It wasn't hard. All bitches craved guidance, whether they realized it or not.

He smiled. Sandra recognized the perversion in his eyes. She subconsciously brought her wounded thumb to her mouth. She had it bandaged today, but that didn't stop her from nibbling on the gauze.

"Get your hand out your mouth," ManMan told her. "That shit's nasty."

Sandra put her hand down to her side.

"Sit down," ManMan told her.

Sandra hesitated before doing as she was told.

"You think I'm ugly?" ManMan asked.

Sandra's heart knocked. Her throat caught. She said, "No," but they both knew that was a lie.

ManMan nodded. "That's why you don't wanna give me none?" he asked, "'Cause I'm ugly?"

"I don't, I don't think you're ugly."

"Then why you hating?" ManMan asked. He approached her slowly.

"I got, a boyfriend," Sandra said.

"Where he at?" ManMan wanted to know. He stopped walking when he was close enough to spread her legs himself, but he told her, "Open your legs."

"He in jail," Sandra said. She was spooked, but her legs began to slide apart.

ManMan saw that her panties were pink, and they were clean. He couldn't see any pubic hairs poking out, which was also a good thing.

"Slide them to the side," he told her. "Them panties."

Sandra started to shake her head. "I don't want–"

"I ain't gon' touch you," ManMan promised. "I just wanna see it."

Sandra continued to shake her head. She was visibly trembling.

"You want me to take this bullshit-ass ring that I can't do nothing with?" ManMan said.

"I'll buy it back from you," Sandra promised.

"That's cool," ManMan said. "I'll hold your ring for you. But I wanna see your pussy first."

Sandra sensed she was about to take a step into the dark side. She convinced herself that this wasn't the same as sleeping with him. She was just showing a little skin. He wasn't even going to take a picture. The most important argument was ManMan agreed to take the ring. The dope was as good as in her hand already. All she had to do was give him a peek. It was no big deal. Even famous people like Farrah Fawcett posed for Playboy. No one thought she was a whore.

Sandra reached down and pulled her panties to the side, exposing her vagina. ManMan liked what he saw. He smiled and nodded and then told her, "Alright."

He turned and walked to the dresser. Sandra closed her legs and held her hands tightly in her lap. When ManMan faced her again, he had three twenty-dollar packs in his hand. He tossed them on the bed next to her. Sandra scooped them up. She stood, but ManMan told her, "Wait," before she could make it out of his room.

Sandra stopped, but she didn't look back at him. She felt him approach. She felt him lift the back of her skirt, and then Sandra felt his hand on her panties. ManMan pulled her underwear down past her butt and stared at her lovely ass for a moment before fondling it. Sandra closed her eyes and clenched her teeth. After a few seconds, ManMan pulled her panties back up and lowered her skirt.

He leaned close to her ear and said, "No more credit, ho. If you come in here again without some money, I'm busting a nut. I don't care if you think I'm ugly. I'm getting some head or some pussy, if you pull this shit again."

Sandra's only response was her rattling bones.

"Gone, bitch," ManMan said.

Sandra hurried out of the room.

ManMan hid her class ring in his dresser, and then he rubbed the hard lump in his pants. He should've made Sandra relieve him before she left, but he knew it would be better when she gave herself to him on her own free will. There was no doubt in ManMan's mind that this day was coming. But that knowledge didn't solve his boner problem today.

ManMan left his room to see if there was someone in the living room who looked decent enough to give him a blow job. He spotted Bridgette sitting in a corner looking desperate and lonely. She was skinny and disheveled, but she was light-skinned and vaguely attractive. Plus Bridgette wouldn't bat an eye at a dick in her face.

"Bridgette," ManMan called. "Get your ass in here."

She jumped up like they were playing Duck-Duck-Goose and she just got tagged. She grabbed her shooter kit and hurried into ManMan's bedroom.

Before he followed her, ManMan noticed another girl sleeping on the floor, her face in a small pool of vomit. There were ten other people in the room, but no one had done anything to help the poor wretch.

"What the fuck wrong with that bitch?" ManMan asked Sammy. "She OD'ed? Why y'all letting her lay over there like that?"

A dozen half-dead eyes rolled in the unconscious girl's direction.

"Get her out of here!" ManMan yelled. He fixed a mean glare on Sammy, his supposed doorman. "Ho, this is your responsibility! Get that bitch outta here!"

ManMan turned angrily and disappeared inside his bedroom. He slammed the door closed. Sammy was sitting on the couch with a straight girl named Cathy. She was close to turning Cathy towards the lesbian side of life, which is why Sammy didn't notice one of their customers was not well.

"Hey, I got two twenty packs for whoever help get that bitch outta here," Sammy announced.

Four people moved into action.

"I'm only giving *two packs*," Sammy reiterated. "I don't care how many of y'all help. You gotta share."

The four people who started to help were not deterred. They hoisted the unconscious girl and headed for the back door.

"Don't leave her in the alley right behind this house, neither!" Sammy warned them. "Say, can you clean that throw-up?" Sammy asked the girl she was hitting on. "I got something for you too, baby."

Cathy got up without asking what her reward would be. *Any* heroin was better than the *no* heroin she had right now. Cathy was also willing to sleep with Sammy, if it put some dope in her pocket. She already prostituted herself for men, some of whom beat her and didn't pay for her services. Sammy looked like a manlier version of Shirley from *What's Happening*, but at least Sammy always paid the fiends when she promised them something.

Three years ago Cathy was just like Sandra. She now understood that the world was different for people like them. And once you become people like them, you can never go back to being a regular person. The only logical course of action, at that point, was to stay as high as possible *as often as possible*, so that you would always see your ugly world through rose-colored glasses.

Anyone in her shoes would come to the same conclusion.

CHAPTER NINE
HATERS AND BAITERS

After two weeks on the job, housekeeper Raquel Rivera had settled into a reluctant groove, and she understood the inner-workings of Jackson Memorial fairly well. The most interesting thing to her was how well-planned and organized everything seemed to be. Everyone who punched a time clock at the hospital had a specific role, and each employee was important to the overall functionality of the system.

Upon entering the hospital, patients encountered admission clerks and triage nurses. The doctors decided if they should get admitted or not, and transporters rolled the patients to their rooms in wheelchairs, stretchers or sometimes in hospital beds. There were people in Bed Control who decided where each patient was sent, people in billing who decided how much the patients should be charged for their stay, and countless other employees who served food, took temperatures, washed linens and repaired leaky faucets.

The thousands of employees at Jackson were all part of a hierarchy of positions, and Raquel was somewhat ashamed to admit that janitors like her were at the bottom of the pile. Housekeepers were called to do the messy work no one else wanted to do. The *disgusting* work.

Some patients had dangerously contagious infections like VRE or MRSA, and Raquel had to be careful not to let her bare skin come in contact with their dirty linens. Lower GI bleeds were the worst. Raquel struggled to keep from vomiting whenever she had to clean up after one of those patients.

But work is work. While growing up in Puerto Rico, Raquel saw her parents take countless odd and sometimes horrendous jobs, day in and day out. They never once complained. As long as they could put food on the table each night, their fatigue was immaterial. Raquel had been in America for more than a decade, but she'd never forget the harsh conditions in her homeland. No matter how stressful things got at Jackson Memorial, she knew that she was blessed to have a home and a job in the great U S of A.

But that didn't mean she shouldn't hustle. Raquel didn't go around looking for trouble, but it was hard for her to say no if trouble found her – especially if it came in the form of a cash offering. On Saturday, March 30th Raquel was cleaning a room in the Meredith Building when trouble came knocking on her door.

Literally.

She turned to see who it was. Raquel was shocked to see a police officer standing in the doorway. Her first thought was that something had gone wrong with her background check. The father of her three children accepted a plea deal last month that sent him to prison for five years for trafficking marijuana. Raquel never sold drugs herself, but she did get questioned when her baby-daddy first got arrested. The sight of Damien made her wonder if the police changed their minds, and they wanted to lock her up after all.

Raquel's hands froze on the bed she was making. A lump caught in her throat.

"Yes?" she said. "Can I help you?"

Damien was decked out in his full police gear, which was the norm. He liked the look of fear that spread across Raquel's face. He'd been watching her since she first got hired. He learned from Amina that Raquel was from Puerto Rico, but she'd been in America for a long time. That was initially a turn-off (Damien rarely made a move on Americanized Hispanics at the hospital), but he decided it wouldn't hurt to check her out.

He couldn't help it. Raquel was alluring. She was young and she was exotic. Watching her mop floors and scrub stains

109

from countertops gave Damien a slight erection each time he saw her. He already masturbated twice this week with visions of Raquel swimming through his mind. Both of these masturbation sessions took place in a hospital bathroom. Damien squirted his seeds on the floor each time, and he left it there, hoping Raquel would be the one to clean it up.

"I didn't want anything," he told her. He stood tall with his thumbs hooked on his utility belt, the fingers on his right hand resting very close to his holstered pistol. "I just wanted to meet you," he said.

Raquel watched him anxiously. She didn't know what to make of this, but her initial reaction was that it was wrong; something was definitely not right. A lot of strangers at the hospital approached her and asked if she could go and clean something, but no one ever said, *I just wanted to meet you.* The fact that this was a cop made it ten times weirder.

"You like your job here?" Damien asked.

Raquel's mouth fell open. She blinked quickly. Was that a threat? Did she do something wrong? It sounded like the policeman would follow his comment with, *Well then you'd better do what I say...* But that didn't make sense either.

In her state of panic, Raquel didn't answer at all. Damien smiled. It was a strange smile, like an arsonist watching one of his fires consume and destroy.

"You not in trouble," Damien said. "I was just wondering how you were getting along. This is a big hospital, a lot of people. Do you like it here?"

His words did little to calm Raquel's nerves. She nodded. "Yeah, it, it's alright..."

"It looks good on the outside," Damien said. "But underneath, this place is *filthy* – and I don't mean the floors."

Raquel didn't respond to that. Was he blaming her for not cleaning something? Why was he talking in riddles? Why was he blocking the doorway like that? Was she under arrest?

"We got some high-tech equipment here," Damien continued. "CAT scans, ultrasounds... You know that MRI machine in the Jackson Building cost over a million dollars..."

Raquel didn't know that. She shook her head.

"But the thing is," Damien said, "no matter how advanced the technology is, no matter how state-of-the-art, they got to hire somebody to work the machines. And that's where the trouble starts. Because a *machine* can't do nothing without somebody pushing the buttons. And the people they hire, they're all flawed. 'Cause people get sick, and they get mad, and they lie and backbite. And they get horny, too. But it's nothing wrong with that. People got to be people, right?"

Raquel nodded. She took a deep breath. Her brain was working overtime, trying to figure out where this was going. She understood that she wasn't in trouble, but this was still a very bizarre conversation.

"People have *sex*," Damien went on. "But then they start running their mouths. They'll tell on *you* for having sex with *them* – like they didn't have nothing to do with it. They tell their stories, and then the hospital's full of sex talk. It's so much of it, it gets to be disgusting, don't you think?"

Raquel nodded again.

"You probably already know about some employees here who had sex with each other, don't you?" Damien asked.

Raquel nodded.

"Are you married?"

She shook her head.

"Got a boyfriend?"

She hesitated.

"It's okay to tell me," Damien said, still smiling. "I'm married. I got two kids."

Raquel didn't say anything.

"I'ma let you get back to work," Damien said. "I just wanted to see how you felt about that stuff; all the sex talk. If I could offer a piece of advice to somebody who's new at the hospital, I would tell them to watch out for all that gossip. It's not good. What two people do behind closed doors is their business. You know what I'm saying?"

Raquel nodded. Her face flushed with heat.

"I take care of people, who don't run their mouths," Damien confided. "Everybody needs some kind of help. And I like helping people. Maybe you need help with something, and I can help you one day..."

Finally Raquel had a clue about where this conversation was going. But so far Damien hadn't said anything that could get him in trouble.

"I don't mind helping people," he continued. "But one thing I don't like is when I help somebody, and they come back to the hospital, with their stories. When people talk, they don't care who they hurt. But I could never let that happen to me. If somebody tries to hurt me or my family, I have a right to defend myself."

Raquel cleared her throat and said, "I don't be telling stories."

Damien's grin grew wider. He nodded and checked the hallway behind him. "Time will tell," he said. "I'll see you later, Raquel."

He backed out of the room and then walked out of her line of sight. Raquel took a slow breath and wiped her forehead with her forearm. She felt like she gave appropriate responses to the policeman's interrogation. But she was still in the dark. She didn't think–

"Hey."

Raquel looked up and saw someone else standing in the doorway. This time it was Brenda Turner, her supervisor.

"Did Damien just leave from out of here?" Brenda asked.

Raquel didn't know how to respond. It was obvious Brenda saw him, but the policeman cautioned her about telling stories. Raquel sensed this was one of those stories Damien didn't want her to tell.

"Come to my office when you get done in here," Brenda said. "We need to talk."

The supervisor walked away, and Raquel finished up the room with cold, trembling fingers. She was both intrigued and terrified about what these people were trying to get her caught up in.

≈ ≈ ≈ ≈ ≈ ≈

Ten minutes later Raquel walked into her supervisor's office.

Brenda told her, "Close that door."

Raquel did so.

Brenda told her, "Sit down."

Raquel did that, too.

Brenda's office was junky, and her hunched back and mean disposition made her look like a junkyard dog. The supervisor took her glasses off and rubbed her tired eye sockets. She put the glasses back on and smiled at Raquel. "You ain't in no trouble, girl. What you looking so scared for?"

"I don't know," Raquel said. She was visibly shaken. "I didn't do nothing, but that cop came to my room, and then you called me to your office. I just want to know what's going on."

Brenda's eyes brightened. "That was *Damien*. Did he say something? Can you tell me what he said?"

Raquel shrugged, not sure where to place her loyalties. Brenda was her boss, but the black man was a cop. Jobs come and go, but from experience Raquel knew that trouble with police tends to linger until it's fully resolved.

"He didn't say nothing," she said. "He just said hi."

Brenda nodded. She looked at the new hire like Raquel might be the solution to a very big problem. "Did he sound like he likes you?" she asked. "Was he flirting?"

Raquel shook her head with uncertainty. "I, could you please tell me what's going on?"

Brenda considered things before she divulged. If her plan was to have any success, she had to get Raquel on her side before Damien got hold of her. If she waited too long, Raquel might cut her off completely, like Amina did.

"Alright," Brenda said. She leaned forward with her forearms on the desk. "I'ma tell you what's going on, but you got to promise not to say nothing to *nobody*. This is serious business. I don't want nobody getting in trouble..."

"I won't tell nobody," Raquel said.

"You got to *promise*," Brenda stressed. "Don't let nothing we talk about leave this office."

Raquel's heart raced. She had to clench her jaws to keep her teeth from rattling. In the past twenty minutes two people urged her not to tell their secrets – which could only mean two big secrets were coming her way. "I won't tell nobody," Raquel repeated. "I promise."

Brenda stared into her eyes. She nodded again. "Be sure you don't."

Raquel nodded, too. She brought a hand to her mouth and nibbled on one of her fingernails.

"That policeman's name is *Damien*," Brenda said. "He a good cop, I guess. I can't really speak on that. But as far as what kind of person he is, I know he ain't no good at all. He think he slick, but I know he been sleeping with a bunch of women at this hospital – some of them is housekeepers..."

Raquel's eyes widened as she put the pieces of the puzzle together. That's why Damien was concerned with all of the "sex talk" at the hospital. He wasn't speaking his mind indiscriminately. Damien came to Raquel specifically. He was *feeling her out*, possibly because she was his next prospect.

Raquel thought Damien was attractive and fine. She wished he would've come right out and said he wanted to hook up, but she understood why he was cautious.

"Amina's one of them," Brenda went on. "At least I think she is. I asked her about Damien. She swear up and down they ain't did nothing, but I know it's something between them two. I see it in her eyes. But don't you go saying nothing to her," Brenda warned. "It'll ruin everything."

Raquel nodded, her brain racing again. Amina and Damien? Wow. That was crazy. Amina was so quiet and respectful. And she was married. Raquel couldn't imagine Amina cheating on her husband, no matter how fine Damien was.

"I think he scares her," Brenda offered. "He might have threatened to have her arrested for something. But she ain't no illegal, so I don't know what he got on her. Maybe he pays her..."

Raquel's heart knocked even harder. That was it! That's what Damien meant by, *I take care of people who don't run their mouths. Everybody needs some kind of help.*

Raquel's mouth fell open.

"Don't get too freaked out," Brenda said. "You gon' find out that when it comes to sex, anything can happen. It's doctors here sleeping with nurses, CNA's sleeping with surgery techs, M.O. people sleeping with damned near *everybody*. When it comes to sex, anything can happen."

This was all shocking and a little scary. But it didn't explain why Brenda summoned her to the office. "What does all this have to do with me?"

"I wanna get Damien," Brenda confided. "I know he gon' come at you one day – if he ain't already. When he do, I want you to help me set him up. Out of all the people messing around up here, Damien's the one I can't stand the most. I don't want him messing with women in my department. I want to expose him and get his ass up out of here. I can't do it by myself, but with your help, I think we can get him."

Raquel was stunned and immediately against her supervisor's plans. And Brenda's explanation for why she wanted to do such a thing was inadequate. There had to be more to the story.

Brenda saw the doubt in Raquel's eyes, but she couldn't tell her the *real* reason she hated Damien so much. If the policeman wanted to sleep with every woman in the hospital, Brenda didn't give a shit one way or the other. But she couldn't stand Damien's *preferences*. He was married to a black woman, but all of the women he slept with (that she knew of) were Hispanic.

Brenda wondered why a fine, handsome brother like Damien wasn't attracted to women his own race. Brenda tried to get with Damien herself a few years ago. He shot her down cold. Maybe she wasn't as young and attractive as she used to be, but if it was just the sex Damien was after, he would've given Brenda a chance.

But no. Damien didn't give Brenda a second glance because she had too much melanin in her skin. His rejection left her bitter. Brenda knew she should probably let it go, but a brother who didn't like sisters – that was just plain old *wrong*. Somebody had to do something about it.

"What I got to do?" Raquel asked. She was pretty sure she didn't want to help Brenda, but it didn't hurt to ask.

"If he try to get with you," Brenda said, "all you got to do is tell me about it, so I can show up and take some pictures. That's it. He won't even know you set him up."

Raquel considered that. It didn't sound too risky. But she remembered what Damien said about taking care of people. If he meant financially, then his offer (if it was an offer) already sounded better than Brenda's. Raquel told her supervisor, "I really don't want to get involved in none of this."

"I can make it worth your while," Brenda said.

Raquel tried not to show it, but she was all ears.

"I got lunch coupons," Brenda said. "They're worth eight dollars apiece. You can use them in the cafeteria, to get free food if you want..."

Raquel wasn't moved by that.

"I'm in charge of your hours," Brenda said. "Maybe sometimes you don't want to come to work, but you still want to get paid for it. I can make sure you get paid, and you won't have to use a vacation day or nothing..."

Raquel raised an eyebrow.

"I can even give you some *overtime*," Brenda said. "Maybe you work three days a week, but I'll pay you for six, or *seven*."

Raquel smiled. She couldn't help it. Brenda grinned, too.

"So we got a deal?" Brenda asked. "You help me out with Damien, and I help you, too. Everybody's happy..."

"Okay," Raquel said, though she knew that wasn't true. Not everyone would be happy if Brenda got her way. But then again, who's to say Damien's counter offer wouldn't be more appealing? Obviously Brenda had this same conversation with Amina, and Amina chose to protect Damien. Raquel wouldn't commit to either side until everyone showed their hand. Ultimately she would only be loyal to herself.

"Alright," Brenda said. She was all smiles. "You wanna take the rest of the day off?"

Raquel didn't have to think about that. "Sure."

"Okay," Brenda said. "You can go ahead and leave. But don't clock out. I'll put your time in for you."

"Why you wanna do that?" Raquel asked. "I haven't done nothing for you yet."

"Just to let you know I'm serious," Brenda said. "If you do right by me, I'll take good care of you."

"Okay," Raquel said. She stood, trying not to show how excited she was.

"Don't forget," Brenda said. "This just between me and you."

"I know," Raquel said. "I won't tell nobody. I promise."

"That's good," Brenda said. "Now get on out of here, girl. Have a nice weekend."

≈≈≈≈≈≈≈

On the ground floor of the Jackson Building, Material Operations employee Rodney Tucker lounged with a new hottie he spotted a couple of weeks ago but never had a chance to meet formally. Tanya Russell was an RN on the oncology floor. She was a redbone with big lips and an unattractive gap between her bunny rabbit teeth. She made up for the gap with a banging body. The fact that she was a full-fledged nurse made her even more desirable.

Rodney knew that all of the nurses in the hospital got paid at least twenty dollars an hour. His last nurse friend used to bring him food from nice restaurants like Cattleman's Steakhouse and Saint-Emilion. Even if he couldn't get Tanya to splurge on him like that, Rodney took pride in his ability to seduce women who out-ranked him in the hospital's hierarchy. His ultimate goal was to bed a doctor and drive her Porsche to work one day.

Wouldn't that be something?

Rodney and Tanya sat on one of the sofas provided for visitors. Tanya had a great sense of humor, but Rodney was already tiring of her horse-like cackle. Plus the more she opened her mouth, the more Rodney decided he didn't care for the gap between her teeth. It was way too distracting. It looked big enough to stick half a peanut in there.

Rodney was about to tell Tanya he had to get back to work when he saw his supervisor exit the cafeteria with a bag full of groceries. Rodney sank down in his seat, but Eva spotted him and immediately headed in his direction.

117

"What you doing over here, boy?" Eva frowned at Rodney, and she frowned at his new friend, too.

"What you talking 'bout?" Rodney said. "I'm on break."

"You not on break," Eva said. "You already had your break, and you had your lunch, too. You need to call the system. I know there's some jobs in there."

Rodney stared at her in disbelief. Tanya looked from Rodney to his supervisor and then back at Rodney again. She decided this was way too awkward.

"Um, I'll talk to you later. Excuse me," she told Eva as she scooted by and headed back to her floor.

Rodney watched her go, and then he got up and approached Eva.

"What's wrong with you? Why you do that?"

"Don't be getting in my face," Eva snapped. "You know you supposed to be doing some work."

"I can sit down for a minute," Rodney argued. "You can't tell me I can't sit down if I'm tired."

"Who was that?" Eva wanted to know.

Rodney was upset, but he saw the jealousy in Eva's eyes, and it made him smile.

"What's so funny?" she asked him.

"You," Rodney said. "You cockblocking."

"I ain't cockblocking."

"You shoulda just told me you wanted some dick," Rodney said. "You ain't gotta be running my friends off. We can hook up."

"Who said I wanted to hook up?" Eva replied. But that was like a fat girl saying, *Who said I wanted cake?*

"What's in the bag?" Rodney asked. He reached for Eva's sack and checked for himself.

"What you doing when you get off?" his supervisor asked him.

"Damn, you got all kinds of goodies in here!" Rodney noticed. "How much ice cream you need? Shit. Let me have one."

He dug for one of her seven pints of Blue Bell, but Eva yanked the bag away.

"Stop, boy. These are for my kids."

"Well give me a lunch coupon then," Rodney said.

Eva rolled her eyes as she reached for her breast pocket.

The lunch coupons were good only at the hospital cafeteria. They were intended for great employees who went above and beyond on a particular task. The only problem was the supervisors who were responsible for the coupon distribution tended to keep them for themselves or give them to their friends (who just happened to be the worst slackers).

"Hey, what's up, y'all? How you doing, Miss Eva?"

Eva and Rodney turned and saw Larry approaching with two wheelchairs in tow; one in each hand.

Eva removed her hand from her pocket without the coupon. "Hey, Larry," she said. "Where you taking those?"

"Eighth floor," Larry said. "To rehab."

"Where my coupon?" Rodney asked Eva.

"Boy, I'm not giving you no coupon!" Eva snapped. "You need to get to work, Rodney. Why don't you help Larry with those wheelchairs? You not doing nothing."

With that Eva walked away with her ice cream and her lunch coupons.

Rodney smacked his lips and shook his head at Larry. "Nigga, you just cost me some coupons."

Larry chuckled. "Man, Eva ain't finna give you no coupons."

"Yes she was," Rodney said. He surprised Larry by taking one of the wheelchairs.

They both headed for the elevators.

"What's up with y'all two?" Larry wondered. "Y'all always fighting, but she never wrote you up or nothing."

"How she gon' write me up, when she all on my dick?" Rodney asked.

Larry laughed. "You think she like you?"

"I *know* she like me," Rodney said. "I can get Eva to suck my dick *right now*."

The men stopped at the elevator, and Larry hit the UP button. The doors slid open with a pleasant *DING*.

"You tripping," Larry said as they rolled the wheelchairs on board.

"No I ain't," Rodney said. He dug in his pocket for his phone when the elevator doors closed. "I recorded her one time. She thought I erased it, but I still got it. Wanna see?"

Larry thought he was kidding, but Rodney pulled up a video and offered his cellular.

"Here."

Larry's mouth hung open. He looked at the phone but didn't take it.

"You bullshitting."

"I'm not," Rodney assured him. "Here. You can see for yourself."

Larry continued to shake his head. "Naw. I don't wanna see that. You, you and *Eva*?..."

"Yeah, we fucking," Rodney confirmed.

Larry felt sick to his stomach. "*Why*?"

"'Cause she wanted to," Rodney said. "She be taking me downstairs sometimes to give me head. But she ain't the only one. A lot of girls up here gave me some head."

Larry was dumbfounded. He knew there was risqué behavior at the hospital, on any given shift, but he couldn't imagine Rodney and Eva getting it on. Well, he could understand why Eva would want to, but not a youngster like Rodney.

"You smashed?" Larry asked. "You really hit that?"

"Yeah," Rodney said. "Plenty times."

"*Here*?"

"I never smashed here," Rodney said. "I mean, I smashed a couple other girls, but not Eva. Not up here. But I been to her house. Usually she'll get us a room."

Larry reached to rub the confusion wrinkles on his forehead.

"I know she nasty," Rodney said. "But she got some good dome. And she be letting me hit it raw, 'cause she got her tubes tied."

As intrigued as Larry was, he didn't want to know anymore about what was going on with Rodney and Eva. He didn't think he could look his supervisor in the eyes anymore.

Luckily the elevator dinged again, announcing they were on the eighth floor.

Larry pushed his wheelchair off, and Rodney pushed the other one. But Rodney didn't step off the elevator.

"You got it from here?" he asked.

"Yeah," Larry said, still in a daze.

Rodney stuck an arm out to stop the elevator doors from closing again.

"Hey, they left the door unlocked in one of the education rooms," Rodney informed. "I already took some trash boxes down there. I wanna get a few computers and drop 'em off by the dumpster, pick 'em up when we get off. Can you help me? I'll give you $40."

"Naw," Larry said. "I don't get down like that."

"Alright, nigga," Rodney said. He withdrew his arm, and the elevator closed, whisking him away to destinations unknown.

Larry pushed both of the wheelchairs, thinking it was time for him and Rodney to stop being friends. The thievery aside, Larry didn't want to associate with a stupid kid who couldn't keep his dick in his pants. Rodney wasn't involved in a love triangle. He had a love *hexagon*.

When everything came to a head, as Larry knew it would, he didn't want to be anywhere near Rodney. He didn't want to catch a stray elbow in the inevitable cat fight, and he didn't want anyone to think that since he and Rodney hung around so much, they must be running mates.

Nope. Larry wanted absolutely no parts.

CHAPTER TEN
NOT SO SECRET

The next day Larry Barnes woke up at ten and took his truck to the carwash. It was the last day of March; a pleasant Sunday morning that made Larry wonder why he wanted to relocated every August. Texas summers were horrible, but the Lone Star State was a great place to be in the spring.

After he got his ride shined-up, Larry returned to his apartment to shower, shave and find an outfit for an unlikely date he managed to secure with a gorgeous medical student named Lola Dego. Larry selected a long-sleeved, pink Polo (because he was secure in his masculinity, and light colors contrasted nicely with his dark skin). He completed the outfit with a pair of khaki Dockers he hadn't worn in months.

Rather than pick Lola up for their date, Larry met her at Romano's Macaroni Grill at one p.m. Sticking to her vegetarian diet, Lola ordered the eggplant parmesan. Larry didn't want to offend by eating meat in front of her, so he ordered the same thing. He was skeptical, but when their meal arrived he thought it tasted great.

"This is awesome," he told his new friend.

Like Larry, Lola looked a lot different than she did at the hospital. She wore her hair down, and she had contacts rather than her bulky glasses. And she had on a skirt. It wasn't tight or anything, but this was the first time Larry saw her bare legs. They were nice and smooth. Lola's blouse offered just a hint of cleavage.

"I'm glad you like it," she told him. "But you didn't have to order that. I eat with people who aren't vegetarians all the time."

"That's not how you acted at Wendy's," Larry recalled.

"That's because that burger..." She shuddered. "*Uck.* That's worse than regular meat – with all that greasy fat."

"I don't eat fast food that much," Larry said.

"It's okay," Lola said. "You don't have to impress me."

"I feel like I do," Larry admitted. "You already have an opinion about what kind of person I am."

"No I don't," Lola said. "I told you, I let go of those hang-ups."

"What about your dad?" Larry wondered. "Does he know where you are right now?"

Lola nodded. "Of course."

Larry was surprised by that. He knew Lola had her own apartment near the university. "What do you mean *of course?*"

"We're very close," Lola said. "He's always been one of those, *Let me know where you are, in case something happens,* type of fathers."

Larry nodded. "I'd be protective too, if I had a little girl."

"Why don't you have any children?" Lola asked.

"I'm careful," Larry said. "I told you my dad didn't raise me. My step-dad was cool, but our relationship was always strained. I was eight by the time he showed up: Too big to cuddle with, and too young for any real man-to-man talks. He didn't know how to respond to me, and I didn't know what to say to him, either. For the most part, we didn't say too much."

"When I have some kids," Larry said, "it'll be with someone I want to spend the rest of my life with. But um, back to your father. What did he say when you told him you were going to see me?"

Lola scooped a rather large forkful of food and chewed on it for awhile.

Larry waited and then frowned. "That bad, huh?"

Lola held up a finger.

Larry chuckled. "Alright, I get it."

Lola grinned.

Larry told her, "You know, I looked up Lola Falana the other day. She was a really good dancer."

"I'm sure she can still dance," Lola said.

"Oh, she's alive?"

His date giggled. "Shows how much research you did."

"I just watched a few videos on YouTube," Larry said. "I didn't pull out the encyclopedia. But I saw enough to understand why your father liked her so much. She's beautiful. A little skinny, but I guess that's what people liked back then. I'm, uh, I'm glad you're not that skinny."

Lola gave him a look. "I don't know how to feel about that."

"It's a good thing," Larry assured. "I think your, um..." He cleared his throat. "I think your proportions are perfect, for you."

"Okay..."

"Why you looking at me like that?" Larry said. "You know you fine."

Lola blushed and took a sip of her tea. "Thank you."

"So, Dr. Dego said it was alright for you to go out with me?" Larry asked.

Lola shrugged. "Why do you keep asking about him?"

"I was wondering if he gave you one of those, *You know I raised you better*, lectures."

Lola laughed. "As a matter of fact, he did."

Larry smacked his lips. "He a hater."

"Don't say that. It's just his culture," Lola offered. "It's my culture, too. In Africa, a woman wouldn't marry or even allow a man to court her if he wasn't of greater or equal status."

"But you weren't born in Africa."

"I know," Lola said. "That's why we're here, together."

Larry nodded. He was glad she was giving him a shot, but overall he didn't feel good about his chances. He'd probably never be Lola's intellectual or financial equal. Did that mean she couldn't respect him as a man? Larry knew he would never play the submissive role in any relationship.

"Enough about me," Lola said, pushing her plate away. "I want to know more about you. What do you do, when you're not at work?"

Larry shrugged. "Nothing really."

"Do you have any hobbies? Do you like to read?"

"I used to read a lot, when I was younger," Larry said.

Lola sighed. "Um, do you like to go out? Ever climbed a mountain or anything?" She smiled.

Larry shook his head. "No. Nothing like that."

Lola's smile looked a little forced.

"I perform my poems sometimes, at open mic shows," Larry offered. "I like to write poetry."

Lola's eyes brightened. "Really? I love poetry."

"That's great!" Larry said and wiped his forehead. "I thought we weren't going to have anything in common."

"Me too," Lola admitted. She giggled. "What kind of poems do you write?"

"All kinds. Mostly spoken word."

Lola's smile grew even wider. "Really? What do you write about?"

"All kinds of stuff," Larry said. "Do you write poetry?"

"Yeah, but I never read it anywhere."

"You should go with me sometimes," Larry said. "I go downtown to a club called Barcelona every Tuesday night, if I'm not working."

"Can you do a poem for me?" Lola asked.

"What do you mean, like *now*?" Larry looked around uncomfortably.

"*Please*," Lola said. She batted her eyes and Larry's heart sighed.

"Dang, you look so good to me," he said.

Lola's smile lit up the whole room.

"Alright," Larry said. He pushed his plate away and wiped his hands on his napkin. "This poem is called, *If I Could Sing...*"

Lola nodded. She put her hands in her lap and gave him her full attention.

Larry cleared his throat and recited his poem from memory. He kept his voice low, and he maintained eye contact with Lola the whole time...

"When a man loves a woman
Sugar pie, honey bun
You got me saying my, my, my

125

If I could, I would write a love song like that for you
I would get you in the mood like Luther Vandross
Show you some sensitivity like Ralph Tresvant
Get freaky with you like Silk
Girl, I would drink you like milk
Make your panties steam
Melt you like ice cream
Damn, baby, I wish I could sing

I would write a love song to show you my fire and desire
I know you've been high, girl
But I can take you higher
I'm inspired by your ebony eyes
The way you purse your lips
Those thick hips, juicy thighs
Jesus Christ!
Come and take me, baby!
I will yield to your will
I'll pay your telephone and automo–bills
No diggity
I'll show you some real love, like Mary J Blige
Or we can creep like T-Boz and Left Eye
I see you telling me no, no, no
But I ain't too proud to beg, ma
I'll get down on bended knee
I will get down wherever and whenever you please
'Cause I wanna be down like Moesha
I'll treat you like a queen – Latifah
Tasha, Kim, Maria or Keisha
We need some U-N-I-T-Y
And I need your sweet apple pie
And if I could sing
I'd spit a rhyme so smooth, I'd make the doves cry
And you'd be proud to tell your homegirls
That boy is mine
And you could ride my pony like Ginuwine

Baby, if I could sing
I'd write a love song just for you

But I can't
So this love poem will just have to do."
When he was done, Lola stared at him in amazed silence for a few seconds. "That was, that was awesome," she finally said.

"It sure was," a woman sitting at the table next to them said.

Larry turned and saw a whole table full of women eavesdropping.

"You're really good," one of them told him.

"Um, thanks," Larry said. He couldn't hide his embarrassment. "You ready to go?" he asked Lola.

She nodded, clearly mesmerized by his creativity. "Will you take me with you, next time you go to Barcelona?"

Larry's heart skipped a beat. Before the poem, his chances for a second date looked bleak. "Yeah, for sure. That, that'd be really cool."

≈≈≈≈≈≈≈

When they got outside, Larry walked Lola to her car. But she shook her head when he lingered there.

"Your poem was wonderful, and I had a great time. But I don't kiss on the first date."

"I didn't ask for a kiss," Larry said, even as his heart sank. "I'm just saying..."

Lola turned and unlocked her vehicle. Larry checked out her figure, but he didn't ogle. He met her eyes when Lola turned back to him.

"So, I guess I'll talk to you later," she said.

"Alright," Larry replied. "But, um, how do you feel about first date *hugs*? I've never even touched your hand, the whole time we've been talking. To be honest, it's driving me crazy."

Lola smiled and she stepped to him without words. The delight Larry felt when he wrapped his arms around her was only surpassed by the joy he felt when she wrapped her arms around him. Out of habit, Larry's hands began to slide down the small of her back. Lola backed away before he did anything inappropriate.

"I wasn't gonna–"

"Mmm hmm." Even her skeptical frown was cute.

"Maybe I was," Larry admitted.

She smiled. "Goodbye, Larry."

He didn't walk away until Lola started her car and waved at him one last time.

Larry wasn't used to dating such conservative women. But he couldn't deny that Lola had him much more intrigued than the last five girls he went out with. He wondered how many dates it would take before he could feel her sweet lips on his. He couldn't even fathom what second or third base might feel like.

≈ ≈ ≈ ≈ ≈ ≈ ≈

That night on the Critical Care/Neuro floor, charge nurse Cynthia Pullman was shocked when a seldom seen co-worker named Sandra Alexander showed up on time and asked what assignments she had for the night. Cynthia was surprised not only by Sandra's presence but also by her appearance. Technically it wasn't Cynthia's place to drill anyone, but she couldn't put any lives in Sandra's hands until Sandra answered some poignant questions.

"I, uh, I didn't expect to see you today," Cynthia admitted. "Your attendance has been so bad, it's getting to be hit or miss with you."

"I didn't call-in today," Sandra said. "I always call-in, if I can't make it."

That made sense, but, "Why are you calling in so much?" Cynthia wondered. "Are you having medical problems? Have you thought about taking a leave of absence?"

Cynthia's eyes were caring, but they were also inquisitive and judging. Sandra's scrub suit was more loose-fitting than it used to be, which was easily explained by the twenty or more pounds Sandra lost since the last time Cynthia really looked at her. To hide her needle marks, Sandra wore a long-sleeved thermal under her scrub top. It was warm outside, but it was chilly inside the hospital, so Sandra wasn't the only nurse who dressed this way.

Other causes for concern were Sandra's gaunt facial features, the dark bags under her eyes and her dry, damaged hair.

And Cynthia couldn't help but notice the bandage on Sandra's left thumb. If Cynthia had to guess, she would say that Sandra looked like an AIDS or cancer patient. If that was the case, Cynthia knew that she could possibly get in trouble if she forced Sandra to talk about it. The one thing Jackson Memorial valued more than anything else was patient confidentiality. That went for regular patients as well as employees who were sick.

"I've been having some medical problems," Sandra said vaguely. "I know it's been bad, my call-ins and stuff. I'm trying to do better. I don't ever want to call in. I'm sorry."

Cynthia's heart melted. Empathy replaced the irritation she harbored for Sandra. Cynthia imagined her coworker trying to get ready for work, but Sandra was too weak to iron her clothes or do her hair. During one call-in, Sandra said she had an upset stomach. Cynthia imagined Sandra hanging on her toilet vomiting, not wanting to call-in but physically unable to function because of whatever disease was eating away at her.

Cynthia made a mental note to discuss the matter with Ruben, to see what help they could offer her. In the meantime she didn't have the authority or sufficient cause to *not* let Sandra work that night. She assigned her two of the easiest patients on the floor, and Cynthia watched Sandra closely throughout the shift. Sandra was a lot quieter and slower than her usual self, but her patient care was not diminished at all.

By seven a.m. Cynthia decided Sandra was a trooper for coming to work despite her health problems. She thought Sandra was a shining example of a woman's strength, courage and perseverance.

Bless her heart.

≈ ≈ ≈ ≈ ≈ ≈ ≈

Cynthia clocked-out at ten after seven and headed for her Trailblazer in the Avery parking garage. She didn't sense anyone following her and was surprised when another nurse approached as she was getting in her car.

"Hey."

129

Cynthia turned and frowned when she saw who it was. She and Janice hadn't gotten along well since Cynthia became one of the new charge nurses on their unit. Plus Cynthia just worked a twelve hour shift with Janice. If Janice wanted to talk about something, why hadn't she done so on their floor?

Cynthia didn't get out of her car, but she left the door open. "Hey. What's up?"

Janice stepped closer and checked to make sure no one else was around before she said what was on her mind.

"You and Ruben sleeping together?"

Cynthia tried to play it cool, but her eyes bugged. She lost all of the air in her lungs, like an unexpected punch to the gut. Most of the blood drained from her face, but thankfully it was hidden behind her dark skin tone.

She and Ruben were extra careful. They didn't work the same shift, and they made sure not to pal around too much on the rare occasions they were on the floor together. Cynthia's mind raced. She tried to figure out what clues they left behind. She couldn't come up with anything. There was no way Janice had proof of anything salacious.

Cynthia shook her head. "No. Why, what are you talking about?"

Janice stepped closer into Cynthia's open door. When they were close enough to touch she said, "You can tell me. I know how it is."

Cynthia stared at her, still in shock. She couldn't have been more uncomfortable. It was only 62 degrees outside, but Cynthia's car felt like a tanning bed.

She continued to shake her head. "That, that's ridiculous. What are you talking about?"

Janice frowned. She considered whether she should divulge her own secrets and decided she had no choice. "I seen the way y'all act when you're together," Janice said. "And the way you was acting when you had to call him in a couple of weeks ago."

Cynthia sighed inwardly, happy to hear that Janice's suppositions were weak at best. "I don't know how you think we act when we're around each other," she said, "but there's nothing going on between me and Ruben. As for me not wanting to call him, I already told you: I don't like to call anyone in on their day off. I definitely don't want to call our manager in."

Janice shook her head and exhaled loudly. She leaned in even closer. "I'm telling you, *I know how it is*." She stared fiercely into Cynthia's eyes. "I know how it is because it was the same for me, when I was with him..."

Cynthia couldn't stop her jaw from dropping.

"I was with him for six months," Janice confided. "He initiated it. I had only dated one white guy before him, but that was in high school. Me and Ruben were serious. At least, I thought we were. I fell in love with him. I thought he was going to leave his wife for me, but he didn't. And I'm telling you, he's not going to leave her for you, either."

Cynthia could barely speak. In addition to the shock, she now felt hurt and betrayed. She knew it shouldn't matter who Ruben was with before they became a couple, but it did. Every one of her major organs felt like it was shutting down. Cynthia's defiance was all gone now. She repeated her denials because her brain was too frazzled to come up with a different response.

"There's nothing going on with me and Ruben."

"*Come on, Cynthia,*" Janice pleaded. "I'm telling you; *you don't have to lie to me.* I know what you're going through 'cause I been there. I been *right there.* I see the look in your eyes. I know how bad you're hurting right now."

"There's nothing going on," Cynthia insisted.

Janice blew out another frustrated sigh.

"He don't come by your house when he get off work?" Janice asked. "He don't love going down on you?" she taunted. "He don't never tell you how much he *love* your black skin, he wish he could mix it up in a bowl and eat it like cake batter?"

The more Cynthia listened, the deeper she fell into a pit of despair.

"He don't really want you," Janice warned. "He got a thing for black girls. *That's it.* He don't love *you*; he loves your black skin. I know because he loved my black skin the same way. I'm trying to help you, Cynthia. I want you to leave him alone before he hurts you like he did me. I don't want him no more – that's not why I'm doing this. I just don't want him to keep running up on

black women with them same tired lines. I don't wanna sit there
and watch you get played."

The nurses stared at each other for a long time before
Cynthia said, "I'm sorry you had to go through that, Janice. But
me and Ruben, there's nothing going on. I swear."

Cynthia had to lie because the moment she told the truth,
she would have to accept that everything Janice told her was the
truth as well. At that point, Cynthia knew she'd break down. She
didn't know how bad her breakdown would be, but *catastrophic*
was a good estimate. Cynthia didn't want to start crying, and she
didn't want to have to depend on Janice to console her.

Rather than compassion, her denials sparked a fit of rage
in her nemesis. Janice's nostrils flared. All of the worry lines in
her face twisted into an angry sneer that looked borderline *evil*.

"Alright, *fine!*" Janice spat. "You wanna sit there and lie to
me when I ain't doing nothing but trying to help your dumb ass?"
She nodded angrily. "Alright. Go ahead and keep fucking him.
Keep sucking his dick! I hope he do break your heart. I hope he
fuck up your head so much, you won't even come to work no more.
Stupid bitch!"

Janice turned and marched away with her teeth clenched.

Cynthia struggled to breathe. She closed her door and
started her car and fled the hospital before the walls closed in
completely and choked the life from her.

CHAPTER ELEVEN
SPIRITUAL WARFARE

The next few weeks passed slowly. They were especially slow for critical care nurse Sandra Alexander. But then again, her whole life was moving in slow motion nowadays.

When she showed up for work unexpectedly on March 30th, Sandra had an insightful talk with her charge nurse. Cynthia didn't demand any documentation of Sandra's mystery illness, but Sandra knew a doctor's note would be requested if she continued to miss days. So she made a plan to stop calling-in – no matter how badly she felt.

This goal wasn't too hard because Sandra only worked three days a week, usually Friday, Saturday and Sunday. That left four days a week for Sandra to shoot dope at will and recline on her couch and watch the world move very

very

slowly.

On the three days Sandra *had* to work (it really was a gruesome chore at this point), she found that if she shot up four hours before her shift, she would sober up enough to not look high when she clocked in. She could usually make it halfway through her shift before her body began to beg for more heroin. The second half of her work day was like a personal hell, but Sandra kept herself going with the promise of more dope when she got off.

Sandra kept one pill of heroin in her car, which she snorted as soon as she got to the parking lot. That was enough to last her until she got to her shooter kit at home. Sometimes the pill she snorted caused Sandra to *nod* or doze a little on the freeway, but so far she hadn't had any accidents. A few people honked at her when she veered into their lane, but that was the worst that had happened.

Overall Sandra reached a point in her addiction where she believed she was in control of the drug, rather than the other way around. According to the text books she studied as a nursing student, this made her a "functional addict." Sandra liked being *functional*, because it meant she didn't have to change her behavior.

Deep down a part of her wanted to stop getting high, but Sandra knew she didn't have the strength to do that. She didn't know how long she would remain *functional*, but she figured she could pull it off for years, maybe even a whole decade. By then she could wean herself off heroin by smoking marijuana instead.

≈ ≈ ≈ ≈ ≈ ≈ ≈

On Wednesday, April 17th, the skies over Overbrook Meadows were dark and menacing. It had been raining off and on all day. By five p.m. there were flood warnings in some parts of the city, but no one was upset about it. The precipitation lowered the temperature a full fifteen degrees. And the springtime showers would leave beautiful flowers in their wake. Next month wild bluebonnets would spring up all across the state. Dogwood trees would add to the splendor when gentle winds scattered their pink and yellow flowers like graffiti.

Sandra alienated herself from most of her friends and family, and she was startled when someone knocked on her door that night. Sandra was even more surprised when she opened it and saw that her visitor was both familiar and unfamiliar at the same time.

Benjamin Miller had been in jail for three months. Before his incarceration, Ben was Sandra's boyfriend. He was the man who introduced her to snorting heroin. Ben hid his shooter kit in Sandra's car at the time of his arrest, so technically he was also responsible for the first needle she put in her arm.

Before he went to jail, Ben was tall and skinny. He kept his head shaved bald, which made him look like a cancer patient in the end stages of the disease. But while he was locked up, Ben had to quit using cold-turkey. And as a guest of the Tarrant County Jail, Ben was fed three square meals a day, which his body readily turned into fat and mostly muscle.

Ben looked so good, Sandra didn't know how to respond right away. He stood six-foot-three. His head was still shaved, and his skin was dark and smooth. Because of his trip through the rain, Ben's tee-shirt was soaked. It clung to his body, exposing swollen pecs and trapezius muscles that were never this pronounced.

But as pleasing as Ben looked, a woeful frown distorted his features because Sandra looked quite the opposite. The last time Ben saw her, Sandra had it going on. She was thick in the hips, thin in the waist, and her breasts were a solid B cup. Now Sandra looked like she'd been smoking crack. Nearly all of her body fat was gone. She was still pretty, but her hair was unkempt and her eyes looked lost.

Tears welled and then spilled from Ben's eyes, because he knew that he was the cause of this. He introduced Sandra to a powerful narcotic, and he went to jail when her addiction was near its peak. It was doubtful Ben could've done anything to stop her if he was free, but without him there to guide her, Sandra let the drug take her too fast and way too far.

Ben reached and pulled her close. He held her very tightly. He whispered, "I'm sorry," into the top of her head. Sandra gradually wrapped her arms around him. She started to cry because she missed him, and she understood how bad things had gotten.

"I'm sorry," Ben said again. "I'm so sorry. I'ma get you better."

Rather than comfort her, his words made Sandra freeze as stiff as a board in his arms. *Get her better?* Sandra wanted a hit of dope *right then*, but she kept her mouth closed. She didn't say anything at all.

≈ ≈ ≈ ≈ ≈ ≈ ≈

135

After taking a shower to get the jail-smell off of his body, Ben changed into clean clothes that had been in Sandra's closet since he got arrested. He then surveyed all of the clutter and missing electronics in Sandra's home as he considered how he could tackle his woman's addiction. He was determined to right his wrongs.

As a former addict, Ben remembered how hard his first week in jail was. He experienced night sweats, full body cramps, nausea, diarrhea, depression and chills. Ben had to endure all of that alone, but Sandra wouldn't have to. Ben was there for her. If he couldn't help her on his own, Ben would talk her into going to rehab. He couldn't live with himself if he didn't at least try to put her life back together.

He went to the living room where Sandra was sitting on the couch watching an old television that she wasn't able to pawn or sell on the streets. Ben turned the TV off and sat next to her. He placed a hand on Sandra's knee. She looked into his eyes and smiled. Ben smiled too, but his was forced and a little shaky around the edges.

"Can we talk?" he asked.

Sandra nodded. "You look good."

"Thanks."

"You got clean, while you were in jail?" she asked.

Ben nodded. "I didn't have no choice."

Sandra chuckled. "Maybe I should get myself arrested."

Ben didn't respond because that didn't sound like a bad idea.

"I look a mess, don't I?" Sandra asked.

"You, you look like you ain't been eating," Ben said. "How long you been shooting?"

Sandra hadn't told him she befriended the needle, but she wasn't surprised that he could tell. "Since you left," she said. "When I picked up my car from the police, I found your kit."

"You pulled up the backseat?"

Sandra nodded. "I knew it was in there somewhere." She chuckled.

Ben sighed quietly.

"So, what's supposed to happen now?" Sandra wondered. "I guess you wanna try to get me clean..."

Ben didn't like her sarcastic attitude. "Yeah," he said. "That's what I want."

"And how do you plan to do that?" Sandra asked.

"Do you want to get clean?" Ben asked.

Sandra shrugged. "I do, but I don't think about it like that anymore. It's a part of my life, like if you lose a leg or something. You learn how to get by. I been getting by."

Ben's heart sank. "So what you're saying is you accepted that you're an addict, and you're okay with it..."

Sandra didn't like the word "addict" without the word "functional" in front of it. "I tried to quit," she said. "I tried a bunch of times."

"Did you ever go to rehab? You can go to a methadone clinic."

"My cousin works at one of those," Sandra said. "I don't want to give them all my personal information, get put in their computer."

"It's all confidential."

"And those people don't ever get clean," Sandra added. "Teachers and policemen, they go in there three times a week. They get their fix, and they go on about their lives. But they keep coming back. They're still junkies."

"But they stop falling," Ben said. "They're not spending all their money, spiraling out of control."

"I'm not either," Sandra said. She actually believed that, so she said it with a straight face.

Ben knew they wouldn't get anywhere until she accepted that there was a problem, so he switched tactics. He grinned at her and shook his head. "You not spiraling out of control?"

Sandra didn't like the new look in his eyes. She became defiant.

"I still have my house. I still have my car and my job."

"You ain't got shit," Ben said. "You walking around looking like a freak, and you got the nerve to say you're doing okay. You prolly about to lose your job. And then what? What you gon' do when you can't get another job because the people at Jackson write in your file that you're a dopefiend. A dopefiend nurse.

"How you gon' get another job when you can't pass a drug test? And who the hell would hire some skinny dopefiend who's *obviously* a dopefiend? You're like one of those anorexic chicks looking in the mirror thinking they still look good. But you know what? You *don't* look good, Sandra. Your house looks like shit, and you look like shit, too."

His words were a slap in the face. Sandra didn't need this. She invited Ben into *her* home. Without her, he'd be stuck out in the rain.

"Just because you went and got yourself clean – wait, I take that back," she said. "Just because you got locked up and got sober because you *couldn't get no dope* doesn't mean you're better than me."

"I know I'm not better than you," Ben replied. "I'm a fuck up. I ain't never did right my whole life. But you a nurse, Sandra. You went to college and everything. You got a future. Even as messed up as you are right now, you're still better than me because once you get all of this turned around, you can get right back on top. You said so yourself, you haven't lost your house or your car."

"*I can't stop!*" Her outburst was sudden and unexpected. "*I tried to stop, and I can't!*"

Sandra's eyes filled with tears. Ben sensed they were close to a breakthrough, so he pressed on.

"*You can stop!* All you got to do is stop acting like a scared little girl!"

"*Shut up! It's your fault anyway!*"

"I know it is!" Ben shouted. His cheeks were slick with tears again. "That's why I can't sit here and let you keep killing yourself. You don't have to be like this no more! You can beat it!"

Tears stained Sandra's cheeks, too. She shook her head fiercely. "No I can't!" Her face twisted in sorrow. She was ugly, and yet very beautiful. "*You don't know!*"

"*I do know!*" Ben growled. "I know exactly what you're going through."

"*Just stop!*" Sandra pleaded.

"*No!*" Ben shook his head. "I'm not. *I'm not gon' stop!*"

"Please..." Sandra lowered her head and sobbed uncontrollably.

Ben was quick to wrap his arms around her. She tried to pull away, but she was so weak, mentally and physically.

Finally she relented and allowed him to comfort her. She cried, and he cried, and the sky cried too. Somewhere in the midst of the tears, Sandra found her willpower, and she muttered, "I wanna quit."

Ben held her tighter. He told her, "I know, baby. I'm here for you. I'll help. I promise I won't leave you again."

≈ ≈ ≈ ≈ ≈ ≈ ≈

Ben stayed with her for the rest of the night. Sandra had a huge monkey on her back, but with Ben there to help her, she found that she didn't have to be a slave to her habit. It may not have felt like it, but Sandra was still in control of her own destiny.

Ben told her that some addicts view their addiction as a form of spiritual warfare. Sandra thought that made perfect sense. The enemy, better known as the devil, wanted Sandra to grieve and turn away from God before she suffered a tragic death. The enemy used a lot of different tactics to corrupt souls. Sometimes it was lust, sometimes gluttony or vanity. In Sandra's case it was drugs.

Ben said the only thing that kept him sane while he battled his demons in jail was an unwavering belief that Jesus would stand by his side, if he believed. Ben said he was never much of a Christian, but he started praying in jail. At first he prayed while curled in a fetal position, his clothes drenched from his night sweats.

Later, when he regained his strength, Ben prayed on his knees. He said a lot of the other inmates thought he was a Holy Roller. Some even came to him seeking solutions for their personal troubles. Ben told them he wasn't an evangelist, and he had precious little knowledge about the bible. All he knew was that when he begged God for help, God listened and gave him the strength he needed. Ben assured his new acquaintances that the same would work for them.

Sandra was never a big-time Christian either, but Ben's story gave her more encouragement than anything else she'd heard in the past six months. She opened her mind and her heart as Ben led her through a sinner's prayer. Afterwards, Sandra got on her knees with Ben and held his hand as he prayed for God to enter the home and cast out the evil spirits that resided there. Ben asked God to bless Sandra and give her the strength to overcome her addiction. He instructed Sandra to tell God that she loved Him, and she gave Him complete control over her life.

They ended the prayer with "Amen," which Ben told her meant "So be it." They were both crying so hard, there was no doubt the Holy Spirit was upon them.

≈ ≈ ≈ ≈ ≈ ≈ ≈

Sandra made spaghetti for dinner. It wasn't ready until ten p.m. By then both she and Ben were ravenous. Sandra hadn't had any dope since Ben arrived earlier in the evening. Even better was the fact that she really didn't want to get high. She couldn't remember the last time she felt that way. It was a welcome change.

After supper Sandra bathed and did herself up because she now had a man to impress. She didn't realize how badly her hair was damaged until she tried to brush it, and the bristles got clumped up with her shedding. Sandra made a silent promise to go to the beauty shop ASAP. But she didn't have the funds for that now. Like many other neglected responsibilities, this too had to wait until her next paycheck.

Sandra put on lipstick and mascara and left the bathroom wearing only a tee shirt and panties. Ben hadn't touched a woman since he got locked up. He quickly decided that his newfound Christianity didn't include a ban on pre-marital sex. He stripped Sandra completely nude and licked every crevice of her body, even between her toes.

Sandra hadn't had sex since the last time she and Ben were together, and she'd forgotten how good it felt to be with a man. All of her horniness had been repressed. Tonight it was unleashed, and it was powerful. She had her first orgasm within twelve seconds of Ben kissing her clitoris. She had another one when he mounted her in the missionary position. She had a third and a fourth when he rolled her over and pleased her from behind.

≈≈≈≈≈≈≈

When they were spent, Ben held onto Sandra like he was lost at sea, and she was a floating piece of timber. Sandra held on to him, too. But as midnight rolled into the wee hours of the morning, she found sleep elusive. At a quarter till four a.m., Sandra had to drag herself from under Ben's arm and leg so she could go to the bathroom.

Ben woke up and went looking for her fifteen minutes later. He saw the light shining under the bathroom door, but Sandra wouldn't respond when he knocked. Even when he raised his voice and pounded with both fists, she remained mute. Ben forced the door open with a heavy shoulder and then a strong kick; right next to the doorknob.

He found Sandra sitting on the toilet with her shooter kit on the counter next to her. She was sweating profusely. She already had her tourniquet secured. Without looking up at Ben, Sandra poked a needle in her arm, found a vein, and pushed the plunger slowly, delivering enough heroin to get her through the rest of the night. When she was done, she calmly placed the needle on the counter, undid the tourniquet and met Ben's eyes.

Ben's bottom lip began to quiver. Sandra expected him to lecture her about how she was letting the devil win. But in a span of five seconds, Ben waged his own battle with Satan, and he too accepted defeat.

"Do, do you got some more?" he asked.

Sandra really didn't have enough to share. But she knew they would get along better if Ben was high, too. She nodded towards the rest of her $20 pack, because the drug was raging through her system, and she couldn't articulate her response.

CHAPTER TWELVE
GUESS WHO'S COMING TO DINNER

On Tuesday April 23rd, Larry picked Lola up at her apartment and whisked her away to for a quick dinner and a night of poetry at an Overbrook Meadows nightspot called Barcelona. Lola and her family lived in the city for the past decade, but she never heard of the place.

From the outside, Barcelona was an unassuming and easily overlooked locale. Every Tuesday night the place was packed with poets who wanted to bear their soul on the mic, usually for no bigger reward than the applause from the audience and maybe a slap on the shoulder when they stepped off the stage.

Larry liked Barcelona because it was one of few places he knew of where black people never got violent or even argumentative with each other. All of the brothers there were into poetry, which said a lot about their culture and literary interests. And the sisters... There was nothing more attractive to Larry than an intellectual woman who liked to read and learn and share her knowledge with others.

Larry and Lola got a seat close to the stage and sipped non-alcoholic beverages under the dim lighting at the club. When the MC called Larry's name, he took the stage and performed another piece he knew from memory. It was a scathing, no holds barred attack on an entertainment giant named Tyler Perry. When Larry was done, the crowd erupted in cheers and snaps. He even got a standing ovation from Lola and several others.

When they left the club, the moon was high in the sky. The air was cool, the mood mellow. Lola let Larry take her hand into his as they made their way through the dark parking lot. He helped her into his truck, and Lola smiled as she fastened her safety belt.

"You had a good time?" Larry ventured.

She nodded. "It was great. *You* were great. That was some poem."

"Aw, it was alright," Larry said.

"Don't be modest. You know you're good."

"Thanks." Larry turned on his headlights and backed out of the parking spot.

"Do you ever travel?" Lola asked.

"Not really," Larry said. "I was in a poetry group a while back. We traveled a little, but not out of the state."

"You performed, everywhere you went?"

"Yeah," Larry said. "I was the youngest one in the group back then. I was always the most *fiery*. Some of the stuff I said, it wasn't even cool back then. Now everybody's saying it."

"You're still saying stuff people might not think is cool," Lola noticed. "Why you hating on Tyler Perry?"

Larry looked over at her and grinned. "Don't tell me I hurt your feelings."

"No. I think you're right. But not too many people talk about him like that."

"I think Tyler Perry could do so much more," Larry said. "He got the attention of black people and white people, too. Why does he keep showing the *worst* about us? I know there are some real-live Madea's out there, but why does he have to throw it in everybody's face? Spike Lee's right; that's some *coon buffoonery*."

Lola laughed. "You're something else."

"I just be thinking about stuff," Larry said.

"That's why it's so impressive," Lola replied. "Coming from the environment you were raised in, you're supposed to be one of Tyler Perry's biggest fans. You're not supposed to step back and say, '*Hold on. This isn't cool.*'"

"It doesn't matter what I think," Larry said. "He's still going to make whatever movies he wants."

"That's not the point," Lola said. "What's important is you know better. And you're not afraid to voice your opinion. That's what makes you special."

Larry chuckled. "You think I'm special?"

"I do," Lola said. "That's why I want you to meet my dad."

Larry's smile froze on his face. "Do what now?"

Lola giggled. "You heard me."

"But, but I already met him. I see him all the time."

"You never talked to him," Lola said.

"I don't have a need to," Larry said. "And he doesn't want to talk to me."

"Yes he does," Lola countered. "He wants you to come over for dinner."

"*What*?"

"He told me to ask you."

"*Why*?"

"We've been dating for almost a month," Lola said. "You knew he'd invite you over at *some* point."

"Yeah, but I hoped we could wait a few decades; 'til he's too old to know what's going on."

Lola grinned. "I'm serious, Larry. I talked to him about you the other day, and he said he wants to meet you."

Larry shook his head. He was happy that Lola liked him enough to try to win her father over. But he was distressed at the thought of sitting across the table from Dr. Dego. He couldn't imagine that dinner going well.

"I don't see the point," he said. "He already doesn't like me. You said so yourself."

"That's because he doesn't know you," Lola said. "All he knows is you work in Material Operations."

"What am I supposed to do," Larry wondered, "recite a poem for him?"

"Do you have one about Ethiopia?"

Larry gave her a look and Lola giggled.

"I'm just kidding."

"Yeah, go ahead and get your jokes out now," Larry said. "'Cause there won't be nothing to laugh about when me and your dad are in the same room."

"So you'll come?"

Larry shrugged. "Might as well."

"Oh, that's great!" Lola leaned over and hugged his arm. "What's your other off day this week?"

"Thursday."

"You wanna do it then?" Lola asked. "I'll ask Daddy if he has anything planned."

Larry shook his head. "He's not going to change his mind about me. You know that, don't you?"

"Larry, you need to give yourself some credit," Lola said. "I know Daddy wants me to find a smart, rich college kid, preferably a medical student. But he's always talking about how he wishes more black men would just get a job – *any job* – and stop selling drugs and killing each other."

"That doesn't mean he wants his daughter to date one of those men."

"He wants me to be happy," Lola said. "More than anything else."

"Are you happy?"

"You make me happy," Lola said. She smiled at him with such a sweet expression, Larry knew he could never deny her anything.

"Thursday, huh?"

"I think so," Lola said. "I'll let you know for sure."

"I don't think I can enroll in medical school by then," Larry said.

"Just be yourself," Lola said with a chuckle. "Don't worry. I'll be right there beside you."

She took his free hand into hers and gave it an encouraging squeeze. Suddenly Larry felt like he had enough strength to take on Dr. Dego, a couple of brown bears and a mighty, African lion, too. That's all he ever needed; a good woman by his side. That's all any man needs.

≈≈≈≈≈≈≈

145

When they got to Lola's apartment, Larry walked his date to the door like a proper gentleman. He was used to Lola's friendly hugs by then, but she surprised him by holding onto his hand after the embrace. She stepped to him quickly and planted a soft kiss on his lips before Larry was aware of what was going on. When it was over, he was a little chagrined that he didn't have time to savor their first smooch.

"Wait. I wasn't ready."

"Yeah you were," Lola said with a giggle. "You kissed me back and everything."

"My lips were just moving, out of reflex," Larry argued.

"What would've been different if you were ready?" Lola wondered.

"Well, first of all, I would've put my arm around you like this." Larry's hand moved to the small of her back. "And I would've pulled you closer," Larry said as he did so. "And then I'd sing softly in your ear," he joked. *Shooby dooby doooo.*

Lola laughed and he did, too.

"You're crazy," she said.

"I like you a lot," Larry told her.

"I like you, too," Lola said.

When they kissed this time, both of them were ready. The warmth and electricity between their lips set off fireworks in their minds.

"That *was* better," Lola said when they separated.

"Told ya," Larry said. "Give me a call tomorrow and let me know if Thursday is a definite."

"Alright," Lola said. "I would call my dad tonight, but I'ma be too busy writing Tyler Perry, to tell him what you said about him."

Larry laughed. "Go ahead. I ain't scared."

Lola unlocked her door and stepped inside. She gave him one more sweet smile before she closed it. "Goodnight, Larry."

"Goodnight, Miss Lola. Talk to you tomorrow…"

≈ ≈ ≈ ≈ ≈ ≈ ≈

Two days later Larry pulled on a pair of black slacks with a white button-down and headed to the fair city of Burleson with the best intentions in mind. He felt a little awkward as he maneuvered his '98 F-150 through Dr. Dego's upscale neighborhood, but Larry tried to remain positive.

All signs pointed to an awkward and embarrassing encounter, but there was a chance everything would work out fine. If not, Larry wouldn't regret giving it a try, for Lola's sake. They had only been dating for a month, but Larry was nearly smitten. Lola was the smartest girl he ever dated. She had more going for herself than any woman Larry knew in his day-to-day life. Deep down he knew he didn't deserve a woman like Lola, but Larry refused to believe that he wasn't good enough for her or anyone else.

Dr. Dego lived in a two story home made of fiery red bricks. Larry thought it looked like a mini castle. He pulled into the circular driveway and parked behind a brand new Mercedes CLS. He hopped out of his truck with butterflies in his stomach. Larry rang the doorbell and was really happy to see Lola when it swung open.

"Hey." Lola wore fuchsia-colored cocktail dress that was not tight or revealing, but still sexy. Larry wanted to wrap his arms around her and nibble the succulent flesh between her neck and collar bone. Of course he restrained.

"Hi," he said. "Am I late?"

"Nope." Lola took his hand and pulled him inside. Larry quickly took his hand back and stuffed it in his pocket.

"You nervous?" Lola asked.

"Yes," Larry admitted. "A whole lot."

The interior of the house was decorated with all of the extravagance one would expect from a husband and wife who were both physicians. There was a strong, African motif that gave the home even more culture and beauty. Larry's eyes were drawn in many directions, but none as important as a shadow approaching from the main hallway.

The shadow was followed by a woman who might have been Lola's sister at first glance. A closer look revealed that she was at least twenty years older than Lola, but the years had been very kind to her. Her skin was dark, with a red tint, like cherry wood. Her maturity was noticeable in a handful of gray hairs and a few crow's feet that appeared in the corner of her eyes when she smiled.

"Hello," she said as she approached their visitor. "You must be Larry."

She offered a dainty hand. Larry shook it tenderly.

"Wow." He was honestly taken aback. "Are you Lola's mom? You're so young..."

"Well, thank you very much," the woman said. "I'm Elani."

"Pleasure to meet you," Larry said. "I brought these for you." He offered her a bouquet of roses he was toting.

Elani's eyes lit up. "Why thank you!" She smelled the flowers and then cradled them like a pageant winner. "He's sweet," Elani told her daughter. "You work at the hospital?" she asked Larry.

Larry felt the temperature rise ten degrees. *Here we go...* But Elani was smiling. He didn't feel like she would judge him. "I've been at Jackson for five years," Larry confirmed.

"That's impressive," Elani said. "Are you hungry? I made enchiladas."

"Yes," Larry said, but he looked confused.

"It's a vegetarian recipe," Elani said. "But you won't be able to tell. I promise." She gave him a friendly wink.

Larry's smile returned. Lola's mother was stately, but still down to earth. She made him feel comfortable. "That sounds great."

"Alright, come on," Elani said and led the way to the dining room. "Isaac is waiting on us."

Larry took a deep breath and followed Lola's mother to, what he would later describe as, his date with Dr. Evil.

≈ ≈ ≈ ≈ ≈ ≈ ≈

Dr. Dego's dining room was as elegant as the rest of his home. His wife brought out the good china and displayed Larry's roses as the table's centerpiece. The vase she put them in was so beautiful, it actually outshined the flowers. Elani served everyone a full-course meal, complete with an appetizer and salad. Dr.

Isaac Dego sat at the head of the table looking just as mean and preoccupied as he did at the hospital.

Larry knew he faced an uphill battle with the doctor, but he didn't expect the evening to be so cliché. Towards the end, he felt like he was stuck in an amateur writer's screenplay, and he was powerless to change the tried and true script that was laid before them.

Lola's mother was an excellent cook. Each dish she placed before them was better than the one before. Larry tried to enjoy his meal, but the tension at the table was so thick it could've been a side dish. Lola and her mom ignored the anxiety and pushed things along as best they could.

They asked Larry all sorts of questions about his life and his interests. Larry remained chipper and upbeat with his responses. Everyone laughed and joked and commented about how awesome the food was – except one person.

Dr. Dego remained quiet through most of the dinner. He would break his silence with an occasional grunt or a *hmph*, but for the most part he just chewed and swallowed and stared at Lola's new friend like there was snot running from Larry's nose.

Lola knew something was wrong. Her mother did, too. By the time they got to desert, Larry was eager to get it over with – whatever *it* was. No matter how hard the women tried, Larry wouldn't feel welcome in their home until the man of the house gave his approval.

Dr. Dego waited until Larry was discussing his poetry influences before he finally said what was on his mind.

"What do you want with my daughter?"

Larry was so happy to hear the question, he couldn't help but smile.

"What is funny?" Dr. Dego asked.

"I've been waiting for you to ask that for the past hour," Larry said. "I'm glad to finally have it out in the open."

Lola and her mother were stunned into silence. The two men locked eyes like bulls; one smiling, the other simmering with anger.

"Well, if you've been waiting an hour to hear the question," Dr. Dego said, "then you must have an excellent response." His accent was thick. It made him sound more pompous than he already was. But Larry already decided he wouldn't cower under the doctor's glare.

"I like Lola," Larry said. "She's smart and funny. She's beautiful. She doesn't have any flaws. I think she's perfect."

"How old are you?" Dr. Dego asked.

"I'm twenty-eight." Larry knew the doctor couldn't say anything about him being six years older than Lola, because Dr. Dego was fifteen years Elani's senior when they got married. The physician chose to attack Larry's ambition instead.

"And you're working an *entry level position* at the hospital," Dr. Dego said. "Why is that, Larry?"

"Dad, stop," Lola said.

"Hush," he told her.

"Isaac—"

"No, that's alright," Larry said, cutting Lola's mother off. "That's a good question. He has a right to ask."

Dr. Dego didn't seem pleased with Larry taking his side.

"I'm a hard worker," Larry told him. "I wasn't raised with a, a mentality to make a hundred thousand dollars a year. I didn't like the situation I was in when I was growing up, and I knew I wanted to do better than that. And I did."

Dr. Dego gave another one of his grunts. "Just enough to get by," he said. "Typical."

"Daddy, stop," Lola said.

Larry leaned back in his chair and chuckled.

"Do you think this is a joke?" Dr. Dego asked him.

"I think you're serious," Larry replied. "But at the same time, yeah, I do think this is a joke. You don't care about the answer to anything you're asking. All you're doing is looking for ways to beat me down."

"Okay," Elani said. "I think we should all—"

"You think you hit the jackpot, don't you?" Dr. Dego said.

"Excuse me?" Initially Larry grinned to show Dr. Dego that he wasn't hurt by any of this. Now he kept smiling because he knew it was irritating Lola's father.

"You think you found the, uh, *cash cow!*" Dr. Dego accused. "You think you, uh, you think you *came up!*"

"Daddy, stop! You don't even know him."

Dr. Dego didn't look in his daughter's direction. He kept his fiery eyes glued on Larry.

"How dare you disrespect me," the doctor said, "with your *smug smile!*"

Larry's mouth fell open. "*I'm* disrespecting *you?*"

"You come into my house, and eat my food..."

"How am I disrespecting you?" Larry wondered. "You haven't showed me one bit of respect since I've been here. You never said hello. Never offered to shake my hand—"

"I'm not shaking your hand." Dr. Dego sounded like Larry might be a leper.

Larry felt his anger rising, which was something he swore wouldn't happen – no matter how badly Lola's father treated him.

"Alright, I'm out." He rose to his feet and placed his napkin on the table. He couldn't force a smile anymore.

"Wait," Elani reached to stop him.

"Larry, hold on." Lola tried to stop him, too.

But Larry had enough of this. He felt like a fool for agreeing to this dinner in the first place. He knew Dr. Dego wasn't going to be civil. He saw it in the doctor's eyes the first time he tried to talk to Lola in the ER.

Larry exited the dining room with two women on his heels. Lola grabbed his arm when Larry reached the front door. But Dr. Dego was out of his seat by then. He marched into the living room and told her, "Let him go!"

"Isaac! You're being unreasonable!" his wife shouted.

"You don't know this man," Dr. Dego told her.

"You don't either!" Elani countered.

"He is *nothing!*" Dr. Dego said. "Bottom of the barrel. No education. No ambition."

"*Daddy!*" Lola was near tears.

Larry knew he should continue on his way and get on with his life, but his pride wouldn't let him. He spun around and threw a finger in the doctor's face.

"*You don't know me!*"

"*Get your hand out of my face!*" Dr. Dego took a swipe at it, but Larry had already moved his hand by then.

"Don't tell me I'm bottom of the barrel! You don't know shit about me!"

"You, you *fuck*!" Dr. Dego's eyes were wide and furious. He was so upset, he couldn't curse right. "You don't use that language in my house! Get out! Get away from here!"

"Stop, please!" Lola was crying. She stood between them with a hand on Larry's chest, the other arm outstretched towards her father.

"Get away from him!" Dr. Dego grabbed Lola's wrist and jerked her away from her troublesome beau.

"*Isaac, you are out of control!*" his wife yelled.

"You can't stop her from seeing me," Larry told the doctor. "She's twenty-two years old. If she wants to be with me, she can. She can leave with me right now!"

Larry stared at his woman, hoping she'd pick up on his cue and break away from her father. But he was surely a fool for thinking that. Lola brought both hands to her face and lowered her head and cried. Both of the men in her life watched her and waited. But Lola wouldn't even look up at Larry, let alone take a step in his direction.

After a few heartbeats, Dr. Dego looked Larry in the eyes. If the doctor wasn't so angry, he would've been the one to smile then.

"She has rejected you. *Now leave!*"

Larry's nostrils flared, but there was nothing else. Even Mrs. Dego remained mute this time.

Larry yanked the door open and stormed outside. The air felt a lot cooler than it was inside the house, but Larry's rage was white hot. His heartbreak was lukewarm. Larry got in his truck, and it took every bit of his will power to *not* plow into the back of the good doctor's Mercedes.

He drove away from the house slowly. Larry held out hope that maybe the college dropout who wrote this shitty screenplay would send Lola sprinting from the house. Larry would see her in his rearview mirror, and he'd stop and jump out of his truck, and they would embrace with the auburn sunset as a backdrop. Soft music would play.

But that never happened.

CHAPTER THIRTEEN
BEN'S ITCH

At the same moment Dr. Isaac Dego called his daughter's new friend *bottom of the barrel*, critical care nurse Sandra Alexander was on her knees in a south side drug house doing something she swore she would never do.

Ben had been with her since he got out of jail, and he'd been a full blown heroin addict ever since Sandra reintroduced him to the drug he thought he'd overcome. Sandra thought it would be better to have Ben high like her (because he wouldn't nag so much). She later realized she made a huge miscalculation.

Sandra wasn't shooting heroin before Ben went to jail. Back then she was only snorting, and she could get by with three $10 capsules a day. But her personal heroin consumption went up to $60 to $100 a day when she discovered the wonders of the hypothermic needle. Ben's habit was just as bad, and he didn't have a job to offset their spending.

Instead Ben relied on daily hustles for his income. Ben's favorite hustle was shoplifting, and he relied on burglary only as a last resort. The moment you break into someone's home and walk inside, you were committing a serious felony. If someone happened to be home at the time, you were committing a *home invasion* – which (in Texas) was much worst. But you could shoplift up to $49 worth of merchandise from any business and only be charged with a misdemeanor if you were caught.

Ben sold his stolen goods to drug dealers and crooked store owners throughout the city. Sometimes he'd bring home close to two hundred dollars. But on average, he was lucky to get fifty bucks a day. Ben was obligated to split all of his dope with Sandra, but she never promised to do the same for him. How could she? More importantly, *why should she*? Sandra was well aware of how much heroin she needed each day. She'd be a fool to willingly give it away knowing she would suffer later.

And it wasn't like she invited Ben into her life. He got out of jail and just *popped up*, like a stray kitten or a discarded baby. He never asked Sandra if he could move back in with her. And if she had to make a decision now, she'd tell him to beat it. Kick rocks. Who needed him? Sandra could go months without sex. And she actually preferred to be alone. When you're high on heroin, the last thing you need is someone trying to strike up a goddamned conversation.

But above all else, the reason Sandra refused to share her drugs was because of the huge price she paid for those $20 packs. While Ben waited outside in her car, Sandra had ManMan's dick in her mouth. The strange thing about that was she didn't think it was so bad; this whole sex for drugs thing. Sandra sucked plenty of dicks in her lifetime. The circumstances surrounding this current dick were bizarre and shocking and even devastating, but at the end of the day it was just another dick. It wasn't even that big.

But Sandra still refused to share her earnings with Ben.

ManMan was so excited to finally have Sandra where he wanted her, he could only hold out for two minutes before his leg started to tremble, and his manhood pulsated and squirted pre-cum. He wanted to let it all go in Sandra's mouth, but this was their first sexual encounter, and he promised to tell her when it was time.

"Oh, okay," he said. Sandra quickly backed away and spit into a hand towel he gave her. She continued to jerk him off. She brought the towel up just in time to catch ManMan's load when he came.

When he was done, Sandra stood and took a seat on the bed. ManMan watched her while he tucked his erection in his drawers and somehow managed to zip and button his pants.

He said, "See, that wasn't bad. Was it?"

Sandra didn't respond. She didn't want to agree with him, and she didn't want him to think she was totally disgusted by him, either. ManMan wasn't unattractive, and he'd always been good to Sandra. At that point she'd much rather have him as a boyfriend than a loser like Ben.

ManMan turned and retrieved four $20 packs from his dresser drawer. He tossed them on the bed next to Sandra. Two of the packs were for the $40 Ben sent her into the house with. The other two packs were for Sandra, for her services.

"I can give you another one," ManMan told her, "if you let me hit."

Sandra scooped up the dope and stood so she could slip them in her front pockets; her two in one pocket and Ben's two in the other. "I can't," she said. "I got somebody waiting for me outside."

ManMan liked how Sandra's excuses had changed over the past couple of months. She used to tell him, "No. Never." Now she gave him practical excuses.

"Who is it?" he asked. "She can come in here, too."

"It's a man," Sandra said. "My boyfriend."

That brought a frown to ManMan's face. "How he gon' be your boyfriend if he can't take care of you? I would've only gave you *one* extra sack, if I knew you was gon' split it with some nigga."

"I'm not splitting it with him," Sandra said. "I'm only splitting the two he paid for."

ManMan grinned. He liked her way of thinking. "So one for him, three for you," he said.

Sandra nodded and headed for the door. ManMan stopped her for what had become his customary fondling. He squeezed her ass and then pulled her butt into his lap. He grinded on her while he reached around and felt her breasts. ManMan slipped a hand down the front of her pants and rubbed her kitty. He didn't insert any fingers, but he got a good feel. The whole encounter lasted twenty seconds.

Sandra used to stand stiffly and shiver while ManMan molested her. But nowadays it was no big deal. She wasn't even thinking about him at the time. She was thinking about how she could do her extra heroin without Ben finding out about it. She didn't want to kick him out of her house because Ben did find a way to get money every day. Things would be a lot better if he could accept the fact that the dope always came one way; *to* Sandra, never *from* Sandra.

Sandra was so preoccupied and comfortable with her prostituting, she didn't realize ManMan was done with her until he chuckled behind her ear.

"Damn, baby, you must wanna stay with me all day."

Sandra snapped out of her daze and realized he wasn't touching her anymore. She looked back at him with a smile. "No, I gotta go."

She left the house without any more delays and hopped into the passenger seat of her car that was still parked on the curb. Ben started it up and eyed her queerly as he drove away.

"What took so long?"

"He didn't have it bagged up," Sandra said.

"But you got it?"

"Yeah, I got it," she told him.

She wouldn't look him in the eyes, which Ben found strange. Even more strange was the fact that most of Sandra's lipstick was mysteriously gone. Ben sensed that something very bad was going on, but he didn't ask what it was. He still felt guilty about introducing Sandra to such a hellacious drug. He understood that anything that happened to her after that point was ultimately his fault.

Ben had enough blood on his hands. He didn't want to add whatever happened in ManMan's dope house to his growing list of woes.

≈ ≈ ≈ ≈ ≈ ≈

When they got home, Ben and Sandra went through their usual ritual of cooking dope and shooting dope. They didn't always stay in the same room, but tonight they sat on the living room couch together, vaguely watching a string of MMA fights on Spike TV.

The twenty dollar packs were never enough to last them all night. By one a.m. they were both fiending again, except Sandra wasn't really fiending. She had two more packs Ben didn't know about. She already took them to the bathroom and stashed them under the sink. Now the only thing she needed was for Ben to preoccupy himself somehow, so she'd have time to shoot up without him.

But that was risky. No matter what drug you're addicted to, other addicts know when you're high. The telltale signs were especially obvious with heroin. Sandra would begin to *nod*; which looked like she was dead tired but trying her best to stay awake. Ben would notice her head bobbing. He'd observe her half-closed eyes, and if he made her talk, Sandra's speech would be slurred. And the gig would be up.

Luckily Sandra didn't have to worry about that tonight. By 1:30 Ben was at his wit's end. He told Sandra he wanted to go to one of the 24 hour Albertsons to steal some steaks. He said he knew a guy who would pay half price for the pilfered meat. The only concern was Ben might not be able to get in touch with his dealer at such a late hour. But that didn't stop him from getting dressed in his baggy "boosting" clothes and leaving the house.

Sandra was worried about him getting arrested again in her car, but she didn't try to dissuade him. As soon as Ben was gone, Sandra secured the door lock, the deadbolt and the chain lock on the front door. She hurried to the bathroom and grabbed her dope and her shooter kit and went to work.

≈ ≈ ≈ ≈ ≈ ≈ ≈

Ben returned an hour later. He used one of the keys on Sandra's keychain to unlock the door. When he couldn't gain entry, Ben fumbled through the keys until he found one that fit the deadbolt. The door pushed open this time, but it stopped again after a couple of inches. Ben frowned when he saw the chain lock. He knew that heroin caused paranoia sometimes, so he gave his girlfriend the benefit of the doubt.

"Uh, Sandra..." He spoke with his face pressed close to the opening. The living room was dimly lit. Sandra's house was junky, but it looked and smelled like home. Ben ached to get inside.

There was no response, so he tried again. "Sandra..." He raised his voice this time, but not too loudly because it was almost three o'clock in the morning. Sandra lived in a nice neighborhood. Any hint of domestic troubles would surely attract her nosey neighbors.

Ben fidgeted with the keys as he waited. He shifted his weight from one foot to the other. He kicked the door, just a little, with the tip of his sneaker. The noise wasn't that loud, so he knocked instead. He looked around anxiously and decided he had no choice but to raise his voice.

"Sandra!" He tried to direct his shout through the door opening, but his strong voice sounded loud outside, too. "It's me," Ben said. "Open the door!"

Inside the house Sandra stood quietly in the living room, just out of sight of the barely open door. She was zooted out of her mind, and Ben was ruining her high. Adrenaline and heroin are two things that absolutely do not mix. An adrenaline rush is more powerful. It could sober a junkie up in minutes.

Sandra was in a happy place, and she didn't want to be sober. She realized she made a huge mistake earlier. What sense did it make locking Ben out when he had her whole key chain? How could she forget something so fundamental? Was her brain fried? Sandra didn't think so, but she didn't have a better explanation.

She moved to unlock the door for him, but then Sandra remembered that she was high. Ben thought she was out of dope, just like him. If she opened the door, he'd notice her inebriation. He'd know Sandra was holding out. He'd demand that she split the pot, and Sandra already decided against that.

She stopped and withdrew her hand from the door. She didn't know what to do, so she did nothing at all.

Ben saw a shadow move inside the house. He knew someone was in the living room listening to him but not responding. It could've been a burglar, but Sandra would be screaming if that was the case. It could've been a killer, but that was even more farfetched.

"Sandra," Ben said. "I know you're there. Why won't you open the door? I got your keys..."

Sandra swallowed hard. Her heart began to knock, which was exactly what she *didn't* want to happen. Luckily she still had a whole $20 pack and half of one hidden in the bathroom. She could get high again when Ben was gone. But how could she get him to leave? She racked her drug-soaked brain for a solution.

With no response from his woman, Ben was left to ponder whether Sandra still wanted to be his woman or not. He couldn't fault her if she chose to dump him. Ben knew he was a leech. He didn't deserve to have a nice roof over his head. He didn't deserve a woman who had a job, a house and a car. His body went numb as he contemplated life without his sponsor. Ben didn't have any family members who'd trust him enough to take him in. He'd have to spend the night on the streets, if Sandra kicked him to the curb.

"Please, open the door," he said, his voice laced with agony. "I got fourteen dollars. Your friend will prolly give you a twenty, if you ask him..."

"Give me my keys. I don't wanna be with you no more," Sandra said.

At least, that's what she thought she said.

What Ben heard was: *"Gih... muh kees... I 'ont whan nuh... be wiffoo... nuh more..."*

His pleading expression changed to confusion, and then his eyes widened, and everything made perfect sense.

"Bitch, you high."

Sandra didn't respond.

"Open this fucking door!" Ben pounded hard with a balled fist. "Open this door! Why you do me like that, Sandra? I split everything with you! Why you do me like that!"

"I don't wanna be with you!" she shouted. "Just give me my keys, Ben!"

"I ain't giving you *shit*!" he growled. "Open the door! Where you get it from?"

"Leave me alone!"

Ben's frantic mind put the rest of the pieces together. *"You fucked him, didn't you? You fucked that nigga today! That's why you took so long! You been holding out all day. You dirty bitch! Open the fucking door!"*

Sandra brought both arms up and pressed the heels of her hands into the sides of her head. Her eyes were frenzied. This is why it was better to be alone. Life was so much better when Ben was locked up. Why did she take him back? She didn't have a lot of experience with drugs, but she should've known that two addicts–

BOOM!

Sandra screamed.

The whole house shook. The door rattled, but it held firm.

"Let me in!"

"Stop!"

BOOM!

This time the door came flying at Sandra. The chain didn't break, but the end that was screwed to the wall came free; taking a two-inch chunk of wood with it.

Sandra screamed again. Ben stepped inside the house looking like Jack Nicholson from *The Shining*.

"You dirty bitch! *Where is it*?!" He was dark and menacing, with big eyes like golf balls. His teeth were bared. Sandra's life flashed before her eyes. She sobered up in a split second. Her fight or flight response kicked in, and she made the obvious decision.

She turned and sprinted down the hallway. Ben was faster. He tackled her. They both fell to the not-so-soft carpet in a twisted pile of boney bones. Sandra continued to scream as Ben rolled her onto her back and restrained her flailing arms.

"Just give me a hit, Sandra! Why you acting like this?"

"I don't have anything!"

"You a liar! You know you got some! Where is it?"

"I don't have anything!" Her eyes bulged. Her gaunt features were horrific.

"I'll buy it!" Ben pleaded. "I got money, Sandra! Give me a fifteen dollar hit!"

"I don't have anything! Get off of me!"

"Aergggh!" Sweat glistened on Ben's face. The veins stood out on his neck and head. He was so angry, he wanted to pummel

and even choke the life from Sandra. But he was sober enough to know that it wasn't worth it – not until he got the dope at least.

He released her and stepped over her body on his way to the bedroom. He turned the light on and looked around Sandra's junky sleeping quarters in dismay. A bag of heroin could be anywhere in the room. But as a burglar, Ben knew that humans are predictable. People still hid their valuables under the mattress or in the nightstand, where it was closest to them. Ben decided to start his search there.

In the hallway Sandra scrambled to her feet and ran to the living room in search of her cellphone. She found it on the coffee table. She dialed 911 with trembling fingers and ran back to the bedroom.

Meanwhile Ben was going completely ape shit. He lifted the mattress and flipped it completely off the bed. Nothing. He yanked the drawers out of Sandra's nightstand and dumped the contents on the bed's box spring. He pawed through Sandra's belongings, growing more desperate by the second. Still nothing.

"Nine-one-one, do you have a police, fire or medical emergency?"

"Some man broke in my house!" Sandra told the dispatcher.

Ben looked up at her and shouted, "I'm not *some man*! I live here!"

"Is he there right now?" the operator asked.

"Yes, he's here right now!" Sandra screeched, looking Ben in the eyes. "It's my ex-boyfriend," she clarified. "He kicked my door in and beat me up!"

"*She lying!*" Ben shouted.

"*He's tearing up my house right now!*"

"*She lying!*" Ben yelled. He began to move in her direction.

"*He's going to hit me again!*" Sandra screamed as she backed away.

"What's your address?" the operator asked.

Sandra gave it to her.

"The police are already in route," the operator told her. "We got several calls. Please remain on the line."

When Ben reached the hallway, he debated whether he should get Sandra off the phone, flee or continue the search for her heroin. Attacking her again was a bad idea. Even in his state of distress, he understood that. Fleeing was the rational choice, but Ben was by no means rational. Plus he thought he had the mystery solved.

Q: Where would an addict hide her dope?

A: In a place where she could go and get high in private.

Q: Where did Sandra go the first time she tried to get high without him?

A: The bathroom.

Ben turned away from Sandra and stepped into the bathroom. He turned the light on. Sandra screamed, *"Get out of there!"* and she dropped her phone. She jumped and clung to Ben's back like a spider monkey, and then he knew for sure.

"Get off me, bitch!"

The next few minutes were like a scene from a *Crackheads Gone Wild* DVD. It was human deterioration at its finest. Ben fought valiantly to remove Sandra from his back so he could search for her drugs. Sandra fought like a wolverine to stop him. The 911 operator listened to the struggle in gut-wrenching horror.

Ben never threw a punch, but he did throw Sandra around the small bathroom. Finally he got so upset, he grabbed Sandra by the shoulders and tripped her. He slammed her hard in the hallway and came down on top of her. He lifted her shoulders from the floor and slammed her down again. Sandra's back and the back of her head impacted the carpet with a soft *THUD*! Her eyes crossed. This was the scene the police saw when they entered the house and rounded the corner with their weapons drawn.

They told Ben, *"Get off her! Put your fucking hands up!"*

Ben was obliged to do as he was told.

≈ ≈ ≈ ≈ ≈ ≈

The EMT's on the scene practically begged Sandra to let them take her to the hospital. Her cuts and bruises aside, they were pretty sure Sandra suffered a concussion during her ordeal. But Sandra was adamant about not going. The EMT's saw her needle marks, so they didn't push it. Drug addicts rarely make good decisions when it comes to their personal health. And there was no law that stated an individual *had* to go to the hospital when someone beat them up.

The police gathered much more information than they needed to prosecute Ben, and they hauled him away in the back of a squad car. By 4:30 a.m. everyone was gone, even the neighbors who came outside to see the result of their 911 calls.

Sandra was glad to finally be alone again. She locked her door, thankful that Ben hadn't done any serious damage to it. She needed to get someone to screw the chain latch back onto the doorframe, but that was not a priority. Tonight was the first time she had ever used her chain lock since she bought the home.

She went to the bathroom to check her visage in the mirror. It didn't feel like it at the time, but Ben messed her up pretty good. Sandra had a contusion on the front and back of her head, scratches on her neck and arms and (most noticeable) a busted bottom lip that was swollen nearly twice it's normal size.

Sandra sighed. She looked terrible, her house looked awful, and her neighbors now knew that her life had taken a bad turn somewhere. Sandra decided that she would take Ben's advice and look into one of the methadone clinics in her area. But then she dropped to her knees and retrieved her heroin from under the sink and decided she would do no such thing.

Before she cooked her dope, Sandra called-in for tomorrow, lest she forget to do it later.

CHAPTER FOURTEEN
DAMIEN EXPOSED

Seventeen hours after Sandra took a few lumps rather than share her drugs, it was nine pm on a wonderful Friday evening. The second shift employees at Jackson Memorial were in a good mood because today was payday. In an hour and a half, they were free to clock out and get their weekend started.

A lot of the youngsters would hit the club tonight and splurge at the bar and later patronize one of Overbrook Meadows' 24 hour Waffle Houses. Others were saving their money for more practical expenditures, like a trip to the beauty shop and maybe a romantic evening with their honey dip on Saturday night.

Larry was one of few Jackson employees who wasn't in a good mood that day, and he was eager to put this shift behind him. Today he had to work in the ER zone. This was never a problem before, but Dr. Dego was on duty tonight. He and Larry locked eyes half a dozen times already. Lola was working tonight as well, but Larry never made eye contact with her. Whenever he caught a glimpse of her lab coat, Larry made sure to change his direction. Sometimes he went a few minutes out of his way to avoid an encounter with Lola.

This didn't seem like something he could keep up for very long. Thankfully all of the Material Operations employees were rotated through the ER. After tonight, Larry wouldn't have to go back again for nearly a month. By then he was sure to have Lola out of his system.

Larry thought he'd always feel animosity towards Dr. Dego, but they were both grown and rational men. They weren't going to disrespect each other at work, and they weren't going to meet at the park for a rumble, either. What they were going to do was *Get Over It*, which was something everyone at the hospital had to do at some point. Nurses and CNA's were constantly bickering with people they had to work with everyday. The Jackson machine wouldn't stop just because someone got their feelings hurt.

Rodney Tucker was another Material Operations employee who wasn't in a good mood that Friday. Larry had been trying to avoid the kid ever since he learned about the dirty video with their supervisor. But Rodney liked to seek wise counsel when the trials of life got him down. While on a leisurely stroll through the ER, he spotted Larry and headed his way.

"Hey, man. What's up?"

Larry was lounging on the Trauma side, waiting for a patient to leave so he could collect a stretcher and IV pole. He started to tell Rodney he was too busy to talk, but that was obviously not the case.

"Uh, hey, Rodney. What's going on?"

"Shit." He leaned on the wall next to Larry. He stuffed his hands in his pockets and shook his head.

Larry sighed inwardly before asking, "What's wrong, playa?"

"Too much," Rodney said. "I feel like I'm getting caught up in some mess."

Larry rolled his eyes. He knew this conversation would lead to more revelations he really didn't want to know about. But he didn't have the heart to tell Rodney to go on about his business and deal with the mess he created himself.

"You talking about Eva?" Larry asked.

"Her too," Rodney said. "But mainly it's Amy and Tanya. They found out about each other, and they stressing me, man. Tanya's spreading rumors about me. People been coming up to me all day, asking if I'm messing with these different girls."

Larry frowned. "Who's Tanya?"

"A nurse I started talking to a few weeks ago," Rodney said. "She works on the cancer floor. She light-skinned, with a big ol' booty. But she got a gap between her teeth."

Larry knew who he was talking about. "And who's Amy?"

"She a CNA on the same floor."

Larry's frown intensified. "You messing with two different girls on the same floor?"

Rodney nodded. "I wasn't really talking to Amy no more. We fucked, but I was trying to leave her alone, so I could holler at Tanya."

"You already had sex with Tanya?"

Rodney nodded again. "Yeah, but I told her I got a woman; me and her could only be friends."

"Amy and Tanya been talking about you?" Larry asked.

"I think so," Rodney said. "'Cause today Amy asked me if I had a girlfriend. I told her I didn't, but I think Tanya told her I did."

"And, who else knows about this?" Larry asked.

"A couple more people came up to me today asking if I was messing with Amy and Tanya," Rodney reported. "And when Eva finds out about them, I know she gon' be hating, too."

"That's what you call it?" Larry asked. "They *hating* on you?"

"Tanya is," Rodney confirmed. "She ain't have no business telling Amy."

Larry brought a hand to his face and rubbed his forehead. "Listen, man, I know you gon' do what you wanna do, but I think you moving a little too fast. It's a lot of women up here, but you can't mess with all of them at the same time – especially not two on the same floor. They gon' talk to each other, and they gon' compare notes. You should know that."

"What about Zach in Nuclear Med?" Rodney said. "He slept with a bunch of girls up here, too. Ain't nobody mad at him."

Larry never spoke to Zach about his personal life, but everyone knew of his escapades. Zach was another Casanova at Jackson Memorial.

"The difference is Zach never talks to them *at the same time*," Larry explained. "And he don't just hook up with them for sex. When he gets with somebody up here, he'll take them out and have a *regular relationship.* When they break up, Zach will wait a little while before he talks to somebody else – so his old girlfriend can't never say he left them for somebody else. You can't compare yourself to Zach, because you're not doing the same as him."

"But I don't want a regular relationship with nobody up here," Rodney said. "I already got a girl."

"Then you should be faithful to her," Larry suggested. "But if you are gon' cheat, why can't you cheat with somebody who doesn't work here? It's two places you don't never want trouble; where you sleep and where you work."

"You right," Rodney said.

Larry was surprised and pleased that he hadn't given his advice in vain. But Rodney wasn't done talking.

"But it's too many good looking females up here," the youngster said. "Everywhere I look is *booty, booty, booty.* And they be *throwing* it at a nigga. How can I turn that down?"

Larry was done giving advice. "You just do," he said vaguely.

"What about her?" Rodney asked.

Larry followed his gaze to the nursing station, where a pretty, young thing named Lola Dego was busy making notations in a patient's chart. Lola had her hair pulled back and her big glasses on, but Larry thought she was still stunning. He would never forget the way she smiled at him after their first kiss.

"What about her?" Larry said.

"Did y'all ever hook up?" Rodney asked.

Larry shook his head. As far as gossip, he knew his interrupted love affair was a doozy. He could tell his story, throw Lola under the bus and have the whole hospital hating her and her stuck-up father. But in doing so, Larry would become the very thing he despised.

Instead he told Rodney, "I never talked to her."

"Why she looking at you?" Rodney asked.

Larry checked again and saw that she was. Lola looked away when he met her gaze. Larry felt his heart break all over again, like she peeled off the scab. He pushed off the wall and told Rodney, "I gotta go pick up some monitors from the basement. I'll holler at you later."

"You need help?" Rodney asked.

Larry didn't really have to retrieve any monitors. He wanted to be alone. "No, I got it," he said.

"Alright," Rodney said and headed in the opposite direction.

On the Quick Trip side of the ER, Rodney encountered two housekeepers speaking quietly in one of the empty patient rooms. He recognized the hump on Brenda's back, and he knew the other housekeeper's name was Raquel. Rodney thought Raquel was the finest housekeeper at the hospital. But he never tried to talk to her because it was beneath him to go out with a mere *housekeeper*. Even assholes have standards.

"What y'all doing?" Rodney asked as he approached the room. He leaned on the doorframe and smiled at the women. They both turned and eyed him with irritation.

"What you want?" Brenda snapped.

"Dang. I just wanted to say *hi*," Rodney said. "Why y'all got an attitude with me? I didn't do nothing."

"We *busy*," Brenda said. "We ain't got time to mess around with you."

Rodney felt he respected his elders, in general. But Brenda was one old bag who never gave him a fair shake. Rodney didn't think he was obligated to continue playing nice with her.

"You not busy," he said. "Y'all both standing in the same room, doing nothing. And the room already clean. You prolly in here gossiping..."

Brenda was doing just that, but she wasn't going to take any lip from a no-goodnik like Rodney.

"Boy, get the hell away from here with all that! Go do *something*! You the worst one in your whole department!"

"And you the worst one in *yours*!" Rodney argued, unaware that he was 100% correct in his assertion.

"Come on, girl," Brenda said with a smack of her lips. "We'll go to my office."

She led Raquel out of the room and rolled her eyes at Rodney as they passed.

Rodney rolled his eyes right back at her.

"Dumb boy," Brenda muttered.

"You dumb," Rodney shot back at her. He shook his head and continued his leisurely stroll to the Avery Building. He wasn't on an assignment, but he knew he'd find something to steal or someone to flirt with when he got there. There was always one of the two.

≈ ≈ ≈ ≈ ≈ ≈ ≈

When they got to her office, Brenda took a seat behind the clutter on her desk and told Raquel, "Close that door."

Raquel closed it and sat across from her supervisor with her knees together, her hands in her lap. Brenda watched her carefully. She was both excited and disappointed about the new development.

"Why didn't you tell me?" she asked Raquel. "I told you to tell me *before* you hooked up with Damien."

"I was going to," Raquel said. "But..." She shook her head. "I didn't know what was going to happen. I was scared. I didn't know what he would do, if he found out I told somebody. I just, I don't know." Her face was red. She looked like she might start crying.

"Calm down," Brenda told her. "It's alright. Just, just tell me what happened when you met him."

Brenda's heart felt like it was going a mile a minute. A sadistic smile crept to her lips, but she got rid of it right away. Raquel was about to reveal the most coveted secret *ever*, and Brenda couldn't look like the sneaky witch she was. No, she had to appear caring and understanding. That was the only way to get Raquel to do her bidding.

"We, we met at the Comfort Inn," Raquel said. She could barely look her supervisor in the eyes. She stared at the papers on Brenda's desk instead.

"Which one?" Brenda asked.

"Off 30. 30 and Beach."

Brenda nodded. "He waited for you, or did he already have the room?"

"He already had it," Raquel said. "He was waiting in the room for me."

"How'd you know which room to go to?" Brenda asked. She missed her first opportunity to catch Damien in the act, but it was actually better this way. Raquel was going to explain Damien's whole M.O., so Brenda would be a lot more prepared when the time came for her to make a move.

"He texted me," Raquel said. "I still got it."

Brenda's smile returned as Raquel dug in her pocket for her cellphone. Brenda straightened her face when Raquel found the incriminating message and looked up at her.

"Here it is."

She handed the phone to her boss. Damien's message was short, but Brenda took her time. She read it a few times before she gave the phone back to Raquel. Damien's message read: Comfort Inn, 2110 W. State, 9:00, Rm 221.

"So, what happened when you got there?" Brenda asked.

Raquel reached to rub her nose. Brenda saw that her fingers were trembling slightly. Overall Raquel looked like she was being interrogated in a foreign jail in some godforsaken land.

"Calm down," Brenda told her. "It's okay. You know I'm not gon' tell nobody."

Raquel shook her head. "I know, but, it, it's embarrassing. I don't want to tell nobody – not even you..."

"But we can't get him if we don't talk about it," Brenda reminded. "You said you wanted to get him, right?"

"Yeah, I do," Raquel said. She frowned. "I hate him."

"That's good," Brenda said. "I hate him, too. Now we need to get on with this, so we can make him pay. I promise you won't get in no trouble. I'll take care of everything."

Raquel nodded and cleared her throat. "When I went in, he, he was sitting back on the bed. He told me to wear my work uniform, and he was wearing his uniform, too."

Brenda's eyes widened. "Why he, he told you to wear it?"

"He a freak," Raquel said. "It's part of his fantasy. He likes to play dress up. He wanted to be the cop, and I was supposed to be the maid."

Brenda's eyes grew wider still.

"Stop looking at me like that," Raquel said. "I feel bad already."

"Oh, I'm sorry," Brenda said. "I didn't mean to. It's just, it's a surprise..." She straightened her face again, but it was hard to remain deadpan.

"I didn't wanna do it," Raquel said. "But when I walked in there, I felt like *anything* could happen, if I tried to say no. I didn't know if he would arrest me, or *rape* me. I just, I felt like I had to do it."

"Do what?" Brenda dared to ask. "What he make you do?"

Raquel brought a hand to her mouth and chewed on her pinky nail. Her lips quavered. Her eyes filled with tears. "I don't wanna say..."

Brenda was on the edge of her seat. She wanted to scream, but she cleared her throat and took a deep breath and spoke calmly. "Tell me what he did, honey. I wanna help you. We're gonna make him pay. I promise."

The tears spilled from Raquel's eyes. Brenda opened one of the bigger drawers on her desk and found a box of Kleenex. She offered it to her employee.

Raquel plucked a few napkins and blew her nose. She wiped her eyes with the back of her hands. Brenda watched her with genuine concern. She was only concerned with her own personal vendetta, but Brenda now wondered if Damien really was the demon she painted him to be.

"He, he wanted me to clean," Raquel said. "He spilled some stuff, and he told me to clean it up."

Brenda was stunned silent. She couldn't do anything but blink.

"Then he started touching me," Raquel said, "while I was cleaning. He said he thought about me while we was at work. He said he wanted to have sex with me at work, but he couldn't, and that's why he liked to do it like that in the hotel. He told me to call him *Mister*. He said it was just for fun; we were role playing.

"But I didn't like it. I felt like, I don't know... I felt like he wanted to control me too much. Like, he didn't really like me; he just wanted to do me like that because I'm a housekeeper. And then, before he left, he gave me two hundred dollars, like I'm a prostitute or something. I felt dirty. He made me feel so stupid."

Again Brenda could do nothing but stare and listen. Her mouth was bone dry. She knew Damien was a freak, but she never expected this level of perverseness.

"I was thinking about Amina," Raquel said. "Why would she do that? I don't understand. Damien, he said he'd give me more money when we hooked up again, if I didn't tell nobody. But I don't want his money. I don't care how much it is, I don't want it.

"My mama," Raquel continued, "she used to have to do that, at her job. She never told my dad. But she told me because I was the oldest, and she had to tell *somebody*. When we came to America, she said it would be different here; I wouldn't never have to do nothing like what she did. But I did it anyway. I feel like, he made me feel like I was nothing. Like he wanted to spit on me, that's how much I mattered to him."

Raquel started to cry again. Brenda didn't comfort her right away because she was lost in her own personal conflict. Brenda's beef with Damien was because of his preference for Hispanic women. But Raquel's story changed everything. Brenda now knew that Damien was simply satisfying his fetish for housekeepers. He didn't put Hispanic women on a pedestal, like Brenda thought he did. Apparently he treated them like shit.

But none of that really mattered because Brenda was a hater at heart. Once she started hating on someone, she would continue to do so until they were no longer in her life. Brenda still hated Damien for the same reason she hated Rodney and a dozen other people at the hospital: *Just because.*

"Don't you worry about that no more," she told Raquel. "It's over now, and we gon' make sure it never happens again."

"How?" Raquel wanted to know.

"You have to trust me," Brenda said. "And you have to do what I say. I told you what to do last time, but you didn't listen."

"I know," Raquel said. "I'm sorry. You were right."

"It's okay," Brenda said. "We can still get him."

"How? What are you gonna do?" Raquel asked.

"Did he say he wanted to meet you again?"

Raquel nodded. "He told me to text him, when I was ready."

"Alright," Brenda said. "So when you text him, how long before he tells you to meet him somewhere?"

"First, he'll text me back and ask when we can meet," Raquel explained. "When I tell him, he'll say *Okay*. And then when that day comes, he'll text me with the address and time and stuff."

Brenda nodded. "So what you need to do is tell me what day you give him, so I can make sure I'm not doing nothing, either. And when he text you with the time and the motel room, send it to me, so I can be there, too."

"What are you gonna do?"

"Just take some pictures," Brenda said.

"But we don't get there at the same time," Raquel said. "You won't see us together."

"Don't you worry about that," Brenda said. "I can get there early. All I need is a picture of him going in the room and a picture of y'all leaving together."

"But I don't wanna be in there with him again," Raquel complained. "I don't wanna have to do that stuff no more."

"Alright," Brenda said. She thought fast. "I'll make a *diversion*. I'll find some way to interrupt y'all."

"How?"

"I don't know. I'll bring my brother. I'll get him to throw a brick in the window or something." Brenda's eyes brightened. "That would be real cool, if Damien runs out with his pants down." Brenda's grin was evil. She didn't think anyone had ever thought of a plan so clever.

Raquel was skeptical. "What if he sees you?"

"I'll be sitting in my car with the engine running," Brenda explained. "I'll take a couple of pictures. If he sees me, I'll drive away. It'll be dark, and I'll put a hat on. He won't know who I am."

"What about me?" Raquel wondered. "I'll still be there with him."

"But he won't know you had anything to do with it," Brenda reasoned. "If he tries to take you to a different room, just tell him you're scared now, and you don't want to. Trust me; Damien gon' have a lot more to worry about than getting his nut off. He gon' be trying to get away from there as fast as he can. He won't be thinking about you."

Raquel thought about it. She couldn't find any more holes in Brenda's plan.

"What are you gonna do with the pictures?" she asked.

"Spread them around the hospital," Brenda said. "They'll get back to his family sooner or later. If not, his boss up here will end up firing him."

"I don't want my face in the pictures."

"Don't worry," Brenda said. "I'm not gon' throw you under the bus, Raquel. If I use a picture with you in it, I'll take your face out first. You gotta trust me."

Raquel did trust her. And she was happy Brenda was so eager to help put the nasty policeman in his place. But there was still the matter of compensation. If Raquel could get something for nothing, she'd be a fool not to take it.

"What about the overtime days?"

Brenda frowned. "Didn't you say you *wanted* to do this, to get him back?"

"Yeah, but it's still a big risk for me," Raquel said. She sniffled and dried the last of her tears. "You said you would give me some overtime days, if I helped..."

Brenda narrowed her eyes. She didn't think Raquel would try to hustle her, but that appeared to be the case. "What day you wanna take off?"

"The rest of tonight," Raquel said. "And I work Saturday and Sunday, but I don't want to come in. You said you could make it look like I was here..."

Brenda pursed her lips. The weekends were always busy because there were six less housekeepers on the schedule. Without Raquel, Brenda would have to clean rooms herself.

"Which day you wanna take off?" she asked. "Saturday or Sunday?"

"Saturday *and* Sunday," Raquel said. "And I'm off Monday and Tuesday. I want you to clock me in on both of those days, too, so I'll have 16 hours overtime."

Brenda inhaled sharply. This was way more than she bargained for. She could make it happen, but their manager would question her about Raquel's overtime. Brenda didn't think she could come up with a sufficient explanation. But if this is what it took to get Damien fired from the hospital, Brenda had to make good on her promise.

"Alright," she told Raquel. "But I'm doing this to help *you*. You acting like I'm the only one who wants to get Damien fired."

That wasn't a question, so Raquel didn't feel obligated to respond.

"Alright, so I'm going to get paid for Saturday, Sunday, Monday and Tuesday?..." she said as she stood up.

Brenda grudgingly said, "Yeah." She was starting to wonder who was getting over on whom.

"And I can leave early tonight?..."

Brenda's nostrils flared. "Go ahead."

"Thanks," Raquel said.

She didn't look upset at all now. Brenda wondered if she'd fallen for a bunch of crocodile tears.

"When are you going to tell Damien you want to see him again?" Brenda asked.

"I'll do it next week," Raquel said. She didn't look back, and she barely slowed down. "*After* you put my time in. I'll check it in the computer..."

Raquel left the office without seeing the look of disgust on her supervisor's face.

That's okay, Brenda told herself. She brought her rough hands together and cracked each knuckle, one at a time. Raquel thought she was running things, but when it was all said and done, she would know that Brenda was (and would always be) the head bitch in charge.

Raquel expected to have her face obscured from the incriminating photos. But that definitely wasn't happening now. As a matter of fact, Brenda began to plot a way to get Damien *and* Raquel fired for their illicit affair. If she kept her around, Brenda sensed Raquel would try to blackmail her at some point.

"*Dirty bitch*," Brenda muttered. Some people didn't know when to leave well enough alone. But Brenda would teach them. She'd show them that she wasn't to be messed with.

CHAPTER FIFTEEN
RUBEN'S PREFERENCES

Later that night, on the Critical Care/Neuro unit, charge nurse Cynthia Pullman was not having a good time at all. Sandra called-in again earlier in the day, and another nurse called-in a few minutes before seven. Cynthia thought they could make it without those two. But a third nurse; Tina, hurt her back while trying to bathe an obese patient. She had to go to the ER for an evaluation, and it was uncertain if she would return to the unit.

To make matters worse, Cynthia had to work with Janice tonight. Cynthia expected her nemesis to complain about the workload, but Janice was surprisingly quiet. After receiving her assignments, Janice hadn't said anything or even looked in Cynthia's direction. As a matter of fact, Janice hadn't spoken to Cynthia since the confrontation in the parking garage three weeks ago. That was good, but it also left Cynthia with a feeling of unease. She didn't think Janice would let her speculations go that easily.

By nine o'clock everyone was getting into the groove of the night. Cynthia expected the worst when she was paged to take a call from the house supervisor. She was not disappointed.

"Hi. This is Cynthia."

"Tina's going home," the sup' said. "She's going to follow up with her doctor tomorrow morning. She's not in a whole lot of pain right now, but her back still hurts. They gave her some meds in the ER, and Dr. Dego is not comfortable with her going back to work tonight."

"Okay," Cynthia said with a sigh.

"And we have two stroke patients down here," the sup' added. "One's going to ICU for sure. I don't know about the other one."

"Alright," Cynthia said. "Any chance we can move out one of our overflows?"

"Everybody's pretty full," the supervisor said. "You have to hold on to them until the morning."

"Alright." Cynthia shook her head. What else was new?

When she got off the phone, she took a seat at the nursing station and went over her assignments again. Cynthia called the four third-shift nurses who were off tonight before she called her manager. Ruben's wife answered on the second ring.

"Hello?"

"Hi. This is Cynthia from work. Is Ruben there?"

"Yes. One moment."

Cynthia didn't feel any apprehension while she waited. Instead she felt completely dead inside.

"Hello?"

"Hey," Cynthia said. "We're down three nurses. I called everyone who's off. None of them can come in. We have eighteen patients and one and a possible downstairs."

"Okay," Ruben said. "I'll come in."

"Alright."

"Are you ok—"

Cynthia hung up before he could finish his sentence.

≈≈≈≈≈≈≈

Ruben arrived on the unit an hour later with his usual charm and knack for turning his nurses' smiles upside down. Tonight he brought a variety of deli sandwiches from the Schlotzsky's downtown. Most of the nurses carried on like Ruben was their savior, but there were two women who didn't leave their seats to say hi or to see what all of the fuss was about. Both of these nurses were black, and they both had Ruben's head between their legs at some point.

After Ruben exchanged pleasantries with his crew, he found Cynthia and asked her to come to his office. She rose from her seat and reluctantly followed him. Janice was seated halfway across the unit. She watched their interactions closely.

Inside Ruben's office, Cynthia was all business. She told him about the nursing assignments she made that night and briefed him on Tina's back injury. She asked Ruben if he knew what was going on with Sandra.

"She told me she has breast cancer," he said, "but I haven't received any paperwork yet. I asked her to bring something from her doctor *today*. Looks like she didn't make it."

"You don't think she's on drugs, do you?" Cynthia asked.

She stood in front of Ruben's desk with her arms folded under her breasts. Ruben sat in an executive chair. His eyes were electric blue. The office door was wide open.

"I did think that," Ruben said. "If she doesn't bring paperwork from her doctor, I'm going to send her to Human Resources for a drug test. I've been documenting her decline. Does she ever look high when she works with you?"

Cynthia shook her head. "She looks tired, and skinny. She didn't really look *high* the last time I saw her. But I guess if she's on an opiate, maybe she was. But I've never seen her falling asleep or nodding."

Ruben sighed. "I guess we'll have to wait and see what paperwork she brings in. I don't think she'd lie about something like cancer, though. That's way too easy to prove."

Cynthia nodded. She started to walk out. "Is that all?"

"No," Ruben said. "Can you close the door?"

She shook her head. "No, I don't want to do that."

Ruben was visibly disappointed by her response. "Well, can you tell me why you haven't taken any of my calls? Is everything okay? Why are you avoiding me?"

"If you don't have anything to say about *work*, then I gotta go," Cynthia said. She kept a straight face, though it hurt her to be cold to him. But the revelations she got from Janice hurt a lot more.

"Cynthia, we have to talk," Ruben insisted. "I don't know what's going on, and there's no way..." He trailed off because Cynthia walked out of his office.

"*Cynthia.*" Ruben called to her, but he didn't raise his voice.

Cynthia didn't stop walking. A moment later she was back on the floor, among her colleagues, and she knew Ruben would have to let it go. For now at least.

≈≈≈≈≈≈≈

Cynthia kept her mind on work for the next seven hours, and she was able to faze Ruben out, even though he was within eyesight most of the time. Whenever they exchanged glances, Ruben had a *What did I do wrong?* look in his eyes. Cynthia kept the same *Leave me the hell alone* look in hers.

At two-thirty a.m. Cynthia took her lunch break. She went to the cafeteria rather than partake in Ruben's free sandwiches. She wasn't surprised when Ruben showed up in the cafeteria while she was paying the cashier. He waited innocently in the background and then followed Cynthia when she left the lunch room.

He sidled up to her as Cynthia approached the elevators. "Can we talk?"

"I don't want to," Cynthia told him. She kept her eyes forward.

The elevator doors opened, and Ruben stepped inside with her. Cynthia reached to push the 4th Floor button, but Ruben sent them to the basement before she had a chance. Cynthia started to protest, but there was a camera in this elevator. It was already strange for the two of them to go to the basement at this time of night. Cynthia didn't want to make it worse by arguing with him in front of whichever dispatcher might be watching.

When they got to the basement, Ruben waited for Cynthia to get off first. The underbelly of the hospital was brightly lit but nearly deserted at this hour. There were cameras everywhere, but none of them were wired for audio. Ruben didn't think there was anything incriminating about him walking and talking with one of his nurses.

"You have to tell me what's going on," Ruben said. He kept his hands in his pockets, his head down, his voice low. "I'm going crazy, Cynthia. I swear to God, I'm going crazy."

Cynthia already decided it was over between them. She wanted to let him suffer longer, but her silent treatment was interfering with their professional relationship. She had to clear the air, so they could get on with their lives.

"Janice told me about you," she said.

Ruben's eyes widened. His face reddened. As angry as Cynthia was, she took a bit of satisfaction in seeing that look on his face. That was the classic *BUSTED!* expression.

Ruben said, "What are you talking about?" while he tried to recover.

Cynthia felt her body heat rising. Even the cold salad she was toting felt warm. Her teeth remained clenched when she told him, "Don't fucking lie to me."

Ruben had never seen her so angry. He didn't think his sweet princess could get this upset. "I'm sorry," he said. "That was a long time ago, Cynthia. It has nothing to do with you."

They made a left at the next intersection, heading towards the Jackson Building.

"How come it don't?" Cynthia asked him. "You have an affair with two black women on your floor, and I'm not supposed to care?"

"I'm not a perfect man," Ruben reasoned. "You know I'm not happy with my wife. I told you plenty of times."

"But you didn't tell me you had another affair," Cynthia said. "You didn't tell me you and Janice had been together. I work with her all the time," she hissed. "You coulda said *something*."

"I, I didn't know how to tell you," Ruben admitted. "That's not the easiest thing to bring up. I never asked about anyone you've been involved with."

"If I was with someone else at the hospital, I would've told you," Cynthia said.

"Okay, I–"

"And I'm not the one who's *married*," Cynthia said. "If you're going to run around having affairs, then you owe it to your *mistresses* to tell them '*You're not the only one. I've had affairs*

*before, and I'm going to continue having affairs, and I'm not
leaving my wife for any of you.'"*

Cynthia's throat caught on the last word. Her eyes filled
with moisture, but she was determined not to start crying again.

"You're not my mistress," Ruben said. "I love you."

"Who else?" Cynthia asked. "How many other nurses have
you told that to?"

"No one."

"What about Janice?"

Cynthia's eyes were fierce. She looked like she might slap
him if Ruben gave the wrong answer. And it sounded like Cynthia
and Janice had compared notes. Ruben knew it would be a bad
move to lie.

"Okay, I was in love with Janice."

Cynthia sucked air between her teeth. She looked up at the
ceiling to keep her tears in. "You dirty sonofabitch."

"That's not fair," Ruben said. He threw caution to the wind
and grabbed Cynthia's arm as they passed an empty waiting room.
He pulled her inside and said, "Please, sit down."

Surprisingly, Cynthia did as he asked. The lights were off
in the waiting room, but they got some illumination from the
fluorescent bulbs in the hallway. Even still, Ruben knew it was
unprofessional for them to sit alone in the dimly lit area. If
anyone walked by, their story would surely be added to the
hospital's rumor mill.

Ruben took a seat next to Cynthia and fought to keep his
hands in his lap. He wanted to hold her, to caress her pain away.

"I know it's wrong for me to have more than one affair."
He spoke with a hushed tone. "I know you're hurt right now. But
I haven't been dishonest with you, Cynthia. I told you I had
problems. You know I've been wrestling with this decision; about
what should happen with my wife and kids. It's wrong for me to
seek happiness outside of my marriage and continue to stay with
my wife. I know that, and I'm sorry. But I don't see what Janice
has to do with this. This is between you and me."

"You're not gonna leave her. You just got a thing for black
girls." Tears spilled from her eyes. She was slow to wipe them
away.

"That, that's not true."

"I talked to Janice," Cynthia reminded. "I know all about you now."

Ruben's brain raced. He tried to remember some of the things he told Janice, but it was no use. His memories of her got pushed to the outskirts of his mind when he and Cynthia began their relationship.

"Cynthia, I think you're taking this the wrong way," he said. "All guys have a preference. Some like tall girls. Some like short girls. I don't think there's anything wrong with me thinking black women are beautiful."

"It is when it's just a fetish."

"Who said it was? I'm old enough to know what I want out of life."

"Then why didn't you marry a black woman?"

Ruben shook his head. "We've been through this, Cynthia. I told you why I married Helen. I told you about the first pregnancy, our parents... This is old news."

Cynthia wiped her tears again. So far Ruben was right about everything. Cynthia was almost too embarrassed to bring up the most damning evidence against him, but there was no way around it.

"What about what you said, about how you love my skin color so much..."

"I–"

"You said you wish you could make it, in a bowl, and eat it. You told Janice the same thing..."

Ruben looked confused for a second, and then he surprised Cynthia by smiling. He lowered his head in embarrassment.

"Okay, you got me. I don't have any *game*, Cynthia. I'm a lame-o. I've got such little game, sometimes I use the same pick-up lines, on different people. I'm sorry if you felt disrespected by that. I didn't mean any harm. I do think your skin is beautiful. I wish I could scrape it off and put it in a freezer bag."

Cynthia gave him a look.

"See! That's why if I come up with a good line, I'll hang on to it for a while," Ruben said with a smile.

Try as she might, Cynthia couldn't help but smile back. But just as quickly, her smile went away again. "What about your wife?" she said. "I don't think you're going to leave her."

"I am," Ruben promised.

"When?"

"I don't, I don't know, Cynthia. Soon."

She shook her head. "I'm sorry, but that's not good enough anymore. If you want me to trust you, you have to give me a date."

Ruben shook his head. "A date? Cynthia, that's not fair. I can't come up with an exact date off the top of my head."

"I don't need an exact date," she said. "But I do need *something*, Ruben. Today's April 27th. How long will it take for you to leave her?"

"I don't know," Ruben said. "At least a couple of months."

"Alright. I'll give you 'til July 1st."

Ruben thought for a second and then said, "Okay. July 1st."

"I'm serious," Cynthia said.

"I'm serious, too," Ruben said. "In a way, I'm happy all of this happened. I know I got complacent, and I wasn't doing what I needed to do. But you're right. There's no sense in dragging this out. I'm not happy with my wife, and I don't need to stay with her."

Cynthia was surprised they resolved this so easily. And she was delighted to finally know the exact date that her man would be all hers. She stood with a bright smile. Ruben stood, too. Without thinking, he wrapped his arms around her and squeezed tightly. He kissed her on the lips before they separated.

"Wow. That was bold," Cynthia said, looking around for the cameras.

"I know," Ruben said. "I feel bold. I feel good. I feel like my life finally has direction again."

Cynthia felt goose bumps all over her body. "I'm so excited."

"Me too," Ruben said as they exited the waiting room. "You go ahead without me. I'm going back to the cafeteria to get some ice cream or something. I'll be back on the floor in a few minutes."

≈≈≈≈≈≈≈

Cynthia and Ruben thought they had everything figured out. But Janice had been fooled by him once, and she would never let it happen again. She watched Cynthia leave the unit alone, and Janice saw Ruben go after her a couple of minutes later. Their twilight rendezvous might have been a secret to everyone else on the floor, but Janice knew full well how cheaters operate.

When Cynthia returned to the unit alone, Janice noticed that she wasn't in a bad mood like she was when she left. As a matter of fact, Cynthia had a pep in her step and a dopey smile on her face. Ruben looked happier when he came back, too. And he went out of his way to avoid interactions with Janice for the rest of the night.

Janice knew the two of them were still an item. She wondered if they were stupid enough to have sex at work. Why else would Cynthia get so happy all of a sudden? If they didn't have full intercourse, she could imagine Cynthia going down on Ruben in one of the single-person bathrooms downstairs. The thought made her skin crawl.

This was probably a good time for Janice to throw up her hands and say *Screw it*, but she was much too bitter to do that. If Cynthia wouldn't stop seeing Ruben on her own, then Janice had to try harder to end their relationship. Not only was it a good thing to do, but it was the *right* thing to do, for everyone involved.

CHAPTER SIXTEEN
ONE MORE

Sixteen hours after Ruben accepted Cynthia's deadline to leave his wife, it was 6:30 pm on Saturday afternoon. The hospital was calm and pleasant. Material Operations employee Larry Barnes was on his lunch break. Larry wasn't on a health kick, but he tried not to eat fast food more than once a week. However, like many people, Larry liked to treat himself with a tasty meal when he was really happy or down in the dumps.

The incident at Dr. Dego's home two days ago weighed heavily on Larry's heart, so he went to Wendy's and ordered the *Dave's Hot 'N Juicy ¾ pound Triple*, which came with three hamburger patties and three slices of cheese. Larry also ordered a large order of fries and a cookies and cream shake.

When his dinner was ready, Larry sat alone in the back of the restaurant. He thought his burger looked like a heart attack in a wrapper. Perfect. The first bite was so heavenly Larry hummed aloud and tapped his foot. He was so involved with his lunch, he didn't notice a pretty, young thing approaching his table until she cleared her throat and said, "Hey."

Larry looked up and was surprised to see Lola standing there. She was as cute as ever, but Larry's heart didn't try to leap from his chest like it usually did when he and Lola locked eyes. In fact, he didn't even care that his cheeks were full of dead meat, and he looked like a chipmunk. He chewed slowly and rolled his eyes slightly.

"What's up?"

"Can I sit with you?" Lola asked. She had one of her school books in hand, her hair pulled back, her big glasses in place. She smelled fresh, even though she'd been working in the ER all day.

Larry shrugged. "Whatever. But I'm not gon' stop eating."

Lola smiled. "That's okay." She placed her book on the table and sat down.

Larry swallowed the food in his mouth and took another bite. He looked into Lola's eyes as he chewed, daring her to object. But she didn't look grossed-out like he expected.

"I, um, I wanted to apologize for what happened," she said.

Larry frowned but didn't respond.

"You didn't deserve that," Lola said. "My dad was wrong. He knows he was."

"It would've been nice of you to say that when he was throwing me out of his house," Larry said. He talked with his mouth full, a big no-no for any woman he was interested in. But Larry wasn't trying to impress Lola anymore. What did it matter what she thought of him?

"I did stand up for you."

Larry shook his head. "No you didn't. Not really."

"I did the best I could," Lola said. "My mom did, too."

"Alright," Larry said. "Whatever." He took a swallow of his shake. Larry found that his burger didn't taste as good as it did a few seconds ago. He sighed and wrapped it up, a little upset that Lola ruined his pity party.

"You can eat it," she said, watching his movements.

"I'll eat it later."

"Okay." Lola looked around uncomfortably. "So, do you forgive me?"

Larry grunted. "For what?"

"For what my dad did."

"I can't get upset with you for something your father did," Larry said. "I can only be upset with you for what *you* did – or what you didn't do."

"What did I do, or didn't do?"

The alliteration in her sentence made Larry grin.

"What?" she said.

"Nothing. You just sound funny."

"How?"

"What I did, didn't do, did do did diddly do da..."

Lola laughed. "Okay, are you going to tell me?"

Larry shook his head. His smile went away. "You know something? I thought you were going to run after me. That's stupid, huh?"

Lola's smile went away, too. She lowered her gaze. "I've only known you for a month."

"I know," Larry said. "That's why I said it was stupid."

"It's not stupid," Lola said. "I almost did go after you."

"That would've made me feel a whole lot better."

"But it would've crushed my father," Lola said. "It would've broke his heart."

Larry stared at her for a moment. Lola was young and beautiful. Her skin was smooth, without any blemishes. Even if she wasn't a medical student, Larry thought she might be too good for him.

"Alright, I accept your apology," he said. "Is that it?"

Lola shrugged. "Do you want that to be it?"

Larry sighed. "Look, girl, this ain't no game. You're not in high school anymore. This is real life, and we both grown. If you got something to say, then say it. Why you beating around the bush?"

Lola was taken aback. "Why are you so mad at me?"

"Because you hurt me," Larry said, a little louder than he meant. He lowered his voice. "Even if you didn't come after me that day, you could've at least called. Two days later you see me in here, and you decide to apologize... That's cool. I accept your apology. I don't have no hard feelings. Is that what you want to hear?"

Lola shook her head. "No. I wanted to know if you still wanted to talk. I still want to see you."

Larry was surprised by that. But he refused to let her get his hopes up again. "Lola, nothing has changed. You're still a rich girl, and I'm just a regular dude with a regular job that doesn't pay that much. Your dad still hates me. We're on opposite sides of the pole. And you're not even a doctor yet. The further you go in life, the further away from me you'll be."

"It's not all about money," Lola argued. "If I like someone for who they are on the inside, what does it matter what kind of job they have?"

"Why don't you ask your father that?"

"And you are successful," Lola said. "You said so yourself."

"I'm successful compared to *my* peers," Larry explained. "Not yours."

"So you just want to throw it all away?"

Larry chuckled. "Throw *what* away, girl? Like you said, we've only been going out for a month."

"You know what I'm talking about," Lola said. "I know how I feel about you, and I thought you felt the same way about me."

Her eyes glossed over. This was almost too much for Larry to bear.

"Lola, I do feel the same way. But I don't want to get hurt anymore." He chuckled. "I know that sounds strange, coming from a guy, but it's true. The chances of you hurting me are way more likely than me ever hurting you."

"That's what I tried to tell my dad," Lola said. "I don't think you would hurt me."

Larry's heart fluttered. It tried to soar, but he grabbed hold of it and held it down. This was more fantasy than real life. It was too outlandish to work out. They already tried and failed.

"You, you really want to get back together?" Larry dared to ask.

Lola nodded. "Don't you?"

"Of course I do," Larry said. "But I can't let people disrespect me, especially when I didn't do nothing to them. I am who I am. Your father is never going to accept that."

"Yes he is," Lola assured.

"No, he's not."

"He is."

"You don't–"

"Larry." Lola reached across the table and held his hand. "You must've forgot that I'm an only child. My mom wanted to have more, but she couldn't. I'm a little spoiled because my dad gives me anything I want. He can't help it. He saw how upset I've been, and he's the one who told me to go talk to you."

Larry's eyes widened. "You tripping."

"No, I'm not," Lola said with a grin.

Larry watched her eyes. He was at a loss for words.

Lola gave his hand a comforting squeeze. "So are we back together, or what?"

Larry's heart jumped again. This time he let it go. "Okay."

Lola's smile lit up the restaurant. "Okay." She grabbed her text book. "I gotta go now."

"You didn't get nothing to eat," Larry noticed.

"I didn't come here to eat," Lola said. "I asked some of your coworkers where you were. They told me to check in here."

Larry beamed. "Dang. You been looking for me?" He narrowed his eyes. "You must really like me."

Lola nodded. She rose from the table, and Larry checked out the way her hips stretched the fabric in her slacks. He checked out her thin waistline, her full lips, and her big, brown eyes. And she was a medical student to boot. And somehow, she was his woman.

Larry wasn't too big on PDA, but he stood and kissed her briefly. Lola was also self conscious, but she kissed him back. Both of them were grinning like children.

"Goodbye, Larry."

Larry returned to his seat but still didn't have an appetite for the dead meat he wrapped up. The shake and fries looked good, though. "Bye, Lola. Talk to you later."

≈≈≈≈≈≈≈

Later that night critical care nurse Sandra Alexander was too preoccupied to go to work or even call-in. For the first time ever she pulled a no-call no-show. But tonight was filled with firsts. Tonight was the first time Sandra was willing to sell her body (all of it) for heroin. And tonight was also the first time ManMan wasn't really interested. He looked her up and down and shook his head woefully.

"Naw, that's alright, shorty. But you can come holler at me when you got some money, though."

189

It was after midnight on what had been a long, hard Saturday. Sandra woke up that morning with no money and a nagging pain in her bones that would only go away when she got her medicine. But Sandra couldn't afford her medicine, and she had exhausted and abused all of the avenues she used to turn to for finances.

Sandra held on to her iPhone for the duration of her spiral into madness, but she sold it today for only forty dollars. She knew that by selling the phone she was cutting off her final link to the civilized world. And she understood that she could no longer go on like this. Sandra decided to go to rehab, but even that was scary.

She knew kicking her habit would be agonizing, and she might lose her job when she asked for the time off. But Sandra probably lost her job already when she told her manager she had cancer. Ruben wanted her to take a leave of absence. He needed paperwork from her doctor to get the process started. Sandra didn't have such paperwork, and she'd been avoiding him ever since.

On one level Sandra understood that everything around her was shit. She was making decisions that could ruin her whole life – not just this year, but for years down the road. But rationality got warped when she was fiending for her drug. Sandra used to view people like her the same way the rest of the world did. She wondered how a crack mother could sell her daughter's virginity. She wondered why an addict would risk prison, AIDS and murder to walk the streets as a prostitute.

Sandra still thought about these things, but as she found herself walking the same path so many addicts took before her, she understood how and why junkies did what they did. But for Sandra all hope was not lost. When she sold her phone today, Sandra made a big decision, probably the biggest decision of her life. She decided that it was time.

Yes, there was no denying it now. Sandra had been attacked, misled, mistreated, disrespected and disavowed. The bank was threatening to take her home and her car. She was on the verge of being fired from the hospital, and there was no one even *trying* to help her. Sandra had no choice but to go to rehab.

But before rehab, there was the ONE MORE phase, which could last as long as an addict wanted it to.

When Sandra scored from ManMan earlier today, that was supposed to be her ONE MORE high. She was supposed to take those $20 packs and make them last for the rest of the day. She was supposed to wake up early on Sunday morning and get her affairs in order before checking herself into an inpatient rehab facility. Sandra had three rehab centers in mind. She'd been preparing herself for this day for weeks.

Unfortunately Sandra's ONE MORE high failed as ONE MORE highs often do. By eleven p.m. she was out of dope and fiending like never before. By eleven-thirty Sandra decided that her ONE MORE high shouldn't end until Sunday morning, since that was the day she planned to go to rehab.

Instead of ONE MORE high, what Sandra really meant was one more *day* of getting high. By midnight Sandra decided that it didn't matter what she did to get drugs on her ONE MORE DAY of getting high, because it was, after all, her last day. What difference did it make if she slept with ManMan now? Everyone was allowed to go all out on their last day, weren't they?

At 12:17 Sandra arrived at the dope house and was greeted by the doorman; a mean lesbian named Sammy. Sammy gave Sandra a friendly smile and told her, "You can come kick it with me, if he don't help you out," before she sent Sandra back to ManMan's room.

A 12:18 ManMan looked Sandra up and down and rejected her offer for sex. This was the same moment Sandra stepped even further over the line and *begged* for her medicine.

"Please, ManMan. I'll pay you back. I swear."

ManMan walked to the front of the room and opened his dresser drawer. Sandra thought he was going to give her drugs for free (which would've been more awesome than a double rainbow), but ManMan dug around in the drawer and found a ring instead. He turned and threw it at Sandra. He threw it hard. The ring hit her on the forehead before falling to the floor.

Sandra wasn't too upset about the unexpected and unnecessary act of violence. She knelt to retrieve the jewelry. It was the class ring she gave him a couple of weeks ago. Sandra stared at it and then looked up at her dealer while rubbing the new sore spot on her forehead.

"Why you hit me?"

"Why you ain't never pay me for that motherfucker?" ManMan wanted to know. He was just a kid, half a decade younger than Sandra. But he frightened her. She respected him like she would a much older man.

"I was gonna buy it back," she said. "I still am. If you give me some time."

"You ain't *got* no more time!" ManMan spat. "I'm through messing around with you. I should beat your bitch ass." He balled his fists. "Gimme my motherfucking ring!" He snatched it from her and returned it to his dresser drawer.

Sandra stood, confused and anxious. She didn't understand why he was so upset with her. It was clear ManMan wasn't going to give her anymore freebies, and Sandra didn't have an alternate plan. She figured if she was going to sell her body anyway, she could do it on the streets just as easily as she could in ManMan's bedroom.

But Sandra didn't know the first thing about working the streets. And giving herself to a complete stranger would be a lot different than sleeping with ManMan. They weren't in a relationship or anything like that, but ManMan played a major role in Sandra's life. She thought they had a special bond, regardless of how twisted it was.

Fortunately ManMan was more freaky than he was upset. The free dope he'd given Sandra over the past few months was a pittance to him. It didn't amount to one percent of his total wealth.

"Take your clothes off," he told her. "All of them. Get butt-nekkid."

Sandra felt euphoria as she stripped off her clothes rather than the shame that should've been there. She knew this was a ghastly predicament, but it was okay because this would be her last time getting high. Anything goes when it's your last time. Everyone knows that.

"If you need to wash your ass, there's a bathroom over there," ManMan said, pointing to the hallway.

"I'm, I'm okay," Sandra told him.

"I'm fucking you in the asshole," ManMan clarified. "If you need to wash that motherfucker, go do it now."

Sandra stopped undressing as she considered this. She made love anally only once. It was not a pleasant experience. But then again, her boyfriend at the time was much bigger than ManMan. Sandra figured she could take ManMan's little dick with no problem. But she couldn't do it sober.

"Can I, you got something I can shoot first?"

"Go get it from Sammy," ManMan told her. "Shoot it in there."

"Oh, okay," Sandra said.

She pulled her jeans back up and went to the front room to collect her rations. Sammy hooked her up with no problem. Sammy even went to the restroom with Sandra afterwards to make sure Sandra cleaned herself up sufficiently.

When Sandra returned to ManMan's room, Sammy went too. Sandra didn't know what the stud wanted, but everything became clear when Sammy sat on the floor and took her pants and boxers off. Sammy lay on her back and opened her legs and told Sandra, "Come on, girl. Bring your face over here."

Licking a female was another first. It was another one of those *I will NEVER do that* moments. But Sandra was too high to care anymore. She dropped to her elbows and knees and gave it her best shot. She thought ManMan was just going to watch, but after a few minutes he pulled Sandra's pants down and did what he told her he wanted to do.

Sandra didn't cry because this was all just a means to an end. Plus today was her last day. Tomorrow she'd go to rehab, and no matter how many group circles she sat in, she would never tell anyone what happened tonight. She'd tell them about her job, and she'd tell them about Ben, but not this.

Not ever.

CHAPTER SEVENTEEN
RUBEN EXPOSED

On Wednesday the following week, critical care nurse Cynthia Pullman and her manager Ruben Watts were still waiting to see the paperwork from Sandra's doctor. But a brand new fire erupted, and Sandra's issues got pushed to the back burner.

Cynthia rarely worked the dayshift, but she clocked in at seven a.m. that morning to cover for a nurse who was out on maternity leave. Cynthia and Ruben limited their interactions during the day even more than they did on 3rd shift, so Cynthia was surprised when he approached her and asked her to come to his office. Her surprise became confusion when he asked her to close the door so they could speak privately.

Ruben sat behind his desk looking a little sickly, Cynthia thought. He was paler than usual, and his forehead was dotted with sweat. He bounced a knee nervously as Cynthia took a seat across from him.

"What's wrong?" she asked.

"It's my wife," Ruben said. "Someone contacted her at work and told her I was having an affair."

Cynthia's jaw dropped. She stared at him in shock. Ruben watched her reaction carefully.

"When?" Cynthia asked.

"A few minutes ago," Ruben said. "She just called me."

Cynthia raised a hand to her head and rubbed her temple. "Wh, who told her?"

"I don't know," Ruben said. "They called her at work."

Cynthia shook her head. Her heart was racing. "That's crazy."

"Yeah," Ruben agreed. He sighed and nibbled on his bottom lip. "Was, was it you?"

There was a pause while Cynthia looked at him like he was crazy. "What do you mean?"

"Did, was it you who called her?"

She frowned. "Why would I do that?"

Ruben shrugged. There was a slight twitch in the corner of his mouth. He looked like he might cry or throw up, or maybe both. "I'm sorry, I had to ask."

"I don't even know where your wife works," Cynthia said.

Ruben looked around the room before meeting her eyes again. He propped his elbows on the desk and clasped his hands together, as if in prayer. "Yeah, yeah you do..."

Cynthia continued to shake her head. "No, I don't."

"I told you," Ruben said. "I told you she works at Fresenius. I told you a couple of times."

"I don't remember that."

"It's–"

"Why are you accusing me?" Cynthia wondered. "You know I wouldn't do that."

"But you, you said you wanted me to leave her."

"Yeah, and you said you would," Cynthia said, growing offended by his accusation. "You said you'd leave her by July 1st."

"I know," Ruben said.

"Today's only May 1st," Cynthia said. "I haven't said anything else about it."

"I know, it's just..."

Cynthia waited, but a few seconds passed without him completing the sentence. "You think I'm so impatient, I'd try to speed things along?" she asked.

"I don't want to argue," Ruben said. "We've been together for a long time, and I can understand if you did feel that way."

"I didn't call your wife," Cynthia said sternly. "I want you to leave her, but we already set a date, and I can wait. Don't ever accuse me of doing something like that."

"I'm sorry," Ruben said. "I just, I didn't know what to think. You understand that, don't you?"

Cynthia did understand. She knew Ruben was anxious and frightened. She let her irritation go so she could comfort and brainstorm with him.

"Who do you think it could've been?" Ruben asked.

Cynthia didn't have to think too hard. "Janice."

Ruben's eyes widened. "Why would she do that?"

"I told you she confronted me a few weeks ago," Cynthia said. "She tried to get me to break up with you, but I kept denying it. She got mad, called me a bitch, and some other stuff. Maybe she decided to try something different, to make us break up."

Ruben nodded. He brought his clasped hands to his face and rubbed his mouth with his thumb knuckles. "Yeah, it might be her."

"Why is she so mad at you?" Cynthia had to ask. "What did you do that would make her go this far?"

"Nothing."

"It's got to be something," Cynthia reasoned. "This doesn't make sense. She wouldn't try to ruin your life unless you really hurt her."

Ruben looked down at his desk as he considered that.

Cynthia waited.

"She's upset because I didn't leave my wife for her," Ruben said. "She, we made plans. And I didn't follow through."

Goosebumps sprouted on Cynthia's arms. She felt sick to her stomach all of a sudden. "Like our plans?" she asked. "Like you leaving your wife by July 1st?"

Ruben shook his head. "No, it's not like that."

Cynthia's eyes watered. She stared deeply into his eyes, looking for deceit.

"It's not the same," Ruben insisted. "I didn't leave my wife for Janice because, towards the end, I knew me and Janice wouldn't work out. We had problems that didn't have anything to do with my marriage. When I told her, Janice got really upset. She said I was a liar... I broke her heart."

Two fat tears spilled from Cynthia's eyes. She felt like she was hearing about her own future. And she didn't like it. She didn't like it one bit.

"It's not the same with you," Ruben assured her. "I love you Cynthia, and I want to be with you. I want to spend the rest of my life with you. It's, it's not the same."

Cynthia continued to watch his eyes. She wiped her tears and sniffled. How do you know when a man is telling you the truth? Can you see it in his eyes, hear it in his voice intonations? Is it something you feel when he's holding and making love to you? Or is it something you just know? Cynthia relied on all of these senses. After a few moments she decided Ruben was being honest with her.

"I love you, too," she said.

"We'll get through this," Ruben said. "I don't know what I'm going to tell my wife, but you and me, we'll get through this. I promise."

Cynthia had a lot of suggestions about what he should tell his wife, but she didn't offer them. Regardless of how she felt about the missus, Cynthia knew that Ruben's wife was a loving and caring woman. She supported and cherished her husband. She bore Ruben two beautiful children during their marriage. It wasn't her fault that Ruben didn't love her anymore. In the eyes of any judge, Ruben's wife would be considered the victim. Women like Cynthia and Janice were the evil bitches who were trying to corrupt a legally binding union.

Cynthia got up and let Ruben figure things out on his own.

"Let me know what happens," she said.

Her manager nodded absently. So deep in thought, Ruben didn't even ogle Cynthia's beautiful ass as she left the room.

≈ ≈ ≈ ≈ ≈ ≈

The day progressed with a lot more stress than Cynthia was accustomed to. She tried to lose herself in her work, but scarcely a minute went by without her thinking about Ruben and Janice and the mysterious call to Ruben's wife. Cynthia held fast to the belief that Ruben wouldn't treat her the same way he treated Janice. But common sense kept invading her thought process; trying to convince her otherwise.

197

By five p.m., Cynthia's brain was nearly fried. She wanted to talk to Ruben badly. Watching him go about his managerial duties without looking in her direction was torture. She knew it had to be this way, but that didn't mean it didn't suck.

Ruben left at a quarter after five, but Cynthia didn't get off until seven. She hoped he would try to contact her before he got home, and he didn't disappoint. Five minutes after Ruben exited the parking garage, Cynthia got a text message from him.

"Call me"

Cynthia hurried to the waiting room, where it was okay to talk on her cellphone.

When Ruben answered, Cynthia heard street traffic in the background and a lot more tension in his voice. "Hey," he said.

"You're on your way home?"

"Yeah."

"Are you okay?" Cynthia asked.

Ruben sighed. "No. Not really. They contacted my wife again. Now they have a facebook account. They asked her to be friends."

Cynthia knitted her eyebrows in confusion. "Who?"

"Whoever called her the first time," Ruben said. "They created a Facebook account, calling themselves 'THE TRUTH.' They sent Helen a friend request, saying they had more information about my affairs. When she accepted, they started giving her details about what's been going on. They told her to check out you and Janice on Facebook. They said, 'These are the kind of women your husband really likes...' Helen, she looked at everything. She's devastated. She had to leave work early."

Cynthia's mouth hung open as she listened. This seemed way over the top. She still thought Janice was behind the exposé, and she knew that Ruben caused her a lot of pain. He was now in a position to inflict the same emotional turmoil on another woman; either Cynthia or his wife.

"Wha, what are you gonna do?" she breathed.

"I don't know," Ruben said. "I'm actually afraid to go home. I don't know what Helen's going to do. I don't know what to tell her. Jesus, this is bad."

"You can go to my house," Cynthia offered, "if you don't want to go home..."

"No," Ruben said right away. "I have to face her. She wants answers, and I have to give them to her."

"Are, are you going to tell her the truth?" Cynthia's mouth was completely dry. She felt perspiration collecting in her armpits.

"Yeah," Ruben said. "I don't, I don't think I have a choice."

"Are you still leaving her?"

"After I tell her what I did, she'll be the one who wants to leave me," Ruben said. "She already said some things, when we talked on the phone."

Cynthia didn't like that answer. Her heart was racing. "But are *you* still going to leave *her*," she specified, "even if she wants to stay with you?"

"Yes," Ruben said. "I love you, Cynthia. I meant what I said about wanting to spend the rest of my life with you. I'm just stressed right now because this isn't how I wanted Helen to find out. I wanted to get a few things in order first, financially. Now it looks like I don't have time for any of that."

"You can come stay with me, if she kicks you out," Cynthia offered again. "You don't have to worry about money. I'll take care of you."

"Thanks," Ruben said. "I know you will."

"I love you."

"Hold on a sec'."

Cynthia was only on hold for twelve seconds, but it felt like a few minutes.

"It's Helen. I gotta call you back," Ruben said when he returned to the line.

"Are you gonna call me tonight?"

"I'll try. But me and Helen have a lot to talk about. I might not be able to get away long enough."

"Go to the bathroom and text me," Cynthia suggested. "Just to let me know you're alright."

"Okay," Ruben said. "I gotta go."

"I love you. And don't forget to tell me what's happening."

"I won't," Ruben said. "I love you, too. Bye."

He disconnected. Cynthia stood there for a few moments before she slipped her phone inside her pocket. She went to the bathroom to wash her face before she returned to the unit. The next hour and a half were nerve-wrecking, but Cynthia made it through her shift without succumbing to the pressure of her sins.

When she got home, Cynthia stayed up until two a.m. waiting for Ruben to call or text her, but he never did. Cynthia slept alone every night, but tonight sleep was elusive. She couldn't stop thinking; wondering what was going on in Ruben's bed. Were he and his wife still arguing? Did she make him leave? Cynthia doubted that because Ruben would've called if Helen put him out. She wondered if Ruben's wife forgave him after he vowed to never cheat again. She wondered if they were having make-up sex at that very moment.

It didn't seem likely, but Cynthia couldn't understand why Ruben hadn't called or texted her. How hard could it be to go to the bathroom and send a quick text? He did it all the time. Cynthia had plenty of messages in her phone from one and two in the morning, when Ruben said he couldn't sleep without telling her he loved her one more time. Was his wife watching him too closely now, or did he *choose* not to contact his girlfriend?

Either way, Cynthia felt like her life would remain on hold until she heard from Ruben again. She knew Janice was in this same predicament one year ago, but Cynthia didn't want to think about Janice. That made everything so much worse.

≈ ≈ ≈ ≈ ≈ ≈

Cynthia didn't think she slept at all that night, but she must have. When her phone rang at eight the next morning, she was startled from a strange dream that might have been a nightmare. She tried to remember what it was about, but the dream was pushed from her memory when she saw Ruben's name on the caller ID.

"Hel–" She cleared her throat. "Hello?"

"Hey," he said. He sounded stressed and fatigued, presumably from a long night of arguing.

Cynthia rubbed the sleep from her eyes. She was fully awake in a matter of seconds. "What happened? How'd it go?"

"Not good," Ruben said. "We're getting a divorce."

200

Cynthia's pulse quickened. While this was the very thing she wanted, it was also kind of scary, now that it was finally happening. "Where are you?"

"I'm at home," Ruben said. "Helen went to her mother's this morning. She took the day off. I've never seen her so upset."

"What happened last night?" Cynthia asked. "What did you tell her?"

"For the first time since we've been married, I actually told her the truth," Ruben said. "I told her I did have two affairs, and everything she learned on Facebook was true. I told her I was still seeing you, and that I'm in love you with. I told her I was going to be with you, afterwards..."

Cynthia couldn't believe it. She stared wide-eyed at the floor until the carpet blurred and began to swirl around. This was what she hoped for, but she didn't expect the burden to be so heavy. She wasn't just sleeping with a married man now. Cynthia was partially responsible for a marriage failing. Her name might be brought up in the divorce proceedings. She knew it was all for the best, but at that moment Cynthia was more afraid than she was pleased that Ruben didn't back down.

"You still there?" he asked.

"Yeah."

"What's wrong? I thought you'd be happy."

"I am," Cynthia said. "I'm just nervous. I, I honestly didn't think you'd do it. When you didn't call last night, I thought you and her were trying to work things out."

"No, it wasn't that," Ruben said. "I did that out of respect for Helen. She was crying. I didn't have the heart to sneak around – not last night." He sighed. "I never thought we'd reach this point. I mean, I've been saying I wanted to leave her for years, but it never seemed like something that could really happen."

"I know," Cynthia said. "That's how I felt."

"I can't wait to see you again," he said.

"When?"

"I don't know. I have to work today. I'm actually running late."

"Can you come over when you get off?" Cynthia asked.

"I'll try."

"Please, Ruben. I need to see you."

"I'll stop by," he said. "But I don't know how long I can stay."

"That's fine. I just want to hold you."

"Okay. I gotta go now. I'll talk to you later."

"Alright," Cynthia said. "I love you."

"I love you. I can't wait 'til we can make our relationship public."

Cynthia frowned. She realized she wasn't one hundred percent ready to go public with Ruben, but she said, "Me, too. Talk to you later."

≈≈≈≈≈≈≈

By one o'clock Cynthia was up and out of the house, trying to enjoy her day off. She did a lot of soul searching after she got off the phone with Ruben. Cynthia decided it was time to take the first step towards her new life. She invited her sister and her best friend to lunch, so she could finally tell them about the mystery man she'd been dating for almost a year.

They were starting to think Cynthia's boyfriend was imaginary. Or maybe Cynthia was gay, and her man was actually a *woman*. Cynthia suspected the news about Ruben would be just as shocking. She had butterflies in her stomach when she and her gal pals squeezed into a booth at the Chili's restaurant on Hulen Street.

Sonya was Cynthia's big sister by two years. She was shorter and rounder than Cynthia, but Sonya had always been the prettier of the two. She was married and pregnant with her third child. Flora had been Cynthia's best friend since their junior year at Finley High School. Flora was tall and skinny with a cute face and a perfect set of boobs she purchased a few months ago.

Cynthia waited until everyone was halfway through their meal before she made her big announcement.

"It's really good seeing you ladies, but there's a reason I invited y'all to lunch today..."

"*Invited* means you paying, right?" Sonya said.

"Yes," Cynthia said with a smirk.

202

"I'm just saying," Sonya went on. "Last time you called yourself inviting me to dinner, you didn't have enough money for anybody's food – not even yours."

"Uh, that's was my *birthday*," Cynthia said.

"I know," Sonya said. "I brought you a gift. But you didn't say anything about feeding you, too."

Everyone laughed. Cynthia shook her head and pushed her plate to the side. "*Anyway*," she said, still smiling brightly, "I got something to tell y'all that's very serious. It's something I've been wanting to tell you for a long time."

"You gay?" Sonya asked.

"No, I'm not *gay*," Cynthia said with a frown.

"It's okay if you are," Flora said.

"We not gon' judge you," Sonya assured her.

"What the?" Cynthia scowled at them. "Y'all think I'm gay?"

"Why else would you have a *boyfriend* for so long without letting us see him?" Sonya made finger quotation marks around the word *boyfriend*.

Cynthia laughed. "As a matter of fact, that's what I wanted to talk to y'all about today. I'm ready to tell you about him."

Her friends' eyes widened. They were eager for this scoop.

"What happened?" Flora asked. "Why are you finally ready to open up? Is he fat?"

"No," Cynthia said with a chuckle. "But it's kinda complicated."

"Because he used to be a woman?" Sonya guessed.

"Girl stop!" Cynthia said. She couldn't stop laughing. "I'm not gay. *God!* How can you not know that?"

"I know you *used* to like dick," Sonya said. "But for the past year, I been wondering about you."

"What's his name?" Flora asked.

"Ruben," Cynthia said.

"Is he fine?" Flora asked.

"Is he a baller?" Sonya asked.

"Dark-skinned or light-skinned?" Flora wanted to know.

"I got a picture," Cynthia said. She dug her cellphone from her purse and found a photo she took in her kitchen one day. She thought Ruben looked really nice, but her friends' smiles disappeared when she passed them the phone.

"Who is *this*?" Sonya asked, her brow furrowed.

"That's Ruben," Cynthia said.

"He's..." Flora frowned, too.

"This a *white man*." Sonya stated the obvious.

"Very good," Cynthia said. "I see you know your colors."

"Stop playing," Sonya said. She tried to pass the phone back to Cynthia, but Flora took it and studied the picture some more.

"I'm not playing," Cynthia said. "Ruben is my boyfriend. He works with me. And yes, he's white."

Sonya didn't know what to say about that.

Flora cleared her throat. "He, um. He's handsome."

Cynthia took her phone back. "Why y'all tripping?"

Sonya was still at a loss for words.

"We, uh..." Flora forced a smile. "I never thought you were interested in white men. But there's nothing wrong with it," she quickly added. "If that's what you want..."

"Hell if it ain't nothing wrong with it," Sonya said. "It would be better if you was gay, long as your girlfriend was *black*."

Cynthia's mouth fell open. "Are you serious?"

"When you start liking white men?" Sonya asked.

"I, I never, who said I like white men?"

"You just showed us a picture of a *white man*," Sonya reminded.

"I mean, I don't..." Cynthia shook her head. "It's not like I got a thing for white men. I like this particular white man, but I don't wanna be with every white man I see. I still like black men, too."

Their waiter approached midway through Cynthia's explanation. He stood, very uncomfortably. His pale skin reddened right before their eyes. "Um, I'll be back," he said and made a hasty retreat.

"Oh my God, this is so embarrassing." Cynthia buried her face in her hands.

"Yeah, it sure is," Sonya said. She folded her arms over her pregnant belly and shook her head in disappointment.

"I know you're not racist," Cynthia told her. "Why you acting like that?"

"I'm not racist," Sonya agreed. "I like white people just fine. But I don't want one in my bed."

"Well, that's you," Cynthia said.

"It, there's nothing wrong with it," Flora repeated. But her expression said otherwise.

"This is unbelievable," Cynthia said. "All this time I thought y'all would be upset about the *real* reason I kept our relationship secret. But you're stuck on his skin color. And Flora, I don't see why you're looking at me like that. You dated white guys in high school."

"I dated *one* white guy in high school," Flora clarified. "But we never had sex or nothing. I also stole lipstick from Tricia's purse one time, but that didn't mean I was going to grow up and be a thief. We all did stupid stuff when we were in high school."

"It was *stupid*?" Cynthia said. "Going out with a white guy was stupid?"

"What's the *real* reason you kept him a secret?" Sonya asked.

Cynthia almost didn't say, but they were going to find out sooner or later.

"He's married."

"*Oh Gawd!*" Sonya brought a hand to her face and tried to rub the shame away.

Flora just stared and blinked. Finally she shook her head and said, "Tell us how this happened."

She sounded like she wanted an explanation for how her best friend lost her leg in the war. Cynthia swallowed her pride and told the whole story. It didn't matter how they felt at this point; she didn't think she could be anymore embarrassed.

When she was done talking, Sonya conceded that "At least he a *successful* white man." And Flora said, "And he is leaving his wife for you." But there was no mistaking that they were both against Cynthia's decision.

The three women left the restaurant a lot less chipper than they were when they arrived. But at least the secret was out. Cynthia was glad the two most important people in her life knew what was going on. She was sure they would warm up to Ruben once they met him.

If not, who cared? It wasn't like Cynthia approved of every man they dated.

≈ ≈ ≈ ≈ ≈ ≈ ≈

When she got home, Cynthia took her dog for a walk, and then she showered and made a taco dinner for herself and Ruben. He was supposed to get off at five, but Cynthia still hadn't heard from him at six pm. She started to call the hospital to see if he'd left yet, but patience had always been the cornerstone of their relationship.

By seven Cynthia's patience was wearing thin. By nine o'clock she had to accept that Ruben wasn't coming. But she didn't understand why he hadn't called or texted her since they spoke this morning. *Jeez, how hard is it to send a fucking text message?*

At midnight Cynthia went to bed with a multitude of questions and uncertainties swirling around her head, much like she did last night. She couldn't shake the thought that Ruben and his wife had reconciled – or maybe they were reconciling right now, with their legs wrapped around each other, their bedroom filled with the scents of their love.

People thought life was hard for a wife who was being cheated on, but no one ever felt sorry for the Other Woman. Sure Cynthia was a cheat, a sneak and a home wrecker. But she had feelings, too. Tomorrow she planned to give Ruben a piece of her mind for keeping her in the dark like this. Well, she would if she could get him on the phone. Cynthia had to accept the fact that nothing was guaranteed at this point. Nothing at all.

CHAPTER EIGHTEEN
INFERNO

When she woke up the next morning, Cynthia checked her cellphone to see if she missed any calls from Ruben. She hadn't. Depression found a nice home in her chest, making her feel sick all over. Halfway across town, Material Operations employee Rodney Tucker felt sick, too. But his pain was more centralized. To be specific, all of Rodney's pain was confined to the shaft of his penis, and it only hurt when he had to pee.

Rodney knew what was going on. This wasn't his first rodeo. He knew what was up two days ago when the pain first started. Back then it was slight, barely an annoyance. But each day the pain grew worse. This morning it was so bad he had to grit his teeth and lean on the sink for support while he urinated. It felt like shredded razor blades set aflame were shooting out of his dick.

When he left the bathroom, Rodney got dressed and went to the John Peter Paul Clinic on Rosedale. The admissions clerk gave him a few papers to fill out rather than ask directly what he was there for. Rodney liked that. There were a couple of young ladies in the waiting room who thought he was cute. Rodney knew they were attracted to him by the way they watched him when he walked in. Their expressions would've changed if they knew he had a blazing inferno in his underpants.

The admissions clerk called Rodney's name after a forty minute wait. She directed him to one of the exam rooms where a doctor was pulling on a pair of latex gloves. The doctor was a man, but that didn't cut down on the embarrassment. He took it upon himself to lecture Rodney during the brief exam.

"What's going on with you, young blood?"

"Nothing," Rodney said.

His doctor was black, but Rodney didn't expect him to use such vernacular. But then again, this clinic was located in one of the poorest parts of the city. It made sense that the doctor wanted to connect with his patients on their level.

"Been swimming without a life preserver, huh?" the doctor said.

"Uh... Huh?" Rodney said.

"Drop your pants," the doctor instructed. He had a sterilized Q-tip in his hand now.

Rodney dropped his pants and underwear.

The doctor took hold of his penis and stared at the slight discharge leaking from it. "A *condom*," the doctor said. "Why weren't you wearing a condom?"

"I usually do," Rodney said. "It was just this one tiiiiii–" Rodney's voice went up a few octaves when the doctor inserted the cotton swab in his urethra. "It was just this one time," Rodney said when he pulled it out.

"It's *everybody's* first time," the physician said. He stepped away from Rodney and went to the counter where he had chemicals waiting to interact with the goo from Rodney's penis.

"Even when I see them two, three times, it's still their first time," the doctor went on. "What's so bad about a condom?" he asked over his shoulder. "You can't feel anything? Is that it? I bet you felt something when you used the bathroom this morning, didn't you?"

"Can, can I pull my pants up?" Rodney asked.

"Yes," the doctor said. He turned back to him, already done with his chemistry project. "You have gonorrhea."

Rodney suspected as much.

"Is this your first time?" the doctor asked.

Rodney started to lie, but he came to this clinic the last time his dick turned into a volcano. He was sure they had his information on file. He shook his head.

"Sit down," the doctor told him. He turned and retrieved a needle, a vial and a tourniquet. He turned back to Rodney and told him, "Let me see your arm."

Rodney took a seat, but he asked him, "What for?"

"I need to get some blood," the doctor said.

"What for?"

"For an HIV test."

"I don't need a HIV test," Rodney said. "I just need some penicillin."

The doctor grinned. "We don't use penicillin anymore. But for someone who knows the drill as well as you, I'd say you definitely need an HIV test."

"No, I'm alright," Rodney said, rising to his feet. "Can I just have my prescription, please?"

The doctor's smile went away. "Son, I'm not trying to judge you. But if you've left yourself susceptible to one STD, you've left yourself susceptible to all of them. You need to get checked, so you don't go around spreading anything to other people. It's the responsible thing to do."

Unfortunately *responsible* was a word Rodney knew by definition only.

"Can I please just have my prescription, Sir?"

The doctor sighed and shook his head slightly. "Go wait out front. They'll give it to you."

"Thanks," Rodney said. He hurried out of the exam room.

≈ ≈ ≈ ≈ ≈ ≈

On the way home, Rodney wrestled with a tough decision: What should he tell his girlfriend, and how should he tell her? Rodney and Trish shared an apartment, and they had sex all the time. Rodney made up excuses to avoid intimacy last night and the night before, but there was a good chance he passed his gonorrhea to her three days ago.

As for where he got the infection, Rodney didn't have to rack his brain to figure that out. Last Saturday he went to Club Tron and met a few sexy ladies on the dance floor. He danced with one of them, which was really just dry-humping to music, and she followed him to his car when the club shut down at two a.m.

Rodney had sex with the stranger in the parking lot and ejected her from his vehicle before her friends took off without her. The whole encounter lasted only ten minutes. Rodney thought the girl's name was Shay, but it could've been *La*Shay or *Shayla* or some other variation. She didn't look *sick* to Rodney, and she didn't ask him to use a condom – which made her a winner in his book. Now Rodney cursed Shay (or LaShay or Shayla) for seducing him with her poisoned pussy. It was getting to the point where you couldn't trust anyone these days.

Rodney's girlfriend was at school that morning, but he knew she didn't have any classes from ten to eleven. Rodney also knew that it would take every ounce of his player skills to keep his woman after giving her gonorrhea, but he felt up to the task.

When he got home, Rodney minced an onion and inhaled the fumes to get his tear ducts working. It's one thing to moan on the phone, but if a girl could actually hear the moisture in your nose, that pushed your credibility up a few notches.

Rodney called Trish at ten-fifteen.

"Hello?"

"Hey," Rodney said. His voice was low and forlorn.

"Hey," Trish said. "What's wrong?" Her voice was immediately drenched with concern.

"I don't know," Rodney moaned. "I don't know what to do no more. I think we should break up."

"Wh, what?" Trish's voice was shaky as the whole world fell from beneath her.

"I'm sorry," Rodney said. "I love you so much. I didn't want it to be like this." He gave her one of his sniffles.

"*Why*?" Trish cried. "What I do?"

"Nothing," Rodney said. "It's not you, it's me. I'm not right for you. You too good for me. I don't deserve you..." Rodney took a breath and let it out in shudders. His heart was pounding, which helped a lot.

"Why are you saying this?" Trish asked. "I love you, Rodney. I don't want to be without you."

"I know," Rodney said. "I don't wanna be without you, either."

"Then why are you doing this?" Trish sniffled, too.

Rodney could hear the agony in her voice. He felt a little guilty because he knew she was in the school's library or cafeteria. There were people walking by and sitting near Trish, watching and feeling sorry for her.

"I got drunk," Rodney said. "Saturday when I went out with James and them... I did something bad, and I can't take it back. I don't deserve to be with you, after what I did. *Oh my God*," he moaned. "I can't believe this happened. James set me up. He knew I didn't wanna be with that girl."

"*What girl?*" Trish cried. "*What happened, Rodney? Tell me.*"

Rodney got up and went back to the kitchen. He inhaled more of the acrid onion scents, and tears squirted from his eyes. He sniffled. It sounded *really* wet this time.

"*They set me up!*" Rodney groaned. "They knew I didn't wanna be with her. They pushed her in the backseat with me. It was James and them, baby. I swear I didn't wanna do it."

"*I told you not to hang around them*," Trish cried. "I told you, Rodney. I *told* you."

"I know, baby. But I didn't listen. And now we gotta break up, because I cheated on you, and I don't deserve to stay with you no more. *I'm sorry, baby*. I'll always love you."

"No," Trish pleaded. "*We don't have to break up! I know it wasn't your fault.*"

In the midst of this emotional exchange, Rodney couldn't help but smile at that. He felt like a salesman watching a loser sign on the dotted line for an obvious clunker.

Ca-ching!

"But I don't deserve you," Rodney said. "We can't stay together after what happened."

"*Yes we can*," Trish wailed. "You not still talking to her, are you?"

"*I don't even know her name!*" Rodney cried. It never hurt to mix a little truth in with a tall tale.

"Then we don't have to break up," Trish reasoned. "If you still wanna be with me, why do we have to break up, Rodney?"

"Because she burned me!" Rodney howled. "I had to go to the doctor today. He say I got burned, and I know I gave it to you, too. *Oh my God, why they do me like that?!* They knew I didn't wanna be with that ugly girl! I love you so much, Trish. I'm sorry, but we can't be together no more – not after what I did to you."

"Stop saying that!" Trish cried. "It's not your fault, Rodney. I know you didn't mean to do nothing. I can go to the doctor when I leave here. My sister had that before. All they did was give her some pills. Why you keep trying to leave me? *I don't wanna break up. I love you!"*

Rodney's heart swelled with glee. "For real, Trish? You mean it? You wanna stay with me?"

"Yes!" Trish gushed. *"I love you, Rodney.* I'll always love you."

"But after what I did..."

"It don't matter. I still love you."

"I'ma make it right," Rodney promised. "I'ma treat you so good, from here on out. I'll *never* do you wrong again. I'm not even going to the club with James no more. I'ma stay home with you every night."

"It's okay," Trish said. "You can still have fun with your friends, Rodney. Just don't get that drunk, baby. She coulda gave you AIDS or something."

Why is everybody so worried about AIDS? Rodney wondered. But that didn't matter. The important thing was he was still the best Mack Daddy of all time. He had to throw his good friend under the bus to get out of this one, but the hell with James. Trish already hated him for *supposedly* giving a couple of girls Rodney's number a few months ago. Rodney had to curse them out when they called in the middle of the night, while he was in bed with his real woman.

"Alright, baby, I'ma let you get back to your school work," Rodney said. "Please stop crying. I don't like to hear you like that."

"I am," Trish said. "I feel better now."

"I'm still gon' make it up to you," Rodney promised. "I'ma get you something real special."

"Okay," Trish said. "I love you."

"I love you, too," Rodney said and he ended the call.

He cleaned up his mangled onion and went to the living room to lounge on the couch for a couple of hours before he was due at work. He called his friend James before he got too comfortable.

"Hello?"

"Say, nigga, I told Trish you hooked me up with that skeezer last Saturday."

"What? Why you tell her that?"

"That bitch burnt me," Rodney said.

"Word?"

"Yeah. I had to go to the clinic today to get some penicillin – or whatever this new shit is they giving out. I know I burnt Trish, so I had to tell her to go get herself checked."

"Why you tell her *I* hooked you up with that ho?" James wondered. "I'm the one who told you that bitch was nasty."

"'Cause I had to," Rodney said.

"Trish already hate me," James complained. "I'm sick of her rolling her eyes at me for some shit I didn't do."

"Nigga, you be telling yo girl you with me sometimes when you ain't."

"I tell her I'm with you," James agreed. "But I never told her you hooked me up with some girl or gave my number to somebody. You be taking shit too far."

"Alright, my bad," Rodney said.

"Y'all still together?" James asked. "She didn't break up with you?"

"Nigga, she begged *me* not to break up with *her*," Rodney bragged.

"You go hard," James said with a chuckle. Then, "Who else you gave it to?"

"Gave what?"

"Your *gonorrhea*, nigga. Who else you fucked since Saturday?"

"Nobody," Rodney said. Then, "This bitch named Eva."

"You gon' call her, too?" James wondered.

"Nope," Rodney said. "That bitch married, so if she come at me with some shit, I'ma tell her she probably got it from her husband."

"You wild," James said. "I'll holler at you later, my dude."
"Alright," Rodney said. "Holler."

≈≈≈≈≈≈≈

When he got to work that afternoon, Rodney was perturbed but not surprised when Eva's whole demeanor changed the moment she saw him.

"Come to my office!" she snapped, her eyes low and menacing.

All of his coworkers in the area gave Rodney an *Ooh, you in trouble*, look. But he sauntered to Eva's office with his usual pimp stroll, showing that he wasn't worried at all.

Inside her office, Eva closed the door and locked it. She backed Rodney into a wall before he could sit down.

"Why my husband got gonorrhea?"

She was standing so close, Rodney could smell coffee on her breath. He used both hands to push her away.

"Get off me!"

Eva stumbled back and came at him again with even more ferocity.

"Boy, don't push me!"

"Then get off me," Rodney said. He had to turn his head to the side to avoid inhaling her funky breath. "Get away from me, Eva! Damn!"

His supervisor took a respectable step back. Rodney noticed her fists were balled.

"*You gave me gonorrhea*," she accused.

"No, I didn't."

"Yes you did!" Eva snarled. "I haven't been with nobody but you and my husband."

"Then you coulda got it from him."

"I got it from *you*, Rodney. And you know it!"

"Whatever," he said. "Get away from me, man."

Eva stood her ground. "You think this a joke?" Her eyes were wide and wild. "I been arguing with my husband all day. We got in a fight because of you!"

Rodney studied her more closely. It was clear that her fight was both verbal and physical. Eva wore enough makeup to

214

cover her slightly blackened eye, but Rodney saw that it was a little swollen. For his girlfriend, Rodney did everything he could to make things right. But for Eva, there was no such compassion.

"All he gotta do is take some pills," he said. "You can get some from the ER right now."

Eva couldn't believe or stomach his nonchalance.

"You weren't even gonna tell me, were you?"

"Tell you *what*?" Rodney said. "I don't know what you talking about. Move. I'm going to work."

He reached to unlock the door. Eva grabbed his arm. Rodney jerked away from her and said, "You better leave me alone!"

"*I can't stand you*," Eva growled. By the look in her eyes, there was no doubt she meant it. "You ain't going to work today. You finna get fired."

"Fired? Who gon' fire me? I know not you."

"I'm your supervisor," Eva reminded.

"Fire me for what?" Rodney said.

"You don't do shit around here," Eva said. "And you stealing. I got plenty to fire you for."

"Alright, fire me then," Rodney dared her. "Let's go to Human Resources right now. You tell them your story, and I'll tell them mine. *Both* of us gon' get fired today."

"I didn't do nothing," Eva said.

"Oh, you didn't? You been sexually harassing me since I been here," Rodney said. "As a matter of fact, I'ma sue this whole hospital, if you fire me."

"Whatever. You can't sue nobody."

"How many times you suck my dick up here?" Rodney said. "How many times you grab on my dick?"

"You can't prove nothing," Eva said. But her eyes darted wildly. She lost fifty percent of her resolve.

"You wanna see what I can prove?" Rodney asked. "Let's go to Human Resources. I'll show you."

Eva was so angry, her whole body trembled. "I'ma get a divorce because of you."

"So?" Rodney said. "That ain't my fault. You shouldn't have been cheating on your husband."

"I'ma *kill* you," Eva stated. She didn't mean to. The threat came out before her infuriated brain could stop it.

"Go ahead," Rodney said. "Keep talking shit. I can't wait 'til we get upstairs. I'm telling them *everything*. I don't care if I gotta tell on myself too, so long as yo ass ain't got no job, either. You ain't gon' have no job *or* no husband."

Eva looked like a rabid pit bull, but Rodney knew she'd been defanged.

"So we going upstairs, or can I go to work?" he asked.

"Get the fuck outta my office," Eva breathed.

"Cool," Rodney said. He unlocked the door and threw one more jab at her on his way out. "Bye, bitch."

≈ ≈ ≈ ≈ ≈ ≈

News traveled fast at the hospital.

Rodney didn't tell anyone he was burning, but Eva confided in one of her friends in the department. Eva's friend couldn't hold the secret for more than an hour. And although each person she spread the rumor to promised not to tell anyone else, the story reached the oncology floor in the Jackson Building. Certified Nursing Assistant Amy Winters called Rodney four times before he returned her call an hour later.

"What?"

"Where are you?" Amy asked.

"I'm here at work," Rodney said. "Why?"

"I need to talk to you."

"We talking right now," Rodney said.

"I need to talk to you *in person*."

"I'm busy," Rodney said. Surprisingly, he was telling the truth this time. With his job on the line, Rodney knew he had to put aside his slacker ways until things settled down. Eva was sure to use the smallest infraction as cause to terminate him.

"*Please*," Amy said. "Tell me where you are, so I can come meet you."

"Nope. I gotta go."

Before he could hang up, Amy asked, "Do you got gonorrhea?"

"Naw."

"People are saying you and your supervisor got gonorrhea," Amy said. "I just wanted to know if I should get checked out, too."

"You can get checked out whenever you want," Rodney said. "What that got to do with me?"

"I wanna know how long you had it," Amy said. "Did you have it last Wednesday, when we did something?"

"If you wanna get checked out, then go get checked out," Rodney repeated. "I ain't got shit to do with that."

"Why you acting like this?" Amy cried. "I didn't do nothing to you."

"'Cause motherfuckers up here starting shit," Rodney grumbled. "How would you like it if people was talking noise about you?"

"They *are* talking about me," Amy said. "How you think I found out? Somebody told me to go get checked."

"Then get checked, bitch! *Damn.* Bye!"

Rodney disconnected and rolled his eyes at a hospital volunteer who was staring at him throughout the phone call.

"The hell you looking at?" Rodney snapped before he walked away angrily.

The volunteer was in her late sixties and a little mentally defective. If she wasn't so shocked, she would've told Rodney the same thing she told everyone else who walked by her station: *Have a nice day, Sir (or Ma'am).*

≈ ≈ ≈ ≈ ≈ ≈ ≈

Amy left the hospital fifteen minutes after her talk with Rodney. Her charge nurse didn't want her to leave early, but Amy was crying, complaining that she didn't feel good, and no one wants to argue with a crybaby.

Amy could've gone to the ER downstairs for her checkup, but there would be no confidentiality there. All of the employees at Jackson Memorial were forbidden to open someone's chart out of pure curiosity, but it was impossible to fully enforce that rule. Anyone with computer access could see all of Amy's medical information with the click of a button.

217

Amy went to the county hospital instead, and she had to wait two hours to see a doctor. After her diagnosis, Amy stayed at the hospital for forty more minutes talking to a grief counselor. Despite the encouragement from the counselor, Amy thought about committing suicide when she got home. Before she did that, Amy was caring enough to call Jackson Memorial and warn Rodney's other lover/victim.

Amy was crying so hard, Eva couldn't make out much of what she was saying. But Eva did pick up the most important phrases, like *"Emergency Room" "No gonorrhea" "Rapid HIV test" "Results in thirty minutes" "**Positive**" "I'm HIV Positive"*

When she hung up the phone, Eva had to leave work early, too. She didn't feel good at all. She didn't want to take a Rapid HIV test like Amy did, but Eva knew it would be irresponsible for her not to do so. Sleeping with Rodney in the first place was irresponsible, but carrying on with her life without knowing how badly he hurt her would be a whole new level of idiocy.

Eva wasn't the brightest apple on the tree, but she wasn't a dummy, either.

CHAPTER NINETEEN
THE SET UP

A few hours after Eva left the hospital with fears about what diseases might be festering inside her, housekeeper Raquel Rivera received a text message from a perverted policeman named Damien Glover. Raquel had been waiting for the text. She called her supervisor and gave her the info about when and where Damien wanted to meet.

"Hello?" Brenda was at work, but she knew today was the big day. She already made plans to leave early.

"He just sent the text," Raquel told her. "It says 'Economy Inn, 8502 E. Lancaster, Room 18, 10:30.'"

Brenda grinned devilishly as she jotted the information on a sticky note. She was a little nervous about her role in Damien's downfall, but mostly she was excited. This was something she'd been trying to put together for over a year. Brenda checked the clock mounted on the wall in her office. It was a quarter 'til nine.

"You got it?" Raquel asked.

"Yeah," Brenda said. "I got it."

"What are you gonna do?" Raquel said.

"We already talked about this," Brenda replied. "I'm just gonna take some pictures."

"Are you still gonna throw a brick in the window?" Raquel wondered.

"I'll do whatever I got to do to get y'all out of that room," Brenda said. "I won't let nothing happen to you. Don't worry."

"But I was wondering, what if I'm over by the window?" Raquel said. "What if I get hit, or cut or something?"

Brenda rolled her eyes. "Well don't be by the window, Raquel. You know it's gon' be a brick coming through there." That sounded like common sense.

"I know," Raquel said. "But what if he has me cleaning over there, by the window? If I tell him I don't wanna clean over there, and then y'all bust the window, he'll know I knew something about it."

"You thinking way too hard," Brenda said. "Ain't nothing gon' happen to you, girl. I promise."

"But, but you won't even be there," Raquel said. "You said you was gonna drive off after you took the pictures. You gonna leave me there with him. What if he does something to me?"

Brenda sighed in frustration. She didn't have time for this. She had less than two hours to get everything in place.

"Raquel, what do you think he's gonna do? They got lights all over that motel – and cameras, too. Damien will be wearing his uniform, and it's liable to be some more people that come outside when we bust the glass. I told you: Damien gon' have too much to worry about than little, old you. Even if he do think you got something to do with it, he can't do nothing about it. Damien ain't no street nigga, Raquel. He a *police*. He got an image to protect."

"But what if–"

"Child, I gotta go," Brenda said. "I gotta get everything ready. I ain't gon' be there on time, if you don't let me get off this phone."

Raquel made a noise that was somewhere between a wail and a moan. "I'm scared," she said.

"You'll be fine," Brenda assured her. "You gotta trust me, Raquel. I'm not gon' let nothing happen to you."

"Alright," Raquel said with a heavy sigh.

"Okay, bye." Brenda hung up before her bait could try to back out altogether.

Brenda leaned back in her chair, brainstorming. She knew Raquel was right about everything she said. There was a good chance Damien would vent his frustration after Brenda sped away. Raquel would be the only one there for him to vent on. Brenda contemplated whether it was right to leave her accomplice out in the cold like that.

Bitch shouldn't have tried to scam me for that overtime, Brenda decided, totally forgetting that she was the one who brought up the overtime as payment in the first place.

Brenda dug her cellphone from her purse and called her good-for-nothing brother Roscoe. Roscoe got out of prison seven months ago, after serving a year and a half for drug possession. Brenda wished she could say her brother got caught *dealing*, but everyone knew Roscoe was smoking rather than selling crack.

Roscoe said he got clean while he was locked up, but it was hard to believe anything that came out of his mouth. At 42 years of age, Roscoe had spent more than half of his life in jail or prison. In truth, Brenda couldn't stand her brother. Roscoe only called when he wanted something from her. The only good thing about having a crackhead in the family was he was always willing to help out with something illicit.

Roscoe was currently living with their sister Roshanda. She was still not happy about taking him in after his latest parole.

Roshanda answered the phone with a grunt. "Yeah?"

"Hey," Brenda said. "Roscoe over there?"

"Naw," Roshanda said.

"Where he at?"

"Hell if I know."

"Dang."

"Why, what's up?"

"I told him I needed him to do something for me tonight."

"What?" Roshanda asked.

"Girl, quit being nosey," Brenda told her.

"I think he went to the corner store," Roshanda said. "You supposed to be picking him up?"

"Yeah."

"You need to keep him over there with you," Roshanda said.

"It's your turn," Brenda reminded.

"I don't trust him," Roshanda confided. "I didn't know it was gon' be like this. I'm scared to leave him here when I go to work."

"He stole something?"

"I know he has," Roshanda said. "I just can't prove it yet."

Brenda laughed. "Tell him to call me when he get in. I gotta go home and change, and then I'm coming over there."

"What are y'all gonna do?" Roshanda asked again. "Can I help?"

"You don't want none of this," Brenda told her. "It's dirty."

"Y'all gon' get in trouble?"

"*I'm* not," Brenda said. "Roscoe won't neither, if he do what I tell him. If he mess up, that's on him."

"You gon' send him back to the pen?"

"That's on him," Brenda said again. "If he get caught, I guess he will go back."

"You dirty," Roshanda said, but Brenda could tell she was smiling. "I kinda hope he *do* go back," Roshanda said. "Might as well get it over with, so I can have my house back."

"That's your brother," Brenda said with a chuckle. "How you gonna call *me* dirty and then say some mess like that."

"*Half*-brother," Roshanda corrected. "We ain't got the same daddy."

≈≈≈≈≈≈≈

Roscoe called Brenda back twenty minutes later. She was on her way home from the hospital.

"Hello?"

"Hey," Roscoe said. "You called?"

"Yeah. Where you been?" Brenda asked. "I told you tonight was the night."

"Just went to get me some wine," Roscoe said. "I'm good."

"You don't wanna stay sober for this?" Brenda asked.

"You ain't even told me what's going on," Roscoe said. "How I know if I need to be sober or not?"

"It's a set up," Brenda said. "I'm trying to catch a dude cheating."

"What I got to do?"

"I'ma take you to a motel where dude is getting it on with a girl I know. I wanna get some pictures of him at the motel."

"How you gon' get pictures, if he in the room?"

"That's what I need you for," Brenda said. "I need you to get him out the room."

"How I'm supposed to do that?"

"You gon' throw a brick in the window."

"In the motel window?"

"Yeah."

"And then what?"

"And then you get back in the car with me, I take some pictures when dude comes out of the room, and then we drive off."

"Why you can't bust the window yourself?" Roscoe wondered. "I can take the pictures."

Because I'm not a stupid crackhead, Brenda thought. "Because the man I'm trying to set up knows me," she said. "He works at Jackson."

"Motels got cameras everywhere," Roscoe said. "Busting a window, when I know it's somebody in there... I can get some time for that."

"That's why I'm paying you," Brenda said. "Make it worth your while."

"How much?"

"Twenty dollars."

"*Hell naw!* I ain't busting no motel window for twenty funky dollars."

"Alright, forty."

"Nope. A hundred."

"You done bust your head!"

"Forget it then."

"Roscoe, you ain't seen a hundred dollars in one place your whole life! What make you think I'ma give you a hundred dollars for this?"

"Do it yourself then."

"Alright, whatever, boy. Bye!"

Brenda disconnected and grumbled to herself the rest of the way home. For that price, she *would* do it herself. But Brenda knew Roscoe was already salivating; thinking about the crack he could buy with her money. She wasn't surprised when her cellphone rang again, just as she pulled into her driveway.

"*What?*" she snapped.

"Alright, eighty," Roscoe said.

"*Fifty fucking dollars, Roscoe!* That's all I'm paying. I ain't playing with you."

"Alright, fifty," he said.

"I'll be there in about forty minutes," Brenda said. "You better be ready!"

≈ ≈ ≈ ≈ ≈ ≈ ≈

At the same moment Brenda's brother agreed to help out with her boneheaded scheme, critical care nurse Cynthia Pullman was three hours into what she would later describe as her *worst day at work ever.*

Cynthia was in a foul mood before she got to the hospital because her boyfriend had ceased all communication more than twenty four hours ago – and this was at a time when Cynthia needed Ruben the most.

The lunch with her sister and her best friend yesterday didn't go as Cynthia anticipated. She didn't think they'd accept Ruben with open arms, but she didn't think they'd be so disapproving either. Ruben's marital status didn't get nearly as much condemnation as his skin color.

Cynthia needed Ruben to come to her yesterday like he said he would. She needed him to hold her and tell her everything was okay: Even if the whole world was against their union, they could take on the world together. But Ruben didn't call or stop by yesterday. He didn't try to contact her today, either.

This morning Cynthia was so heartbroken, she thought about skipping work. But she knew the hospital was the one place she could get some information about her shifty lover. The first thing she asked when she got to work was whether Ruben had come in today. Cynthia was crushed when the dayshift charge told her, "Yeah. He just left, about an hour ago."

That set off another whirlwind of turmoil in Cynthia's mind and her heart, but it was too late to go back home. She decided that if she didn't hear from Ruben tonight, she would call him in the morning before she left the hospital – the hell with what his wife had to say about it.

≈≈≈≈≈≈≈

The unit was fully staffed that night. Cynthia was shocked when an extra nurse appeared at ten o'clock, virtually out of thin air. Cynthia was stunned more by Sandra's appearance than the fact that she actually came to work.

"Oh my God, Sandra. Are you alright?"

"Yeah, I'm fine," Sandra said. But anyone with two eyes could see that was not the case.

Sandra was thin the last time Cynthia saw her. Now she was borderline skeletal. Her cheeks were sunken. Her eye sockets were dark and starting to sink in. Sandra's clothes were ill-fitting and wrinkled. And Cynthia noticed a few old scars on her face. Sandra was dressed in the proper scrub attire, but she had to be out of her mind if she thought Cynthia was going to put a couple of lives in her hands tonight.

"Come to my office," Cynthia said, so she wouldn't have to embarrass Sandra any more than she was already embarrassing herself.

When they got to the quiet room, Sandra sat down nervously. Cynthia took a seat across from her. Cynthia tried to be compassionate, but she had a look on her face like she was watching a monkey taste its own stool. She didn't know how to be politically correct at a time like this.

"Girl, what the hell is going on with you?"

"I'm sick," Sandra said. She couldn't look Cynthia in the eyes. "I got cancer."

"You're supposed to have some paperwork," Cynthia said. "Did you bring it?"

Sandra shook her head. "I forgot it at home. I'll bring it tomorrow."

Cynthia shook her head as well. "Sandra, I don't think I can let you work without seeing that paperwork. We already covered for you tonight anyway. I don't need any more nurses."

"I didn't call-in today," Sandra said.

"You didn't call in the last two times you were scheduled to work," Cynthia said. "But you didn't show up. We figured you weren't going to show up tonight, either. We have no idea when you're coming to work, so we took you off the schedule."

"That's not right," Sandra said, though she already suspected as much. She didn't really want to work tonight anyway. She just needed to be there long enough to snatch a few vials from the Pyxis drug station at the front of the unit. Sandra knew she would get fired and lose her nursing license if she accessed those drugs illegally, but that didn't matter anymore.

Ever since she sobered up and realized how low she sank in ManMan's drug house the other day, Sandra decided death was a better alternative to her current lifestyle. Her only desire at that point was to die high. Sandra even prostituted herself on the streets yesterday, but she survived the massive amount of heroin she injected. Later she hit the streets again for more money, but Sandra got arrested. She spent the last twenty hours in the Overbrook Meadows jail.

Life could never go back to normal now because, once convicted, Sandra's record would forever show her to be a prostitute. ManMan slapped her in the face this afternoon when she went to him begging for just *one more* freebie. Even his lesbian doorman wasn't interested anymore.

Sandra knew that she could get morphine from the Pyxis machine at work if they were stupid enough to let her clock-in tonight. A lethal dose of morphine would give her a heroin-like high before it put her to sleep and then stopped her heartbeats. The Pyxis would keep track of everything she took out, but Sandra hoped to be deceased by the time they realized what she'd done.

The only question was would she have an opportunity to steal the morphine? From the looks of it, probably not.

"I can't let you work tonight," Cynthia told her. "I'll be honest with you, Sandra; you look like you might be on drugs."

"You can't send me home just 'cause I got cancer," Sandra said. She was never this irrational before. Wandering through a dangerous wasteland will change a person.

Cynthia narrowed her eyes. It was within her authority to make Sandra leave, but if this cancer story turned out to be true, Sandra's complaint might be justified. Cynthia was pretty sure they took Sandra off the schedule without notifying her.

"Hold on," she said.

Cynthia left the office and went to the nursing station, so she could make a phone call without Sandra eavesdropping. She knew she should call their manager for something like this, but Cynthia was too upset to talk to Ruben. The first thing she would say to him was *What the hell is going on? Why haven't you called me?!* Rather than make a fool of herself, Cynthia called the nursing supervisor instead.

"Hello?"

"Hi, Andrew. This is Cynthia in Critical Care/Neuro."

"Hey, what's going on?"

"I got an employee up here who I don't know what to do with. We took her off the schedule because she's been calling-in a lot, and we couldn't get in contact with her. But she showed up tonight wanting to work. She says she has cancer, but she hasn't brought any paperwork yet. I don't think we're supposed to let her work until she brings that paperwork."

"Have you called your manager?"

Cynthia grimaced. "I, um... I tried, but I couldn't get a hold of him."

"You need to try again," Andrew said. "If she's not supposed to work, that's your manager's decision."

"I think she's on drugs," Cynthia said. "I was wondering if you could send her down to the ER for a drug test."

"Why do you think she's on drugs?"

"Because of the way she's been calling-in," Cynthia said. "And she's three hours late tonight. She has a few bruises on her face. She's really skinny... You can look at her and tell she's on drugs."

"I thought you said she had cancer."

"That's what *she* says."

"I'll come up there," Andrew said, "but I got another problem I have to deal with first. Tell her to sit tight until I get there. In the meantime, you need to keep trying to get your manager on the phone."

"Okay," Cynthia said. "I will."

She hung up and went back to the office. Sandra looked up at her with the most desperate expression imaginable. Cynthia knew for a fact she was on drugs. She didn't want to be the one to cost Sandra her nursing license, but Cynthia had a job to do. And from the looks of it, Sandra already ruined her own life.

"The supervisor's coming up here to talk to you," Cynthia said. "You can tell him why you think you should work tonight."

"How long is it gonna be?" Sandra asked.

"Shouldn't be that long," Cynthia said. "Just sit tight."

"I can–"

"*Cynthia!*"

Their conversation was cut short by a shout, which was followed by bright white and blue lights flashing all over the unit. Cynthia stuck her head out of the office and saw half of the nurses on the floor converging on one of the patients' rooms.

"*Two's not breathing!*" one of the nurses told her. "*It's a code!*"

Cynthia rushed to help the ailing patient just as the hospital operator made the dark announcement on the overhead paging system.

"CODE BLUE... CRITCAL CARE/NEURO... FOURTH FLOOR... CODE BLUE... CRITICAL CARE/NEURO... FOURTH FLOOR..."

Sandra rose from her seat and approached the office door. She saw the chaos, and she knew that for the next twenty minutes or so everyone on the floor would be busy either observing or trying to help the dying patient. Surely this was a sign from God.

Sandra left the office and headed straight for the Pyxis station, like she'd done many times in the past. She entered her employee ID and waited. The machine did not reject her. This too was a sign that this was how things were meant to be.

CHAPTER TWENTY
ROBOCOP

Brenda and her crackhead brother Roscoe pulled into the parking lot of the Economy Inn on Lancaster at 10:25 pm. Before finding a nice hiding spot, Brenda circled the lot, looking for room 18 and also checking to make sure she knew the escape routes.

The motel wasn't that large, and it was only one story. The parking lot was horseshoe-shaped with one entrance and one exit, both on Lancaster. The manager's office was set up like a toll booth, so tenants could pay on their way in without exiting their vehicle. The manager was at the window when Brenda rolled by, but he didn't stop her or question why she wasn't paying for a room. Nearly every couple who visited this locale came in separate vehicles, so Brenda hadn't done anything out of the norm.

Rather than one large hotel-style building, all of the rooms at the Economy Inn were freestanding, like a row of tiny houses. Brenda noticed there was a brand new Camaro parked in front of room 18. Right away she knew this was Damien's car. The Camaro was fiery red, the perfect blend of beauty and power. This was the kind of ride that would stroke Damien's massive ego and also draw plenty of attention from the opposite sex.

"Damn," Brenda said. "I wanted to beat him here." She turned and glared at her brother who was slumped down in his seat. "You made me late, fool."

"Whatever. I was ready when you got there."

"What are you doing?" Brenda asked as she backed into her desired parking spot. She had to park directly behind the manager's office to get a good view of room 18. Because the property was so small, Brenda came to a stop less than twenty-five yards away from Damien's Camaro. That was both a good and a bad thing.

"Nothing," Roscoe said, but he was crouched so low, he could barely see out of the passenger window.

"Why you trying to hide?" Brenda asked him.

She put her car in park but left it idling. She checked the time and then scanned the property again. There were approximately 30 rooms at the Economy Inn. Most of them were occupied. There were a lot of cars in the parking lot, but no one was in the vehicles or walking around at that moment.

"You see somebody you know?" Brenda asked her squirrelly brother.

"Uh uhn," Roscoe said and he sat up a little.

Roscoe was 42 years old with fair skin like a walnut shell. Brenda used to think he was handsome, *way* back in their school days. A hard life of drug abuse and prison stints changed all of that. Roscoe was missing both of his bunny rabbit teeth and a couple more choppers from the bottom row. His cheeks were covered with stubble, but Roscoe was never able to grow a proper beard. The result was a cluster of badly spaced hairs on his face and upper lip that were short and curly.

Roscoe's left eye didn't open fully (that started a decade ago, but Brenda never inquired about the cause), and both of his eyes had a red tint to them, even when he was stone-cold sober. The only positives Brenda could note was Roscoe kept his hair shaved low, and (tonight at least) he didn't stink. His breath reeked of Thunderbird, but that was a lot better than the funk that usually jumped off his tongue.

"It's the manger," Roscoe said, checking his side-view mirror. "He told me not to come here no more."

Brenda gave him a look that said, *I'm not surprised by that, but you still disappoint me, sir.*

"I didn't do nothing," Roscoe said. "They said I was loitering."

"When was this?" Brenda asked.

"A couple of months ago," Roscoe said. "I was in that room over there..." He nodded towards room 26. "I got high, and they said I was zoned-out, walking around scaring people. I don't remember it though."

There was so much to say about what Roscoe just told her, but Brenda didn't comment. Roscoe once broke his leg while running from the police. When Brenda inquired about that incident, Roscoe told her he jumped off a two story building while running from the police. When Brenda asked why he was on a two story building, Roscoe said he liked to go up there because the pigeons looked after him while he slept because he was their friend.

That was the day Brenda stopped asking about her brother's strange tales from the hood.

"He can't see you now," she told him. "Sit up. You look suspicious."

Roscoe reluctantly straightened himself in the seat. He looked around nervously. "They got cameras," he said. "They be watching all the time. He'll see me, if I get out the car."

Brenda shook her head. Leave it to Roscoe to throw a monkey wrench in the works at the last minute. If throwing a brick at a motel window wasn't seriously illegal, she would do the whole thing by herself. But Brenda couldn't risk an arrest that might cost her her job at Jackson Memorial.

"You—"

Brenda's phone rang.

"Hold on," she told Roscoe while she answered. "Hello?"

"It's me," Raquel said.

"Hey. You here yet?"

"I'm pulling in now."

Brenda turned and she saw the bright headlights of a Ford Festiva approaching. When the car passed, Brenda recognized Raquel behind the steering wheel. "I see you," she said. "You just passed us. Here," Brenda said to her brother. She gave him her digital camera and told him, "That's her. Take some pictures when she get out the car."

"Who's with you?" Raquel asked. "Where you at?"

"We parked behind the office," Brenda said.

"How I turn this on?" Roscoe asked.

"Boy, push the goddamned button," Brenda told him. "Shit. *Hurry up.*"

Roscoe fumbled with the camera. He stole and sold quite a few electronics in his lifetime, but he never kept one long enough to familiarize himself with it. "What button?"

"*This one!*" Brenda snapped. She reached into her brother's lap and turned the camera on.

"Who's with you?" Raquel asked again.

"It's my brother," Brenda said. "But he don't know how to work this camera. I gotta get off the phone, so I can take the pictures."

"I got it," Roscoe said.

"Shut up, boy," Brenda told him.

"I'm scared," Raquel said as she pulled to a stop next to Damien's Camaro. "Are y'all gonna get me out of here in time?"

"We will," Brenda assured her, though she was almost certain they would not. She still had to talk Roscoe into getting out of the car in full view of the motel's cameras. And she knew he'd try to haggle over his payment again. All told, it might take up to ten minutes before the crackhead summoned the courage to throw a brick through the window of room 18. Raquel might have a dick in her mouth by then. But that wasn't Brenda's fault.

"Everything will be fine," Brenda promised her. "When you get in there, just give us about two minutes, and that window will be broke."

"What if he don't come outside?" Raquel wondered.

"He will," Brenda said. "Who's gonna stay in a room when somebody's throwing bricks through the window? What you think he's gon' do, crawl under the bed and hide?"

"No, but what if–"

"Girl, it's too late for all of that now," Brenda said. Beads of sweat blossomed on her forehead. She couldn't believe she was this close to ruining Damien's life. "Everything's gonna be fine. Now let me get off this phone, so I can take the pictures."

"Alright," Raquel said with a sigh. "But if you don't get me outta there..."

Brenda waited to see what her punishment would be. She grinned when Raquel couldn't complete the sentence. *Yeah, that's right, bitch*, Brenda thought. *You got nothing. Now shut the hell up, and go suck that dick!*

"You got to," Raquel pleaded. "Please get me out of there."

"*I am*," Brenda said. "Trust me. Now gone on and do your part, and let me do mine. This will all be over in a few short minutes."

"Alright," Raquel said. "I'm getting out of the car now."

"Okay, bye," Brenda said. She disconnected and snatched her camera from Roscoe's grubby hands.

"Wait, I figured it out," he protested.

"I already told you *I'm* taking the pictures," Brenda said. She pointed the camera at Damien's car, zoomed in, and got a couple of shots of the Camaro parked in front of room 18. She zoomed out and got a few shots of Damien and Raquel's cars together. Brenda took five more pictures when Raquel exited her vehicle. The housekeeper was so nervous, the first thing she did was look back to see if she could spot Brenda's car. Normally that was a big no-no, but Brenda needed a good shot of Raquel's face.

"Perfect," she whispered. She took six more pictures as Raquel entered the motel room.

"I still think *I* should take the pictures," Roscoe said when his sister lowered the camera.

Brenda's eyes narrowed, but she was grinning. "Why you wait 'til the last minute to start all this arguing?" she asked.

"'Cause I didn't know you was talking about the Economy Inn," Roscoe said. "If you woulda told me, I woulda told you I can't go in there. If they see me, they'll call the police."

"Roscoe," Brenda reasoned, "no matter what motel we go to, they'll call the police if they see you bust out a window."

"Yeah, but the manager over here will call the police as soon as I get out the car," Roscoe said. "If he see me, I'm done."

"It's dark out here, Roscoe," Brenda said. "The only camera that can see your face is the one they had in the office. The rest of them are way up high. They won't see nothing but a skinny black man."

"You just saying that 'cause you not the one who got to do it," Roscoe complained. "You ain't the one that's going to jail."

"That's why I'm paying you," Brenda said. "I never told you to do it out of the goodness of your heart."

"Fifty dollars ain't enough."

Brenda chuckled.

"What?" he said.

"I can read you like a book."

"It ain't enough," Roscoe repeated. "You know it ain't."

"Ain't nobody going to jail," Brenda said. "Quit making this sound harder than it really is. All you got to do is throw that brick in that window..." She pointed at the brick on floorboard between Roscoe's feet and then at room 18. "...then get back in the car," Brenda said. "You lucky to be getting fifty dollars for that."

"What if he chase me?" Roscoe asked.

"If you can't make it back to this car before he catch you, then you deserve to get caught," Brenda said. "He gon' have to pull up his pants and everything before he come outside."

"What if he chase *you*?" Roscoe said.

Brenda gave him a dumb look. "How he gon' chase a *car*?"

"What if he jump in his car and chase you?" Roscoe ventured. "You can't outrun that fucking Camaro..."

Brenda thought for a moment and realized she hadn't accounted for that. She was glad she brought a true criminal with her, but she didn't show it. "What you think we should do?"

"You gotta slash his tires first," Roscoe suggested, "so he can't chase you."

Brenda played the scene in her mind: Roscoe would throw the brick. Damien would open the door and see Roscoe fleeing the scene. Brenda would get a few pictures of Damien while Roscoe jumped in the passenger seat. Damien might try to chase Roscoe on foot, but he was more likely to assess the damage to his car first. That would give Brenda enough time to make her getaway.

Slashing Damien's tires was not only a good idea; it was a great idea. Brenda wondered why she didn't think of it first.

"That's good," she mused. "You got a knife?"

"Yeah." Roscoe pulled a jackknife from his pocket and opened the three-inch blade. It was cheap and made mostly of plastic, but it would get the job done.

"Alright," Brenda said. "Slash the tires before you throw the brick in the window."

Roscoe's eyes widened like he took a hit of crack. "Why *I* got to slash the tires? I thought you was gon' do it."

"I can't get out the car," Brenda said for the umpteenth time. "Damn, Roscoe, what it take to get that through your head? *You* gotta slash the tires and break the window, too."

"Uh uhn." He shook his head. "Not for no fifty–"

"I'll give you *sixty dollars*," Brenda said. "Now hurry up and do what you got to do. That man might be in there hurting my friend right now."

"That's her fault," Roscoe said. "Didn't nobody tell her to go in there. Gimme the money first."

"Nigga, you don't trust me?"

Roscoe shook his head. "Nope. Ain't no sense in me lying. Gimme my money *first*."

Brenda cursed him under her breath, but she snatched her purse from the backseat and found three twenties. Roscoe grinned like a jack-o-lantern when she gave him the money. He could already taste the crack he was going to smoke tonight. And he now had enough money to invite a crackhead female to his little party. Roscoe didn't like to share, but a female addict would work hard for her high. No doubt.

"Alright," Roscoe said. He stuffed the money in his pocket and pushed his door open. He exited the vehicle with a brick in one hand and his knife still open in the other. "Leave this door open," he told Brenda, and then he crept like a goblin towards his destiny.

Out in the night air, Roscoe had to fight a strong urge to drop the brick and take off running, leaving Brenda and her friend to deal with this mess on their own. Roscoe didn't care about burning his sister; he did that plenty of times in the past.

The only reason he didn't pull the crackhead move was because Roscoe knew he wasn't in the best of shape. Any prolonged physical exertion might give him a heart attack. What sense would it make to die with unspent crack money in his pocket? Roscoe decided it was better to go along with the plan and let Brenda drive him to safety.

Back in her car, Brenda wondered if she should've told Roscoe that Damien was a cop, and he was sure to be decked out in full policeman gear. She decided that leaving her brother in the dark was the right move. Every good commander knows that a soldier only needs enough information to complete the task at hand. Roscoe was already spooked enough.

≈ ≈ ≈ ≈ ≈ ≈ ≈

Inside room 18, Officer Damien Glover was having the time of his life.

But he was still cautious, always vigilant.

Damien chose the Economy Inn for tonight's tryst because the motel was located in the hood, and one thing you're certain of in the hood is *anonymity*. The motel's manager didn't care about Damien's uniform any more than he cared about the thirty or more dopefiends he rented rooms to every night. The junkies in the area were a little worried about Damien, but once they realized he wasn't there to arrest them, they tried to forget about him while they did their thing.

Everyone at the motel was there for something illicit. The Economy Inn constantly played host to drug deals, beat downs and even sexual assaults. Rarely were these crimes reported. It was enough to drive a good cop mad. But Damien was a bad cop, so he fit right in.

But even with his badge and uniform, Damien worried about being victimized at the motel. His main worry was his most prized possession; his 2013 Chevy Camaro. His car was easily the most expensive vehicle in the motel's parking lot. The candy apple paint job drew even more attention. Damien had his ride wired with the best alarm he could find, but the thieves in Overbrook Meadows were a skilled and resourceful bunch.

Damien knew they would try him one day, so he lounged on the motel bed with one ear facing the front window. Raquel was on her hands and knees scrubbing a stubborn jelly stain from the carpet. Damien leaned with his back on the bed's headboard. He watched Raquel's ass sway rhythmically.

Damien liked Raquel, but not as much as he liked Amina. For Amina, being submissive was second nature. It seemed like a stretch for Raquel. She complied with everything Damien told her to do, but Raquel appeared to do so grudgingly.

236

It was still a turn on.

Damien rubbed his growing erection while he watched her work. Tonight he wanted to break Raquel's will completely. He wanted to see her cry. He wanted her to cry while sucking his dick. He wanted to humiliate her so badly her head would immediately snap downwards the next time she saw Damien at the hospital. Her eyes would remain glued to the floor whenever he came around.

And when they hooked up a *third time*, Raquel's shame would overwhelm her. She would tremble when Damien undressed her. But her body would respond to him sexually. The conflicting emotions would drive her crazy. It would be—

Damien lost his train of thought. He sat up and turned towards the room's front window. He waited, listening intently. He looked back at Raquel and saw that she was no longer working on the stain. She was watching him.

"What's wron—"

"*Shhht!*" Damien held a finger up to silence her.

And then he heard it again. The sound was faint, but it doesn't take much to rouse maternal instincts, especially when Damien was already worried about something happening to his baby. What Damien heard was a *whoosh* sound. If he didn't know any better, he'd think someone was puncturing and letting the air out of his $200 tires.

Damien's eyes grew wide with disbelief and then dark with anger when he heard the third slice. He glared at Raquel. She finally wore the look of total fear that he'd been waiting for, but it was too late. Damien slipped off the bed and popped the button on his holster. Behind him Raquel gasped as he drew his handgun. Damien looked back at her and spoke softly.

"Don't move."

She didn't. Raquel's face was completely white, her hands frozen in the soapy carpet.

Damien moved quickly and quietly to the front door. He released the deadbolt slowly. He held his gun in his left hand; the barrel pointing towards the ceiling. He eased the door open with his right hand. He didn't have any expectations, but the last thing he thought he'd see was a filthy crackhead kneeling next to his beautiful ride. Three tires were already flattened. As Damien watched, Roscoe stabbed the last tire and worked the blade in the hole to make it bigger.

Damien's jaw dropped. The contents of his stomach flipped. He'd never seen anything so horribly *wrong*. Stealing was one thing, but a crackhead wantonly vandalizing his property was unheard of. It was unjustifiable, and there would be hell to pay. Without a doubt, this bastard would get the living shit stomped out of him.

Damien's breathing was rough as he stepped out of his motel room. His nostril's flared. His eyebrows bunched, creating a sneer that was two parts angry, one part evil. Damien trained his gun on the perp just as the crackhead looked up at him.

"Get the fuck away from my car!"

Roscoe's eyes grew as big as doorknobs. He stared at the policeman in amazement. He pulled his blade from the last tire and slowly raised his hands. He tried to tell the officer, *Please, don't shoot*, but he was too terrified to get the words out. All Damien heard was, "Pluh, puh, plea, pluh, pluh..."

"Drop the knife, asshole!"

Damien stepped closer to the junkie. He walked sideways, flanking him, checking out the damage to his car as well as the threat posed by the dopefiend. Roscoe dropped the knife and raised both of his arms as high as he could. This did little to calm Damien. His baby had four flats. It didn't make any sense. What had he done to deserve this? What was the point? How dare this two-bit, piece of shit motherfucker!

Damien's foot flew up, seemingly on its own accord. He kicked the dopefiend square on the chin and watched as his bottom row of teeth collided with the few still left up top. There wasn't enough room for all of them. Roscoe screamed as one of his cavity-plagued canines snapped. His bottom incisors dug into the newly exposed gum tissue, and his mouth rapidly filled with blood.

"Aaaah!"

Roscoe fell to his back and threw both hands over his mouth.

"Owww! Stop!" he begged.

Damien was just getting started.

"I said drop the knife!" he belted, even though the blade was a good three feet away from the writhing junkie. With his gun still trained on the perp's midsection, Damien drew his taser with his free hand. He aimed for the dopefiend's chest and pulled the trigger. Compressed air launched two probes from the weapon that easily dug into the junkie's flesh. A split second later 50,000 volts of electricity jumped from the gun to the victim. Roscoe began to jerk and jiggle like he was having a seizure.

"Ow! Uh, uh! Owww! Owww! Oww! Oww! Oww!"

"Drop the knife!" Damien yelled as he advanced on him. He kicked Roscoe in the ass and then kicked him in the balls when the perp rolled onto his back.

"Drop the knife!" Damien demanded, because that's what good cops do when they're kicking ass. He kicked again and again, in the ribs, the back of the head, the face. *"Drop the knife, motherfucker!"*

"Please! Stop, please! Oh, oh, oh!"

Inside her car, Brenda watched the scene in wide-eyed horror. She had her camera up and ready to take pictures, but she was so shocked when Damien walked out of his room, she hadn't taken one shot. And then the beating started. Brenda's heart thundered. She thought Damien was going to shoot Roscoe, but the beat down seemed much worse. Brenda flinched with each blow. Her car was filled with a low, whining moan that she didn't know was coming from her at first.

By the time Brenda got a hold of herself, Damien had tased Roscoe. The policeman continued to vent with hard, well-placed kicks to Roscoe's head and gut. Brenda felt bad for her brother. She wanted to rescue him, but Damien was like a demon in a police uniform. Brenda knew she had to get the hell away from there. The hell with Roscoe, and the hell with Raquel, too. Shit just got way too real.

Brenda dropped her camera, and it rolled to the floorboard. Her hands trembled as she gripped the steering wheel and put her car in DRIVE. Brenda's foot trembled, too. She stomped on the gas a moment before she realized she was in NEUTRAL. The sound of her engine was like a jet taking off in the parking lot, but she didn't move an inch. Damien looked in her direction. Brenda screamed and squirted a little urine in her panties.

"*Oh, no, no, no, no, no no...!*" she moaned.

She got her car in DRIVE and tried to hightail it out of there. Damien was coming for her. He dropped his taser and ran towards her car as Brenda bolted from the parking spot. She jerked the steering wheel to the left, heading for the only exit.

Brenda thought she'd have an easy route to safety, but Damien didn't give up so easily.

"*Stop, or I'll shoot!*"

Brenda checked her rearview mirror and was mortified to see the deranged policeman chasing her. Damien had his gun pointed at her car at first, but he lowered his arm and ran full out as she increased speed.

"*Oh, stop! Please! Leave me alone, leave me alone! Help me, Jesus! Help me! Help me, please!*"

Brenda thought this had to be a dream. She didn't know if Damien saw her face or not, and she was devastated to see that no matter how fast she went, he was still chasing her. In her rearview mirror, she saw him coming. Damien's face was stern and rigid. His arms and legs pumped rhythmically as he sprinted. Brenda thought he ran like the liquid metal cop from Terminator 2. No mortal could move like that. She thought Damien was Robocop.

Her eyes glued to the rearview mirror, Brenda didn't realize she was exiting the motel until she hit a hard dip on Lancaster Ave. The front end of her car slammed into the pavement hard enough to crack the axle.

WHOMP!

Brenda jerked the wheel to the right as hard as she could and barely avoided plowing into the street's median.

By the time she got her car and her nerves under control, Brenda was going 70 mph on the busy thoroughfare. The Economy Inn was a mile behind her. Her face was slick with sweat. There was smoke seeping from under the hood of her car, and she couldn't take a breath without nearly choking on it.

"*I'm sorry, Jesus,*" she panted. "*I'm so sorry, Jesus. Please forgive me. Please forgive me...*"

Brenda hadn't been to church in over a year. But if ever there was a time to get religified, this was it.

≈ ≈ ≈ ≈ ≈ ≈ ≈

Back at the motel, Damien was upset that he didn't get a good look at whoever was driving the crackhead's getaway car. But all was not lost. He sensed this ambush was motivated by revenge rather than theft, which meant Raquel had something to do with it.

The housekeeper was trying to sneak out of the motel room when Damien returned to his vehicle. It was too late. Her opportunity for escape had passed. Damien told her, "Don't move, bitch," as he knelt to retrieve his stun gun. Roscoe was still rolling on the asphalt, mumbling, crying and bleeding all over the place. Damien rolled him onto his stomach and planted a heavy knee in his spine as he handcuffed him.

Roscoe begged for help, so Damien stood and tased him again. The junkie's screams filled the night air. Damien seemed not to notice. He turned his attention to Raquel who was completely petrified. Ever since their first date, Raquel sensed this crazed policeman would one day kill her. She now knew that her fear was justified.

"You set me up, didn't you?" Damien asked as he approached her.

Raquel was a blubbering mess. Tears streamed down her face. She heard sirens in the distance. She knew those police were coming to help Damien – not her.

She nodded. *"I'm sorry. Please don't hurt me."*

"You gonna tell me everything you know, ain't you?" Damien asked as he re-holstered his pistol and his stun gun.

"Yes," Raquel said. *"Please don't hurt me."*

She backed up until she encountered the front end of her car. Damien followed her. He didn't stop walking until his bulletproof vest pressed against her. He looked down at Raquel like Satan himself, with the full moon glowing brightly behind him. Raquel dropped to her knees and begged for her life.

"I'll tell you everything. Just, please... Don't hurt me, Mr. Damien. Please, don't hurt me..."

Alone without vision or moonlight. The dark
Is overwhelming. I'm cowering. I'm floundering. I'm stark
Naked. This place is beyond freezing. My shivering
Bones are Morse code, quickening. I'm withering
Away. I'm decaying. I'm rotting. I'm rotten
I'm blinded by the signs. All warnings forgotten
Thick cotton fills my veins. Down my neck drips dark stains
From my ear leaks the liquefied remains of my brain
And I've gained no deep visions; only cell loss and fission
No keen insight. Division. There's pressure. There's tension
This calamity is passionately blameless. I'm tasteless
With each breath I taste death. I'm aimless. I'm wasted

CHAPTER TWENTY-ONE
RUBEN RESOLVED

It took nearly thirty minutes to stabilize the patient who stopped breathing on Cynthia's unit. The nursing supervisor had to come to the floor as well as the on-call neurologist. Code Blues sometimes ended tragically at the hospital, but in this case the patient had all of the support he needed. Cynthia was glad for that because, although it wouldn't have been her fault, she never wanted a patient to die on her watch.

With the crisis averted, the nursing supervisor had time to deal with Cynthia's other problem. Except her other problem was missing. Cynthia led the supervisor to her office, and she scratched her head in confusion when she saw Sandra's empty seat.

"She's not here."

"Where is she?" the supervisor asked.

"I, I don't know," Cynthia said. She backed out of the office and looked around. She and the supervisor walked around the unit. "She was there just a second ago," Cynthia told him.

The supervisor remained mute until they searched the whole floor and couldn't find Sandra. Andrew wasn't an unpleasant boss, but he was never known to have a lot of patience.

"What do you think happened to her?" he asked.

"Maybe she's in the bathroom," Cynthia guessed.

"Are y'all looking for Sandra?"

Cynthia and Andrew turned to face a new nurse named Shannon.

"Yes," Cynthia told him. "Have you seen her?"

"Yeah, I think she left," Shannon said.

"When?" Cynthia asked.

"During the code," Shannon said.

"Oh," Cynthia said. "I guess that problem solved itself," she told their supervisor.

"I can take one of her patients," Shannon offered, "if you need some help..."

"No, that's alright," Cynthia told him. "Sandra didn't have any patients."

Shannon frowned. "But, I saw her at the Pyxis, taking some meds..."

Cynthia's heart sank. Her jaw dropped as well.

"When?" their supervisor asked. "When did you see her at the Pyxis?"

"Right before she left," Shannon said. "About twenty minutes ago."

"Oh my God," Cynthia said.

"Check it," the supervisor told her. "We need to find out what she took."

The two of them walked to the Pyxis machine, and Cynthia requested an audit for Sandra's employee ID number. Her heart sank even further when the machine displayed the info.

Andrew read the screen aloud. "Morphine."

"I knew it," Cynthia said. "I told you she was on drugs."

"Call security," Andrew instructed. "If possible, we need to catch her before she leaves the hospital."

"I can't believe this," Cynthia said as she hurried to her office. Her heartbeats were hard and quick. This was almost as bad as a patient dying while she was in charge.

Andrew followed her. "Did you get in touch with Ruben yet?"

"No," Cynthia said. She took a seat behind her desk and reached for the phone.

"What's going on with him?" Andrew wondered. "Did you leave a message when you called earlier? Doesn't he have a pager?"

Cynthia's fingers were trembling. Her earlier lie had come back to haunt her. "I, I didn't call him yet."

"You said you called him before the code."

"I'm sorry," Cynthia said, looking down at her desk. "I didn't."

Andrew gave her a stern look of disapproval. "Well, are you going to call him now, or do I have to stand her and watch, to make sure it gets done?"

"I'm sorry," Cynthia said. "I'm calling him now..."

Contrary to his sarcastic comment, the nursing supervisor stood in the doorway anyway, to make sure Cynthia followed orders this time.

≈ ≈ ≈ ≈ ≈ ≈ ≈

The hospital security and the dispatch office worked together to track Sandra down. The Overbrook Meadows police also got involved at the supervisor's request. Sandra didn't clock-in when she entered the hospital, and she definitely didn't dispense medications to any of the patients on the unit.

The supervisor wanted to give Sandra the benefit of the doubt; maybe it was a crime of opportunity. But Cynthia thought Sandra came to the hospital specifically to steal the morphine. Either way, this was one of the worst things that had ever happened on the critical care unit. If the press got hold of the story, it would be a public relations problem for the whole hospital.

The dispatch office traced Sandra's steps from the moment she entered the building. There were cameras everywhere. The film was stored digitally, but looking through it was a daunting task. The hospital's security team searched for Sandra on foot. Dispatch notified them by radio each time they put another piece of the puzzle together. Cynthia had a radio, too. The conversations she picked up over the airwaves were alarming.

Dispatch announced, "We got her on camera forty-five at nine-fifty. She came in through the Meredith building..." Then, "She left her floor at 10:21 and got on the visitor elevators. She went all the way down to the basement..." Security responded, "We got three guys down there now. We're checking the bathrooms. There are a lot of exam rooms down there. It's gonna take awhile, if we have to check all of them."

Later dispatch declared, "Alright, scratch the basement. We got her exiting the Avery Building at 10:26." Finally security ended the search with, "We found her. She's in the Avery parking garage. Sixth floor. She's out of it. Needle still in her arm. We need some help over here. Call a code. I don't think she's breathing."

Cynthia, along with the nursing supervisor, two CNA's and two physicians, rushed to meet the security team in the parking garage. Cynthia didn't do much to help. She stood on the outskirts of the crowd as the doctors assessed the employee who was now a patient. Sandra was unresponsive. Her eye sockets were dark. She looked very, very small. The CNA's loaded her onto a stretcher, and the whole group rushed Sandra to the ER.

Cynthia watched all of this in wide-eyed wonder. It was heartbreaking, and it was bizarre. It was impossible for her to maintain objectivity. As a nurse, she witnessed countless tragedies at Jackson Memorial. She saw everything from still-born babies to homicide victims with severe head wounds. But Sandra wasn't a stranger. This was someone Cynthia worked with for years. She laughed with Sandra, stressed with her and even confided in her at times.

Like most people who never got high, Cynthia couldn't understand why someone would do this to themselves. Why would Sandra throw away her career and possibly her life over something so fleeting? Cynthia was too numb to cry. She knew the tears would come later, when she got home and had time to fully process everything that happened tonight.

≈ ≈ ≈ ≈ ≈ ≈ ≈

Ruben showed up when they got Sandra to the ER. He didn't have to come in tonight, but he was a good manager. He knew Cynthia couldn't run the floor efficiently and deal with Sandra's crisis at the same time.

Cynthia was in Sandra's exam room when she locked eyes with her *maybe* boyfriend. Ruben looked like he jumped out of bed and left the house within two minutes. But he was still handsome. His wrinkled clothes and five-o'clock shadow gave him a rough and rugged look.

He told Cynthia, "Hey," and she nodded back, but they couldn't communicate too much in the ER. The doctors who stabilized Sandra were still present as well as the security guard who found her, the policemen who wanted to arrest her and the nursing supervisor who wished this whole thing would simply disappear.

Cynthia wasn't offering Sandra any patient care, and with Ruben on the scene, there was no longer a need for her to stay. She went back to her unit and gave the worried nurses up there an update on Sandra's condition. She didn't want to tell them about the drug abuse, but they had already talked amongst themselves. Everyone knew about the theft from the Pyxis machine.

An hour after Cynthia returned to the floor, Ruben walked in looking stressed and exhausted. He gave the nurses another update: "She's going to pull through. She, um, she did OD. It's too early to say how much damage she caused herself. The doctors are optimistic, but until Sandra wakes up and starts talking, they can't say if she'll have any, um, lingering effects."

The nurses asked a few more questions, but Ruben didn't give them anything else. "I wanna thank all of you," he said. "I know tonight's been crazy. I appreciate the way all of you handled yourselves. I have the best group of nurses in this hospital, no doubt about it. I couldn't have asked for a better crew."

The nurses were pleased with his endorsement. They didn't ask any more questions about Sandra's condition, her theft or the consequences for her actions. Ruben went around the unit and touched bases with each member of his team to see how their patients were doing and also to make sure they weren't too freaked out about tonight's calamity.

He should've spoken to Cynthia first and foremost, but Ruben avoided her with a passion. He didn't ask his charge nurse what time Sandra got there, what Sandra said when Cynthia spoke to her, or what instructions Cynthia gave her. Eventually Ruben had to go to his office to deal with some of the paperwork from Sandra's debacle. He closed the door, indicating he didn't want to be disturbed.

Cynthia waited exactly twelve seconds before she barged in without knocking. Ruben sat behind his desk wearing a look of shame and foreboding. Cynthia closed the door, but she didn't approach him. She folded her arms under her breasts and took a deep breath. The first tear fell before Ruben offered his explanation.

"I'm sorry," he said. He brushed his hair back with his fingers and wiped the fresh droplets of sweat from his forehead. It was hard, but he managed to look Cynthia in the eyes.

"Sorry for what?" she asked, but she already knew. Both of her eyes were leaking now. She didn't immediately wipe the tears away.

"Me and Helen, we're going to stay together," Ruben announced.

Cynthia suspected as much, but hearing it from him was still devastating. She felt her heart rip in two, yet it still managed to pump hot, lonely blood through her body. She was short of breath. His words hit like a sucker punch to the gut.

Cynthia's nose started to run. She wiped it with the back of her hand. She folded her arms again and took slow, shuddering breaths. She stared at Ruben's electric blue eyes until her tears made them look like pools of cobalt agony.

"I'm sorry," Ruben said. He shook his head. His face went from pale to pink to red, right before her eyes. "I wanted to call you, but I promised Helen I wouldn't. I'm sorry, Cynthia. I..."

He didn't finish his sentence because Cynthia turned and walked out of the small room. She had to get out. She couldn't breathe in there. She wanted to scream, and she wanted to attack Ruben. She wanted to lie down on the floor and simply die.

A few nurses saw Cynthia when she left the manager's office, and they didn't know what to think. They assumed her tears had something to do with Sandra. Maybe Cynthia mishandled the situation, and Ruben had to reprimand her. From the looks of it, Ruben might have *fired* her. That didn't make sense, but they had never seen Cynthia so upset.

The last thing the nurses suspected was that Ruben had done something wrong to cause Cynthia's distress. In their eyes, Ruben was the best manager in the hospital, possibly in the whole state of Texas. He was above reproach. If he made one of his nurses cry, then she must have done something to deserve it.

Whatever the case, they weren't going to get an explanation from Cynthia. On her way out of Ruben's office, she snatched her purse from the nursing station and headed straight for the elevators. They took too long to get there, so Cynthia took the stairs down. She didn't clock out, and she didn't ask to leave. She was supposed to be in charge of the unit tonight, but she knew she would face no disciplinary actions for her abrupt exit.

After the anguish Ruben caused her, the least he could do was turn a blind eye to Cynthia storming out of the hospital, her hopes and dreams shattered, her whole life in disarray.

It was the very least he could do.

CHAPTER TWENTY-TWO
THE FINAL CHAPTER
WHO'S RODNEY?

The next day was Sunday, May 5th. It was a beautiful spring afternoon, but not everyone was free to lounge in front of the TV or spend time with their family. Most of the departments at Jackson Memorial never closed, and the hospital was as busy as ever.

But just because the doctors and housekeepers had to work on such an awesome afternoon, didn't mean they couldn't find time to enjoy God's day of rest. Larry and Lola sat outside of the Avery Building on a bench provided for patients who were waiting for a ride home.

Larry had a surprise for Lola, and he was a little nervous about giving it to her. He purchased the gift with no occasion in mind. Now he felt like a pauper trying to impress a princess with a shiny trinket.

Larry selected a charm bracelet for his woman because it wasn't too expensive, and it was personal. Among the charms on the wrist-wear was a tiny stethoscope, a cute, little syringe, a medicine bottle with "Rx" on it, and the rod of Asclepius, which was a snake entwined around a staff. Larry wasn't sure about the snake charm at first, but the woman at the jewelry store assured him it was a widely accepted symbol for medicine. The only non-medical charm on the bracelet was a shiny, quarter-inch microphone.

Larry had more than four thousand dollars in his savings account, but he didn't buy Lola any of the expensive, diamond encrusted rings and necklaces the woman at the jewelry store tried to steer him to. He knew Lola liked him for who he was and not who he'd be pretending to be with an expensive gift. The charm bracelet cost $75, which was a lot of money, considering Larry only made ten dollars an hour. That was nearly a full day's pay.

He presented the gift to Lola at six p.m., during their lunch break. Every piece of jewelry Lola currently wore was more expensive than Larry's bracelet, but you would never know it by the look in her eyes. Lola studied each charm. She looked up at Larry with a bright smile.

"It's beautiful," she said. She leaned closer and kissed him softly.

They never did any serious making-out at work, which was for the best because Lola's kiss set Larry's soul on fire. He immediately missed the feel of her soft, sweet lips when she backed away. He stared into her eyes and smiled warmly.

"You like it?"

"It's perfect," Lola said. "But, um, what's this?" She fingered the microphone.

"That's for the future," Larry told her. "Did I tell you I was psychic?"

Lola shook her head, grinning. "No, you didn't tell me that."

"I am," Larry said. "I predict you'll be a great slam poet one day. I wish you would memorize your 'New Day' poem."

Lola chuckled. Her poetry was something she kept close to her heart. Her dad never thought it a wise investment of her time. Larry considered it a huge honor when Lola gave him one of her journals to read. He thought she had talent. He hoped she'd nurture and share it with the world.

"Is this a microphone?" Lola asked, studying her bracelet.

"No," Larry said. "That's an ice cream cone."

Lola looked confused.

Larry chuckled. "Yes, it's a microphone. One day, when you finally take the stage, you'll realize you have a calling."

"A calling *other* than being a doctor?"

"The life of a poet is much more fulfilling."

"Really?"

"Sure," Larry said. "You might save a person's *life* as a doctor, but poets make people think and smile, for a few minutes. What's more important?"

Lola laughed. "Clearly the three minute smile is *way* more important."

"I know, right?"

"You're cute," Lola told him.

"Cute like a kitten, or cute like a powerful lion?"

"Both," Lola said. "You make me laugh."

"And you like the bracelet?"

"Definitely." She offered her arm. "Can you put it on?"

Larry nodded. He secured the bracelet around her wrist and held her hand for a moment.

"I forgot to ask, what's the occasion?" Lola said.

"Just because."

"Because you like me?"

Larry grinned. "Yes, and because you're so fine." He felt Lola's hand was growing warm. Or maybe it was Larry's temperature that was rising.

"I'm going to read a poem next time we go to Barcelona," Lola said.

"Really?"

"Of course. I can't walk around with a microphone on my bracelet, if I never take the stage."

"Are you going to memorize 'New Day'?"

"No, but I'll read it. The paper will be shaking so hard in my hand, everyone will know how nervous I am."

"Use a clipboard," Larry suggested. "It's harder to tell if a clipboard is shaking."

"That's a good idea."

"And I'll be there to encourage you."

"I know."

Larry kissed her again. He couldn't help it.

"I'm sorry," he said afterwards.

"It's okay," Lola said. "No one's watching us."

"Are you ready to go?"

Lola checked her watch. "Yeah. I guess I'd better."

"Do you want me to walk you?" Larry asked. "Your dad's here today, isn't he?"

"You can still walk me," Lola said.

"You sure?"

She nodded and rose to her feet. "Come on."

Larry's chest swelled as he walked with Lola to the ER. They didn't hold hands or express any signs of affection once they entered the building, but anyone who saw them together knew there was something special going on.

Dr. Dego knew it to. Larry felt nervous when they got to the Trauma side of the ER, but Lola's father didn't frown or cut his eyes like he used to. Larry knew Dr. Dego wasn't fully pleased about his daughter's persistent boyfriend, but Lola was right about him accepting Larry, even if it was grudgingly.

Dr. Dego seemed to sigh inwardly as Larry and Lola approached.

"I'll talk to you later," Larry told her.

"Okay, bye," Lola replied.

Larry tried to get the hell away from there. He was surprised when Dr. Dego called to him with his heavy, Ethiopian accent.

"Larry."

Larry stopped and slowly turned back to him.

Dr. Dego took a deep breath. "I am sorry, for what happened at my home."

Larry wanted to accept his apology, but he was speechless. He stood uneasily, not sure this was really happening.

"I would like to invite you to my home again, for dinner," Dr. Dego said.

Larry didn't realize Dr. Dego stuck out a hand to shake until Lola elbowed him in the arm and said, "He'd love to come, wouldn't you, Larry?"

"Uh, oh, yeah," Larry said. He shook the good doctor's hand. "Yes, I would like that. Thanks, sir. That's, that's really cool."

Dr. Dego nodded. "Lola will tell you the date." He turned and walked away.

Larry stared at Lola when he was gone. Her smile was ear to ear.

"Told you he liked you."

Larry didn't think that was the case, but there was definitely progress.

"Talk to you later," Lola said and hurried to catch up with her father.

≈≈≈≈≈≈≈

Larry's head was still in the clouds when he ran into Rodney on his way out of the ER. Rodney was milling about, looking a little depressed, Larry thought. He tried to hurry past him, but Rodney said, "Hey, man," and Larry was obliged to be cordial.

"What's up, youngster. You in the ER zone today?"

"Yeah," Rodney said, then, "What's up with you and that medical student? I thought y'all wasn't talking..."

"We not," Larry said. "Not really."

"I saw you and Dr. Dego over there," Rodney informed. "That nigga actually shook your hand, like he was giving y'all his blessing..."

Larry still couldn't believe that happened. He couldn't help but smile.

"Why you don't wanna tell me about it?" Rodney wondered.

"'Cause it's too much talking at this hospital," Larry said. "Everybody wants to know somebody else's business. That's why it's so many people here who don't like each other."

Rodney nodded. "I feel ya."

Larry nodded, too. He started to walk away, but Rodney stopped him again.

"That's what's happening to me. Today prolly be my last day up here."

"People talking about you and Eva?" Larry asked.

Rodney hesitated. He wished that was the worst of it. He was surprised Larry hadn't heard the rumors yet. Their whole department was talking about it. Last night Rodney received a couple of text messages from Amy and a few prank phone calls as well.

Amy told Rodney he needed to get checked for HIV. The prank callers brought the same news, except they weren't so nice about it. A couple of females called him a *"Nasty motherfucker!"* and a *"Sick dick nigga."* Another told him, *"You got the Monster, punk! Go get checked."* Yet another urged Rodney to *"Stop passing yo AIDS around, nigga! Just cut yo dick off completely!"*

Rodney didn't think he was infected – in fact he knew he wasn't – but why would Amy lie about something like that? Even if Amy contracted the virus, that didn't mean Rodney had it, too. Amy was a known whore. She could've picked up HIV from anywhere.

Rodney knew he should get checked, just to be sure, but he couldn't muster the courage to do that. No one wants to know they're dying – especially from an STD that was easily preventable. Rodney knew he'd go crazy if he went to the doctor and got a bad diagnosis. Magic Johnson said HIV was no longer a death sentence, but there were a million Africans who would strongly disagree.

But Rodney didn't have the Monster. That was the bottom line. He didn't give it to Amy, and he refused to consider that he might have given it to his girlfriend Trish. That was unthinkable. Trish was a good girl. She had a full life in front of her. Rodney loved his dick dearly, but he would take the prank caller's advice and cut it off before he told Trish to go get checked for HIV.

"They talking about me and Eva and everybody else," Rodney said. If Larry hadn't already heard the awful stories, Rodney wasn't going to be the one to tell him.

"Maybe leaving here would be a good thing for you," Larry said. He wouldn't normally encourage someone to give up, but the women at the hospital were catty. Once they got riled up, they would never let a rumor die. If they hated Rodney today, they would make sure every new crop of employees learned to hate him as well.

"You need to start from scratch," Larry suggested. "Go somewhere where nobody knows anything about you. And don't get off to a bad start like you did here. Just because a girl offers you some ass don't mean you got to jump on it. Women will respect you a lot more if you *don't* sleep with them. Plus it's all kinds of diseases out there, Rodney. You can't be slinging your stick all willy-nilly. You'll end up with some shit they can't get rid of with just a pill..."

Rodney's eyes widened. He wondered if Larry knew what was going on, and he was only pretending to be in the dark. If that was the case, Rodney knew he had only himself to blame.

"I gotta go," Larry told him. "My lunch break will be over in fifteen minutes, and I haven't eaten yet."

"Alright, man. I'll..."

Rodney lost his train of thought when a housekeeping supervisor walked by, her eyes big and full of fright. One of the policemen who worked part-time as a security guard was quick on her heels. Rodney knew the muscle-bound cop was named Damien.

Damien was trying to have an important conversation with the housekeeper, but Brenda didn't want to talk. She flew by Larry and Rodney, her white sneakers squeaking on the waxed floor. Damien followed her with the slow persistence of Michael Myers from the Halloween movies.

"Why you running?" he taunted her.

"Leave me alone," Brenda said.

"Damn, what's up with that?" Rodney wondered.

"I don't know," Larry said, looking after them. It was quite a bizarre scene.

Brenda rounded the corner on the Quick Trip side of the ER. She didn't know where she was going. She was nearly panicked. Her forehead was slick with sweat. She knew she couldn't outrun Damien, and she hoped she wouldn't have to. They were in a crowded hospital. There was no way he would assault or even yell at her in front of so many people. But if that was the case, why was he chasing her? He was already drawing a lot of attention.

Damien's blood flowed white hot as he pursued the hunch-backed warthog. He knew people were watching them. At this point, he didn't give a damn. He was a cop, first and foremost. Part-time security jobs were a dime a dozen. Who cared if he got fired from Jackson Memorial?

Damien didn't think Brenda would have the nerve to show her face at the hospital after what happened last night. When he saw her today, Damien lost nearly all of his composure. *Revenge* was the only thing on his mind. If anyone dared to interfere, they could get some, too.

He chased Brenda to the Quick Trip side, where she tried to test his cool by walking to the nursing station. The area was crowded with doctors and scribes and other employees. Brenda didn't have a reason to be there, but her gray scrubs worked like a cloak of invisibility. Housekeepers had free range of the hospital, and people barely paid attention to them.

Brenda thought Damien would retreat when he saw all of the nurses around her, but the policeman was still in ROBOCOP mode. He walked up to her and stood stiffly with his hands on his hips, his thumbs hooked on his utility belt. Brenda reluctantly turned to face him. She nearly screamed when she saw the look in his eyes.

Damien looked deranged. Brenda knew this wasn't a mean glare he perfected over the years. It was real life. After watching him beat her brother mercilessly, Brenda understood that getting on Damien's bad side was the biggest mistake she'd made in the past decade. It might have been the biggest mistake she *ever* made.

"You through running?" the cop asked her.

Brenda looked around frantically. A few nurses were watching them now, but no one intervened.

"Leave me alone," Brenda told Damien. "I didn't do nothing to you."

"You owe me eight hundred dollars," Damien told her. He spoke calmly, but he looked like he was on the verge of striking her.

"No, I don't. Leave me alone."

"Gimme my money, or you're going to jail, bitch."

Damien's use of profanity brought more unwanted attention. He didn't care.

"I don't owe you nothing," Brenda said. She briefly locked eyes with a few bystanders. The shocked look on their faces emboldened Brenda. She knew they wouldn't stand for this – not in the middle of the ER.

"You got your brother to slash my fucking tires," Damien barked. "Now you gon' pay for them."

"Hey." The ER charge nurse was Theresa Session. She ran her unit with an iron fist, but Damien's uniform and his demeanor gave her pause. She approached the employees cautiously. "This, this isn't the place for that," she told Damien. "Y'all need to—"

"Did I say something to you?" Damien spun on her, his eyes on fire. "Did I ask you for any help?"

The color drained from Theresa's face. "You, y'all have to take this somewhere else."

"Yeah, we're about to," Damien said. He returned his attention to Brenda. "Come on, let's go."

"I'm not going anywhere," Brenda said. She tried to sound defiant, but her voice rattled with fear.

Damien removed the handcuffs from his belt. "You wanna do this the easy way or the hard way?"

Brenda's eyes grew even wider as she stared at the restraints. She knew full well what Damien's *hard way* was like, and she wanted nothing to do with it. But she wasn't too keen on the easy way either. Brenda didn't want to go to jail at all. And despite what happened last night, she was pretty sure Damien didn't have the right to arrest her. She didn't slash any of his tires. If he wanted to prove otherwise, he should take her to court.

"Leave me alone!" she pleaded. She begged the charge nurse to, "*Please, help me! This man done gone crazy.*"

Damien reached for Brenda's arm. She jerked it away roughly.

"Stop!"

"Leave her alone!" Theresa shouted. "You, this isn't right!"

There were more than a dozen people watching them now. Most of them had known Damien since he started working at the hospital five years ago. They were inclined to give him the benefit of the doubt.

"Get out my business!" Damien told the charge nurse. He reached again and caught hold of Brenda's arm this time. She fought valiantly to free herself.

"*Help!* This man ain't got no business touching me! *Somebody help me!*"

Theresa threw her head back and hollered, "*Security!*" just as Damien performed a classic takedown maneuver that sent Brenda crashing to the floor.

"*Oof!*"

Brenda's shoulder took the brunt of the impact, but she felt the pain all over her body. Damien rolled her onto her stomach. Brenda was disgusted to find her lips on the same filthy floor she'd been mopping for more than eight years.

At that point she no longer doubted that Damien was arresting her. Brenda kept screaming because she knew he was going about this the wrong way. Just because Damien was a cop didn't mean he could arrest anyone he wanted to. He had to file a complaint and secure a warrant first.

"*Help me! Please, I didn't do nothing!*"

"Stop resisting!" Damien growled as he struggled to secure the handcuffs. "You wanna get tased?"

"*Security!*" Theresa shouted just as two members of the security team burst through the crowd.

They were fully prepared for any unruly patient or visitor, but the guards stopped cold when they saw who it was. Confusion washed over their faces as they looked from Damien to the housekeeper and then at each other.

"Whuh, what's going on?" one of them asked.

"*Help me!*" Brenda screamed. "*Get him off me!*"

"She's under arrest," Damien told his colleagues.

"She didn't do anything," Theresa said, but the guards didn't make a move. Interfering with a police officer who was performing his duty was a serious crime. Neither of the guards got paid enough to make a decision this decisive.

By then nearly everyone in the ER was migrating to the Quick Trip side to see what the hell was going on. Larry was generally against gossip and scandals, but he and Rodney were among the rubberneckers. This wasn't some run-of-the-mill argument. It was outrageous. It was impossible *not* to watch.

With everyone's attention diverted, it was fairly easy for an unknown Hispanic man to slip into the ER with an employee ID that didn't have his picture on it. The stranger wore a heavy jacket, despite the warm weather outside, and he was disheveled and reeking of alcohol. He didn't have a wristband that identified him as a visitor or a patient, and he didn't know how to find the man he sought.

All he had was a name and a description. He tried his luck with that.

"Is Rodney here?"

The stranger's skin was dark, but his accent wasn't thick. His hands were rough from a lifetime of manual labor. He looked to be in his early forties.

The closest person to him was a CNA named Twyla Perkins. Twyla was on her way to the Quick Trip side, to see what the commotion was. But she was accustomed to helping visitors with directions.

"What?" she asked the stranger.

"I'm looking for Rodney Tucker," the man said. "Do you know who's Rodney?"

Twyla frowned. "Rodney?"

"From Equipment Operations," the stranger said. "He works there, but today he works in here; in the ER."

"You mean *Material* Operations?" Twyla asked.

The man nodded. "Yes, Material Operations. Who's Rodney? Is he here?"

Twyla smelled alcohol on the stranger's breath, but it didn't fully register at the time. Also strange was the fact that a forty year old Hispanic man wanted to speak with a twenty-year old black man from Material Operations. Twyla doubted the two were friends. Plus the M.O. employees didn't provide patient care or have any direct dealings with visitors.

Later Twyla would admit that she didn't give the stranger her full attention because she was distracted by Damien and Brenda's situation. Instead of asking what he wanted Rodney for, Twyla looked around until she spotted the knucklehead in a crowd.

"There he go right there," Twyla said and pointed. She called to him. "Rodney! This man's looking for you."

Larry and Rodney turned around at the same time. Larry surveyed the deadly scene in a split second. He saw that Twyla was standing next to a Hispanic man, and Larry saw that the stranger had a gun. Larry's first thought was, *Why would Twyla point Rodney out to a man who had a gun?* But then Twyla looked at the stranger again, and she screamed, and Larry realized the man didn't have a gun in his hand when he entered the ER. Of course he didn't. He must've whipped it out just now, just for Rodney.

The man didn't speak. He pointed the gun at what he wanted dead and started shooting. The sound of gunfire in the ER was surreal, but all gunfire sounds surreal if you're not on a battlefield.

Larry was scared stiff. At first he thought he was the target, and his whole life flashed before his eyes. He didn't move at all until after the third shot. When he did move, Larry's immediate reaction was for self-preservation. He ducked and threw his hands over his head, as if this was a tornado drill. Larry's second move was to save Rodney, but he was too late. Rodney was already on the floor, crumpled, screaming and bleeding.

POP!
POP!
POP!POP!POP!

By the seventh shot it sounded like everyone in Overbrook Meadows was screaming and running – all in one direction: *Away* from danger. The ER looked like Spain's *Running of the Bulls*. The only person who wasn't running was the gunman. But when his gun stopped spitting fire, he too got moving.

The stranger didn't know the ER very well. He was drunk, and he didn't plan his escape route like Brenda did at the Economy Inn last night. The shooter saw exit signs, and he ran towards them. But he had no idea if those exits would lead to his car that was parked near the ER's side entrance.

The shooter did have one thing going for him: He was armed, and everyone on the ground floor heard the gunfire. People parted for him like the Red Sea. After twenty crazed seconds, the gunman burst through a set of double doors and was greeted by warm sunshine. He tucked his weapon in his jacket pocket, but he didn't have time to find his getaway car.

Damien charged through the double doors a second later. He knew this situation warranted lethal force, but he didn't slow down long enough to draw his pistol. Damien tackled the shooter, and he went to town on the perp's head once he fully mounted him. Damien's fists were hard and heavy. He swung so fast, it looked like he had too many arms, like Leonardo Da Vinci's *Anatomical Man*.

The third blow sent the shooter to sleepy land. Damien kept swinging because he didn't know where the weapon was, and for the first time in a long time he felt genuinely threatened by this individual.

"*Drop the gun!*" Damien yelled as he pummeled the limp body, because that's what good cops do when they're kicking ass. He didn't stop swinging until he was physically exhausted, and the shooter's face looked like raw meatloaf.

Two security guards exited the hospital a moment later. They had to restrain the assailant with a zip tie because Damien couldn't find his handcuffs on his belt. When he remembered where he left them, he couldn't help but smile inwardly.

Everyone in the ER greeted Damien like a hero when he returned to assess the damage. Even the charge nurse apologized for siding with the housekeeping supervisor a few minutes ago.

EPILOGUE

Two days later Larry sat on the corner of his bed wearing jeans and a tank top. He used the remote to turn the television to the nine o'clock news. Larry's breathing was slightly labored. His muscles were tense from a set of fifty pushups he just completed. When Channel Six's star reporter, the handsome Chad Collins, appeared on the screen, Larry dropped to the floor to do another set of fifty.

"Tonight we have *more breaking news!*" Chad announced. He sat alone in the Channel Six newsroom looking dapper in a tan suit with a white shirt and blue tie. His blonde hair was short and tapered on the sides. His deep blue eyes were piercing and hypnotic. It was hard to look away. Every night millions of viewers were captured by Chad's gaze and held hostage from commercial break to commercial break.

"There's been *another* arrest involving the *scandal* at Jackson Memorial Hospital that culminated in a shooting in the ER on Sunday evening," Chad reported. "*This woman,*" he said, with all the flair of a Vegas magician, "*Mrs. Eva Valdez,* has been charged with facilitating the aggravated assault and attempted murder charges that were leveled against this man, *Mr. Joseph Valdez.*"

Larry strained his neck but couldn't see the television from his vantage point on the floor. He stood and shook his head at the mug shots Channel Six had on display.

Larry wasn't a fan of reporter Chad Collins. He thought Mr. Collins added too much hype and sensationalism to what were often sad and tragic events. But when it came to getting to the meat of a story, Larry had to admit that no one did it better.

Eva's mug shot was disheartening. Larry couldn't stare at it for too long. He studied the man's picture instead. Channel Six had been parading Mr. Valdez's mug shot since he was arrested on Sunday night. Larry couldn't stop looking into the shooter's cold, dark eyes whenever the news came on. Even now he felt his heartbeats quickening. Larry took a seat on his bed and watched the rest of the report in silence.

"No, it's not a coincidence that these two individuals have the same last name," Chad said. "They are in fact *husband and wife*. Police believe Mrs. Valdez – an employee at Jackson Memorial – facilitated and possibly *orchestrated* Sunday's shooting by giving her husband her hospital ID badge. That badge allowed Mr. Valdez access to Jackson Memorial's ER. The police believe Mrs. Valdez gave her husband instructions on where to find the shooting victim, another employee named Rodney Tucker..."

Larry swallowed roughly. He brought a hand to his face and rubbed his mouth subconsciously.

"If you haven't been keeping up with the events that unfolded this week," Chad went on, "the police are investigating a shooting at Jackson Memorial Hospital that occurred at approximately six p.m. on Sunday night. Mr. Joseph Valdez was arrested on the scene with a gun in his possession. Three people were injured in the shooting, but only one of them sustained injuries that were considered life-threatening. The intended target, a Jackson Memorial employee named Rodney Tucker, was upgraded from serious to fair condition this afternoon.

"As for a possible motive for the shooting," Chad said, "the police believe Mr. Tucker, Mrs. Valdez and Mr. Valdez were involved in a deadly love triangle. The police suspected Mr. Valdez had some type of help getting into the hospital, and his wife's arrest appears to tie up that lose end."

Both of the mug shots dropped from the screen. They were replaced with the picture of a police officer Larry recognized as Damien. Damien was in full gear in the photograph, and he looked thinner than Larry remembered him. He guessed the picture was at least five years old.

"We also have more breaking news regarding the policeman who apprehended Mr. Valdez on Sunday," Chad told the viewers. "This man, *Officer Damien Glover*, was suspended by the police department, pending an investigation into what many witnesses are calling an unlawful arrest that occurred in Jackson Memorial's ER a few minutes prior to Sunday's shooting. Police Chief David Stearns had this to say at a press conference this afternoon..."

They cut away to footage of the stressed police chief standing behind a podium. He spoke into a dozen microphones as members of the media took photographs and filmed the scene for their news agencies.

"There's more to Officer Glover's story than what's in the papers," Stearns said. He was a big man with rosy cheeks and a handlebar moustache. He wore a black Stetson with his police uniform. "Officer Glover's been with the department for six years, and he's been an outstanding officer. An asset to the force. Pending the outcome of an internal investigation, he may be disciplined for this incident. But I don't believe it will cost him his career."

"Witnesses are saying he tackled a Jackson Memorial employee and put her in handcuffs," one of the reporters blurted. He was out of view, and he didn't have a microphone to amplify his voice, but everyone heard him. "Is that true, Mr. Stearns?"

The police chief began shaking his head before he responded. "No, that's not true at all. The incident was captured on the hospital's security cameras. I have viewed the video myself, and I can assure you no one got *tackled*. Officer Glover did perform a takedown maneuver when the employee resisted arrest, but he didn't *slam* or throw her to the ground, like some of you are reporting."

"So you do acknowledge Officer Glover *took down* an employee and placed her under arrest?"

Mr. Stearns' face reddened even more. He knew he was going to get an ulcer from this. "No, I will not confirm that," he said. "The employee was never formally arrested. Officer Glover *attempted* to make an arrest, but she was not placed in a police car or taken to jail at any point."

"But why did it happen?" a female reported asked. "Why did your officer assault this woman?"

The police chief reached to wipe the sweat from his face. *"There was no assault,"* he said sternly. "Everything happened just as I said: Officer Glover approached the individual and *attempted* to arrest her. He did take her down when she resisted, and he did secure handcuffs on that individual. But there was never an arrest, and there was never any assault."

"But what about—"

"The most important thing here," Mr. Stearns went on, "are the mitigating factors that led up to that incident. The employee in question is not innocent. She committed an offense that called for her arrest. Officer Glover did not go through the proper channels to secure an arrest warrant, and that is the *only* thing he did wrong on Sunday."

"What did the woman do?" another reporter asked.

"I'm not at liberty to discuss that," Mr. Stearns said.

"Would you characterize Damien Glover as a loose cannon?" a reporter asked.

"No I would not," the police chief said emphatically. "I think some of you are forgetting that Officer Glover singlehandedly took down an individual who pulled a gun at the hospital with the intent to kill at least one person. Three people were injured in the shooting.

"Officer Glover apprehended the suspect at the risk of his own safety. He prevented the gunman from escaping and hurting even more people. We're all disappointed in his actions regarding the Jackson Memorial employee, but we refuse to let that override the courage and dedication shown on that day and over the last six years."

"Was Officer Glover fired from his job at Jackson Memorial?" someone asked.

"I have nothing further," the police chief said and stepped away from the podium.

Channel Six cut back to Chad in the newsroom.

"So there you have it," he said. "The hero cop who took down the shooter is under investigation himself for an unrelated incident regarding a *still-unidentified* employee at Jackson Memorial. The police chief is offering scarcely little information about why that arrest – or *attempted arrest* – might have been justified. Mr. Stearns is clearly standing by his officer.

"For more information, we have Gabriella Sands, who's broadcasting live from Jackson Memorial Hospital..."

The screen split in half to make room for a shot of the beautiful Gabriella, who'd been gathering information at the hospital for the last few hours.

"How are you doing, Gabriella?" Chad asked her. "Anything new?"

"I'm fine," Gabriella said with a bright smile. She was a light-skinned Hispanic with dark, curly hair. "Chad, I've been at Jackson Memorial for the better part of the day. Not surprisingly, the administrators here are very tight-lipped. I spoke with the hospital's president, Mr. William Hawkins, and he released the following statement..."

Gabriella read from a clipboard:

"While we understand that the events that occurred at Jackson Memorial Hospital on Sunday were tragic and alarming, we have taken steps to ensure that similar incidents will not happen in the future. Jackson Memorial is still a safe place to visit, as a patient and as an employee, and we will continue to provide the excellent patient care and community service that we have been providing Overbrook Meadows since 1911. We will survive this crisis as a family, and we will emerge as a stronger and more cohesive unit."

"That's beautiful," Chad said, his voice laced with sarcasm. "What about the nurse who stole drugs and overdosed at the hospital on Saturday night? Did the president say anything about her?"

"Only that they were investigating the matter and getting the nurse all of the help she needs," Gabriella replied.

"What about the cop who roughed up one of their employees?" Chad pressed. "What did the president say they were going to do about him?"

Gabriella couldn't help but grin at Chad's demeanor. "I spoke with the Human Resources department. They indicated Officer Damien Glover's employment at Jackson Memorial has been terminated."

"Are they going to sue him or the police department?" Chad wondered.

"At this time no one has mentioned a lawsuit," Gabriella reported. "But I did interview one employee who was able to shed more light on the love triangle that led to Sunday's shooting…"

"That's great," Chad said. "I'd love to see that."

"She had to speak on a condition of anonymity," Gabriella explained, "because the hospital asked all of its employees to restrain from discussing these matters with the media…"

There were a few seconds of dead air while Channel Six cued Gabriella's interview. When it began, Chad and Gabriella were replaced with a shot of a Jackson Memorial employee who was wearing black scrubs; the color designated for Material Operations. The camera view was cropped to show only the employee's torso, from the neck to the waist. His or her employee ID badge was conveniently missing.

Off camera Gabriella asked the anonymous individual, "What do you know about the shooting in the ER?"

"I know the whole thing," the headless person said. It was a female. She gesticulated with her arms as she spoke. "I work in Material Operations. That's the same department Eva works in. I know she been having an affair with Rodney – that's the boy who got shot – and then on Thursday she said Rodney burned her."

Larry's eyes widened. He knew the story already, and he couldn't believe someone in his department defied the hospital's gag order. Even worse, Larry recognized the snitch's voice right away. It was Roshida Fuller, one of the girls Eva used to pal around with in her office.

"Rodney burned who?" the reporter asked. "What does that mean?"

"Rodney burned *Eva*," Roshida said. "He gave her gonorrhea. And then Eva turned around and gave it to her husband. And Rodney burned this other girl, too. And she took a HIV test and found out he gave her AIDS. And so Eva took a test and found out she got AIDS, too. And when Eva told her husband, he got real mad and said he was gon' kill Rodney. But he didn't even take a test to see if he had AIDs. He just assumed that if his wife had it, he must got it, too."

Larry shook his head in disappointment. Why did they always interview the most ghetto Negro they could find?

"So this is all about someone spreading HIV?" Gabriella asked.

"Yep," Roshida said. "But I think Eva was wrong for setting Rodney up because she the one who was sleeping with him in the first place. If he gave her something, and she gave it to her husband, that's *her* fault. She shouldn't have set Rodney up to get shot like that. And Eva's husband shot two more people that didn't have nothing to do with it. That ain't right."

The interview concluded abruptly. Roshida was replaced with the split screen of Chad in the studio and Gabriella standing in front of Jackson Memorial's ER. Chad wore the same look of awe Larry was wearing.

"Wow," Chad said. "That is amazing."

"It is," Gabriella agreed. "But for the record, I haven't spoken to anyone who would substantiate that employee's claims."

"I'm sure it's all true," Chad said. "I must say, Jackson Memorial sounds like a wild and crazy place to work."

Gabriella smiled and nodded. "That's probably an understatement."

"Thanks," Chad told her. "You do good work."

"You're welcome," Gabriella replied, and her camera was dropped from the shot.

"Well, we still don't have all the answers," Chad told the viewers when he had their full attention again. "But we will keep you updated on this *breaking news*."

He half-turned in his chair. The camera shot widened to reveal another reporter who had apparently been sitting there the whole time.

"Interesting story, huh?" Chad asked his colleague.

"Very," the other reporter said. "Almost as wild as the Mavericks overtime win in Miami last night!..."

Larry turned the television to a station that played classic R&B music only. Smokey Robinson was singing a mellow song called *Cruisin'* as only he could. Larry dropped to the floor to finish his set of pushups.

He tried to enjoy the music, but the news report had Larry's mind racing. Channel Six took a lot of jabs at the hospital. They had been doing so ever since the story broke on Sunday night. But Larry thought Jackson Memorial was a great place to work. The shooting in the ER was the first and only incident of such violence since the hospital opened its doors a hundred years ago. And Damien's trouble with the housekeeping supervisor was also a rarity. Chad Collins made it sound like rogue cops were the norm.

Channel Six didn't say anything about the many lives that were saved at Jackson Memorial every day. They didn't talk about the state of the art equipment or the talented neuro and trauma surgeons. Every time the corporate office did a poll, 89 percent of the employees at Jackson Memorial said they were happy with their job, and they would recommend the hospital to their friends who were looking for employment.

The events that occurred last week certainly gave the hospital a black eye, but sometimes you have to shake the tree to get rid of all of the dead and rotting fruit. Eva got fired for her role in the shooting, and Rodney was terminated for stealing and for overall good-for-nothingness. Cynthia requested and was granted a transfer to Trauma ICU, and Sandra was now getting the help she needed to beat her heroin addiction.

Brenda and Raquel both got fired for their away-from-work antics, which created an abundance of overtime in the housekeeping department. Amina took full advantage, and gradually she was able to wean herself off the dirty money she was getting from a dirty cop. She still thought about him, from time to time, but Damien stopped calling Amina after he was fired from hospital.

As for Larry, he emerged from the drama with a nice promotion. He took over Eva's role as the second shift supervisor in Material Operations. Larry now had his own office (which used to be Eva's), and his pay got bumped from ten to seventeen dollars an hour. His max pay was now $25 an hour, and Larry was sure

he'd reach it one day. He was a hard worker, and he was reliable.
And no one could question his integrity.

Larry shot to his feet when his bathroom door opened. He
sat on the bed and tried to look relaxed, but Lola saw him rise
from the floor. She eyed him curiously.

"What are you doing?"

"Nothing," Larry said. He folded his arms over his flat
stomach. His chest and arm muscles rippled under his dark skin.

Lola grinned. "Were you doing pushups?"

"Um, no," Larry said.

She giggled. "Yes you were. You're trying to look all buff."

"I am buff," Larry said. "I don't have to do pushups for
that." But he was a little short of breath from his workout. A few
beads of sweat glistened on his exposed pectorals.

"It's okay," Lola said. "I'm very impressed." She stood
before him and admired his physique openly.

Larry wished he could do the same, but Lola's body was
completely concealed under one of his bathrobes.

"What took you so long?" he asked her.

"I had to put on my outfit," she said with a grin. "Then I
had to put on some make up, and do my hair..."

"You did a great job," Larry said. "You look amazing."

"Thank you."

"Can I, um, can I see your outfit?"

"Yes," Lola said. "But I'm nervous."

Larry was too. Tonight he would fully explore her body for
the first time. Larry didn't think Lola needed to wear lingerie for
him, but she wanted everything to be perfect. She made plans to
spend the night. She even brought a bottle of wine and candles to
set the mood.

Larry reached and carefully removed his robe from her
shoulders. Lola stared into his eyes as he pulled the garment off
completely and tossed it onto the bed. Larry's heart sighed when
he saw her lingerie. He blinked quickly. Thankfully the glorious
vision did not disappear.

Lola's outfit consisted of two pieces: A babydoll top that
was red and sheer, offering a glimpse of her succulent cleavage
and her smooth stomach. The bottom was a lacy thong. Larry's
breath caught as his gaze rolled down her body. Lola did a slow

spin for him. Larry exhaled slowly when he saw her luscious cheeks. He'd been admiring Lola's ass in jeans and slacks for a long time. He knew she had it going on, but he didn't know she was *this* fine.

"Oh my damn," he muttered.

Lola was smiling when she faced him again. She leaned on him and placed a hand on his chest. She kissed him slowly and passionately. Larry reached for her. The feel of her perfect ass in his hands made his heart flutter. He hardened as he fondled both cheeks.

"It's real," Lola whispered.

"Damn right," Larry said in the same hushed tone.

"You want some wine?" she asked him.

"Not if I have to let go," Larry said. He pulled her hips closer until she could feel how badly he wanted her.

Lola's smile went away. She sucked his bottom lip and nibbled it.

"Yeah, I do want some wine," Larry decided.

"Okay."

Lola took a few steps back, and then she turned, heading for the kitchen. Larry's head swam. He watched her ass until it was completely out of sight. He went to the nightstand to retrieve a three-pack of condoms, not sure if they would make it back to the bedroom.

THE END

BY KEITH THOMAS WALKER

ABOUT THE AUTHOR

Keith Thomas Walker, known as the Master of Romantic Suspense and Urban Fiction, is the author of a dozen novels, including *Fixin' Tyrone*, *Dripping Chocolate* and *The Realest Ever*. Keith enjoys reading, poetry and music of all genres. Originally from Fort Worth, Keith is a graduate of Texas Wesleyan University. Visit him at www.keithwalkerbooks.com.